Prologue

THE KILLING TIMES

David Fraser, biographer of *Alanbrooke*, historian of the British Army with *And We Shall Shock Them*, social commentator in *The Christian Watt Papers* and novelist with *August 1988* and *A Kiss for the Enemy* was once one of Britain's most senior generals. He is married, has five children and lives in Hampshire.

DAVID FRASER

The Killing Times

FONTANA/Collins

First published in Great Britain by
William Collins Sons & Co. Ltd 1986
First issued in Fontana Paperbacks 1987

Made and printed in Great Britain by
William Collins Sons & Co. Ltd, Glasgow

The man had walked from Wimbledon underground station to the Common, a brisk walk on a pale, cold December afternoon. He was well wrapped up in a heavy black overcoat with fur collar, a garment reaching almost to his ankles and having about it a hint of capes, a flavour of coaches and posthorns, a style of something now twenty if not sixty years obsolete. The man was thus hardly dressed fashionably for the year 1911, in the strict sense of the word – and yet there was a suggestion of fashion, or at least of elegance about his tall-crowned bowler hat with its curly brim, about the gold band round his umbrella handle, about his beautifully polished and well-made shoes. He had walked fast. He needed to keep warm, to get his blood moving. A park bench in December was a chilly prospect. And this might take some time.

The man appeared to be about forty-five years old, with a handsome, rather heavy face, a full, dark moustache, an air of solid prosperity. In his left hand he carried a copy of the *Morning Post* – no doubt brought or bought for reading on the train, for he looked as if the journey to Wimbledon might have taken some time. This was, surely, a denizen of SW1 or W1, a creature from north of the Thames.

Wimbledon Common had a large number of wooden benches, of designedly 'rustic' appearance, scattered here and there among the clumps of gorse and shrub, among the well-grown trees, overlooking limited but agreeable expanses of undulating turf, clear for a little from the frost which nightfall would bring once more. The man, without hesitation, marched up to one of these and sat down. The bench was dry. The afternoon, however, was

9

chilly and he did not remove his gloves before opening the newspaper. He glanced at his watch and then tucked it away beneath his massive overcoat. He blew his nose. Then he appeared engrossed in his paper.

'I think the *Morning Post* 'Chasing articles are better than the Flat, don't you?'

The figure now seated beside him had arrived as if from nowhere. There had been no footfall, no shadow of approaching presence, no salutation – or at least the first man had heard none, so absorbed was he in his reading. Even now he only glanced sideways, without much sign of curiosity or even civility. He saw a man of, it seemed, about his own age, cleanshaven, hair grey – perhaps prematurely grey, for the face was as unlined as it was unremarkable. Nondescript grey suit, grey overcoat, soft grey hat with broad ribbon of darker grey. Grey gloves, a woollen scarf of indeterminate hue. A man without colour. His voice, intruding on the other's solitude, was flat and sounded bored. He seemed to be talking purely as if to show that he was capable of producing sound. There was a hint of the foreign in his accent.

'I don't know,' said the man who had walked from the underground station, 'I've no interest in racing. I sometimes had a bet on the old King's horses out of loyalty! Absurd, really – still, he did win the Derby for me!' He grunted, returning to his paper.

'He did win the Derby for you?'

'That's what I said.'

There was a short silence after this. The grey man said quietly, 'You have asked for an immediate meeting. Why?'

'I need instructions and advice.' The first man's voice, too, was quiet, almost inaudible.

'Advice?'

'Advice. There's been a reference – a direct reference – in a London paper to some of our friends, some of our friends across the sea. It was ten days ago. To most people it would have meant nothing. But the newspaper article gave – as examples of the – er – sympathies, attitudes the journalist was describing – mentioned four names.'

The grey man gave no indication of interest.

10

'Four names. Accurate. They couldn't have been associated by chance.'

'We agree,' said the grey man, without emphasis, 'we agree. The article to which you refer caused concern. Please continue.'

'As it happens, I know the journalist in question. I know him quite well.' The man from the underground station waited, as if expecting a response. Grey man said nothing.

'His name's Drew. For some reason he's got it into his head that I've – that I've got something to do with all this. He's trying to find out more from me. Immediately after he wrote that article, he approached me. He asked me to – to confirm and expand the detail. Naturally I told him I'd no idea what he was talking about.'

Two children, accompanied by a stout, bad-tempered-looking nurse, moved past the bench kicking and scuffing. They looked bored.

'How many times have I told you not to do that to your shoes? There'll be no toecaps left.' The children ran a few paces, turned, jumped, walked backwards, escaping as far as they could from the deadening routine of even-paced, eventless promenade. Their nurse's scolding voice died into the distance – 'Wait till I get you home, young madam!'

The man in the black overcoat from the underground station said grimly, 'He pretended not to believe me. In fact, he pretends to know – enough – to bully me into telling him more. I've told him to go to the devil, of course.'

'Of course.'

'Recently, he's been at me again. He says he can – well, show us up. Nonsense, of course. But he knows a bit, he's a scribbler and he's dangerous.'

'Have you any suggestions?'

'It's like this.' The man in the black overcoat, who had so far spoken in a low, hurried voice, now sounded stronger, more robust and deliberate. He appeared one who, having wrestled with a delicate, even dangerous situation, at last sees his way clear and intends, by force of character, to follow it.

'It's like this. This journalist fellow can be shut up. With money.'

'A dangerous precedent, surely?'

'I think not. Having accepted money he'll be entirely vulnerable to a rumour spread around potential employers – receiving a bribe to suppress his own journalistic integrity, that sort of thing. He's got a high reputation and a rumour like that could crack it. But he likes money and only money will shut his mouth or break his pen in the immediate future. He's talking about another article.'

Grey man appeared to be considering.

'Money? How much?'

'A considerable sum. Of course, I've had to sound entirely non-committal in all this, just listened, talked vaguely. He talked vaguely too, said he stood at the moment in need of a particular "loan", that he didn't enjoy these articles, this "investigation" he calls it, would be glad to drop them – he's a freelance, you know – get down to serious writing, that kind of claptrap. But these articles are paying well. It was clear what he was driving at.'

'How much?'

'Five thousand. Unless he's to be – extinguished – I really think it's the only way. That's why I need advice. He'll get in touch with me again.'

There was a long, long silence in the cold afternoon on Wimbledon Common. The sun threatened to end its brief visit to London, to sink beyond the rim of Kingston Hill. For the first time, black overcoat shot a penetrating look at grey man. The latter was gazing over the Common as if deep in meditation. When he started talking it was in a gentle, almost dreamy way.

'In itself the article did little to harm us. Four names – the individuals concerned, as you will have supposed, are behaving correctly, indignantly, talking about going to law. A little mud, as you say here, will stick to them. The general interest we have in the area in question is self-evident, and the main background points of Drew's article could have been – and probably have been – set out by any topical novelist. An alarmist, topical novelist, constructing a fiction about the wars of the future. You have many such.'

12

'Quite so. But I'm afraid he's got a bit more, somehow. I'm pretty sure the next article will be nearer the bone. That's why I asked for this meeting.'

'And why are you so "pretty sure" of that, as you put it?'

'Well – things he said –'

'No,' said the grey man, and the December air was warmer than his voice. 'No, let me tell you why. It is because this journalist's information came from you. And the information for his next article, if there is one, will also come from you. That is why you are "pretty sure", my friend.'

'No! Good God, you've got the wrong – I assure –'

'Please listen. The information for the article came from you. Your object was to worry us. With idiotic simplicity you supposed this worry would lead us to produce a considerable sum of money. The money would be divided between this journalist and yourself.'

'You must tell them. I swear –'

'Swear what you will, my friend. We are strangers to each other but I am perfectly well aware of what you have been doing and what you have planned. Now, listen carefully. Your contract is concluded.' Grey man paused for a moment, as if for emphasis. In the same even tone he continued: 'If other articles – and other names – appear, you may be assured of one thing only. The authorities here in England will be acquainted, confidentially, exactly and fully, with the part you have played in this little matter.'

The man from the underground station, the man in the black overcoat with the fur collar, sat absolutely motionless. After more than a minute he said, almost inaudibly, 'You've got it wrong.'

'I think not.'

'Got it wrong! And suppose *I* decided to talk to what you call "the authorities here"?' Grey man had stood up, as if bored by a conversation which had run its course. Now he turned on the other a look of mild enquiry.

'Yes? Let us suppose that, shall we?'

'No, of course not!' Black overcoat had also stood up and was looking not at grey man but at his own feet. 'Of course not! I'd never – you know I've done everything I've undertaken – loyally – carefully! But you – your people – have got this wrong, they really have!' His voice was trembling. He went on, looking at the ground, scratching it with the ferrule of his neatly rolled, gold-banded umbrella. He said, 'I can't just be dropped! It's all a mistake, as I've told you. I don't know where this fellow got his stuff from, I promise you. And I can't just be dropped – I've got certain commitments. Certain difficulties.' He was, it seemed, trying to speak judiciously, with dignity. But his voice was ill-controlled.

Grey man appeared to consider.

'You mean you are on the point of bankruptcy, from your wife's extravagance, your own follies and so on. Despite your – remuneration – you have been spending beyond your means. Of course. Naturally we are aware of that. It is not our business. I repeat – your contract with us is over. Your reputation is intact unless you, yourself, do it harm. We wish you good luck.'

'Good luck! Is that all?'

'Good luck. And if you attempt to, shall we say, embarrass us further, rest assured that everything, *everything* will be explained to our excellent colleagues in your Government. It's perfectly easy to convey information to them, as you know.'

'I'm surprised you've not threatened to – extinguish – me yourselves,' said the other, without smiling and very low.

Grey man said politely, 'Naturally, it remains an option. But you must not exaggerate your own importance. All you have to do now is to keep silent and you may live long – impoverished perhaps, but long. Besides,' said grey man with something that sounded like a chuckle, unamused, chilling: 'Besides, there is a saying in England, is there not – "Why keep a dog and bark yourself?" Were we ever to wish to dispose of you, my dear friend, there is quite enough known about you, isn't there, to persuade our British friends to handle you for us.'

At this, black overcoat gave what might have been intended as a disdainful smile but looked like an animal's snarl. Grey man

14

made as if to walk away, and then turned as if remembering something of little consequence, just worth a mention.

'Incidentally, my superiors, although they've finished with you, have no desire to be ungenerous. You've been a fool but there's a small terminal payment. Provided you don't try to be embarrassing. Provided your journalist friend is not encouraged by you to be embarrassing.'

'When? How much?'

The other smiled thinly. 'Less than you might have hoped for – far, far less – had you gone on sensibly, had you not surrendered to greed! But – they're still discussing this – you might hope for a thousand. And no more articles.'

'It's not enough.'

'Probably not.'

'When?'

'When? Oh – not quite yet!' With a stiff motion of the hand, a gesture of farewell seemingly mixed with admonition, the grey man melted into the thickening dusk as unobtrusively as he had first appeared.

Part I

FRANCIS

CHAPTER I

Francis Carr was slightly more susceptible to women than the other young bachelors in the Embassy. They were all, of course, periodically teased about some imagined tenderness for one of the many charming ladies met on the 'diplomatic circuit' in Berlin. The wives of the senior members of the Mission had particularly watchful eyes. Their raised eyebrows – not only for romance but for the general conduct and suitability of their young compatriots – were among the principal hurdles which an honorary attaché had to jump without calamity if, like Francis, he aspired to make a career in diplomacy, to become a fully fledged member of the Service. Francis had been at His Britannic Majesty's Embassy in Berlin for nine months. He was a probationer, a person of no consequence. He had, however, attracted favourable comment. The Ambassadress had been heard to say –

'Francis Carr has charming manners. Of course, I was fond of his mother, and he's got a good deal of her in him.'

And the First Secretary had remarked to his wife, 'Young Carr's an obliging boy. Quick on the uptake.'

'He's very young, isn't he, darling! Blushes when a pretty girl speaks to him! He gives me the impression of falling in love once a week!'

'Perhaps – but don't underrate him. There's something there. Shrewd. And although he may find the girls painfully attractive – after all, he's twenty-three, why not? – I think there's quite a cool, calculating mind at work as well. I suspect he'll be all right.'

Francis had already impressed with his sharpness, and his ability, refreshing and a little disconcerting, to say exactly what

19

struck him as true even when running counter to fashionable dogma. He had a concise and fluent pen, too. Immediately after arrival, in September, Francis had found himself having to do some devilling on the Anglo-French Treaty of 1904. Berlin had been making enquiries about the dimensions of Britain's undertakings to France – supposed by the British Parliament and public to be diplomatic support only, but secretly and implicitly extended by Staff talks in the preceding five years, so that were France ever at war, Britain would find herself a great deal more committed than was generally supposed. It was a delicate matter and even the Counsellor had been uncertain. A man had been ill with influenza and Francis had been set to work. His experience had been nil, his research thorough, his quickness of mind impressive and his written minute – which was seen, virtually unamended, by the Ambassador's own eyes – drew highly favourable comment. The First Secretary had felt a twinge of envy. He, a thorough, rather heavy man, was known to be inelegant on paper. Now he said again, generously and sincerely –

'Yes, he'll be all right.'

'Well,' said the First Secretary's wife, 'he's perfectly nice-looking. More than one can say for some who've been pushed out to you by desperate or influential relations!'

Francis was, indeed, 'perfectly nice-looking'. He was fair-haired, the kind of man who, it might be guessed, would go 'thin on top' earlier than most, and with a light, slightly girlish complexion. His pale youthfulness was only tempered by his eyes. They were blue and very penetrating. His colleagues in the junior ranks of the Embassy found it easy to like him, but one of them said to another soon after his arrival, 'He's a cold fish!'

'I don't agree. He warms up when an attractive woman comes into the room! We were at the same dinner party last night and he was the life and soul of it – the Brandinis, the Italians. They found him immensely *simpatico*, I could see. Brandini had his arm round his shoulders after dinner, cuddling him like a rather simian sort of uncle, and Madame Brandini looked as if she'd have liked to do the same!'

'I dare say. But he can look at you like a human iceberg if he doesn't care for something you say. Look at you, through you and out the other side. I'd not like to have him as an enemy.'

Parham, the Counsellor, did not greatly care for honorary attachés. In those days it was an accepted route into the Diplomatic Service for young men with what were unabashedly called 'decent connections' to be taken into an Embassy without commitment on either side. If they passed the scrutiny of their superiors – and their superiors' wives – they were encouraged to enter the career. A knowledge of at least two European languages was essential and good French was mandatory: French was the universal language of diplomacy.

Parham sent for Francis one April morning. Parham was the sort of diplomat, oddly produced now and then by Britain – perhaps only by Britain – who seemed to experience as his dominant emotion an ineradicable distrust of foreigners, particularly the inhabitants of the country to which he was accredited. Distrust, in Parham's case, was perhaps too strong a word. It was, rather, that he appeared absolutely incapable of imagining how others thought or felt unless, in education, nationality and background they exactly resembled Philip Parham. Francis had not been drawn to him. Parham's supercilious xenophobia might have been explained as an allergy to all things German – 1912 was not a good year for Anglo-German relations – but a colleague remarked, disloyally, that he had served with Parham in Brazil and his attitude to the natives had been exactly the same. Now he looked at Francis without enthusiasm.

'Carr, this isn't the sort of thing which normally reaches my desk, but there's a personal connection. I once knew this lady's husband quite well, although I don't know her herself. Mrs Henry Gaisford is arriving here in Berlin on Thursday, the day after tomorrow.' He eyed Francis, as if mention of Mrs Gaisford might arouse some inappropriate reaction, to be instantly quenched if detected. Francis looked and felt blank.

'We've been asked to be helpful. Poor Gaisford was an Oxford contemporary of mine, a good man. He died suddenly, just before Christmas. This is his widow. Apparently there's some business connected with Gaisford's estate which has meant her

21

coming to Germany – he was a City man and had some sort of commercial connection with people over here, it seems.'

'I see, Parham.' Whatever the difference in rank or age they addressed each other by surnames in the Embassy – except for the Ambassador, of course. 'Sir' would have been regarded as vulgarly deferential. 'Mr Parham' would have implied one thought oneself an office boy rather than an equal, a gentleman. Christian names were used little.

'I see, Parham.'

Parham was at least twenty years older than Francis, who saw him as an ancient, fussy and decrepit. His contemporary, Gaisford, had presumably died of old age and Francis's twenty-three-year-old heart did not lift at the thought of being helpful to some middle-aged widow, no doubt palely incompetent in black bombazine and expecting an attaché at the Embassy to act as a fag. It was clearly this, Francis thought, that Parham had in mind. There might also be expense in it! There were no rewards in the Service for such as Francis, until accepted and qualified. He existed on a slender allowance, while the temptations of Berlin were vivid and demanding.

Certainly without enthusiasm, and without much interest, Francis was also mildly perplexed. Why did Mrs Gaisford propose to visit Berlin simply because her late husband had business dealings with people in Germany? How could that demand the presence of a widow? It sounded like the concern of an agent, a solicitor, rather than a lady. Parham, too, seemed to feel there was more to be said. He spoke irritably.

'I gather Gaisford had – er, interests – here which are taking quite a lot of sorting out for his executors. The lawyers have agreed to her – Mrs Gaisford's – suggestion that she come out to have some, er, personal discussions. I believe there may be difficulties, and that she may –' Parham dropped his voice, as one using indelicate language, and a look of distaste appeared – 'may find herself less, er, happily placed than people supposed.' Francis nodded. Nothing he had heard made the assignment more attractive.

'Financially, that is,' Parham breathed with an inhibiting frown.

22

He went on: 'She's got a lot of people to see. Her lawyer knew of my acquaintance with Gaisford and told her he'd write to me. Would you look after her, Carr? Give her lunch, see she knows how to make the contacts she wants, that sort of thing. She's probably helpless, I don't expect she can speak a word of German.' Parham said that Mrs Gaisford would be staying at the Hotel Excelsior.

Francis thought it peculiar, since Parham's involvement stemmed from friendship with the deceased Gaisford, that he showed no sign of intending to take any personal hand.

'I suppose you'll be calling on her yourself? Shall I arrange something?'

'No, we're leaving Berlin that day, we're spending Easter in the Black Forest. I'll let you have a letter for her, of course. I gather she plans a short visit and by the time we return, I expect she'll have left. As I say, I've never met her,' Parham added. 'Gaisford only married about three years ago, as it happens. She's – I believe Mrs Gaisford is a good deal younger than poor Gaisford was. He went very unexpectedly – and at no age at all.'

A contemporary of Parham's of no age at all! Francis murmured that he would do anything he could and left the room. Later he wrote a note to Mrs Gaisford and had it delivered, with Parham's, to the Hotel Excelsior. It said that Mr Francis Carr hoped he could be of some service to her and that he would call at the hotel on Friday. Her widow's status and her presumed maturity – even though she was 'a good deal younger than poor Gaisford' – meant that an invitation to luncheon would be proper, expected, and (Francis sighed to himself) expensive. But it would be better to meet the lady first.

At four o'clock that Friday, Francis walked up to the reception desk at the Hotel Excelsior. Yes, Mrs Gaisford had arrived. Yes, she was in her rooms – she had a sitting room on the second floor. No, she had no visitor with her. Francis sent up his name. A page shortly afterwards approached where he was sitting in the hall, bowed and said that Frau Gaisford wished to come down, and would be with him directly.

Five minutes later he heard a voice say, 'Mr Francis Carr?' very softly. Veronica moved towards him, hand outstretched, a gentle, appealing smile on her face.

Francis Carr was, as the First Secretary had observed, a shrewd man – shrewd for his years and shrewd in any company; shrewder than contemporaries had yet discerned. Even the Ambassador, set in a position of almost divine eminence over lesser mortals in the Embassy and generally presumed to be ignorant not only of the characters but even the names of underlings such as probationers, was quite sure of Francis's perceptiveness. The Ambassador happened to be aware of who had drafted the major part of that very incisive minute on Anglo-French collaboration which he had read in September. The Ambassador also knew Francis's family, although not well, and had marked him, genially, from first arrival. And when he had been in the Embassy three months, the Ambassador summoned him.

'I'd like to have a word with young Carr. See how he's getting on.'

The Ambassador felt benign. After a few agreeable exchanges and enquiries about relations, he indicated that the interview was about to end.

'Glad you're getting on so well. No problems, I hope?'

To his astonishment he found a pair of very pale blue eyes fixed on his in a way which somehow did not convey subordination, and heard Francis say very quietly, 'Yes, sir. There is a problem.'

'Anything I can help with?' said the Ambassador, feeling immensely benevolent but also irritated and resentful. He was not the King's representative to sort out the lives of honorary attachés.

'It is simply this, sir. Last night I dined with the von Karsteins. He's in the *Auswärtiges Amt*.'

'I know.' There was an edge to His Excellency's voice.

'After dinner another guest – a German who perhaps I'd better not name – started talking to me confidentially, facetiously, and offensively. He'd drunk too much brandy – a lot too much. I broke clear as soon as I could. I could see our host had noted it all and was angry. The fellow left early.'

'Well?'

'The man's remarks were about yourself, sir. They were deplorable, and I refused to listen, turned my back and left him to himself. I thought it right to tell you personally, since you've kindly seen me this morning and given me the opportunity.'

The Ambassador nodded. After a short silence he heard himself ask, very softly, 'What did he say?'

'He said that it was well known that your private view about this last summer's events was closer to Germany's than to our own Foreign Secretary's; and he said that everyone in Berlin knows that you regard Sir Edward as a weak Foreign Secretary with poor judgement.' Sir Edward Grey, the British Foreign Secretary, had been accused of feebleness that summer in face of what seemed a studied German act of discourtesy, when a British note of protest at German actions in Morocco had not been answered for three whole weeks. Some thought the original British reaction ill-judged. Others – or, in some cases, the same – reckoned that whether London was right or wrong, German manners were deliberately provocative and that Grey lacked backbone.

'And you very sensibly declined to listen to this improper and insulting stuff. Was that all?'

'No, sir. He said that your attitude is sufficiently well known because of your close friendship with a certain German lady.' Francis named her.

There was a long silence. At the end of it the Ambassador said, still very softly, 'Well, my boy, what did you think of all that?'

'I thought, and think, that the man, although near-tipsy, wanted to see whether I was prepared to hear, without objection, stuff like that about you. I imagine that had I, a member of your Mission, acquiesced even by silence, I would have been listed as one susceptible to some sort of advances. Worth trying.'

There was another silence. Then the Ambassador said, 'Thank

25

you, Francis. You did well. And your judgement was perfectly sound. Nor has this been particularly easy for you to tell me. I'm grateful.'

So acquaintances were right in supposing that despite an appearance of innocence, Francis Carr had a cool head. He was capable of a good deal of hardness. But they were also right that his head could be turned more easily than many by a woman. Long afterwards he sometimes reflected that he would have had an easier youth if he were one of those men who had never desired Veronica, whose blood did not race at the touch of her hand, the smell of her skin; who did not (despite all sense) indulge feverish hopes from the glance she would shoot out with a half-smile when she said goodbye. Then he asked himself if such men existed – and smiled a rather grim, secretive smile. Could any man boast that invulnerability? Cosmo Paterson, perhaps, who made his contempt for her so clear. But Francis would say to himself that Cosmo, whether consciously or not, had probably wanted her too.

Veronica Gaisford at that time was twenty-two, a year younger than Francis and (as he later discovered) exactly half the age her husband would by then have attained. She wore black, of course, and she looked enchanting. He guessed, correctly, that Veronica never looked anything but enchanting, yet black suited her best of all. She had very pale skin and fair hair – not exactly red, but a rich gold rather than ash blonde. Her wrists and ankles were particularly slender. They looked fragile – misleadingly so, for in fact her beautiful limbs were exceptionally strong. Most striking were her eyes – grey and very expressive, so that when they were fixed on a man's face they conveyed a sense, however improbably, that they wanted never to leave it. She spoke more with her eyes than any woman Francis had ever met. Her voice was low, but there was generally a touch of laughter hinted by it. Veronica laughed a good deal – quietly but sometimes irrepressibly. She had that gift, too, so rare and so irresistible, of giving her whole attention to a person, of devoting careful thought to whatever was said, slight or profound, and of responding in the same kind. No human being, Francis would think with mixed feelings, could more instantly and sympathetically match a companion's changing mood. No woman was quicker at anticipating feelings, putting another's half-formed thought into succinct and often amusing form. And he quickly discovered, and never changed the opinion, that no woman could be more fun.

Veronica was of medium height, slim and straight. After they parted, on that first occasion, Francis told himself that she was beautiful. He was not sure that her quality was exactly beauty in the visual and artistic sense, and he never saw a photograph of her which was better than a pallid distortion of the reality, a shell without a creature within. Reflecting on this long afterwards, he suspected she had sat for no skilled photographer – and perhaps the technique was less adventurously developed in those days, its products comparatively lifeless. But whether or not Veronica was formally beautiful, the impact she made was unmistakable. Men's hearts quickened whenever she appeared, however dark the circumstances. Francis's heart first beat faster that afternoon in the Excelsior. And afterwards he said, head aswim, 'She is beautiful!'

'Mr Francis Carr?' Veronica Gaisford was smiling at him. They exchanged some introductory sentences. 'You are much too kind – I never expected you to leave the Chancery, to call on me who have no sort of official standing or business! Or are Chanceries always closed in the afternoon? I don't know about such things.'

'If not closed, often deserted! We work in the mornings. Then we lunch – sometimes that goes on a long time. We call it part of our duties, you see! Sometimes I ride in the afternoon – but it's not unknown to work! Not that what I do is work, exactly.'

'Really? I think you're being deprecatory! You must explain to me a little of what you do, the position you have. I know I mustn't waste your time, but immediately I saw you sitting here, before you saw me, I thought –' She checked herself. 'No, I nearly committed an impertinence!'

Francis laughed.

27

'Please tell me what you thought! That I looked too young and insignificant to be of any importance in His Majesty's Diplomatic Service?'

'No. No! Oddly enough I at once said to myself, I can't tell why, "He is anxious. He is a very private person, not easy to know, and there is something anxious about him." I hope I was wrong!' She smiled, and, for a second, placed her fingertips on his sleeve.

Francis immediately wanted to talk, wanted to talk about himself. 'Yes,' he thought, 'how perceptive she is! I *am* anxious at the moment.' The cause of this anxiety was unexciting to a stranger. Very simply, he was short of money and uncertain of his future. He did not know whether the Diplomatic Service was the life for him, nor how he was appearing to his colleagues. He needed to feel little anxiety on the last point, but despite his good sense and considerable abilities, Francis lacked confidence. He was unsure of the impression he was creating, a little introspective. Furthermore, his health – he had always suffered from a form of asthma and it seemed to have worsened in Berlin – was doing nothing to improve his spirits. None of this was likely to intrigue Veronica – not, of course, that he yet knew her name was Veronica. He said –

'I've got no interesting anxieties, I'm afraid, Mrs Gaisford. I'm only attached to the Embassy, a sort of probationer, a person of no consequence. But I don't want you to feel you've been badly treated by being entrusted to such an underling, so I mustn't exaggerate my insignificance, I suppose.'

'I'm flattered,' said Veronica softly, 'that you should be giving me your time. Mr Parham wrote, as you know.'

'Mr Parham is Counsellor, an important person, you see! He will have told you that they're away from Berlin –'

'So he has, as you put it, entrusted me to you. I'm *so* glad! Shall we order some tea?'

Francis thought this an excellent idea. When it had been arranged, Veronica said, 'I mustn't be a bore to you, Mr Carr. But I have such confused impressions of Berlin – it's my first time here – that it's truly wonderful to have the chance to talk to somebody who knows it, to test my impressions, ask the questions I need to ask. You see, I have to pay a number of visits here, talk to some alarming-sounding people about my late husband's affairs. It's a daunting prospect, I can tell you.'

'Of course it is. Mrs Gaisford, I may be able to help a little. I know this city quite well now, I've been here since last autumn –'

'You're very kind. But I won't let you be used by me. I'm quite ruthless, you know. I exploit my friends horribly, especially if I like their company.' She smiled charmingly and with mock apology as she said this. Francis, with a flash of perception, felt it might be true. This was a woman of power.

He asked, delicately, if she would like to tell him the people she needed to see, and whether she wanted him to make any enquiries about them. He had no wish to be obtrusive – officious.

'That you could never be! I think – yes, I'm sure – that I'm quite well informed on these people.' She explained that under her husband's will a life interest in certain property in Germany was to pass to her. Suddenly she looked withdrawn and a little frightened.

'My lawyer in London has advised me to come here, to find out what that life interest will amount to. I have to see a German lawyer, a Herr – Herr Finckheim, *Rechtsan . . .*'

'*Rechtsanwalt.*'

'Yes, I'd forgotten. I speak German quite well. I had a German governess – ghastly! Then I must visit a Bank Director. And there's a colleague, a sort of German partner of my husband's, here in Berlin. I want to see him first. I've never met him but he's written two very charming letters. His name's Brendthase – Herr Wilhelm Brendthase.'

Francis thought he would find out what he could about Herr Brendthase from Commercial Section. Veronica said next, in a low voice, 'I know I shouldn't bother a stranger with my problems, but this visit matters a great deal to me. You see, due to various *quite* unexpected circumstances, my husband's English estate – well, it's largely melted away.' She looked vulnerable. Then she said, 'But let's talk about Berlin.'

They talked a little about the city, about commonplace things, what one tipped taxi-drivers, the hours offices opened, the peculiarities of contact by telephone in the German language. Berlin had impressed her, with its massiveness, the huge stuccoed buildings, the open spaces and broadness of the avenues, even dwarfing the boulevards of Paris; the considerable distances between places, the cleanliness, the uniforms, the sense of burliness and prosperity, the harsh, staccato voices under the cold sky. A great, grey, masculine city, forever on guard.

'Do they despise women here, for their feebleness? Will they do me down because I'm not a man?'

Francis felt protective.

'Not exactly. But there is something in that fear, yes.' Veronica moved her hand across her eyes for a moment. He said, 'Mrs Gaisford, I very much hope you will have lunch with me one day.'

'That's very kind, Mr Carr.'

'It would be delightful for me. Perhaps I can help a little as your – business gets further on.' Francis's fear of expensive hospitality now seemed vulgar and inappropriate. All he wanted was to see Veronica again.

He also wondered about the Excelsior. It was not a cheap place for a widow in difficult circumstances. Perhaps when Veronica said that her late husband's English estate had 'largely melted away' she was using relative terms. Perhaps a rich man was simply rather less rich than the world had supposed. An hour passed quickly. They arranged a date for luncheon.

Two mornings later there was a note at the Embassy.

'Dear Mr Carr,

Really – this is the twentieth century and I must *insist* on calling you "Francis". I am an old married woman, after all, and I feel I know you better than in fact I do. I was happier, after our talk, than I had been for rather a long time. Perhaps you have the gift of reassuring people just by the atmosphere you project – despite what I thought and impertinently said about your

30

anxiety! Anyway, you did me good and I look forward very much to next Thursday and our luncheon.

I have seen Herr Brendthase. I am deeply troubled by what I learned from him. I will explain further when we meet.

Your grateful friend,

Veronica Gaisford.'

Francis arrived in good time at the restaurant in a small street off the Kurfürstendamm. It was a cold, clear April day, with that icy-blue sky which only northern Europe produces, and with the shiver of east wind which tells Berliners that no mountain barrier lies between them and the Urals. The great plains, the forests, marshes and lakes extended eastward in those days into ancient Prussia, covered the Prussian provinces of Poland to the Vistula and Bug rivers. Berlin would always feel something of a frontier city, a place standing not far behind the march once held by the Teutonic Knights against the Slav.

The restaurant was warm, the windows misted, white table-cloths agleam, the low partitions between the tables creating intimacy. Francis had suggested a quarter to one – Berliners tended to eat punctually – and he only had to wait five minutes to hear swing doors revolve, and to sense rather than watch the head waiter moving towards his table, bowing, escorting. He rose. She smiled at her escort who bowed even lower and then straightened, back particularly erect, expression solicitous and content.

'Francis,' she said, 'I have a lot to say. But I can only say it if you do as I do. I mean, you really must call me Veronica.'

Veronica's news was bad. Brendthase had made the financial situation disagreeably clear. Gaisford's stake in their joint business was apparently worth very little. There were, Veronica explained in a rather muddled sort of way, considerable holdings of stock which looked important on paper. They were, it had been explained to her, now of small value and the income they produced was at present negligible.

'I can't believe it! My husband was so clever, so successful,

31

everybody thought. First, he left almost no money in England. Now this – this death blow! And right to the end I'm sure he was getting a good deal of his income from Germany. Everything's gone down, suddenly. A death blow!'

'I'm sure it won't be a death blow! Perhaps when it's gone into further –'

'I saw Herr Finckheim, the lawyer. My own lawyer took trouble to check on him. He has a high reputation for cleverness and honesty.'

Francis, too, had done some checking. with the same result.

'Herr Finckheim, I knew, could give me an objective view on what Herr Brendthase had told me. You see, I don't understand one thing about business, but the awful thought came to me that they – Brendthase – might have in mind to acquire my – my husband's – share in these companies cheap if I was depressed and desperate. They might be calling the value down. Brendthase did say something about – "It might be possible to dispose of your husband's holdings, but not, I fear, for very much money." I'm ashamed of such a beastly suspicion. It's just that I know so little.'

Veronica's eyes shone. Francis thought that her reactions about business might be as untutored as she declared, but were not exactly sluggish.

'Anyway, Herr Finckheim – he's rather an old stick but quite nice really – he spoke to all sorts of people and came back with some sort of estimate price that my husband's property here – his stake in various companies – might fetch. It's awfully little.' She frowned and added, 'I still can't understand how, in that case, we – he – seemed to be getting a large income from the German end right up to – well, until last year, anyway.'

'Do you know what sort of business he and Brendthase did?'

'Oh, shipping things, some sort of agency. Is that the right word?' she said vaguely. 'I know there was a lot of business between Europe and South America. Henry knew South America very well – he was there for years before we married. It all seems to have gone wrong.'

'Perhaps it's gone wrong quite recently.'

'Perhaps. Anyway, Herr Brendthase didn't put any of this in letters to England. What he wrote was quite – cryptic. Charming, but cryptic. That's why, after talking to people at home, I thought I'd better come here.' She looked across the table suddenly, very directly, and said, 'And I'm glad I did.'

Francis asked, delicately, about her immediate circumstances. He found he was blushing.

'Mrs Gaisford – Veronica –'

'That's better.'

'Veronica, it's awful cheek to say this, but the Excelsior's quite an expensive hotel. If you – as you've had rather disappointing news – perhaps we could find something –'

She smiled. 'Quite right. But I now have no need to stay in Berlin. I'm leaving on Sunday. I've seen everyone here. I've made lots of notes. I shall go and consult my lawyer in London – he's also my husband's executor, you see. Then I must see about selling the house.' She explained that she lived in London – a house, a 'little house' she called it, in South Street, Mayfair. A very expensive quarter. A very smart address.

'And then?'

'I must buy something really small and see how economically I can live.' She looked withdrawn, considering. Francis supposed that the proceeds of the sale of a house in South Street would produce a tolerable income. As if with the same thought she murmured, 'It's a nice long lease.'

Francis found that he had reached out his hand in a gesture of support and protection, and that she had placed hers in his, leaving it there. Now she pressed his hand and sighed. He felt slightly out of breath.

'Veronica, may I call on you when I return to London? I'm only attached to the Embassy here for another six months.'

'Of course, Francis. That would be lovely.' She told him an address which would 'probably always find her'. He suddenly realized how little he knew of her. An adventuress? Nonsense – their introduction, after all, had been effected by the appallingly respectable Parham.

They started telling each other something about themselves.

33

Francis had been brought up strictly, conventionally, always taught that his circumstances would be poorer than most of his contemporaries. 'You'll always be hard up,' his father had frequently said, almost with relish, 'but it's not the main thing that matters. Learn to live economically.' It was true and Francis did not resent it, but he grumbled inwardly at the implication that joylessness was his necessary fate. There was no joylessness in Veronica. Veronica was different. Veronica had an Irish father and an English mother and had been brought up in County Galway, 'allowed' as she put it, 'to run pretty wild'. An only child, she was orphaned at the age of seventeen when her mother died after a painful illness. Her father had died in the hunting field when she was eight years old.

'He taught me to ride. A lovely man.' Her heart, she said, was always to some extent in Ireland. Yet she had married the (it sounded) very English Gaisford. Francis suspected that neither parent had left much in the way of worldly goods behind them, and Gaisford, by Parham's account, implied if not explicit, had been able to make matters right in that direction. Francis wondered what he'd been like. He said –

'My own father died just before I came out here. Quite young.'

'I'm sorry.'

'I'll be in London when I go back. I'll be looking for rooms, hoping to work at the office – the Foreign Office – if they've not chucked me out by then. Veronica, I would certainly be a happy man if I could look forward to seeing you in England.'

'Anyway, Francis, this isn't goodbye, even in Berlin,' she said gently. 'Herr Brendthase is giving a little dinner for me tomorrow evening, and he's asking you.'

'Me?'

'You. I do hope you can come. He says he's got a son who's in the Army here in Berlin, who knows you.'

Francis stared, nodded and said, 'Of course.' It had never occurred to him. Gerhardt Brendthase! A quiet, charming man a few years older than Francis, a Lieutenant in a Saxon Guards Regiment, now attached to the Imperial General Staff in Berlin.

They had met at various receptions and liked each other. Francis had never connected him with Veronica's acquaintance. He supposed that he had already formed the instinctive view that a Lieutenant in a Household Regiment of Saxony would be unlikely to have close relations in the commercial world, and had thus subconsciously rejected the association. Berlin society was snobbish and hierarchical. Saxons of Brendthase's kind tended to be as closed a caste as the Prussian Junkers themselves.

So Brendthase was a Saxon! Possibly that, thought Francis, had produced a touch of softness which worked against ruthless commercial success! And Gaisford had suffered thereby.

Next evening, Herr Brendthase entertained. The party consisted of the Brendthases – Frau Brendthase spoke little and looked anxiously at her husband most of the time – and their son, Francis's friend Gerhardt, tall, slender, fair-haired, with beautiful manners. Making up numbers was a middle-aged lady introduced as Frau von Kattwitz, widow of an official in the *Auswärtiges Amt* – presumably to make Francis feel at ease. Frau von Kattwitz had travelled widely and had no doubt been promised a British diplomat. Disappointingly, Francis thought, she got him.

'In what Embassies have you served, Mr Carr?'

'In Berlin, Frau von Kattwitz. I am, at present, an honorary attaché only. I hope to make the Service my permanent career.'

She frowned. He did not appear serious! Frau von Kattwitz said, 'It means hard study. Hard, hard study.'

Francis reflected on his life in Berlin. There had been many long, joyous evenings – music, wine, coffee, singing. There had been stiff, demanding receptions, honorary attachés expected to marshal, to ease the task of their superiors, to be unfailingly pleasant. There had been rides in the Grünewald, sunlight speckling the beech leaves, pretty girls, a memorable visit to the Masurian Lakes and to Königsberg. Hard, hard study? He thought not.

'Yes indeed, Frau von Kattwitz, you are right. Hard, hard study.'

Veronica was asking Gerhardt Brendthase about his life.

'I suppose you have a lot of parades and so forth, being a Guards Regiment? Royal birthday reviews, that sort of thing. Do you enjoy that?'

'Yes,' said Gerhardt Brendthase seriously. 'Yes, I do enjoy it. Just now, of course, I am here in Berlin, in an office. But when I'm with my regiment I do enjoy that side of things.' Quietly and simply he started telling Veronica about the Emperor's birthday parade as celebrated in the garrison city in Saxony where his regiment had their home.

'The Emperor's birthday is in January – there's generally snow on the ground. When the cathedral clock begins to strike and the first gun of the saluting battery fires, the huge procession begins its round of the troops. Very cold! They play the *Prasentier Marsch*! Six thousand men are standing, presenting arms.'

Egged on by Veronica, he talked about the King's birthday, the King of Saxony. They were all listening, smiling, nodding.

'That's in May. Our regiment comes last into the Palace Square, it's edged with chestnut trees. We march on just to a drum and fife band. Then it stops playing and for four paces you hear nothing but the fifteen hundred pairs of boots of our regiment, crunch, crunch, crunch, crunch – then the bands strike up our regimental march, a sort of hunting song. It's wonderful! Weber composed it for us.'

'Your uniform is grey?'

'Dark green – it looks black from a distance, the collars and cuffs are black.' He smiled. 'The people shout, "*Die Schwarzen, Die Schwarzen*!"'

Francis watched Veronica's face as she gazed with encouraging enthusiasm at Gerhardt Brendthase. He could not suppress the feeling that this gift of absorbed attention was insufficiently discriminate. What were Browning's lines in 'My last Duchess'?

> 'She liked whate'er
> She looked on, and her looks went everywhere!'

But Veronica was superb that evening. She was a woman of extraordinary vitality, so that every word she uttered, every small movement she made, every expression that crossed her face, all, in a certain harmony, enhanced her physical beauty and conveyed enchantment, power and life. She wore a narrow-waisted black dress, with bare shoulders towards which every man's eyes went as if drawn by magnetic force. She glowed and shimmered.

Brendthase listened with indulgent pride to h:s son's descriptions. He was also, Francis could see, closely studying Veronica, and her effect upon others. Sometimes he shot a penetrating look towards Francis himself. More generally, and unusually for a German paterfamilias, he acted in conversation as the prompter of others. He seemed to enjoy hearing his son talk.

Gerhardt spoke simply, with infectious enthusiasm, without arrogance. He isn't boring, Francis thought. He made them see and hear the scene, the spring leaves on the chestnuts, the mighty column of perfectly drilled troops, the thrilling, blood-stirring crackle of the trumpets as they deafened the cheering crowds with the wild melody of Weber's march. He made them, with his quiet, vivid sentences, share that pride in corporate discipline which – Francis rather grudgingly found he believed – must animate every one of *Die Schwarzen*. How not?

Both the elder Brendthases murmured, assenting, approving, their expressions rapt now, the same look that could be seen on a hundred thousand faces in the Unter den Linden when the Kaiser rode back from review. Perhaps it was the same in London? Francis was uncertain. Relations between Germany and Britain were not happy in those months of 1912 and there was a good deal of hostile feeling and talk in both countries, each with a strong sense both of threat and of invincible rectitude. And for more than a decade Imperial Germany – land power by clear tradition, with Brendthase's compatriots ready to be mobilized by the million – had been building a mighty, ocean-going navy, challenging Britain at sea.

Francis listened to Gerhardt Brendthase's gentle rhapsody on the pleasures of the military life in time of peace, unsure of his reactions. His ambivalence of feeling had more than one cause. He observed, with an unreasonable spasm of jealousy, how the young Saxon's voice shook very slightly as he talked, how his breath quickened as he sometimes raised his eyes to meet Veronica's.

Agreeably, Francis said to him, 'Does any nation combine thoroughness and practicality with so much emotion and feeling as yours? You do nothing by halves, do you!'

Gerhardt Brendthase smiled. 'I think you are right.'

'Well, I hope soldiering can be confined to parades and martial music,' said Francis, a little awkwardly. Perhaps, on reflection, it was undiplomatic for a diplomat to imply that there could even be a doubt in the matter.

Brendthase the elder nodded to this heavily, however, and said, 'Why not? Why not? England and Germany, above all, need to understand each other,' and Francis shied away from more serious talk with a smile and an inclination of the head. He thought Veronica's eyes were on him and that he did not imagine a small sigh.

When they parted that evening, Veronica whispered, 'Francis, I have had another *business* talk with Herr Brendthase. I can't tell you how thoughtful and kind he's been.'

Francis helped her with her coat. 'How?'

'He says it's possible one of the – enterprises – my Henry, my husband, had invested in may still be converted to something really profitable. Something about a limited offer of shares in a new venture, to people who held preference stock in the old – I don't understand it.' (But, he thought, she had a remarkably accurate and retentive memory all the same.) 'He might be able to do something about that. I might even come again – Frau Brendthase has been angelic and asked me to stay with them.'

Next day Veronica left Berlin.

Francis's duties with Veronica were, of course, known to colleagues at the Embassy. The morning after she left, one of them, older by several years, took his arm.

'Well, well! Mrs Henry Gaisford! Did she refer to it directly? Awkward for you – there was a good deal in the English papers. I think it was when you were taking that holiday in the east.'

'I don't know what you mean.'

Parham was back at his desk the following Wednesday. Francis went to his office and told him he thought Veronica's business had gone as well as could be hoped, but that she had undoubted problems and worries. Parham looked uninterested.

'No doubt, no doubt . . . To tell the truth, I heard Gaisford had been in pretty deep water. Thank you for coping, Carr.'

'There's one thing.' Francis wore a slightly embarrassed, albeit courteous smile, to rob his reproach of impertinence.

'One thing?'

'One thing you might have told me. You might have told me her husband cut his throat.'

CHAPTER II

Soon after he returned to London, just before Christmas, 1912, Francis wrote to Veronica. He had, after her departure from Berlin, decided that he was not in the least in love with her, that he had no intention of pursuing her. Despite the unsettling effect she had on him when he was actually with her, Francis did not feel desperate or driven to make a fool of himself, to write tormented letters, hope feverish and futile hopes. Susceptible he was, but sense would always have a habit of breaking in. Nevertheless, there was something about Veronica which made Francis restless until he saw her again, and this something survived eight months of Berlin without word of her. He was, of course, callow. He would not, at that time, have articulated the words 'in love', even to himself, without some thought of a serious, even a permanent relationship. With such as Veronica, he would have presumed in those days that this must include the possibility of marriage – and it was incredible that Veronica would contemplate marrying someone like insignificant and penniless Francis Carr. This was not so much reasoning – for he never put the matter to himself – as instinctive reaction. Of course, although unsophisticated, Francis was not so absurdly innocent as to neglect the thought of a casual 'affair' – Veronica was a widow, and although vulnerable to gossip was, by some standards, fair game for those so minded. Francis was far from a puritan. But, somehow, although sure he was not 'in love', the disturbing effect the thought of Veronica had on him was a matter of the heart, and he associated these feelings with old-fashioned concepts and words – love, honour, commitment, permanence.

And as he admitted to himself, the idea of Veronica filled

Francis not only with desire – he recognized that and it was fitfully strong; not only with a stirring of the emotions, but also with unease. There was something of the witch in her, he thought. Was it – would it ever be – possible to trust her? When she caught one's words in mid-air, when she said, 'Yes, ye., you put that *exactly* right!' – would she not say the same to another man in an hour? Her pressure on one's hand – was it not practised and meaningless? Was she a seductive but superficial creature? He wasn't sure.

Veronica never answered the letter. It appeared later that it was not forwarded. She had sold her house in South Street and moved, as Francis discovered afterwards, to an address in Ebury Street, a different matter altogether.

The Marvell brothers were always favourite cousins of Francis Carr, both enjoying a distinction Francis felt he lacked. Alan, the elder, was a soldier, a cavalryman, posted to India at the beginning of 1911, two years before all this. He was a vigorous, handsome young man, tall, dark-haired, muscular, with something a little daunting about him – a dominant creature, even a shade brutal although this was not betrayed by his excellent manners and apparent good nature. Alan did all things well. He was quick-witted without being intellectually showy; it was said that his brother officers in the cavalry regarded him with awe as some sort of genius. The unkind remarked, of course, that he stood out there among the exceptionally brainless and uneducated, but in any company Alan would have impressed by the sharpness and rapidity of his mind. He read widely and, in some company, even liked talking about books. As a boy he had been a promising scholar and when he had – to the surprise of many – decided he wished to join the Army, he had been very easily at the top of the Army class. Alan's brains, however, did not make him unpopular, as could have happened in the England and the Service of those days, for he was also an excellent horseman, a good shot, and genial company although there was always a sense, with him, of one who did not suffer fools gladly,

41

a man whose toleration was limited. Francis admired him but sometimes felt a poor thing, lacking robustness, by comparison.

The Marvells' mother was Francis Carr's mother's first cousin. In material terms, Mrs Marvell had done better for herself. Bargate, the Marvell home in Sussex, was an agreeable, sprawling, unpretentious place, and while not deemed rich, the family seemed to live comfortably on their own land. Everything at Bargate was very well done, and since the ownership of land was far from lucrative at that time, they had, the world supposed, certain other reserves. Francis's father, David Carr, had died just before his son went to Berlin – in the same year as Alan Marvell's father, both at a surprisingly early age, leaving the two widowed cousins, close friends. David Carr used to snort about Cousin Marvell of Bargate. 'Money running out of his ears,' he would say, privately, in the family circle, since discussion of people's financial circumstances was held to be in poor taste. 'Money running out of his ears! His father blued a lot with those ridiculous additions to the house, but he's got more than enough to come and go on!' These comments, however, were not evidence. David Carr always felt himself to be poor and, being human, he looked on the life at Bargate with some envy. By the world at large, the Marvells were thought of as discreetly well-off. Alan's regiment was an expensive one for a subaltern of those days, although military life in India was financially easier than elsewhere. His mother lived at Bargate and looked after things for him with quiet competence. Alan was, at that time, twenty-four.

John Marvell, the younger brother, also dark, but slender and built to a slighter scale, was a young man of striking good looks. He was two years younger than Alan, to whom he was deeply and admiringly devoted. To Francis, John was the more congenial of the two. He was younger than his cousin, less intimidating than his brother – one with whom everyone felt instinctive sympathy. John, underneath a light, often bantering exterior was a resolute young man when he made up his mind, but he had a certain deprecatory modesty, often expressed with humour and always with charm, which contrasted with Alan's vigorous assur-

42

ance. Like his brother, John Marvell had that quality which Francis could only describe to himself, a little enviously, as distinction. When he was persuaded by another to be serious, when somebody said to him – 'No, John, I mean it, and I want to know what you really think,' he would pause to consider his reply, eyes thoughtful, mouth quizzical, something always arresting about him. John 'filled a room' when he entered it – less perhaps than his brother, but very perceptibly. 'A charmer,' people said, a little uncertainly, 'a real charmer, John Marvell. Do anything for you, too, but I'm blessed if I ever know what he's really thinking.' He moved with a certain nervous, impulsive force which drew eyes to him.

Of Alan's fondness for John there was no doubt. It was not a demonstrative age, but there was something in Alan's smile and eyes when he looked at his younger brother which was not there at other times.

Francis had a note from John Marvell early in June 1913.

'Did you know I had become a publisher? It's rather enjoyable so far, although I don't know whether I'll be any good at it. Will you come and lunch here ("here" was his publishing house, small but certainly distinguished) and meet some of the nice people I work with? Ladies, too! We're having a very fashionable party indeed, rather dashing in fact! Do come if you can.' He named a day and Francis was delighted to accept.

Francis had now spent six months in England. The Diplomatic Service of those days was amiably deficient in what a later age would describe as 'career planning' – let alone in scientific methods of assessing suitable entrants. Berlin's climate did not suit Francis, his asthma worsened and he was sent home – home to London, to a number of undemanding tasks in the Office compatible with his rather delicate state of health. Until 1914, he was not due to be a full member of the Service. He was still on trial and still virtually unremunerated, but had not been rejected. Whether he was useful to the country, Francis found difficult to judge. He did various duties, of an assistant private secretary character, which somebody had to do. He did them, and even suspected this himself, extremely well; and by employing a man in return for the possibility of a future rather than for cash in the hand, the Government, he told himself equably, was getting a reasonable bargain.

Although he had greatly enjoyed Berlin, Francis was delighted with the pattern of life in peaceful, social, luxury-loving London, a London particularly kind to a young man with a passport into society. Like all his contemporaries, he accepted the current conventions without particular question – indeed, with a good deal of gratitude. In every European capital city the small observances of life were demanding. As a bachelor, living in a small set of rooms off St James's, Francis often changed his clothes several times a day. To the office he usually wore a morning coat, its tails having replaced a full-skirted frock coat in fashion some years before, at least among the young. After leaving the office and returning to his rooms before going to a club (even impecunious Francis belonged to several) to play bridge or billiards, loiter, gossip, his morning dress was replaced by some sort of suit, dependent on season and climate. This, in turn, was exchanged for evening clothes – as often as not a tail coat, white waistcoat and white tie – before dining. These habits varied somewhat with the time of year, as did the amount of entertainment a young man could expect. During 'The Season', which started in the spring and continued until the end of July, there were almost always dances – often several dances each night – to which Francis was invited, as a young single man in London. Often, too, these were preceded by dinner parties to which he was also invited. There were frequent luncheon parties as well. Entertainment and a satisfying amount of food and wine were, therefore, virtually free.

This suited Francis, who had little money. Rooms, lunches, clothes and club subscriptions could just be funded. An excellent, Irish, retired butler and his wife, Mr and Mrs Flannery, kept the rooms – there were four bachelor sets in the house – and looked after their clothes. Francis lived well on a small income although there was little over for entertaining or travel. The hospitality of the rich acted as a pleasant redistributor of wealth among such as him.

Furthermore, the 'weekend' had become part of the scene. It was referred to in a hostess's letter of invitation as 'Friday to Monday', to avoid the insulting suggestion that the week might be occupied by toil, leisure reserved only for its end. Francis was often asked to some house in the country, a train journey's distance from London, where, for three or four days, a collection of people of all ages assembled, ate, drank, played tennis, croquet, billiards and bridge, gossiped, flirted and passed the time. Some houses – rarely those at which he found himself – were centres of political talk and intrigue, others were entirely dedicated to sport of some kind. The best, he discovered, were those presided over by a hostess who simply delighted in bringing individuals together, in stimulating their conversation and their enjoyment of each other. A good many houses, of course, were plain dull. Francis sampled most kinds. On occasion, Flannery, by agreement and for a small fee, left his wife in London and came with him in the guise of manservant. It was all great fun and Francis's asthma bothered him less and less.

Taxis had largely replaced horse-drawn cabs in London, and Francis, leaving the Office later than he had hoped, found one for the short distance to Jermyn Street. The driver, perched on his seat in the open front part of the machine, manoeuvred past three carriages and moved into and down the Mall with what seemed reckless speed. The taxis in Berlin had been rigorously controlled as to velocity, and Berliners, like Londoners, were still abusing the noise and fumes of the now ubiquitous motor car.

The room in which John and his colleagues entertained their guests for luncheon was small, panelled, and apparently crowded with people who knew each other but certainly didn't know Francis. John took his arm on arrival.

'You must meet one of my colleague's guests, a quite remarkable fellow, Cosmo Paterson. I don't think you know him.'

Francis had heard of Cosmo Paterson, who was associated with some curious tales. In one of them he had, when at Oxford, spent a long vacation prospecting for gold in a remote part of South America, had actually found some, had obtained a concession and then lost it at a gambling session in São Paulo, all before term started in October. In another story, Paterson had fought a duel in Romania, challenged by a man he had knocked down for saying that Great Britain was rapidly becoming a third-rate power because of the luxury and laziness of its people. Francis had never met Paterson, but everybody had heard of him. He doubted whether the popular accounts of those exploits had much substance – but England liked its heroes in simple form in those days and Cosmo Paterson fitted the type.

Rather to Francis's surprise, Paterson was small, fair-haired, and appeared attractively quiet and modest. He was about twenty-six, perhaps a year or two more, and although John Marvell's description of him as 'quite remarkable' turned out to be true, he made no attempt to impress. Only his eyes were immediately arresting – pale blue, very penetrating and extraordinarily restless. Francis was reminded of Stevenson's description of Alan Breck Stewart's appearance in *Kidnapped*: he whose eyes 'had a kind of dancing madness in them that was both engaging and alarming.' They shook hands and Paterson said, 'I know about you. You've been living in Berlin.'

'Yes – do you know it?'

'Never been there. But you've got a friend here, someone who knew you in those days, heard you were coming, been talking of you.'

Francis had not so far been introduced to anybody and had not spotted his Berlin acquaintance. At that moment, Paterson's arm was taken by a stout man of about thirty-five with a very pale face and red hair. He nodded in a bored sort of way at Francis and spoke to Paterson with an appearance of intimacy.

'Now, Cosmo, I want to hear what exciting things you've been up to recently!' He swung Paterson towards him, simultaneously half turning his back to Francis. It was a manoeuvre of exclusion. Cosmo Paterson, without apparent effort, freed his arm, smiled pleasantly at the red-headed man, and said to Francis –

'Do you know Dominic Drew? Printer,' he said to the other,

46

'This is Francis Carr. Diplomat. We were talking about Berlin.'

'Really!' said Drew, whom Paterson had called 'Printer'. He spun the word into a drawl, sustaining the deliberate effect of boredom, of finding it tedious not to have Paterson to himself. 'Really! And what, I wonder –'

But at that moment an entirely distinctive voice, low, gentle, remembered, said, 'Francis!' Francis turned sharply and found himself looking at Veronica. Almost immediately they moved into luncheon.

Veronica was sitting between John Marvell and Francis. On Marvell's other side was a large, forceful lady whose name Francis never caught but who was, he gathered, the wife of one of John's older colleagues. Francis heard her addressing John pleasantly but with authority on the book scene of the day, and suspected that this neighbour's opinion might matter. Veronica looked at Francis, a smile in her eyes. It was as it had been.

'Francis, do you know everybody here?' It was not a large table but conversation was loud and everyone seemed to be speaking at once. It was possible to exchange quiet words without ill manners.

'No. I've never met anyone except you, and my cousin, John Marvell. My host.'

'My host, too. I only discovered last week that you were cousins. I asked him to invite you.'

Francis did not welcome this information. It implied a closeness of relationship with John which disturbed him. And why did Veronica and he need the contrivance of an intermediary in order to meet? Why –?

'Veronica, you never answered my letter. I wrote just after I returned to London. Last Christmas, in fact. To the address you gave me. I got no reply.'

'Francis, I never got a letter from you. Never!'

'Oh dear! I said I'd write and I did. I hoped you'd – that we'd meet.'

'Well, we've met.'

'Yes, but I've been back six months.'

'Never mind. I still live in London.' She told him of the house

47

in Ebury Street. She told him, too, that she had spent several months in Ireland, mostly in Dublin, earlier that year. 'It's always been home to me. I feel alive there. It refreshes me.'

Her eyes danced when she said this. Francis remembered the catch in her voice when she'd talked in Berlin about her childhood, about Ireland – talked evocatively, with a strong touch of romanticism. Then Veronica started questioning him about the European situation, softly, intelligently, and he was struck as he had once been in Berlin by how perceptive she was, while disclaiming any understanding of affairs. She flattered Francis by assuming he was an expert on Germany, but there was nothing gross in the flattery.

'Francis, please tell me about this Turkish business.'

The Treaty of London, signed only a few weeks before, had ended the latest Balkan war. Turkey, Germany's most recently acquired ally, had been gravely weakened. The Serbs, hated and distrusted by Germany's Austrian partners, were cock-a-hoop.

Veronica said, 'I imagine they feel pretty sick about it all in Berlin, as well as in Vienna, don't they?'

'I think perhaps they do.'

'What does Grey think?'

'I suppose,' said Francis, a little taken aback, 'that Sir Edward, as usual, will try to mend fences with everybody and be soothing. I expect his line will continue to be that Germany has got no reason to think there's some great plan to surround her with a hostile array of France, Russia and Serbia, all supported by the British fleet. If that myth could be laid to rest, I don't think Turkey –'

Veronica had been listening carefully. She interrupted.

'The English aren't very good at seeing things from other people's standpoint. You may not agree, Francis, but I think it's a national characteristic. And weakness.'

'We do our best. In the Office.'

Veronica sighed. She looked beautiful.

Francis felt that he could not, at that moment, possibly ask about her personal affairs – whether things had turned out better for her than had appeared likely in Berlin. She seemed quiet, serious. He saw Dominic Drew's eyes on her from across the table, and was less than overjoyed when Drew leant forward and used her Christian name. Francis had already decided he disliked Drew. Now Drew talked with his mouth full and spat a few particles of dressed crab towards their side of the table.

'Veronica, I intend to take you to –' Drew mentioned an exhibition, much talked about. Cubism. Francis was unversed in modern art. With pleasure he heard John Marvell interrupt from Veronica's other side, voice agreeably sardonic.

'Braque and all that! Tell me, Drew, do you really like it or do you simply feel the need to admire novelty – because news is your business?'

John's remark might be Philistine – a Philistinism Francis shared at that time – but it told him what he had not previously known, that 'Printer' Drew was a journalist.

'The latter, of course,' somebody called out with a laugh, with what sounded as if it might be relish at the thought of Drew not having things all his own way. 'The latter! Printer's a creature of fashion, not of artistic insight. He'd never boast otherwise, would you, Printer?'

Drew joined in the laugh, recognizing that he was being goaded for a response to which they would listen; to which they, having goaded, would, as it were, be bound to listen. It was the sort of opening he never missed. He started talking about the Cubists, about Paris, talking with mocking contempt for those of the company who might be unfamiliar with the names he dropped, talking with the odd hint of scandal, talking if not with artistic understanding (that Francis certainly could not tell) at least with mastery of jargon. Talking outrageously, talking amusingly. He was winning this round easily. After an admirable performance which went on several minutes, he was master of the luncheon table. It was unlikely that many had assimilated, perhaps even understood, all of what he said but thenceforth he provided, as it were, the conversational centre of gravity. Lunch continued. At one point Drew looked again at Veronica.

'You'll come, then? Thursday?'

'Yes, I think that will do.'

'I'll call for you,' Printer Drew said. 'Let's say three o'clock.' There was no interrogation in his voice. Francis suddenly noticed that Cosmo Paterson had been looking hard at them both, eyeing first Drew, then Veronica, with a half-smile on his face, paying no attention to his neighbour (they were sitting at an oval table).

Then a remarkable thing happened.

Cosmo – Francis was already thinking of him with curiosity and something like affection, by that name – rose from the table without word or explanation and walked round until he was standing immediately behind the chair of Printer Drew. Then, without the slightest warning, using a lot of force, he overturned the chair backwards so that Drew crashed to the ground in a sprawl of flailing arms and legs, to the accompaniment of a sort of screech. There was absolute silence. Cosmo stood with a somewhat theatrical pose over Drew, who was scrabbling about on the floor prior to heaving himself to his feet. A man opposite Francis was wearing a monocle which dropped from his eye. Cosmo's right arm was raised, as if imploring an audience to listen carefully to some exquisite and elusive sound.

'Please note,' he said with a contented smile, 'that Printer is entirely unharmed. The trick is to give no warning, so that the body is relaxed. I was, of course, ready to catch and steady him if he showed the slightest sign of falling badly. He was never in any danger of hurting himself. I promise you you weren't, my dear fellow.'

Cosmo was the luncheon guest of a senior colleague of John Marvell, a grey-haired man who, Francis suspected, did not actually know his guest very well. Now he looked speechlessly at the chairman of the firm who had been sitting at the end of the table as if in a trance, peered at Cosmo and said, rather breathlessly – 'I think, Mr Paterson, that we'd better be going.'

They had reached the pudding stage of the meal. It was not a strong speech but the grey-haired man clearly felt that nothing less would be appropriate, and hoped, rather desperately, that after one exhibition of violence Cosmo might be prepared to return to the norms of conventional behaviour and leave.

'I agree,' said Cosmo, to what felt like a sigh of universal relief,

'I agree, I have to leave now. Thank you all so much for a charming luncheon.'

Printer Drew, now upright and breathing heavily, brushed off a few vestiges of food: he had spilt these from a spoon clenched in his right hand during the fall. Everybody avoided his eye. He was not a man, however, to let such an incident die upon the air, unmarked. The moment for hitting Cosmo, unthinkable though such brawling might have seemed in front of ladies and between morning-coated gentlemen in St James's in 1913, had clearly passed. Anyway, something about Cosmo suggested it might have been a hazardous reaction – although Drew was by far the bigger man. Now he found his voice. He spoke into what was still a great silence. Cosmo and his host had not yet moved to leave.

'Why the hell did you do that, Cosmo? You lunatic, murderous fool!'

'Oh, why did I do it, you ask?' said Cosmo with a gentle smile, 'I did it to make Mrs Gaisford laugh!'

The appalled hush around the table was broken again, by the gentle sound of a woman laughing; Veronica, weakly, apologetically, and very musically laughing.

Francis himself left soon afterwards. People excused themselves uneasily. The smooth surface of life had been awkwardly, absurdly cracked and there was uncertainty as to how to behave. Printer Drew made some remarks to nobody in particular about Cosmo's notorious instability, and said goodbye after reminding Veronica of their arrangement. Veronica herself was held for a few minutes in deep conversation by John. Francis went up to them and was surprised to see how concentrated was the expression on John's face. He thanked his cousin for lunch.

'It was enjoyable. And surprising.'

'Odd thing to do. He's a bit mad,' said John, without rancour. He added: 'Poor old Drew! I don't – still, it's rather a rotten sort of thing to undergo!'

Veronica giggled. Francis said to her, 'I'll try to force myself on your company now I've found you. I hope you'll dine with me one evening.'

'Thank you, Francis, I'd like that very much.'

John shook his hand and asked if he could find his way out. It was plain that he hoped for a few minutes yet of Veronica's company. After Francis had walked a hundred yards up the street, he heard his name called.

'Carr!'

It was Cosmo Paterson. He came up and slipped his arm through the other's.

'Come on, let's walk, it's a lovely afternoon.'

'I'm going back to the Foreign Office.'

'Splendid! I'll do the whole distance with you.'

They walked towards St James's Palace. After a minute, Francis said, 'You made quite a sensation.'

'Yes, I wanted to see how Drew would take it. And I wanted to make him as ludicrous as I could in front of Veronica Gaisford.'

'Do you know her?'

'Yes, I know her. Known her on and off for several years. Ireland. Here and there. Cousin of hers used to be a good friend of mine. Veronica Gaisford, yes, I know her.' He gave something like a sigh and added, without change of tone, 'She's a destructive woman, a bad woman in many ways.'

Francis was prepared neither to concede nor dispute this. Cosmo added quietly, 'She's a real little lady for asking questions, too. People talk to her. People who should know better. Still, she deserves better than Drew.'

'Is there any question of her getting Drew, whatever she deserves?'

'Oh, he's after her. You could see today, and it's well known. He's proprietorial. Or predatory, rather.'

'Perhaps she's taken with him.' Francis hated saying it.

'Perhaps she is a bit, although God knows it's hard to understand a woman's fancies. But I don't think so. I think he's got – I think she's frightened, hard though she is. There's something –'

But as Francis turned to look at him, sick in heart at what the other said with such nonchalant assurance, as he opened his mouth to question, as he tried to keep his voice steady and said, 'But look!' Cosmo suddenly stopped dead in his tracks and asked, 'What day's today?'

'Tuesday. Listen, about what you were saying –'

'*Tuesday*?' shouted Cosmo. 'My God, I'm late already.' The clock on St Ja.nes's Palace struck three o'clock. 'My God, a cab, a cab, my kingdom for a cab!' yelled Cosmo, striking Francis's shoulder in friendly farewell. Francis watched him race like a sprinter into Pall Mall.

CHAPTER III

The weekend spent with the Winters was the watershed of the business as far as Francis was concerned. Nothing was the same thereafter. Mrs Winter's letter arrived soon after the extraordinary luncheon at which he had met Drew and Paterson for the first time.

The Winters lived in Hampshire, and Francis knew them quite well – a hospitable pair with no children and a large, rather ugly house set in beautiful country near Petersfield. Adrian Winter, a man of about fifty, had held a seat in Parliament for several years but had given up, due to some unsuspected form of ill health, it was said. He now seemed perfectly fit again, although not very energetic. He appeared content to do and say little, smiling agreeably, dispensing ample hospitality, treating his guests, whatever their age, with an easy intimacy which in the past had won the heart of many an uncertain elector. He played the part of backdrop to his more formidable wife's energetic essays in entertainment.

Mrs Winter was large and somewhat overpowering, but exceedingly kind. She pretended to regard any young bachelor as grist to her matchmaking mill. She could be rather awfully playful.

'Now, Francis Carr, I think I've got exactly the right answer for you – she's enchanting, and a real little ambassadress in the making! Now, my dear boy, you must show some initiative –'

Her young men ran out of deprecatory smiles, but she had a generous heart. Her food and wine were excellent. Francis had first met the Winters with the Marvells at Bargate and had no hesitation in accepting Mrs Winter's invitation to stay 'From Friday to Monday, in the middle of July'. He hardly knew what he felt – plain jealousy, he said to himself with honesty, more likely than not – on reading one sentence in her letter,

> 'John Marvell will be here. Also Veronica Gaisford, whom I know you have met. *Entre nous*, I'm a little anxious there. I'm not sure she's right for ·lear John! I'd like to hear what you think if we can have a quiet, discreet little talk together! John is one of the most distinguished young men I know, and deserves much. I know how fond you are of the Marvells . . .'

But before that weekend at Faberdown, the Winters' house, Francis saw Veronica again.

It had been a particularly hot and sultry day, and Francis felt the need for more air and space than the London parks provided. He had no particular arrangements for the evening and decided to take the underground train to Richmond and stroll for a bit in Richmond Park. Quite a lot of people had the same idea, and as he cleared the borough of Richmond itself and climbed to the lovely expanse of the park, he saw that a number of couples and the occasional solitary were ambling in the same direction. He had forgotten that there was so much of a walk – a hot, sticky walk – between the station and the edge of town, and after about half an hour, having reached a satisfying stretch of parkland, he thought he'd sit for a while and cool off.

In spite of their encounter at the extraordinary Marvell luncheon, and Veronica's easy friendliness on that occasion, Francis had not yet written to her to suggest any further meeting. He wanted to do so, but was unsure what he felt about Cosmo's account of her connection with Printer Drew, as well as about what he suspected of John Marvell's feelings, a suspicion confirmed by Mrs Winter's letter, just received. The situation must be unpromising for himself, he thought – and to what promise, anyway, did he aspire? To take even the smallest step towards courtship of Veronica, however tentative and uncommitted, was likely to lead to pain and little else. Yet he wanted to, despite earlier and sensible resolve. To his annoyance, he found he could not rid himself of the picture of Veronica, nor drive the sound of her voice, her laugh, from his ears, nor forget the fleeting touch, the fragrance of her.

During the months which had passed after that first encounter in Berlin, months of a change of scene, new duties, new faces, Francis had effectively persuaded himself that Veronica was simply one of many attractive married women (albeit in this case a widow) met all the time in the course of life and particularly in London. There had been nothing special about her. But he knew that there had, and the knowledge had been immediately confirmed by that meeting at luncheon, although a year had elapsed. Her tone, her smile when she said 'Francis!' had instantly dispelled the consoling illusion that Veronica was like others. She conveyed something – a sheer *quality*, he said to himself, it's like an electric force – which was unique in Francis's experience, and he was disconcertingly reminded of the fact within minutes of their meeting again. Here was a woman disturbing enough to break a man's heart, he thought, not simply to make me itch with desire, however strong, but to turn me weak and helpless and destroy both my will and my peace of mind. Yet it sounds as if she has two – it's probably at least two – pretty successful suitors. And she is, he thought, well beyond my reach. I cannot hope to rise and fly towards that sort of star.

Richmond Park was not infested with park benches, symbols of urban values. Francis wanted a piece of turf on which to stretch, ideally with some shade and no other human being, and thought he saw exactly the place. A small clump of fine trees crowned the small hillock he'd been traversing. He'd seen nobody climbing towards them, and he trudged up the rather steep slope towards a sharp crest. Most of the trees were just beyond it. He reached the top.

Then he stopped. He'd been beaten to it, he thought with irritation. The clump was smaller than appeared from a distance, and although it would be absurdly easy to find a place, relax, without any sense of 'butting in', nevertheless the presence of the couple sitting on the ground about fifteen yards beyond and below him was inhibiting. Those two, a man and a woman, were talking earnestly, seemed so absorbed in each other. The lines of their bodies conveyed something peculiarly intense. It was not the intensity of love but there was an urgency about it, of that Francis felt sure. These people had sought solitude with set purpose. They were sitting a little apart, with nothing of the appearance of lovers. A quarrel? He thought not. These speculations flashed through his mind as he decided to slip away. If he had had to find a word, afterwards, to convey their attitude as evidenced by their backs, and the possible character of their conversation, he thought he would have offered 'business-like', but the impression had been formed in no more than five seconds.

Francis felt an intruder. Instinctively he started to move quietly back down the slope which he'd climbed. The man and woman were engrossed in their conversation. Neither turned their head. Francis had not been seen or heard. Then the woman laughed, and Francis froze, listening now to her voice as she spoke more loudly. There was no doubt. It was Veronica.

Francis felt a grotesque lout for his instant resentment. Why shouldn't Veronica go for a walk in Richmond Park on a summer evening as well as he? He felt fiercely inquisitive about her companion but, again, it was no business of Francis Carr with whom she passed her time. They were now out of sight – the crest was sharp and a very few backward steps had taken his head below the brow of the hill. The glimpse he'd had of the man's back, however, had made it clear that it was not Printer Drew. This was a slender back, and the hair he had seen beneath a curly brimmed bowler was very fair. It was not Printer Drew. Nor was it John Marvell.

Francis hated himself for what happened next. He moved again cautiously to the crest of the little ridge. He moved up, inch by inch, until he could see Veronica and whoever was with her while his own head was the only part of him that could be visible if they turned – and could quickly be ducked behind cover. He spied. They were sitting on a fairly steep downward slope. It was improbable – and not particularly easy to do – that they would suddenly swivel their heads and peer upwards in his direction. Heart beating, he spied. It was, he knew, unpardonable.

Veronica seemed to be talking with animation, the man offering only an occasional remark. Once Francis saw him take something from his pocket. A cigarette case? A paper? Veronica, too, seemed at one moment to be fumbling in her handbag. Then the man, for the first time, turned so that Francis saw his profile clearly. He laughed and took his hat off for a few seconds, patted his hair before replacing it. A little later he inclined his head towards Veronica, it appeared interrogatively. They were speaking softly but Francis was as sure as if he'd heard, that the man was proposing departure. They would certainly move forward, down the hillock in the opposite direction from where he was concealed. He would, he thought, wait among the trees until they were completely clear, make his own way down, across the grass of the park, rejoin the road that ran between the principal gates, and walk back to Richmond and its station. A minute later he spied again over the crest and saw that they had indeed gone. He could not watch their progress because of the trees.

But the sight of Veronica, even so secretly, even from a little distance, had its customary, heart-wrenching effect on Francis. The man, without question, had been Gerhardt Brendthase.

When Francis arrived at Faberdown, collected by the Winter car and chauffeur from Petersfield Station, Mrs Winter showed that she intended to waste no time in getting down to what she had anticipated in her letter – a 'quiet, discreet little talk'. He could not envisage it quite like that since Mrs Winter was an impetuous, temperamentally indiscreet and exceptionally noisy woman; but her desire for a tête-à-tête was very clear.

It was tea-time on Friday. Francis gathered that John Marvell was coming by car and had offered to drive Veronica down. He knew about John's car. It gave perpetual trouble but John loved it dearly. Perhaps, he thought, John was a man to whom both people and objects were treasured the more for the challenges they provided.

Two other couples were due to arrive by a later train. They would be nine in the house. Mrs Winter had invited a girl to square up numbers, but something had got muddled and the girl had misunderstood and supposed she was being bidden for Saturday evening only.

'As if I'd do that!' said Mrs Winter to Francis as they settled. 'Silly child – not that she's got far to come, but of *course* I wanted her here from this evening. But she's got something today she promised to do with her crazy brother.'

'Who is she?'

'Paterson, Hilda Paterson. Her elder brother is that extraordinary Cosmo Paterson. Hilda's different, a quiet, sensible sort of girl. Pretty, too. She adores her brother and of course any arrangement made with him couldn't be broken. She's coming at lunch-time tomorrow, with another girl, until Monday morning.' Mrs Winter added, 'Cosmo's driving them over – they all live in east Sussex. I've *not* asked him to stay. Lunch, of course. Now, Francis –' She put her hand on his sleeve. 'I want a little talk about John Marvell. Do you realize how besotted he is with Mrs Gaisford? Veronica Gaisford?'

Francis said he expected she was right. 'I've only seen them once together, you know. We – Veronica and I – were both lunching with John.'

'I heard about it,' said Mrs Winter forcefully, 'and Cosmo Paterson assaulted that Dominic Drew creature! Extraordinary behaviour! And you all just sat and watched! When I was young it would have been *unthinkable* – a gentleman – and ladies there – really –'

'Well, it all happened very quickly. Then Cosmo left, almost at once –'

Mrs Winter wanted to shift the conversation to John and Veronica but perceived that the London lunch party made a good point of departure for her investigation. Her intelligence about what was going on was, Francis knew, generally pretty good.

'I heard that Cosmo Paterson said he did it to amuse Veronica Gaisford! Now, why say that?'

Francis shrugged his shoulders. He was not keen to share with his hostess Cosmo's curious speculations made outside St James's Palace.

'I've no idea. She did laugh, I admit.'

'She laughed!' said Mrs Winter nodding. 'She laughed! Yet I happen to know that she has the name of a – a c.ose friend – of Mr Drew. Yet he's knocked down –'

'Not knocked down. Cosmo pulled his chair away.'

'Whatever happened, he was, I suppose one could say, "*floored*",' said Mrs Winter smiling, pleased with the felicity of her expression, 'and Veronica Gaisford laughed! Do you know what I think?'

Francis didn't.

'I think she's rather heartless. She loves admiration.' Mrs Winter seemed very much at home with Veronica's character, interspacing her remarks with complimentary words about her beauty which made Francis's heart beat with recognition. He could see Veronica's face again, hear her laugh, feel the touch of her hand. Mrs Winter was running on fast. 'She'll lead men on, then she'll enjoy their downfall, humiliation even, because it makes her feel free. Proves to her she's got the upper hand.'

'You don't give her a very good name, Mrs Winter,' Francis said, but he was rather enjoying this, it was curiously consolatory. 'Not a very good character. Yet you've invited her here!'

'Of course I have. She's often been to Faberdown, I've known her since she was a child. Her father was a charmer and I used to stay there when she was small – stayed with them in Galway. She was allowed to run completely wild, you know. Never mind, I'm fond of Veronica and I was very sad when she had that ghastly tragedy – her husband –'

'I never knew much about that.'

'Money. And everybody thought he was so well-off. Some sort of breakdown, poor man. Nobody could sympathize more with Veronica than I did. Years younger than him, of course. Gaisford had a sort of heavy charm, fleshy, rather *courtly*, if you know what I mean. Veronica was taken by it, felt secure with him perhaps, felt herself rather poor and lost and lonely, that sort of thing, wanted to marry somebody solid, substantial. I'm not sure who introduced them but everybody knew Gaisford, he went about a good deal. The thing is, she's *tricky*, Francis, she needs handling. She's very attractive – and not very vulnerable – in spite of being hard-up. And her reputation – well, my dear boy, you're young and of course I wouldn't have her here if there were anything – but Veronica ought to be *careful*. People have got vicious tongues, you know.'

'Yes, I do know.'

'I shouldn't be talking to you like this, Francis,' said Mrs Winter, who was enjoying herself greatly. 'It would have been unmentionable when I was a girl. But I feel I know you so well. Don't *you* fall for her, my dear! You couldn't cope at all.'

Francis smiled politely, profoundly insulted and grimly aware of the accuracy of her remark.

'And I know how devoted you are to John. I can *not* believe that he is the right person for someone like Veronica.'

Francis thought of John, generous, bantering, good-hearted to a fault. Mrs Winter might have a point, and Francis was gratified that his cousin had joined him in the group of males their hostess reckoned inadequate to Veronica's forceful temperament, although he had a certain respect for the steel in John's nature.

'People are saying,' said Mrs Winter, 'that he's serious. That he's actually asked her to marry him.' She dropped her voice a little but it still reverberated with considerable strength round the fairly large room where they were sitting alone with the tea table. 'She won't, I think. She's hard-up. He's a younger son, he won't have much money although I expect he'll be good at whatever it is he does. He's immensely good-looking, he's capable, he's amusing. But I think Veronica will go for something – something bigger. If she hasn't already. Then John will be hurt, although he will be good at hiding it. Perhaps he has already been hurt.'

'Yet he's driving her down.'

'His suggestion. Oh, he's besotted all right. She keeps him on a string and he's besotted – whatever the pain,' said Mrs Winter with a sentimental sigh.

'Well, there's not much anybody can do about it. Perhaps

you're wrong, Mrs Winter. Perhaps Veronica's – fond of him. Perhaps –'

'She may be,' said the lady with an air of finality, 'but she has an eye for the main chance. And I don't call John Marvell the main chance. You wait. And you watch.'

In spite of the emotional strains beneath the agreeable surface, the sense Francis had that Veronica, John and he were involved in a pattern which promised trouble – in spite, indeed, of a certain hope that this would be so, for he could not easily contemplate the prospect of Veronica's happiness with another, however estimable that other – Francis remembered the evening as pleasant. And when he looked back, from later life, on those long summer days of 1913 and 1914, gilded by memory, evenings at Faberdown had an honourable place, stresses and sufferings forgotten, only beauty and gaiety and elegance recalled. The house was ugly, but inside the rooms were well proportioned and Mrs Winter's taste in decoration was surprisingly good and less over-exuberant than her personality might have suggested. Adrian Winter had collected some agreeable Dutch pictures of the second rank, and there was always a great profusion of flowers, competently rather than exquisitely arranged. Veronica, that evening, glowed and chattered, never still. The eyes of most men went to her more often than they needed. Mrs Winter presided with a smile which sometimes had a sour edge to it.

John Marvell was very quiet, laughing less than most of them at Veronica's remarks, looking at her intently now and then; and Francis, despite himself, was very aware of both of them. There was no direct clue, he thought, as to what of a deeper character had passed between those two. If John had been hurt by her rejection, or was in despair at her tantalizing equivocations, he showed no particular sign of it, chatting sensibly and amusingly to the rest of the party. It was rare that Francis didn't meet, at Faberdown, people with whom he had at least some sort of acquaintance, but on that occasion all were strangers to him except John and Veronica. One pair were the Dick Dempseys – sporting, often photographed, personally unmemorable. The others were a young married couple called Fox. At dinner they were an uneven number and Francis sat next to John, who most of the time talked to his other neighbour, Mrs Fox. Once he turned and, with his usual quizzical smile, said to Francis, 'Come and lunch again soon. I'll try to arrange another little circus act to entertain you.'

'Cosmo Paterson's an extraordinary fellow!'

'He is indeed, and coming to lunch here tomorrow. My colleague – the man who invited him – was terribly upset. I told him everybody expects that sort of thing from Cosmo, would be disappointed if something didn't happen. Francis, I want to talk to you some time.' He said this quietly and seriously.

'Well, why not? Here we both are.'

'Here we both are, as you say. We'll have a walk and a talk together during these two days.' He turned again to his companion on the other side.

After dinner Veronica came up, radiant in appearance, with her eager, confiding smile, looking as she had when she moved towards the table where Francis was awaiting her once in the restaurant in Berlin. The memory was intensified by the fact that again, although by choice now rather than the conventions of recent mourning, she was wearing black. She looked superb in it, the dress silky and gleaming, her bare arms and neck slender, smooth and perfectly displayed.

'Francis! It's always so lovely to see you. I thought you were going to invite me to dinner. Has that idea been discarded?'

'Certainly not.'

She lowered her voice which had been bright and sociable. 'Francis, I'm anxious to talk to you. Quietly.' She looked uncertain for a moment. The light had gone out of her face.

'Of course.'

John, Veronica, to say nothing of Mrs Winter. Francis Carr is in demand, he thought, for quiet, discreet little talks at Faberdown.

'You were always so reassuring. So helpful. So wise.'

'Well, anything I can do, of course –'

'I need a bit of wisdom at the moment. You supply it, I always felt that.'

'Veronica –'

She said softly, 'I'll arrange something. Tomorrow perhaps.' Then she moved across the room, away from him. He was, he thought, always watching her move away. But that was Veronica.

Later that evening there was some general conversation. Somebody started to talk about Ireland. In the previous year the leader of the Conservative Opposition, Bonar Law, had made a speech to a huge rally of Unionists somewhere in Oxfordshire, saying that he would support Ulster 'to any length imaginable' in resistance to the Irish Home Rule Bill which the Liberal Government had introduced in return for Irish support in the House of Commons. The Bill was anathema to Ulster's Protestants, and thoughout 1912 and 1913 there was a certain amount of talk as to whether the Army might be used to 'coerce' Ulster; and, if that were mooted, what individuals in the Army would think about it. There were many Irish officers, from both north and south, and the great majority were Protestants, many with pretty strong feelings. Apart from these, however, there was fairly widespread distaste at the idea of 'forcing' (whatever that might mean) loyal British citizens into a constitutional arrangement they so evidently disliked.

'Surely the Government couldn't order our soldiers to act against their own friends and relations,' somebody said, 'against people as loyal to the King as you and me! It would be horrible. Like the Civil War. What do you suppose Alan thinks, John?' Alan Marvell, soldiering in India with his regiment, was now understood to be homeward bound later in the year.

'I don't expect they've been bothering much about Irish Home Rule in India.'

'I can't see Alan thinking it right to use soldiers to force this Bill on Ulster against the local peoples' will,' said Adrian Winter, who knew him. 'He's too fair minded.'

John spoke carefully. Young though he was, they all felt his force.

'I don't see why not, although it's not the way I'd put it. We're told the Ulster Volunteers are arming – illegally – so that they can resist a Home Rule Bill passed by the British Parliament, if it *is* passed.'

'Oh, it'll be passed. The Lords' teeth were drawn by the Parliament Bill. Asquith's got his majority in the Commons – just.'

'Well, all right, the Bill will be passed. If the Ulster Volunteers resist its provisions by force, is that what you'd call being loyal to the King? And in that case, what could the Government do but meet force with force? I don't see that's "coercing Ulster" as people call it. The Ulster Volunteers – Carson, Craig – would have become rebels, wouldn't they?'

'For their own land, their own ideals –'

'Like all rebels,' said John, drily. 'And I would have thought it a proper job for the Army – no doubt unpleasant but perfectly proper – to fight rebellion.'

There was a silence, not particularly friendly. John did not help the atmosphere by adding, 'Anyway, surely nobody supposes the Opposition cares a rap about the feelings of Ulstermen. They simply want to embarrass the Government. With luck, turn it out.'

Adrian Winter coughed. Veronica said lightly, 'I'm sure *you'd* never "coerce" anybody, John, never force them to do something against conscience, never even try to persuade them!'

There was something like a smile in her voice. Perhaps a challenge. John looked at her and then at his feet and said, very low, 'Well, I might.'

Throughout the preceding conversation Veronica had sat with a half-smile, taking no direct part. With her 'heart in Ireland' as she'd once told him, Francis thought she might have contributed more directly than the others, English all; and perhaps done so, one way or the other, with passion. But she sat silent, looking thoughtful, until her playful and certainly personal remark to John.

'I heard,' said the lady who'd sat next to Francis at dinner, Mrs Dempsey, 'that that peculiar Cosmo Paterson has been mixed up in smuggling arms to the Ulstermen, can you believe it?'

'I certainly can,' said her husband, 'it's entirely in character.' He chuckled appreciatively.

Mrs Winter said, 'Cosmo Paterson's sister, Hilda, was meant to be here this evening. She'll be with us tomorrow and I don't want her embarrassed. She adores her brother. If she knows anything about these illegal activities –'

'Illegal they may be,' said Dempsey, 'strictly speaking. But nearly half the House of Commons and most of the House of Lords would cheer them on!'

'Perhaps. Still, they're highly dubious, in my view, whatever the rights and wrongs of the politics. And Hilda is likely to be worried for Cosmo, troubled about it. She's most unlikely to look on it as a matter for cheering. I know her, she's particularly level-headed. But she'd be utterly loyal to Cosmo. He's lunching here but going afterwards, and I forbid the subject of Ulster unless Hilda brings it up herself. Which is most improbable.'

Soon afterwards they all dispersed to bed. Dinner had been delicious, but for some reason Francis was feeling extremely unwell.

Faberdown was a house of long passages, all somewhat resembling each other, and it was Mrs Winter's custom to have a card on each door with a guest's name inscribed thereon in her own rather stylish calligraphy. Although Francis had stayed there several times, he still found it easy to take the wrong turning and the cards were a help. Bathrooms were few and, unless one was lucky, remote; as a young bachelor of no great status, Francis generally had a longish way to travel. He had had a bath before dressing for dinner that evening and had noticed that the room adjoining the bathroom had no card on the door. Next to it he had seen 'Mrs Gaisford', and then a corner, followed by two others, both needing to be passed by a dressing-gowned Carr.

At about two o'clock in the morning Francis woke up, feeling, as he could not disguise from himself, perfectly ghastly. There was no doubt about it – something had disagreed violently with his stomach. He knew that he might easily be sick, and wished to heaven he was not in a room so far from bathroom and lavatory. There was nothing for it but a long emergency trudge through the darkened house. The gaslights in the passage would be on, turned low, but there was quite a stretch to negotiate and

Francis's sense of geography was always fallible. He took a candle, providentially placed on the dressing table, unsure of ability otherwise to generate light in the bathroom itself. Gas could let one down, he thought queasily. The matter was urgent and he crept out, trying not to make the sort of noise which would waken fellow guests. In something like silence he rounded the first corner and heard deafening snores. Not, he thought he remembered from Mrs Winter's cards, John Marvell. Mr and Mrs something else, perhaps. The light was very dim and Francis felt worse every second. Round the next corner, then the third. Bathroom last door on the right. There was practically no light here and he moved cautiously, door by door, almost feeling his way. Eventually, he reached what he thought was the bathroom door and pushed it, immediately to stub a toe on the lavatory pedestal. He lit the candle – the gaslight was intractable – and settled down to be rather ill. His evil stomach condition, however, had been driven almost from his mind.

Passing, silently, the room which he knew to be Veronica's – one with no neighbour except the untenanted chamber between it and the bathroom in which he now sat and suffered – Francis had heard, unmistakably, the sound of whispering. He had – he could not avoid it – listened too, momentarily, to a soft but recognizable giggle and a deeper, masculine murmur.

He sat in the bathroom for a long time. Richmond Park. Faberdown. Hell.

Eventually, relieved somewhat in body but bothered in mind, Francis decided to go back to bed. He deliberately made a good deal of noise pulling the plug and unlocking the bathroom door, with no attempt to mute it. He wanted to be sure he stood no chance of seeing John Marvell's dressing gown slipping ghost-like down the passage before or behind him. He was no longer in danger of being sick, but he was not in the least happy.

After breakfast next morning, the men at Faberdown were left for a bit to their own devices. All the ladies breakfasted in their rooms. John took Francis's arm.

'Let's walk to the farm. Adrian's proposed a little expedition after everyone's down, but that won't be before eleven.' Adrian Winter was proud of his Jersey herd. Unless they gave him the slip, they both knew he would certainly want to accompany them to show it off. Francis was unsure how much he would enjoy a confidential talk with John at that moment, but the latter seemed determined and something was apparently occupying their host elsewhere.

'Come on.' John still had his cousin's arm and steered him towards the back drive. Francis glared at him. He must have been in Veronica's room last night. Francis found himself resenting very bitterly any man who'd been as close to her as had, he judged, his well-loved cousin John Marvell.

Francis had to step out more sharply than he enjoyed to keep pace with John who had a rapid, springy stride, the stride of a man who was temperamentally averse to inactivity, impatient to be doing, an enemy to hesitation. John Marvell was what people called a 'sound' man, as well as a 'charmer': he had a name for good judgement, and in assessing situations and persons he was perceptive and far from hasty. But there was within him a certain restlessness, a nervous energy which could be deduced from his physical movements. He walked fast.

After a little he said, 'Francis, I want to talk to you about – about Veronica. I know how helpful you were to her in Berlin. She says you were splendid. Just what she needed.'

Francis thought he was likely to have little part to play in this conversation. That suited him, he reflected.

'I can talk to you, Francis, because you know her, you've seen a little of what she's been through – or you've been able to guess it. That ghastly business with her husband – then humiliating money worries. You've probably got some inkling of the sheer, indomitable courage she's shown and goes on showing.'

'She obviously has great spirit.'

'Most people look at her and probably see a – a beautiful, popular, lively woman –'

He paused, as if awaiting confirmation.

'Certainly.'

68

'– and that's all they see. They don't, of course, know that Veronica's not only been through hell, but is still suffering hell.'

'When I met her first she'd just lost her husband.'

'Exactly. I don't expect she told you the whole story of that.'

'We never discussed it.'

'I'm sure. And she herself, of course, knew very little of the real truth at the time. Poor, poor, darling!' He muttered the last words, and Francis saw that his cousin was under considerable emotional pressure. They had nearly reached the Winter farm and the confidences, if they were to come, had better move forward from this extended celebration of Veronica's moral quality.

Francis said, in as common-sensical a tone as he could manage, 'John, I imagine you love her?' They'd never talked to each other of feelings. One didn't.

John didn't look at him but after a few more paces said, simply, 'Francis, I absolutely worship her.' He chuckled, in a way Francis found hard to bear and said, 'She's the most enchanting, wonderful woman I've ever dreamed of –'

'And the most delicious in bed, I wouldn't wonder,' Francis thought, meanly and enviously. He looked impassive and, he hoped, sympathetic. John sounded powerful and confident.

'I want to marry her. And the remarkable thing is, Francis, that she actually – is actually fond of me, too! Would you believe it?' But he didn't sound astonished. He laughed with pure joy. He was transfigured. He glowed.

'I congratulate you.'

'But there are difficulties. Rather hellish difficulties. You see, the poor darling girl has got herself into a bit of a fix. Now I want to swear you to utter secrecy.'

'Of course.'

'Not a word of this must be known to anybody.'

'You can trust me.'

John sighed heavily. 'Well,' he said, 'I'll give you the summary of the story. It's like some penny-dreadful in parts. You'll hardly believe it, but I'll give you the outline.'

CHAPTER IV

John, Francis thought with irritation, was an unsatisfactory narrator, because whenever he said something about Veronica which might be interpreted in a remotely critical sense, he instantly qualified it, ruminated as if some point had only just struck him, and added things like, 'I wish she were here. I'm not sure I've got that bit right.' This was unlike John, a clear-headed and decisive man, but Francis reckoned it was an inevitable consequence of the complexity of parts of his story. And although he told it with his usual lightness of touch, it was clear that John's emotions were strongly involved and the fact tended to work against lucidity. The story Francis ultimately absorbed thus owed something to John's recounting *en route* to the Faberdown home farm, and quite a lot to later conversations with Veronica and others. It was a peculiar tale, and Francis had expected nothing like it when John first proposed 'a walk and a talk'.

It seemed that Henry Gaisford, Veronica's husband, than whom she had been 'years younger', in Mrs Winter's phrase, had had a lot of contacts in South America – a whole network of business acquaintances with whom he was in frequent communication. Between them they knew most of what was going on in the world of commercial transactions and shipping movements between British and South American – and, John thought, between most European and South American – ports. There was nothing extraordinary or clandestine in that, of course. It just so happened that Gaisford was well placed to discover or collate information of that kind.

Gaisford's business interests – negotiating exports, imports and loans – started to go badly for him in 1910, the year after he married Veronica, who was only twenty at the time and, Francis imagined as he listened, no doubt knocking him off his feet. They lived in considerable style and Gaisford started to feel anxious. Then things got worse very quickly. Gaisford tried to recoup with unsuccessful high-risk ventures and got in ever deeper water. By the end of 1910, it appeared that he was in desperate difficulties. Most of the world – and, John emphasized, Veronica – knew nothing. They still managed to live pretty comfortably in South Street. Gaisford kept up a brave front both to the world and in his home, although Veronica now said she knew he 'had a lot of business worries', and he would get almost hysterical about even minor extravagances.

Then, in the following year, 1911, the sun seemed to come out again. Money was plentiful. Gaisford was prosperous – or, at least, seemed unpressed by anxiety.

Early in 1912 he cut his throat. Veronica found him.

As John talked, Gaisford never materialized as a personality in Francis's mind. He pictured a heavy, rather conventional, perhaps somewhat rapacious figure, something of the Soames Forsyte in him (Galsworthy's *Man of Property* had been published four years earlier and formed many of their images). Mrs Winter had described him as both fleshy and courtly. Anyway, when Gaisford decided to quit the world he did it in a messy, orthodox way with an old-fashioned razor in his dressing room; and Veronica found him.

Afterwards it was discovered that his business and his investments were either defunct or valueless. Nobody was sure how he had survived the last two years. Everybody muttered. And everybody pitied Veronica.

What had in fact happened, John explained, was this. In 1910 Gaisford was contacted by 'somebody in the German Embassy'. He was invited to a gathering of one or two visiting German businessmen – among whom, anyway, he had a pretty wide acquaintance and had often done a good deal of business. At this particular gathering he was introduced to a German, ostensibly a shipping agent.

'In reality,' said John as they trudged towards Adrian Winter's cows, 'the fellow was some sort of spy! He made – I expect at some subsequent meeting the same people arranged – a proposition to Henry Gaisford. You'll hardly believe it.'

In return for 'certain confidential services', Gaisford – about whose personal difficulties the Germans were remarkably well informed – would receive a substantial income from Berlin. This would be disguised as profit from a number of joint commercial ventures he was to undertake on Berlin's orders – ventures entirely above board, to all appearances. John stumbled some-what over this bit but Francis thought he understood. He thought of Herr Wilhelm Brendthase, 'a sort of German partner' of Gaisford. He was fascinated. That sort of thing was outside the experience of most people in those days, even at fourth hand or from the newspapers. Gaisford some kind of agent of Germany! Of a power already regarded, with varying degrees of apprehension, complacency or frivolity, as likely to be England's enemy one day! That was certainly the mood in the Foreign Office, where Francis worked. And for most people the question simply was, why had the Kaiser built that huge Imperial navy? Francis wondered how much the British Government knew about Gaisford. He had never had the remotest contact with anybody even on the fringe of such a world, but he thought he knew whom to ask. At present, however, he felt entirely bound by confidence. He interrupted John.

'What "services" was Gaisford to provide? I suppose that's the crux. He wasn't in Government service. What secrets, if any, did Gaisford know – what did he know, what could he do, that anybody in Germany couldn't achieve by perfectly open and legitimate means?'

It was at this point that John's account became somewhat confused, and Francis ultimately pieced things together for himself. It appeared that the Germans wanted to expand their already formidable network of information about shipping and commerce between Europe and South America. They already had a huge range of contacts in their consuls, agents, expatriate businessmen and so forth. So did the British. The Germans wanted to expand theirs, and they wanted to penetrate and even control those of their rivals. They wanted to ensure that every activity connected with the movement of necessities between Europe and South America was known to them. Others would see part of the picture, as they went about their business; the Germans alone would see it all, because everybody in a position to collate, to assemble the parts of that picture, would be on the payroll. Knowledge must precede action. Knowledge is power. If war threatened, they, the Germans, would see clearly, while others – and others meant England – would be partially blind. To achieve this there had to be penetration of institutions, suborning of officials, shipping agents (these above all) and members of business houses. It was, perhaps, a remarkable effort for a rather small return, in terms of what could not be learned simply, openly and without expense. But they are, Francis acknowledged, a thorough people.

And Gaisford could help. Gaisford could supply a large part of the target area at which this German operation had to be directed. He knew who knew what, who mattered, how every individual system and agency worked, who was too inflexible in attitude, who might be receptive to a gentle suggestion, and who best might make it. He knew it in the course of his legitimate business and he knew it more comprehensively than most men. Furthermore, he could update his information, keep his paymasters abreast of change, supply names. Gaisford could help.

He agreed to do so. For a fee.

John said, 'Veronica, of course, knew absolutely nothing of this, suspected nothing. You can imagine how ghastly it was for her to discover – her husband a traitor! One can't use any other word. This information isn't going to be used to help England, exactly, if there's a war! And Gaisford must have known that as clearly as anybody. He wasn't an innocent.'

'You've not told me how she *did* discover. Nor why he cut his throat.'

'Those two things go together. One day, some months after her husband's death, Veronica got a letter from Dominic Drew. She had met "Printer" once or twice, read his articles in the Press, didn't know him well. The letter asked for a meeting.

Veronica was intrigued by a certain atmosphere of mystery projected by Drew's note and she agreed to meet him.' It was not clear to Francis from John's account whether this took place before or after Veronica's visit to Berlin. It transpired, however, that everything John was relating came from Drew – or, Francis reflected, more accurately it was Veronica's account to John of what she said Drew had told her about her own husband.

Drew, according to John, told Veronica that he had discovered what her husband had been up to – that he'd had suspicions and played on Gaisford's anxieties with practised skill, pretending he knew more than he did. He'd spoken to Gaisford about the latter's friendship with certain Germans and his knowledge of South America, and had then let off a shot in the dark, suddenly saying, 'Well, you're well paid for it,' or some such words – a remark which, if challenged, might have been excused as being simply a rather vulgar reference to the rewards of commerce. Gaisford had collapsed. He'd assumed, quite mistakenly, that Drew had actual proof that he, Gaisford, was on a German payroll. It was, John thought, highly improbable that Gaisford could have faced criminal proceedings. He had passed information which was presumably in some cases confidential but in no sense could be officially secret, and any painstaking journalist might have discovered as much. Gaisford had received payment – for what might almost have been bluffed through as a commercial service.

Nevertheless Gaisford reckoned, certainly correctly, that disclosure would mean the end of his business career such as it still was. It would also mean the end of his social life, which he greatly valued; Francis remembered Mrs Winter's voice – everybody had known Gaisford, he 'went about a good deal'. It would be the end of Gaisford, the well-to-do, respectable, solidly patriotic, rather fashionable man. Motive was what people would perceive. The sense of being threatened by German ambitions world-wide was pervasive at that time, and a man 'in German pay', whatever the technicalities, could expect no mercy from society.

And now outcast, disgraced and penniless, Gaisford would, Francis suspected – although John did not refer to it in his tale

74

– have been unlikely to keep Veronica. He could imagine a ponderous, unworthy and ultimately tragic man deeply in love with his wife. It was all bitterly clear.

Disclosure would also, of course, terminate his usefulness to the Germans, and his payments from them. Gaisford had everything to lose. The threat from Drew's knowledge was real. Together with a now ascendant Drew, Gaisford had hatched a scheme which could suit them both.

Gaisford would give Drew a certain amount of detail (he probably discovered at this point, John thought, how little Drew really knew, how much had been guesswork). Gaisford would give Drew enough to write a knowing and, in the atmosphere of 1911, sensational article on the theme – 'Why are the Germans so active in South America?' There would be some dropping of names, all set against the background of the importance of the South Atlantic sealanes and commerce in case of war. The article would include some of what Gaisford could tell Drew, but by no means all. Drew understood very clearly (although the extent to which Gaisford confided this to him was doubtful. Drew, as Francis guessed then and confirmed later, was always ready to invent or adorn a story to suit his ends) that Gaisford proposed to use the article to extract more money from the Germans – to 'buy Drew off' from a second article.

For Gaisford was once again in serious difficulties. The Germans had him on a string, and unless that string was thickened it could break. Drew published his article, which drew a lot of correspondence from the large number of readers who thought of little but the threat of war with Germany. The article created a certain sensation. People like to be chilled.

'I can't remember what paper it was in,' said John. 'I know I didn't see it myself, although I remember people talking about it. He writes for several papers on and off. Freelance.'

'And then?'

'And then Gaisford cut his throat.'

That had been the gist of Drew's conversation with Veronica. The story, of course, was entirely discreditable to himself but he apparently neither saw nor told it in that way. He assumed, he said, that the Germans turned down Gaisford's attempt at extorting more money for the same services. Perhaps they saw through it. Gaisford must have felt darkness closing in. Too many people had power over him. He had nothing left to sell. He desperately needed money. He decided to quit the stage.

Francis hated hearing of suicide. He could imagine too vividly the loneliness, the despair. Francis might be cold on occasion but he was never insensitive. Gaisford must have gone with a poor conscience.

And Veronica found him.

John muttered that Francis had heard nothing yet, and Francis observed that he didn't see why any of this awful business put Veronica herself in a fix. He felt a certain confused scepticism.

'Of course, it's horrible for her – her husband some sort of German agent – and one who died after trying unsuccessfully to cheat his masters, by your account! Very nasty. Poor Veronica. But it's past –'

'Not quite past. You see, this brute, Drew –'

'Yes, why tell her all this? Did he obscurely feel the widow had a right to know?'

'Not a bit.' John spoke with great vigour, a frown on his handsome face. 'Not a bit. He started to apply pressure on her. First, he was ingratiating – tried to be charming, sympathetic, to build up an atmosphere of confidence, of shared secrets between them, then suggested another meeting, dinner with him.'

Francis was beginning to see it.

'Gradually she felt more and more trapped. First hints – then pretty clear threats to expose the whole thing. Pressure, the brute. Pressure on a woman. On Veronica.'

John was walking rather faster.

'She says she'd die of shame to see her husband's name – her name – all over the newspapers again, with the story I've just told you. She says she could never face people again, she'd change her name, go abroad. It was bad enough – when it first happened. She was pestered then. Now – it makes her desperate. Unreasonably so, you may think.'

Francis did think. Veronica, by this story, had done absolutely nothing amiss and it seemed a clear case for Wellington's classic response to threat of scandal – 'Publish and be damned'. People, of course, cared greatly for appearances. Publicity was equated with vulgarity. Veronica, however innocent, indeed unaware, would have a name from which people would prefer to stand aside, unconnected. Fingers would be pointed. All the same, Drew's hold over Veronica because of her late husband's misdeeds must, in the end, be considered tenuous. It could secure, perhaps, small gains. Not more.

Francis said, 'You should tell Drew where he gets off. Tell him to go to hell. Take a strong line. The whole story shows him up as a near-criminal or worse, and the idea of him publicizing it must be bluff. Anyway, what does he want from her?'

'He wants to marry her.'

Francis was already half-suspecting this.

'And she? Doesn't she loathe him? Can't she at least make him see there's no possibility of marriage – the blackmailer and his reluctant victim! Hardly a good match.'

'Of course not. She's disgusted by him, anyway. He's a brute, unimaginable.'

'Quite so. And I should think it not impossible to make him see – besides telling him to do his worst – that he'd be unlikely to enjoy marriage on that sort of basis.'

John said nothing. Francis wondered how strong, in fact, was Veronica's revulsion from Printer Drew, and expected that John wondered too. He pursued his point.

'If you – or she, if she's capable of it – tell him to do his worst, he wouldn't, you know. He'd know he was beaten. He'd have nothing left to extort with. And surely he could be threatened with some sort of action – defamation or something – to scare him off publishing the story just out of spite?'

John thought not. He said that Veronica was absolutely opposed to any confrontation between himself and Drew.

'I don't want to take action she's against, Francis – terrifically against. We've got to cope with this thing together.' Francis suspected that wishful thinking might be playing its part, that John, himself, might still be uncertain of the profundity of

Veronica's love. Now John said, 'I'm sure he's got something else, too, besides what I've told you, something which bothers her. She says not, but I sense it. Perhaps she's mentioned in a letter of Gaisford's which Drew's got –'

This sounded very far-fetched, thought Francis. He said, 'Well, why not? And why should she suppose he's got a letter of Gaisford's? I can't understand you –'

'I don't know what it is, Francis,' John said, irritably, 'I'm just sure she's got some very strong additional reason for not wanting me to confront the damned fellow! She says, "No, that would never do," very decidedly. She's a most intelligent person, you know.'

'So what do you – or she – propose?'

'Well,' said John. 'First, I'd like to persuade her to let us, all three, talk about it. She likes you. You're my cousin. Alan's in India – he gets back in October. I can't wait till then, it's driving me mad. Three heads may be better than two. And you, better than I, may be able to make her see that if all this were in the open there'd be nothing left to fear.'

Francis supposed Veronica's suggestion of 'a talk' had, unknown to John, been made on the same premise – that another pair of eyes might help inspect their problem. Francis now told John that Veronica, too, had indicated she'd like a discussion. John did not look entirely pleased. He said, unnecessarily, 'You're not emotionally involved, you see. That may help.'

'Naturally I'll do anything I can. You know my view, and I'll repeat it to her, you or anyone – that somebody should tell Drew to do his worst, preferably knocking him down at the same time! And that Veronica should make it clear – perhaps clearer – that in no circumstances whatsoever has she the smallest intention of marrying him, whatever he does do or abstains from doing. Has she discussed any of this with a lawyer?'

'Good God, no.'

'I can't see why you say that. It would seem to me a sensible first step, but if she won't and you won't –'

John shook his head violently.

Francis said, 'Well, I could quite see at your lunch party, John,

78

that Drew regarded Veronica rather as his property.' He made the remark with a touch of malice. He added, 'That must be intolerable not only to her but to you as well. Had you known he was going to be there?'

'One sees him about a good deal. I manage to show nothing.'

He said it with contempt, even with annoyance. Francis looked at his cousin. What a delightful-looking fellow he was! Surely no woman could seriously prefer an overweight, articulate intriguer like Printer Drew, to the young, admired John Marvell? Or could she?

The Winter Jerseys, fenced by the immaculate wooden timbers of the rich, came into view. John thanked his cousin for his support and said that he would try to persuade Veronica to agree to a talk between the three of them. They walked back to the house in silence.

Immediately before lunch, John murmured, 'Veronica's happy I've talked to you. She agreed I should. I think she was relieved. But, next, she wants to talk to you herself. By herself.'

If, thought Francis, you drive obsessed by the ditch, you find yourself in it. If you can't get the picture of a particular fence out of your mind, your horse hits it. Three of the party must have had a similar sensation halfway through lunch that day. Dick Dempsey started it. During a brief silence over the rest of the lunch table, they heard him describing to Mrs Winter with absurd gusto to what abject cowardice a visit to his dentist reduced him.

'Real torture. Fellow called Andrews. Devonshire Street. Good, though. I went there last week.'

'Really,' said Mrs Winter, 'don't remind me of it, I dread dentists as much as you do.'

'I find myself tilted back in that chair, huge light suspended over my head, gazing out of the enormous window at the row of attics in the back premises opposite, and I feel just like the wretched chaps must have done on the rack! Here comes the pain, no it doesn't; is it going to be worse than last time, yes it is! Every second a minute. I'd be rotten under torture!'

'I go to Andrews, too,' said Cosmo Paterson. Cosmo was behaving decorously. He had arrived at the wheel of a large, open car which seemed especially noisy, even for those days. He had come with his sister, Hilda, and a neighbour of the Patersons called Angela Forrest. They were both pretty, agreeable girls, and Angela Forrest especially so, Francis thought. In later years, she often told him that she had not heard his name on introduction and went for some time under the impression that he was called Arthur Clark. Hilda Paterson was not wholly unlike Cosmo to look at – hair a little darker, but small and neat. In personality, however, she was a good deal more tranquil. Cosmo was not in the least aggressive, but most people felt from him, as Francis did, a sort of electric force even when he was silent and motionless. There was no doubt about it, he made others slightly uneasy. He gave an impression of being capable of doing absolutely anything, if the mood or the motive gripped him. Hilda, on the other hand, was a restful person. People felt at peace with her, although her remarks were sharp and pointed. Francis sat next to her at lunch and immediately sensed two things – her strength of mind and her love for her brother; two remarks and one intercepted glance made both entirely clear. Cosmo talked quietly to Angela Forrest, his neighbour, and appeared to say little to Veronica who sat between him and their host, Adrian Winter. They were even numbers at table now: twelve.

'I go to Andrews, too.' Cosmo gave a sympathetic grin in the direction of Dick Dempsey. The latter said –

'I suppose I shouldn't say it, but I've found one of Andrews' customers who's even more abject a coward than I am. That fellow Dominic Drew. He was in the waiting room when I came out, having got it over. You know how there's always a bit of a wait between victims, while the torturer sharpens his instruments! I had a word with Drew. He was in a blue funk! Worse than me! I couldn't resist saying – "He's in vicious form today, Printer!" I know Drew, you see.'

'You brute!' said his wife. 'Deliberate cruelty!'

'I suppose it was! Drew said, "I haven't got much to be done," but he was green about the gills.'

Nobody spoke. Veronica, John and Francis went to some lengths to avoid each other's eyes.

After lunch Cosmo left very rapidly, declining a rather perfunctory suggestion from Adrian Winter that he should stay, 'borrow some gear' and play tennis.

'No thanks, I've got to get back.' Both girls were due to travel to London by train on Monday morning. Cosmo knew, without disturbance or surprise, that Mrs Winter looked at him askance. He was in the habit of disappearing abruptly from any conventional gathering, in pursuit (or so others imagined) of some private, possibly clandestine, business. Mrs Winter looked relieved. Ireland had not been mentioned.

People changed for tennis, John showing himself slightly less preoccupied now, perhaps because he had shared some of his anxieties with another. He had chatted with animation to Hilda Paterson at lunch, sitting on her other side. They were both going to play tennis. John was skilful at the game.

'So is Hilda,' said Mrs Fox, who knew her well. 'She's got a devastating backhand.'

Veronica excused herself from playing.

'I'm going to inspect your lovely garden.'

'I'll show you the garden with pleasure,' said Adrian Winter.

'My dear, you must sort out the tennis fours and see fair play,' said his wife firmly. They had two courts, fresh cut, in lovely condition. By agreement, Francis was excluded from the opening sets and took, without too much contrivance, a long walk round the extensive garden with Veronica. Mrs Winter sat exclaiming, in a large hat, beside the tennis courts.

Francis, Veronica beside him, rounded the corner of a yew hedge. As ever, his heart was beating somewhat faster because of her presence. A faint smell of jasmine. A moment imagined often.

'I'm glad, Francis, that you had a talk with John.'

'I was appalled at what he told me, Veronica. Beastly pressure from that cad – worry –'

'I always seem in some sort of trouble, don't I?'

'Veronica, I think you should see a good lawyer. And I think you should allow John to see that fellow and tell him, in no uncertain terms, to leave you alone for good, and to publish what he likes, you're untouched by it.' Francis added, 'And you may find that a lawyer can stop him doing that, or anything else, anyway. Defamation, menaces, that sort of thing. I don't for a moment think he's got the sort of hold over you that you and John suppose. It's been inflated in your minds. He, himself, is the one who's vulnerable, if his story is true. It's time to prick the bubble.'

Veronica sighed and strolled on looking straight ahead. She said very softly, 'I don't want John to see Dominic.'

Just that, thought Francis. 'Dominic'. Not 'him', or 'Printer', or 'that man'.

'I can understand that. You're afraid of a fearful row, violence even, loss of control. Of course John must hate him, of course you don't want to make matters worse. And John's a strong character, I'd not like him as an enemy. But somebody's got to see Drew. Somebody's got to have it out.'

'Francis, do you know the first thing Dominic would tell John?' Francis shook his head.

'He'd tell him that I've been his mistress for the last few months.'

They walked in absolute silence. Veronica, still speaking without expression in a careful, factual way said, 'He – persuaded me, threatened me. That would, as I'm sure you understand, destroy John. He has no idea of it.'

It was a strait-laced age, at least outwardly. Francis was unsure of his own reactions. He remembered his long session in the Faberdown bathroom the night before. She had not been alone in her room all that time.

'Veronica, I know John loves you very much. He's made that awfully clear to me. We're not in the habit of exchanging confidences but I've never seen him feel anything so obviously or so deeply. I'm certainly not the only person who's aware of that.' Francis thought of Mrs Winter.

'Yes, I think he does,' she said, frowning slightly. 'Of course, that's why I don't want him – shattered – by what I've just told you.' She had indeed told Francis – told him with complete openness. She'd made no attempt at saying, 'This is a secret, nobody in the world must know.' She knew he was safe.

'But – do you love John, Veronica?'

'I think he's the most charming, most considerate man I've ever known.' It wasn't an answer. She added, smiling – 'And the best looking!'

'If you're sure Drew would – would tell John what you've told me –'

'He would. To hurt him. And me, of course.'

'Then don't you think it possible – wouldn't it be inevitable one day – that you should tell John yourself? It's all in the past. It's pretty hellish to have to do that, of course, but John knows, now, the pressure you've been under. He might want to kill Drew, I agree! But, short of that, wouldn't it clear the whole thing up?' Francis added, 'After all, it would finally draw Drew's sting.'

She looked at him with a faint smile. Then she put her hand on his arm with a very familiar gesture.

'You're always so dear and so wise, Francis. I'll think about it. It's not easy for me.'

Francis thought of Printer Drew's possessive manner to her at lunch in London. That had been only a month ago. He said, as easily as he could, 'After all, it's over now, presumably.'

Veronica said nothing.

'Presumably?' Francis waited.

'I – saw him – last Wednesday.'

'For the last time?'

'We're – lunching – next Wednesday. In his rooms. He – sort of bullied – me.'

This was all becoming intolerable, thought Francis. He saw John Marvell's face, handsome, quizzical, twisted with desire as he had talked of Veronica and her predicament. He was this woman's lover. So was her blackmailer. They both wanted to marry her. And, damn her, Francis too wanted her very badly at exactly that moment, walking through the Winters' rose garden, her slender fingers caressing his forearm, her eyes wide open, beautiful – considering, contemplating, no doubt, another nocturnal visit from John at Faberdown, as well as luncheon next Wednesday in Printer Drew's rooms.

Francis said, rather feebly, 'I see.'

After a few more paces, Veronica said, 'I know what you're thinking. I aim to make it the last time I see him. Somehow. But he'll – Dominic – will start threatening again. I have to be very careful how I manage all this, you see, Francis. I've got rather a lot to lose.'

Francis said, 'I suppose you mean you've got John to lose,' and she answered, 'That, certainly,' and sighed.

Then she said – and Francis knew that it was more significant than the words she used, that it was the missing piece in this jigsaw puzzle, that it mattered and was odious to contemplate – 'Dominic's not too bad, you know. He's determined that the world's against him, that he'll brazen his way despite everybody. But he's – he can be rather fun. Intelligent.'

Francis thought of a greasy, overweight man sprawling on the floor after his chair had been tipped over. Rather fun!

Veronica added, 'I suppose I rather fell for him. A lot of women have, you know. It – it passed quite quickly.'

It was not the first time Francis had discerned how a woman can lose her heart and give her body to a man whom other men find repulsive, but it was the most disagreeable of such occasions. He wasn't sure what, if anything, she wanted from this talk. After a silence he heard himself saying –

'Have you seen anything more of your contacts in Berlin, by the way? I remember you thought you might have to return there to see Herr Brendthase again. How did that go?'

'Yes. I paid Berlin another visit.'

'Herr Brendthase was helpful?'

'Yes, he was.'

'Was his son there, my friend Gerhardt? A nice fellow, I'd like to see him again.'

'Yes,' she said uninterestedly, 'he was rather nice, wasn't he.

No, he wasn't there. Just the father. They – he and his wife – were kind.'

No word, thought Francis, of a more recent encounter, no allusion to a long, long talk sitting on the turf, not two weeks back, in Richmond Park. Veronica next disconcerted him by a show of something not unlike irritation.

'You're a terribly detached person, aren't you, Francis? Consoling, and thank you for it, but rather one of life's spectators. Has anybody ever told you that?'

As a matter of fact, similar comments had sometimes been made by others and never failed to annoy Francis, who reckoned that balance and objectivity were not the same as indifference.

'I don't think I can say more, Veronica. I can't help, can I? You know what I think. I think you should tell John the truth. That you should see a lawyer. That John, whatever it costs him, should speak to Drew. And that you should never see Drew again. Unless something like that is done I don't see how you can extricate yourself from this mess.'

'Thank you, dear Francis. You make it very clear, as usual.'

'And if you delay, you'll hurt John more in the end. And yourself, of course.'

She said nothing and squeezed his arm with a sigh. It was time to return to the tennis court. He had, Francis supposed, done his duty. But had he? Was it right to do anything, say a word, to help her, to help them? To advance, in the slightest degree, the chances of his cousin marrying this many-faced, delicious woman, on whose word he doubted if any man could for an instant rely? He touched her hand on his arm with his fingertips and she smiled into his eyes, a hint of mockery in her own.

CHAPTER V

John told Francis that Veronica was thinking over what Francis had said to her.

'She's immensely grateful.'

Heaven knew for what, Francis thought irritably. John said he'd keep him informed, although by then Francis felt he wanted to be at a distance from the whole confused and somewhat grubby business. There was no change in John's own tone. He was head over heels in love and it was obvious to Francis that Veronica dominated every corner of his working mind, most hours of every day. Strong and gifted though he might be, John Marvell was not a free man.

As the weeks passed, Francis wondered whether Veronica was still betraying John with Dominic Drew – whether under threats of a kind he still found difficult to take seriously, or whether because she still greatly enjoyed it, he didn't feel like speculating. He was away for all of August and the first half of September, and it was not until autumn, 1912, that he heard anything of the Marvells again. He didn't suggest a meeting of any kind to Veronica. The time for that, he thought, had passed.

But in the second week in October somebody said to Francis, 'Alan Marvell, your cousin, is back from India.' A week later he received an invitation to stay at Bargate. Alan's and John's mother, known to him as Cousin Helena, was in a state of irrepressible delight at Alan's return. She was a kind woman who loved both her sons, and although it may not have been accurate to describe Alan as the favourite, he always so dominated his surroundings that, once he was present, family life inevitably centred on him. And he was, of course, the eldest – the proprietor, the possessor – although, enjoying the Army, he entrusted much to his mother (an active woman, still under fifty) and was lucky in her competence, just as she, most people thought, was lucky in his trust.

There were two guests at Bargate that weekend in early November, beside the Marvell brothers and Francis, and both had been at Faberdown. One was Hilda Paterson: the Paterson house was not far from Bargate. The other was Veronica.

Francis arrived at Bargate on Friday evening, by train. Veronica was driven down by John. Alan had gone over in his own car, a rather splendid affair, and collected Hilda. When these two swept into the house, arriving last, Francis noted, as ever in the past, Alan's forcefulness and charm, increased by two years' maturity in India, making him seem dominant and instantly attractive. Everybody jumped up, moved towards them – Francis saw with surprise, for he had not particularly recalled it, how pretty Hilda Paterson was. But all eyes were on Alan, his mother laughing with pleasure to see the pleasure of others in her magnificent elder son. Soon it was as it had always been, thought Francis. Everybody in the house seemed to say, casually, 'Where's Alan?' if he were not in a room. Everybody seemed to be waiting for him to speak, looking at him for approbation. 'I suppose he's a spoilt chap,' thought his cousin Francis, fearing him more than a little, 'but he's formidable.'

They had an agreeable, companionable, informal sort of dinner. When Francis arrived, his cousin Helena said – 'There's nothing for you young people to do, I'm afraid. I simply want Alan to pick up the threads gradually, and meet people.'

But later that evening Helena said to Francis, 'I want to show you some things in my sitting room, Francis, dear. Things which I believe might interest your mother.'

It was a subterfuge. Helena had always been fond of Francis, and she took his arm, led him into her 'little room' as she called it, her refuge, sat him on a small sofa and settled herself beside him. He was unsurprised by what followed.

'Francis, my dear, how well do you know Veronica Gaisford?'

Francis told her briefly, keeping his voice steady. It was easier than it would have been some months previously. Francis's feelings about Veronica were becoming very mixed indeed.

Helena smiled at him. 'You find her attractive, as they all do, my dear!'

Then she talked for a little, talked about John, and Francis knew that he was moving into that delicate situation where a friend's confidence can easily be betrayed, where probing is undertaken and affectionate treachery invited, and all for the best of motives. Helena, however, was not particularly concerned with asking Francis questions, and he was convinced from the way she spoke that she knew nothing of the matter of Drew. Nor, of course, Francis said to himself, could she possibly suspect that John and Veronica were – had been for some time – lovers. Cousin Helena, thought Francis, a person of the utmost propriety, would be terribly shocked. In this he was probably wrong. Helena, nevertheless, wanted to talk about John. She described her own first contact with Veronica. John Marvell did not find it easy to confide in his mother. He had, it seemed, invited Veronica to Bargate on one previous occasion.

'A friend of mine, a widow, Mother, who's had a rather tragic life –'

Francis could imagine the exchange. How Helena Marvell had nodded, speculatively. How, after the visit, she had said to her second son, no doubt rather abruptly –

'Veronica Gaisford's charming. She's got real quality.'

'Mother, I'm delighted you felt it –'

'But I don't think you should lose your heart in that direction, dearest boy. She's not domesticated. She's *untamed* beneath all that elegance and charm.'

'Untamed, Mother?'

'Untamed. A creature of the wilds. A beautiful creature of the wilds. And, my darling, I don't recommend you to set up as a tamer. Even you.'

John had smiled, passed it off lightly without argument or

avowals, but Francis knew that he would have been hurt. And when, some months later, his mother said,

'We must have some young faces in the house for Alan's first weekends – he'll be asking them himself soon enough. Any suggestions?' John had said –

'Why not Veronica Gaisford? You liked her. I'm sure Alan will like her.'

'All right. And Francis Carr. And another girl – I'll ask Hilda, she's always excellent company.'

It was clear from Helena's account that John had not said, 'By the way, Mother, I intend to marry Veronica Gaisford!' Nevertheless, Francis guessed that John had decided to try to force the pace during this weekend. It was obvious he longed beyond expression to bring Veronica to his home as his fiancée, his love, his wife. From casual exchanges between all of them earlier, Francis supposed that it had been difficult for them to meet in recent weeks. Apparently Veronica had been away from London throughout August and September. No doubt it seemed to John an age since she had lain in his arms.

Helena was talking on. Alan, earlier that day, had said to his mother, 'Tell me more about this Mrs Gaisford who's coming.'

And Helena had replied, 'A friend of John's. Between ourselves, I know he wants to marry her.'

John's feelings were not difficult to discern, and Helena was discerning. To Francis she was frank about it. She had said to Alan, 'I don't know if it's a good idea. But I think he's got it rather badly, poor boy.' Love was, as often as not, referred to as a disease, like measles. Especially by someone like Helena Marvell.

To all this, Francis nodded easily, equivocally, gave away nothing. Helena said, 'Oh well, I expect everyone will be sensible. An old woman like me fusses too much!' An attractive forty-nine year old, she was certainly no old woman, and she was shrewd, but she had not enlisted an ally and she knew it. She sighed, patted Francis's cheek, and soon afterwards they rejoined the others.

*

Francis wondered whether John or Veronica would take the opportunity to bring him up to date with their concerns. Was Veronica still being blackmailed, if that were a fair description? She looked radiant. Was John still distraught on her behalf? He seemed at ease and happy. Francis decided that they must have taken his advice and 'seen off' Printer Drew – that their lives had now entered calm waters, and that they had expressly or tacitly agreed not to mention the matter to him further. This assessment – formed by the time they all went to bed on Friday evening – was, however, disturbed by John after breakfast next morning. He and Francis found themselves alone for a little in the inner hall at Bargate, a large, comfortable, panelled room where the morning papers were always read. Bargate was a pleasant hotchpotch of architectural styles with a Jacobean core and those Victorian accretions whose expensive construction had aroused David Carr's frequently expressed, snorting contempt. The inner hall was in the Jacobean core. It was the heart of the house.

For a little, on that Saturday morning, the inner hall was populated only by John, Francis and two Labradors. The cousins were both looking at newspapers. Quietly, without warning or looking away from his paper, John said, 'Veronica's at last about to shake that fellow off, you know.'

'I'm delighted to hear it. Are you going to see him?'

'No, I don't think I'll have to. Just as well, I'd lose my temper. She's definitely decided to tell him she intends to see him no more – no more, ever again – and that if he publishes filth about her husband, let alone her, he can go ahead and do it. And that she'd naturally consult her solicitor as to what to do if he *did* publish. She says she's sure he'll surrender. She's found her resolution at last.'

'What a relief!'

'You helped greatly, you know. We had got the whole thing out of proportion.'

'I thought so.'

'When you think it over, what could he really do?'

'I agree.'

90

'I doubt if there'll be any need to go to law. I tell her he's likely to accept the situation when he sees she means it.'

'And what,' Francis said, 'are your own plans?' He wondered to what extent Cousin Helena would regard him as a betrayer, by his implicit encouragement of John's love, his assistance in the problems of that love.

John smiled, a little uneasily. He said that Veronica still needed to 'sort herself out a little'. 'I'm not pressing her, the darling girl. She's lived with worry for a long time. I want her to take her time. She's been away for a while. To tell the truth, I've hardly seen her for the last two months.'

It was clear from his voice that he was as much in love with Veronica as ever. Francis said to himself that she was treating John badly. There was surely no particular reason why they shouldn't openly become engaged to be married. Obviously Helena Marvell would disapprove, think Veronica 'wrong for him', but that was a matter which John would need to face and dissolve or forfeit everyone's respect – and, Francis knew, face it he would. An engagement there must, presumably, be. John obviously longed for it, and the shadow of Drew's threats would fade when exposed to the light of frank defiance. Francis supposed that what he suspected, with some revulsion, to be Drew's powerful, sexual hold over Veronica was also a thing of the past. John still knew nothing of that, presumably. For him she simply intended to see no more a detested, threatening scoundrel. She had found her courage. Of her own feelings – and conceivably, actions – Francis felt less sure. And that, perhaps, was the impediment?

Before lunch, Francis had almost his first words alone with Veronica. There was chatter in the inner hall and he could talk without being overheard by others. She looked at him with a Veronica smile as he went up to her. She was expecting it.

'I gather from John that things are pretty well sorted out,' Francis said softly and lightly.

'Pretty well. Not quite.'

'No more Drew.'

'I think not.' At that moment Francis knew perfectly well that she was lying, at least in part.

Then, on Saturday evening, Alan fell in love with Veronica.

Both Francis and Helena Marvell, simultaneously, could tell as certainly and as simply as if somebody had smashed a wineglass on the floor. Alan suddenly looked at Veronica across the table at dinner, a long, stern look, without a word spoken. This coincided with a silence, a break in the general conversation. Francis saw Veronica raise her eyes to meet Alan's. They both looked immensely grave. Neither looked away. Francis found his own eyes moved to Cousin Helena, and hers had turned to him. Nobody looked at John.

After dinner, Veronica and the others went to bed rather early. Alan sat entirely silent by the fire. John gave Francis a whisky and soda, and chatted of this and that. From his talk with Helena, Francis knew that she had told Alan how she reckoned John wanted to marry Veronica. Sadly, he thought, that's unlikely to make much difference. Some things are stronger than all the loyalty in the world, and the sword-thrust to the heart a woman like Veronica could deliver was one of them. Francis wondered whether to say to John, when they went to bed that night, 'Make an excuse, tell some lie, drive Veronica back to London immediately after breakfast tomorrow. Get her away from here and keep her away, unless you want to lose her!'

Neither then nor at any later time did it occur to him that if Alan wanted Veronica, he wouldn't win her. John was handsome and effective. John had been her lover, was still, presumably, her lover whenever opportunity offered. But Alan was a conqueror, had always been a conqueror. And Francis had seen the look on Alan's face, marked his silence. He wanted her all right. She had hit him straight between the eyes, and there was a great deal of trouble on the way.

Next morning Alan said to Veronica, 'A walk round the garden before church?' He smiled at her. Francis and John were in earshot but excluded. Understanding each other and hating it they followed Alan and Veronica's exit by the garden door. And there a curious thing happened.

Most unusually – for Bargate was a particularly well-ordered establishment – somebody had been painting an upper window-frame and had left a tall ladder in position, unnoticed throughout Saturday because round a secluded and not much passed corner of the house.

Veronica called out, 'Have I seen this bit?' and darted round the corner where her foot caught the base of the heavy ladder, which began to fall ponderously. Veronica cried – 'Oh!' Alan instantly leapt forward. The ladder, about to crash, was caught in his very strong grip, in mid-flight. Veronica had moved clear, hand to mouth.

Alan held the ladder for a second, breathing deeply. It was heavy, he had caught it near the falling end and the weight had been considerable. Then, without a word, he moved it up again, into position. Veronica laughed delightedly. Her eyes sparkled.

'Alan, it's most unsafe. Shouldn't we carry it away?'

'No. That's for someone else to do – and be told off for not doing it yesterday. You might have been hurt.'

'Or someone might have been, anyway.'

'Not someone. You.' He said it quietly, but John and Francis, unnecessary spectators, heard clearly and saw that he cared nothing. Then Alan smiled at Veronica, his very sweet, special, Marvell smile and said, 'We did that rather neatly, don't you think? Would you like to do it again?'

Veronica laughed once more, a particularly joyful laugh. As they walked on slowly, towards a small, sunken, terraced garden, she slipped her hand inside Alan's arm. He looked down at her, completely careless of John and Francis, following a few paces behind. Francis felt John's reaction as if electricity had run between them. John had seen his brother's face, drawn his conclusions, there could be no doubt of it. The brothers were very close. Alan, although the more dominant, the leader, the master, nevertheless always asked John's opinion, relished his humour, valued his judgement, his objectivity, listened to him with care; would always consult him in the major matters of life. But not in this. In this situation, a brothers' war was inevitable.

It could only be a matter of time now, Francis thought, before ambassadors were withdrawn.

As far as Francis was concerned, the stabbing fact of Veronica's effect upon Alan was all that mattered about that weekend. It was, he reflected, inevitable. Veronica was entrancing. Alan had, for several years, been confined to the limited society of the English in India. Like all the Marvells he was susceptible – hard and dominant, but susceptible. 'When they fall,' Francis's mother used to say, 'they fall heavily, that family. And quickly. Very quickly.' Francis thought he had witnessed exactly that. He could, with antennae sharpened by pain, not all of it on behalf of John Marvell, feel Alan's eyes watching Veronica, noting her every movement, every expression. And Veronica, he knew, was conscious, every minute of the day, of Alan's eyes.

The sense that a drama was being born, even if not yet enacted, was not confined to Francis. He was playing backgammon with Hilda Paterson before they went up to change for dinner on Sunday. Nobody was leaving until Monday morning. Alan had discovered that he, too, had business in London – and would be unable to drive Hilda home. A plan involving trains had been made.

Hilda threw double fours, moved her pieces expertly, and said, without particular emphasis – 'Mrs Gaisford alarms me.'

Francis had imagined many adjectives in connection with Veronica, but had not thought of alarm as an emotion she was likely to induce.

'Really? Can you tell me why?'

'Is there ever a minute when she isn't working something out? I feel her mind is active, planning or dissecting something all the time! Terrifying!'

'I think you exaggerate! She's a fairly light-hearted person, you know. Perhaps a bit capricious – but not exactly a – a female Machiavelli, as you imply. She's something of a romantic, impulsive, that sort of thing. At least that's my impression.' Francis laughed as he said it. He knew what Hilda meant.

'I don't know about a female Machiavelli,' said Hilda, considering the board and debating whether to offer her opponent a double which would bring the stakes to eightpence, 'but she's got power all right.'

Francis thought of that as he returned to London. 'She's got power.' Power over men, certainly; the power of immense physical attraction, humour, charm and – there could be no doubt of it – a certain amount of ruthlessness, although he had been sincere in referring, as well, to Veronica's romanticism. Power that was nevertheless insecure, lacking material support, alert for opportunity. He had seen this in Berlin, he presumed it from what he had learned and guessed of her marriage to Gaisford. Yet he had been invited to believe that this woman of power had been, herself, threatened, reduced and forced to accept as lover a man she once had 'rather fallen for' but now had good cause to dislike, a man she later obeyed simply because she feared the social embarrassment he claimed to be able to create for her if she denied him. Was that a woman of power? The more Francis thought of it – and he'd not been able to avoid thinking of it a good deal since the summer – the more he found himself convinced that, whatever she said, Veronica still had quite a taste for Printer Drew. Then why take up with John Marvell? Why tell him a pack of lies – if they were lies – to excuse a relationship with Drew which had been based on pleasure, not blackmail? Why take John Marvell, too, as a lover – and let him believe she loved him, would one day marry him? A desire for more 'position', whatever that was, than Drew could offer? John hadn't got much of either position or money – certainly less than Drew, who was a pretty successful journalist. But perhaps Drew, despite what she'd told John, didn't really want marriage, and Veronica did, and had seen her chance.

Perhaps, again, there were small bits of truth in all these suggestions, none of them totally excluding the others. Perhaps Veronica half-loved John, admired him, found it difficult to rid herself of the habit of Drew, while finding some aspects of his character repellent – but only some (Francis had been sceptical, even at the time, when John in his first disclosures had said with vehemence 'she's disgusted by him'). Perhaps she wanted to be married, was under a certain amount of pressure (as recounted) from Drew, and exaggerated it to John to justify her delays, her uncertainties, which might have their root in a good deal of fairly profound feminine emotion. And perhaps she had lied – or, again, exaggerated – about the degree to which she'd given Drew his marching orders, hoping that time would ease the situation, that her own mind would clarify, that Drew might get bored with it and her (but perhaps she dreaded this, too); that something would turn up.

Now Alan had turned up. In his assessment of Alan Marvell's feelings, Francis was in no doubt whatsoever. And he was used to Alan getting what he wanted, and easily exercising power. It had always been so.

Exactly one week later, on reaching his rooms after the weekend, Francis found that the Saturday post had brought a letter in an unfamiliar hand.

'Dear Carr,

We met under rather peculiar circumstances last summer lunching with John Marvell, and had no opportunity for a chat. I was fascinated by what little I overheard you saying to someone else about life in Berlin, and I do hope you'll allow me to take that further and will agree to have lunch with me one day. I have to be away from London for three weeks. How would Thursday, 11th December suit you?

Yours sincerely,

Dominic Drew.'

This would, Francis thought, suit him perfectly well. This curious cat's cradle of relationships, in which he played a peripheral but not entirely detached part, might be clarified a little by exposure to one of the principals, of whose activities and emotions he had so far heard only at second-hand. But before the lunch took place, John Marvell asked Francis to come to see him. And Francis could tell from his cousin's voice, that he was an unhappy man.

John sat his cousin down and at first said little. It will come, thought Francis. It will come. He told John that, out of the blue, Drew had asked him to lunch.

'I don't care for it, thinking of what you and Veronica have told me, and what a swine the man is. But I didn't want to refuse, in case you both think I might use the opportunity in some way. Otherwise, of course, the last subject I'd ever discuss would be Veronica. From what you say, he may, like the cad he is, bring it up. I've no idea why he's invited me. Not, I fancy, just for a little gossip about Berlin.'

John said, 'I'm sure he'll talk about this business. He's not in the least a gentleman, he'll say anything. You'll probably feel like knocking him down. Try not to – it wouldn't help. He obviously knows you're a friend, a relation of mine. And Veronica will have mentioned you to him, in the context of her visit to Berlin.'

Bound to have, Francis thought. Bound to have few secrets from Drew. It had been – perhaps was – that sort of relationship. Not that Francis was much of a secret, he thought, a little bitterly. He said, 'Anyway, you tell me Drew's out of the contest, or about to be. So there's nothing to worry about.' He at once regretted using the word 'contest'.

John said nothing. Francis guessed what was the matter without the slightest difficulty, and it wasn't Drew. Worse, from John's viewpoint. He was unsmiling and silent. He'd suggested the meeting and there had to be something he needed to say. Francis thought he'd better force the pace.

'Do I understand that you and Veronica will shortly be announcing your engagement?'

'Not exactly. Francis, I thought that when we got past the ridiculous blackmail idea – which was grotesque anyway, the more I think about it the more I ask myself what on earth Veronica had to fear – when we passed that, we could face the world, get engaged, get married. I'm getting on pretty well in my

97

publishing life, we'd be hard up but we'd manage. I want to tell my mother it's settled, have things in the open.'

'And Veronica's reluctant?'

'Yes – she still says, "Give me time!" Hang it, there's been plenty of time. And she's assured me she's now told Drew she's no desire to see him again.'

'She's had that interview, has she? It was pending but had not taken place when we were all at Bargate.'

'I've asked her. She's been rather difficult to get hold of lately – poor darling gets appalling migraine, you probably didn't know that – and I couldn't reach her by telephone or at the house. But I write to her, just a note, pretty well every day and of course she writes back –'

When pressed, Francis thought. Not, perhaps, spontaneously or immediately now –

'– and in her last she said, "I've seen D.D. He's accepted the situation."'

Francis said, 'John, it's natural you're impatient. But I remember, at Bargate, that you said you didn't want to press Veronica. You actually said – "I want her to take her time."'

'Well, now I don't. That was before she settled it. Now she's done so. I think I'd be right to – push a bit.'

Francis looked at his cousin. They were sitting in John's charming rooms in Davies Street. It was a cold evening, winter well underway.

'John, are you sure?'

'Naturally. You know what I feel about Veronica.'

'Are you sure she's the wife for you? I know you're in love with her. But marriage goes on a long time.'

John said, 'Francis, I know, I really know, that she –' He stopped.

Francis thought of a dark passage at Faberdown, Veronica's smothered laugh heard through a flimsy, panelled bedroom door. He perfectly understood that to John such evidences of passion as he had obtained might seem irrevocable, decisive, impossible to doubt. But Francis doubted. He said briskly, 'Well, I expect she's out of sorts. You'll have to be persevering and keep your balance. It's a great thing Drew's out of the way. Seen Alan lately?'

'He's going to Ireland in February.'

'Whereabouts?'

'About thirty miles from Dublin, he says. A lot of the cavalry are there.'

They sat silent for a minute.

'Francis, in spite of what I've been saying, there's a difficulty on my side.'

'Really?'

'Yes. You see, it's clear to me that Alan's fallen for Veronica.' He said it flatly. It had been obvious from the start that this was what he wanted to talk about, and Francis was glad of it. Anything would be better, he thought, than self-deception, and a wound now might avert death later. John was, of course, confused. He would say neither to Francis nor to Alan – 'I've slept with this woman. I know she loves me. I know she wants me. I know I can make her happy. I don't want anybody else to muddle it.' John, thought Francis, was entirely honest. It was a conventional age: he and Veronica had overstepped one convention. It was inconceivable to him that this might not be as important as he fancied. Charming he might be, but he was not a sophisticate. And he was in love, that fearful condition. Francis felt old and wise.

He also felt a certain exasperation. John would 'protect' Veronica's reputation, whereas if he spoke out freely, said to his brother, 'She's been mine: I know all about her,' Alan, angry and hurt though he might be, would possibly decide he preferred to avoid shop-soiled goods. That was how he would probably express it to himself – and John could be the beneficiary. But that line of conduct would never be contemplated by John – it needed, thought Francis, a Printer Drew to act on realistic calculations of that sort. Meanwhile, these two brothers would muddle their way into a situation of unhappiness and tragedy.

Francis said, 'Does Alan know that you, yourself, want to marry Veronica?' He knew the answer, of course, but not whether John knew it.

'Yes. I've not talked much about it, but he knows.'

'Well?'

'Alan and I have not seen much of each other of recent weeks.'

'And Veronica? You say you're sure of her love?'

John looked out of the window and said grimly, 'I was.'

'John, I return to what I said before, when I asked you if you were certain about marriage. You're unsure of her now, just because your brother's fallen for her as well! You've no idea what he really feels, or how she'd react. For God's sake, she can't have seen Alan more than a few times. Your – your connection with her has been going on for ages. Yet you're uncertain.'

John said nothing.

Francis said as roughly as he could, 'Well, if you're right, she'll just have to choose between you, won't she?'

John didn't respond with resentment, but with something like resignation. He said, dully and without his usual smile, that he supposed she would. Francis left him, sad for his sadness and knowing that he was leaving a beaten man, although acknowledgement of defeat might not come for a little time.

When they parted, John said, 'Thank you, Francis, you're the best of friends at a time like this,' and Francis felt something twist his gut.

Long afterwards Francis recalled that conversation to John, recalled it when it could be presumed pain had disappeared. John told him that he'd not then been able to bring himself to describe one scene between himself and Veronica, a scene that had been played two weeks earlier and which he rehearsed endlessly in his mind, seeking from it comfort he knew was not there. It had been a Sunday, and Veronica, elusive these days, had consented to be driven out of London for 'some fresh air and a good walk'. John had suggested Buckinghamshire – a walk in the Chilterns.

'Much too far! It'll take hours.'

John protested that if they started early they could have a

walk, sandwiches in the pocket, and drive back at the end of the afternoon, to reach London for dinner.

'I promise you, the car's going splendidly! We'll cut church – I'll call at nine o'clock.'

'All right.'

He was utterly happy for an hour or two. Veronica looked at him, smiling, as they bowled along. She had shouted at him above the noise of the open car. John had grinned at her, 'Can't hear!'

'I said, "You're heavenly when you're carefree!"'

They had walked among the great beeches above Princes Risborough. Veronica, long skirted though she might be, walked with the energy and almost with the stride of a man. Her cheeks were flushed. They climbed to a crest and she pulled off her hat and sat on a tree stump, gasping from the exertion. They had climbed fast, John in the lead and Veronica determined not to be out-distanced. She laughed in his face.

'Why must we ever go down? It's perfect here.'

It was, indeed, a perfect day – a clear sky and surprisingly warm. Visibility was excellent and every clearing in the beeches had disclosed a fresh view over the Vale of Aylesbury.

'I agree! Let's never go down!' He turned her to him and put his arms around her, holding her tight, kissing her cheek, her eyes, her lips. After a moment she gently pushed him away.

'I'm afraid we ought to be getting back, all the same.'

'Darling, darling Vee. Why?'

'No, my dear – no, really, John, darling. I mean it. We ought to go.'

'Vee, Veronica, must this go on, can't we –'

'There are a lot of things about me you don't know –' She sighed. 'John, I love you, you know. In a way. But – well, I really don't feel that we –'

'Veronica,' he said, voice trembling, 'I've made you happy, haven't I? And you know what I feel! I'd die for you. And –'

'Yes, and I'm grateful. But life's a complicated business, darling John. An awful lot of things have to be taken into account.'

There was a short silence and they walked a little way. John said softly, 'Are you telling me to get out?'

'Oh, my dear, I could never – But – you see, my dear, as I said, there are a good many things about me you don't know.'

'Are there? Are there really?'

'Yes, there are.'

'And does that matter?'

'I'm not sure.'

John said – 'It's Alan, isn't it?'

And Veronica said, very softly and with a break in the voice, 'I'm not sure.' Then she said, angrily, 'Come on, we must start down, it'll be dark soon.'

They had driven back to London in silence. And Francis, long afterwards, could envisage them, envisage it all.

Printer Drew gave Francis lunch in the Ritz Grill and a very good lunch it was. 'Journalists' in those days brought to minds like Francis's the sort of half-apologetic, half-pushing scribblers sometimes portrayed on the stage to help a plot along. There were, of course, rich and fashionable writers for the newspapers, but to many people, 'journalist' was synonymous with 'reporter', and reporters, it was felt, snooped. This, of course, was snobbish travesty and Drew, by contrast, was definitely of the rich and fashionable variety. Everybody knew him. He, too, snooped – but he wrote the results with audacious skill.

He made himself charming, and Francis had to keep reminding himself that this man, according to the evidence, had been forcing Veronica into bed with him by threat of blackguarding her late husband, and, perhaps as effectively, by threat of exposure that he'd forced her into bed with him! Or so the story ran. Francis looked at his host, moral outrage struggling with physical jealousy, and tucked into his *Sole véronique*.

'A glass of Chablis?'

'Thank you.'

Drew showed a highly intelligent interest in Berlin although he'd never been to Germany. The possibility of war was often discussed in those days, but often with a certain sense of fantasy. There were the Germans, immensely powerful in military terms, their huge, confident army of *Pickelhaube*-wearing warriors, so often witnessed by Francis marching up the Unter den Linden; their huge, newly created fleet, challenging Britain in her own, surely God-given element. There were the French, hating the Germans, neurotically planning revenge for 1870. There were all the others – the remote, numerous, enormously unstable Russians, periodically throwing insurrectionary bombs at each other and ruling an immense and mutinous empire. There was Austria-Hungary, equally sprawling, equally wracked internally, or so the British supposed, not unhappily. But there didn't really seem much reason why the peoples of the European nations, apart from a number of crackpot revolutionaries, should start killing each other.

There'd been diplomatic coolnesses – even one crisis – when Francis was at the Embassy in Berlin. But no war. Talk of war always seemed absurd to Francis's generation. All the ingredients were there – conflicts of national interests, domestic pressures, huge armaments, strategic plans which demanded pre-emption as the only method of averting defeat, 'if war came'. But why on earth *should* the match ever be struck? To strike it involved a deliberate choice to kill rather than argue. It was hard to believe, in the civilized world of 1913, that such a choice could possibly be made. Francis found he was enjoying lunch.

Drew was less optimistic.

'You're a rational man, Carr. You work in the Foreign Office, a rational atmosphere I should think, dedicated to talking about problems, postponing crunches rather than anticipating them, seeking a way forward for a little, rather than a final solution.'

'Certainly. That's diplomacy. When wars start, diplomats retire. They exist, largely, to prevent them.' Francis felt lofty and experienced. Next year he was due to be absorbed into the profession itself.

Drew was too old a hand at flattery to look amused at these authoritative sentiments from a twenty-four-year-old honorary attaché. He nodded respectfully.

'As a newspaper man I see more than you, perhaps, of the irrational. I see how the emotions and weaknesses of human beings in places of authority or influence can suddenly topple any sensible course of action. You hope for history to be guided at least a bit by reason. I see it, all too often, driven by mood.'

Francis thought of the Kaiser. 'And some rulers, I suppose you'd say, are moody!'

'Not only rulers. Whole populaces can be gripped by mood. Democracies are even more violent than autocrats when they get excited.'

'And what's going to excite them about foreign policy? Domestic matters, wages, conditions, certainly.' England had been gripped by a series of particularly damaging and intractable strikes during the previous three years. They appeared to order such things better in Germany. People said that what would later be called 'industrial relations' in Britain had never been worse.

Drew said, 'The British may not take much interest in foreign affairs most of the time, but they have periods in history when they ignite: when they decide that their country needs the sort of rowdy enthusiasm generally reserved for some more parochial cause like a football team or a trade union! Then their patriotism becomes formidable.'

'It happened to some extent in the war, I agree.' They meant the Boer War, recalled by Francis from boyhood, concluded twelve years earlier. 'But a lot of people were in two minds about it. Hardly a crusade, in spite of all the patriotic songs.'

'Well,' said Drew. 'If there were trouble threatening in Europe it might be different.'

'I should think the public reaction would be to want to stay out of it. Unless the Germans, for instance, tried to be impertinent at sea. As long as there were no nonsense in that quarter, I doubt –'

But Drew had already decided to change the subject. His last remark had been intended to close the European topic for the present. He nodded now, implying nothing, and said, 'Of course Veronica met you in Berlin, didn't she? Veronica Gaisford. You were helpful to her, I remember.'

'Not very. She managed very well without much assistance from me.'

'Not what she says, my dear fellow. I understand you saw each other at Faberdown in the summer. I hardly know the Winters. Veronica mentioned it.' He said it carelessly, but he was looking at Francis shrewdly. Drew had the knack, which no doubt helped make him so formidable a journalist, of getting into a person's thoughts with a piece of swift guesswork, hazarding a remark and detecting by every nuance of reaction whether his shaft was on target. Now he said with what sounded like an easy, amused chuckle, 'Did she complain about me?'

'I don't remember any complaint.'

'But she spoke of me, perhaps?'

Francis shook his head as if puzzled. He was never an expert dissembler and Drew was watching him carefully.

'May I take you a little into my confidence, Carr? I feel I know you better than I do, because Veronica has always talked about you with such admiration. Of course, when she met you first she'd just lost her husband. He was no good at all, you know.'

'Did you know him?'

'I did indeed. We met quite often. I – I had to do some pieces at one time on an area where he had a good deal of experience and he was an interesting man in many ways. But then it all went wrong. He behaved very badly. Frankly, I was able to help a bit, in seeing that some things didn't come out about that which might have – might have hurt Veronica.'

'I see.'

'I first saw a good deal of her at that time. What I want to tell you is this. Between ourselves, she and I have, for a long while, understood each other. Understood each other very well.'

Francis concentrated on the delicious duckling which had succeeded the *Sole véronique*. He disliked the mixture of anxiety and relish in Drew's voice. And in his talk of Gaisford what a revolting humbug the man was! Drew was speaking softly.

'We've agreed to get married one day. She's an enchanting person. She has her absurdities, of course – you've probably experienced them. This Irish nonsense – really, she becomes

105

passionate – and entirely unrealistic. But that sort of thing makes her all the more delightful.'

Some sort of reaction was necessary. Francis again said, 'I see.'

Then Drew showed why he had suggested lunch. His light, amused tone changed. His face, pudgy and to Francis highly unattractive, evinced something like strain. He was still looking hard at his guest. Then he dropped his eyes to his plate where his own duckling was untouched and took a large gulp of the claret they were now drinking. In a different, rather strangulated voice he asked if Francis had seen Veronica lately. Francis saw no point in not telling him frankly, and in an easy conversational tone said that they had both stayed at Bargate a few weeks ago.

'Of course, the Marvells are cousins of yours, aren't they?'

'They are.'

Drew was now sweating disagreeably. There was no doubt about it, thought Francis, he was suffering. He wanted information and he had thought – not an unreasonable guess – that he might get it from Francis Carr. To do so, he needed to show more of his hand.

'Carr, what I'm now going to say is very confidential. You may think it most peculiar to say it to a stranger, but you know Veronica. The truth is – we've had a small misunderstanding.'

'Ah!'

'She professes, at the moment, to say that she wants to see no more of me. And this quite suddenly. It has happened before, I may say. We're both temperamental people which is probably why we understand each other so well. It's generally quickly over and the less notice taken the better. *Donna e mobile* and all that. May I ask you – did anything extraordinary happen when you saw her last?' Francis had, when asked, told him when that had been.

'No. Nothing extraordinary.'

'Naturally, I know that the Marvell brothers were both there. I know John Marvell slightly. Of course, you and I first met lunching at the same table – with his firm.'

'Exactly. John was at Bargate. And his brother Alan. And

my cousin Helena, their mother.' Francis tried to revert the conversation to a mildly uninteresting, family level; to imply that it had all been domestic, dull. It was not that he wanted to spare Printer Drew, but he had no desire to discuss the Marvells in the same setting as Veronica except in very superficial terms. At the same time, he knew there was something convincing about the way Drew had referred to a misunderstanding with Veronica which had 'suddenly' arisen. This did not, thought Francis, match the painful and protracted efforts to shake off his blackmailing pressure which John had described and Veronica implied. Perhaps Drew did not classify that resistance as a misunderstanding – and had it, in reality, amounted to much?

Either way – and there were, Francis reflected, probably a good many ways – it sounded as if Veronica, whatever she'd attempted before, had now really decided to break with Drew. And he had taken it hard, of that there was no doubt. He looked at Francis now with a certain coldness, and Francis knew that Drew knew that Francis knew more of all this than had been implied; knew, too, that his luncheon guest would say little more. Drew could find no way to scoop something more out of the unsatisfying egg cup of information so far displayed.

He said – 'You obviously know that John Marvell, himself, is an admirer of Veronica.'

Francis smiled, rather fatuously, and said, 'I think we're all admirers.'

Drew said quietly – half to see its effect and half to satisfy himself – 'She likes him. Everyone likes him. Nothing more, of course. We often talked about it.' Then, recovering composure, 'We must be going. I've immensely enjoyed this.'

When they said goodbye, when Francis thanked him, shook his hand, watched him hail a cab, he walked off into St James's Street and found, to his astonishment, that he was sorry for the man. With part of himself he loathed him, but he was sorry for him. Of Drew's suffering there was little doubt. Veronica, once, had 'rather fallen for him', as she put it, and Francis, with reluctance, found this easier to believe after two hours in Drew's company. And he – had he 'fallen' for her, heavily and painfully?

It certainly appeared so. And that he'd felt he'd won her was as certain as that he'd lost her now. And he knew it.

A few days later, Francis told John that he'd seen Printer Drew, who obviously knew Veronica had done with him, although pretending to himself and others that it was temporary. He didn't say that Drew had indicated this was a new and, to him, surprising development. He reckoned John had enough to hurt him, without having to meditate on the extent Veronica had deceived him about Drew, if she had. That was past. Prudence was entirely justified.

They spoke on the telephone. John said, 'Thank you for telling me about it. I think I've got the right to tell you, in confidence, that Alan's engagement to Veronica will be announced in next Tuesday's *Morning Post*. All very quick. I hope they'll be happy.' He rang off.

CHAPTER VI

Alan had conducted a whirlwind courtship. From his first meeting with Veronica to the announcement of the engagement was just under eight weeks. Francis wrote to him, conventional and insincere lines of congratulation, saying that he knew what a prize had been won and could imagine how happy Alan must be. To Veronica he wrote briefly, saying that he was delighted she and Alan had found each other. This was entirely untrue. Francis thought the whole business very bad. He was intensely sorry for John, whose heartbreak would be bitter and concealed. He thought his cousin Alan was acquiring a wife from whom much trouble could be expected. Veronica had, Francis acknowledged, 'done well for herself', but how she would settle down to the life of a cavalry officer's wife – even a rich one – was uncertain. And once again, he acknowledged to himself, Francis felt absurdly and discreditably jealous. He wondered whether her old lover, Drew, would make some sort of a scene – try to put pressure on her again, perhaps, by threats of a disagreeable publicity about her first husband which would upset the Marvells? Try to induce her to think again, by exposing to Alan her previous connection with himself, Drew? These were the ploys attributed to Drew by Veronica, as reasons for keeping John Marvell uncertain but in tow. Had they really happened? After seeing Drew, Francis was less sure. He also suspected that Alan, albeit probably strait-laced in matters of sexual mores, would be less easy to upset than John, and at any hint of menace from Drew would deal with him pretty summarily. All in all, Veronica might turn out to be 'settled' now. There was still, however, the picture of her back, sitting on the turf in Richmond Park, talking so intently to Gerhardt

Brendthase. This was a deep one, thought Francis, that his cousin was about to wed. Fascinating certainly, but so sharp it would all be too easy to cut oneself. Badly.

Veronica answered his letter affectionately, saying that Francis had, as usual, been a tower of strength 'in all that tiresome business, now past and, thank heaven, to be dismissed utterly from mind by my present happiness.'

Alan wrote to him that the wedding was likely to be in June. To Francis, a six-month engagement seemed protracted, particularly since Veronica, as a widow, might have been expected to be rather quicker off the mark – and he could not believe Alan was not impatient. Engagements were often lengthy in those days, but in the circumstances Francis was surprised. John, however, enlightened him. He saw John as much as possible. John knew that Francis realized what he must be going through and his cousin's company was some comfort.

John had told Alan that he himself had been very much in love with Veronica but that he had to accept Alan was the right man for her and 'wished them happiness with all his heart'. He may have had few alternatives, thought Francis, but it was obvious that he had behaved thoroughly well, as he invariably did. But he was wracked, that was painfully evident. This woman, even if fleetingly, had been his mistress, his promised one, had given him to believe she loved him, had lain in his arms. It was easy to imagine that the taste of Veronica would linger long on the palate, and Francis pitied John a great deal. Alan had taken his *démarche* with a certain kindly complacency. He had known what he was doing to the brother to whom he was devoted. He had taken his woman with eyes wide open, he had challenged and won. It had all happened with terrifying suddenness. This was love; and love is war.

John explained that it was Veronica who had insisted on deferring the marriage until the summer. He and Francis were having dinner together.

'Gaisford only died at the beginning of 1912. She thinks two and a half years the minimum period that should elapse before remarriage. At first she spoke of three years.'

110

'That seems rather overscrupulous! And surely rather unfair on Alan?'

'He'll do whatever she wants. At first she wanted to defer announcing it until July and marry at Christmas. Alan's persuaded her to agree to announce it now, and marry in July.'

At least Veronica wasn't trying to rush him! Francis decided not to think about it much. The whole thing was their business and there was no immediate reason why they shouldn't manage it successfully. Francis confessed to himself that he had derived a certain rather dangerous satisfaction from peripheral involvement with the affair of Veronica and John. Veronica still made his heart jump, and he couldn't resist any circumstance that produced a shared interest between them. There was unlikely to be any of that now, and he would, he told himself, be the better for it.

Meanwhile John was being crucified. Everybody was saying, with the sort of heartless sniggers that are usual on such occasions, that 'poor old John Marvell has been cut out by his own brother'. Now John was doing his best to give Francis the family news in a matter-of-fact way.

'Alan's off to Ireland, of course. Veronica's going to stay with friends over there, part of the time. To be near him. But they'll be married in London.' John was to be best man. Alan had insisted. Love drives out other sensitivities.

They talked of other things, and found that both had accepted an invitation to stay in Sussex for the same weekend in February. A hunt ball.

'I suppose it's near Bargate?'

'Not really. It's not a bit of the country I know. Nor have I hunted over there.' Their hosts were the family of Angela Forrest, who had lunched at Faberdown on that day when John and Veronica had confided their problems to Francis. He had been glad to get Mrs Forrest's letter. He had liked Angela, and had the impression that she had liked him. Hunt balls were not Francis's favourite occasions, but he thought this one might compare favourably to some.

'The last sort of thing I feel like,' said John, 'is a hunt ball!'

With a terrible burst of self-revelation he said, 'It's no good, Francis. Whenever I pass a woman in the street I hope, somehow, it's going to be her. And whenever the post arrives I hope, hope like a madman, there'll be a letter from her to say that this engagement between Alan and her is just a foolish mistake. Oh God!' He put his head in his hands. Francis had never before seen his cousin so lacking in composure, so naked and revealed.

Knowing that it was too late for the question and the answer to affect the matter, speaking only from a nagging curiosity, Francis said, 'John, I'm not prying but I'm pretty sure I know how much there's been between Veronica and you. Does Alan know? Don't look at me with that haughty look, old boy! I've been a bit mixed up in this, remember? I repeat – Does Alan know?'

'He does not,' said John quietly and sternly, 'and she – Veronica – does not wish it— ever. We – we had a talk. Hard to bear – but we had it. Of course she wants to – to keep our concerns private. And precious. So do I. For ever. I'll share a lot with Alan. But not that.'

Francis managed to write 'Angela Forrest' as often in his ball programme as was discreet: perhaps rather more often than was discreet. Mrs Forrest's eyes were sharp, and although the hunt ball was less rigorous than the London Season, where débutantes were brought straight back to their chaperones after a dance, it was, by later standards, a pretty disciplined affair. Francis had hunted as a small boy but couldn't afford to do so now, and, probably from a certain envy, found that the boisterous camaraderie on these occasions of people who knew each other and didn't know him, was not particularly enjoyable. But tonight, he reckoned, was different. The principal difference was connected with Angela Forrest, small, neat, with a delicious little turned-up nose and a mischievous expression. Francis tried to remember if Mrs Winter, at Faberdown, had involved her in any matchmaking designs. He thought not. It was incomprehensible!

Berlin had, Francis fondly believed, taught him to waltz almost as well as Vienna might have done. Angela's dancing flattered.

The setting, in Francis's experience so often unsympathetic, delighted him that night. The ball itself was held at Anstice Park, the home of Lord Anstice, a man of enormous wealth, ennobled by King Edward VII. People were malicious about Anstice, as they were about the large number of very rich men whose style of life ostentatiously outdid all but the grandest of the more ancient grandees.

'His grandfather,' they used to say, 'hadn't an "h" to his name.'

'He lent King Edward money, of course.'

'Nonsense, that was his father, when the King was Prince of Wales. Anstice got the deferred reward.'

Lady Anstice, of better breeding than her husband, was a handsome woman who spent the money and who possessed the looks and the nerve to get accepted in London society. The old King had looked favourably on her, too.

John Marvell, who knew a good deal about Sussex, was contemptuous of this sort of talk. He said to Francis before they went up to dress, 'I look forward to seeing Anstice Park. It's a beautiful house from all accounts, and they say the Anstices have very good taste. If it wasn't for Anstice, the place would have fallen down. His father bought it from the Baltrys. They were broke, entirely through their own fault. They did nothing for the county or the country for two centuries. I get irritated when I hear people sneering at Anstice because he's new. He and his family have got energy! They've succeeded! Why can't they love a place like Anstice, and do well by it, just as much as those who conspicuously failed to make anything either of their lives or their lands for ages?'

Francis was disposed to agree.

'The worst thing about England,' said John, 'is its profound reverence for cultivated and self-effacing failure.'

'Hardly the hallmark of the Edwardians, John!'

'Agreed, and I'm not defending vulgarity for its own sake. But we're too damned modest and well bred.'

John was himself modest and the best bred of men, and, while understanding him well, Francis sighed inwardly. Nothing, he thought, would be to John's liking these days, not parties or philosophies or people. Nothing would be to his liking until a certain ghost was exorcized.

Anstice Park was, indeed, lovely. They congregated in a hall from which a curved, divided staircase climbed to three splendid rooms where supper was served and dancers wandered, talked, laughed and cooled off. Dancing was in the largest room in the house, on the ground floor and leading off the hall. The band was excellent. It was also very loud – too loud for some tastes, but helpful to the spirit of the evening since the sound pulsed throughout ground floor and staircase, penetrating as far as the supper rooms. Even when temporarily exhausted, feet were tapping. Most men wore hunt coats – the hunting pink of the local hunt whose ball this was, here and there a dark blue, a green or a canary-coloured coat. It was a splendid sight – somehow more so, Francis thought, than other hunt balls he'd attended. It was energetic work, too. He had brought two spare collars and a fresh pair of white gloves in a small bag left in the cloakroom, and the evening wasn't halfway through before he needed them. He thanked his stars that asthma had hardly bothered him since his return from Berlin, and danced with immense enthusiasm.

The other circumstance which made the Anstice ball both agreeable and interesting for Francis was the Forrest party. They had dined early – the Forrest house was about half an hour's drive from Anstice Park – and had then been packed into two stately Forrest motor cars.

'Such fun,' Mrs Forrest said. 'Anstice would have been much too far for the horses. People grumble about changing from their carriages but really one can do all sorts of things one never used to.'

'Where's the meet tomorrow?'

'At Anstice again. We're not going. I suppose we should have mounted you, John.'

'Not a bit of it, Mrs Forrest.' Although John had ridden all his life and rode well, he was the reverse of what is generally thought of as a 'horsy' man, and nobody was surprised that he disclaimed any desire to hunt next day. Francis, indeed, had been astonished to hear from John a week before that he had, of all things, applied for a commission in the Yeomanry and was intending to join them in annual camp. John was not only distinctly 'unhorsy'; he was also unmilitary, in some indefinable way an individualist, a man aloof from the herd, very evidently a man of peace. That he had the courage and energy to be a soldier if so minded none could doubt.

'Do you hunt, Mr Carr?'

Francis shook his head. He had, anyway, ascertained that Angela had given up hunting when a schoolgirl. They were not a particularly sporting family.

One of the chauffeurs, an elderly, apple-cheeked man, had been the Forrest coachman. He showed no signs of welcoming the transition to petrol.

'Albert takes us all the way at the *same pace*,' whispered Angela, 'and he slows down for the last half-mile so that the car isn't sweating on arrival! We'll be fearfully late!'

The other chauffeur was Albert's nephew. He looked lively, and all could see his appreciation of the car. It was made sternly clear to him by Albert that his task was to follow, and that the two vehicles would proceed in convoy. Mr Forrest counted them off into the two cars. A girl called Pamela Finch was staying: she, John, Angela, Francis, and Mr and Mrs Forrest mounted and were tucked into rugs.

Also in the party were Hilda and Cosmo Paterson.

During the ball, Francis strolled without a partner through one of the upper rooms. Tiresomely, Angela was dancing with some rather loutish neighbour, claimed as an old friend. Francis wandered and admired. John had been right about Lord Anstice's taste. Great wealth can always procure beauty but a good eye had assembled these tapestries and pictures, displayed them in the way they were, and decorated the rooms which had certainly been done anew from top to bottom since the departure of the feckless Baltrys, of ancient lineage and indifferent sense of responsibility.

'Hello, Francis.'

It was Cosmo. Francis said, 'Is Hilda enjoying herself?' He felt a little guilty. Hilda was charming. He had danced once with her. As a member of the same party he had certain obligations and she might have been neglected. He had, too, only had one dance with Pamela Finch.

'Hilda's dancing with Marvell. They're getting on pretty well.'

Francis thought, sadly, that this was outward appearance only. John must be moving through the rooms, dancing, talking, even flirting, like an automaton, a body whose soul was elsewhere.

Cosmo said, 'I've been wanting a bit of a crack with you. About to dance?'

'Not the next two.'

'We may have to go on talking tomorrow. Or later, anyway. Rather a long story.' His eyes were bright, as usual. He'd greeted Francis on arrival with the Forrests as an old friend. He was still driving the car which had once brought Angela and Hilda to Faberdown, but Mrs Forrest had sternly forbidden him to conduct any of them to Anstice in it. Now he took Francis's arm. 'A glass of champagne, don't you think?'

They sauntered, glass in hand. Anstice was a huge house and despite the numbers the rooms were uncrowded. It was possible to breathe, to wander undisturbed.

'You remember when we first met, that time lunching with Marvell? We walked together down St James's Street, remember?'

'I most certainly do. You had just pulled Printer Drew's chair from under him, and left the lunch table rather quickly.'

'That's it. And when we parted, at the bottom of St James's Street, I said to you – "I think she's frightened." Remember? I was talking about Mrs Gaisford, of course, who had been going on with Drew. The one that's going to marry your cousin.'

Francis didn't care for this description but it was entirely just.

'I remember perfectly.'

'I reckoned Drew had some hold over her. Instinct. May be unimportant now, of course. On the other hand, it may not.'

Francis felt he would like to stop this conversation in its tracks. He wished neither to confirm nor deny Cosmo's suspicions, presumably about to be voiced. That he was in a position to do so he did not doubt. He said, 'I think Drew has faded from the scene now, you know, I'm glad to say. I think all that's in the past.'

'Maybe. But I reckon I've got an idea of what Drew knew about her that made her scared. You see,' said Cosmo, 'I think the little lady has been playing some rather dangerous games.'

Francis braced himself for a repetition of scandal touching the late Henry Gaisford. It was perfectly possible that Cosmo, with his rackety, uncertain background, had come upon tail ends of that story. It was also – and a good deal more disagreeably – likely that he knew or suspected Drew's relationship with Veronica: he spoke of her 'who had been going on with Drew'. Earlier he had, Francis remembered, referred to Drew being 'proprietorial' towards Veronica, and his dislike (or envy, like many men?) had apparently been sufficient to make him indulge in that rather brutal piece of horseplay at the publishers' luncheon party. But none of this, surely, justified or explained his words now – 'some rather dangerous games'. This was, inevitably, intriguing. Francis suspected Cosmo had something of an animus against Veronica, perhaps an obsession, and wondered how well he knew her. He had referred to her at their first meeting as 'a bad woman'. Francis felt Cosmo was not an objective witness, for whatever reason, but wanted to hear what he had to say.

Cosmo seemed in no hurry about this. Francis suspected he was not a dancing man, that his duties in that direction sat light upon him. He wore a hunt coat, which suited his small, neat frame. His eyes were very bright and he gave, as ever, the feeling of a coiled spring, ready for release and likely to fly, dangerously, in some unpredictable direction. Francis awaited whatever Cosmo wanted to disclose with a certain unease but a good deal of curiosity, never bored where the conversation touched Veronica. Cosmo's first remarks, however, clarified nothing except aspects of his own character.

'When I reckoned Drew was twisting the little lady's arm, behaving like a real cad, I thought he might have to be frightened off. Know how I thought of doing it?'

117

'No.'

'Do you remember, at Faberdown, somebody talking about how scared Drew is at going to the dentist? Same dentist as I use, as a matter of fact.'

'I remember.'

'When I next submitted myself to torture in the old Devonshire Street chair, sitting back with my jaws open, I saw that one was a sitting duck to anybody in the back attic windows of the houses opposite. Telescopic sight, probably. Rifle. Predictable timing – access to dentist's appointment book – no problem. Hot weather, always had the window open. Quick getaway.'

'You contemplated murder?'

'No, no! I thought Drew, with his nose for a good story, would see at once what a good crime it would be. I would tell him – anonymously, of course, as a "well-wisher" – that certain people were out to get him unless he dropped anything to do with the Gaisford story. I'd tell him that I believed there was knowledge of his dental appointments – I happened to know he's having a positive orgy of fillings and the like, to repair his disgusting mouth. I'd tell him he was in danger through the window. He'd start jumping about. Not police, I think, although that wouldn't matter. He'd change appointments. Start looking ridiculous, sweating. Chances were he'd leave the whole Gaisford business alone. Funk would fight it out with whatever his desires were. It was my bet that funk would win.'

Francis digested this. It sounded slightly insane and, having witnessed what looked like the depth of Drew's feelings for Veronica, Francis doubted whether he would have been deflected by so far-fetched, not to say criminal, a manoeuvre. But it was interesting, he thought, even amusing in a bizarre way, as a light on Cosmo's own character. All this, too, for a cause in which, as far as was known, his own feelings and interests were in no way engaged. He was a rum card all right! There was something about him which made Francis doubt if he was simply showing off. Francis smiled, disbelievingly, and said, 'Well, I don't know whether it would have worked but I don't think it's necessary now.' He noted that Cosmo talked of frightening Printer into

118

'leaving the whole Gaisford business alone'. That still sounded like Henry Gaisford's wrongdoings. There was no indication yet of Veronica 'playing some dangerous games'. Francis felt there was more to come.

'Let's have another glass of champagne.' Music rose and fell, amid a distant hubbub. Francis looked at his dance programme. Plenty of time. A footman passed with a tray of glasses.

Cosmo said, 'I don't know if you ever heard that I've had a good many contacts in Ireland over the last two years?'

Gun-running to the Ulster Volunteers was what people said, some scandalized, some excitedly admiring. Francis told Cosmo he knew nothing of that.

'Yes. Certain business deals with the Ulster boys. They're perfectly determined, you know.'

'One gets that impression. But in the last resort I suspect everyone will find some sort of compromise, some formula. I'm sure that's the Government's hope.'

Such, certainly, was Foreign Office belief.

'Perhaps,' said Cosmo, with what sounded like sadness at the prospect of a really good conflict being aborted, 'Perhaps, but meanwhile the Ulster boys are getting as ready as they can.'

Francis said nothing. A servant of Government, albeit very junior, he knew a certain amount that it would be improper to share.

'Readiness in war,' said Cosmo, 'isn't only a matter of weapons. It's information. What soldiers call Intelligence.'

'Of course. And your Ulster boys have developed their Intelligence, have they?'

'Done their best. Question of penetrating the other side, the Fenians, you see. Done their best.' 'Fenians' – Cosmo used the old-fashioned term.

'You mean the Irish Republican Brotherhood? Surely Ulster's quarrel in the first instance would be with the British Government?'

'Maybe. But then there's the second instance, isn't there! Anyway, if the IRB decided to go for more than London's likely to give them, the Ulstermen would like to know. Knowledge of

IRB – useful card in dealing with London. Bunch of rebels! Traitors!'

'The Government, surely, are perfectly well aware of the aims of the IRB, the Hibernians and so forth. The Home Rule Bill is intended to take the wind from the sails of the extremist Republicans. That's what it's about.'

'Yes, yes,' said Cosmo, finding himself deflected, 'of course. Point is, there's a lot of foreign interest in the IRB.' He looked at Francis carefully. 'Foreign interest. German. First contacts made in America, of course.'

This was by no means unknown to Francis's superiors. His end of the conversation would have to be circumspect. At the same time they had not yet reached Veronica.

'I dare say. The Germans would fish in troubled waters.'

'They certainly would. "England's difficulty, Ireland's opportunity", all that. And my Ulster friends have found out a good deal about the IRB contacts with Germany, I can tell you.'

'Then I hope they've taken steps to share their knowledge with the Government. Whatever their view of the Home Rule Bill.'

'Not all of it, I suspect,' said Cosmo with candour. 'You don't play out all your trumps, do you, unless it's near the end of the hand. What sort of a deal is Ulster going to get from this Government, that's what they want to know. Looks as if things will move pretty fast now. Feeling's running pretty high.'

In November, not three months before, Bonar Law, leader of the Conservative Opposition, in a speech in Dublin, had referred to James II, who had fallen because, in Ireland, his cause was legitimate but 'his own army would not fight for him'. How exact was the intended analogy nobody knew, but there was no lack of fuel, that year, being poured on the flames of Irish feeling, whether North or South, about Home Rule.

Francis said nothing. He didn't yet see it, but there was a disagreeable feeling somewhere below the bottom of his stiff shirt front. Cosmo sipped his champagne with enjoyment.

'Point is, the Germans have got some surprising contacts. IRB are ragamuffins, good for the rough stuff, but with limited contacts in civilized society, and most of those notorious. In

120

addition, you see, the Germans have got a number of friends who can be relied on to keep their ears close to the ground at, shall we say, a higher level. People who, for whatever reason, think Ireland's interests don't coincide with England's. People who sympathize. Some would be active, I imagine. Some would just keep their contacts – their German contacts – informed. Some, I suppose, might even be in positions to influence opinion. But all in touch with the Germans. And playing an orchestrated German game.'

'All for the love of Ireland!'

'In part. Money, too.'

'You're talking of treason, of course.'

'Am I? Everyone's entitled to an honest political opinion. Everyone's at liberty to talk, to try to exert influence. And we're at peace with Germany.'

'And I hope will remain so. You're saying that your Ulster friends know a good deal about this network of German agents, contacts, sympathizers, call them what you like. And for their own reasons are sitting on their information.'

'They're not so naïve as to suppose the Government don't know a good deal of it. But – yes, they reckon it might come in useful to them, to Ulster as well.'

'And –?'

'Names,' said Cosmo thoughtfully. 'They've shared a few names with me. Asked my views.'

'And you've discussed these names with – with the appropriate authorities here?'

'Can't quite do that. Not in present circumstances.'

And then Cosmo talked for some minutes, quietly, effectively, convincingly. The music, distant and enticing, continued to throb. Then Cosmo said, 'See you later. On with the dance!' and a moment later he had disappeared.

CHAPTER VII

At the end of February, 1914, Alan Marvell went to Ireland, to a Staff appointment which promised to give him much pleasure. An exchange of letters had already established that he would have no difficulty in obtaining a generous spell of leave for a summer wedding. Wretched at leaving Veronica, albeit temporarily, but full of enthusiasm for a new life, he crossed the Irish Sea. He had, he reflected, been given a job in Ireland at a troubled time, fraught with new and numerous rumours, in particular as to what the Cabinet planned to do over the Irish Bill.

The newspapers were full of a plan they said they had discovered 'on unimpeachable evidence', whereby the Prime Minister intended to suggest that any Irish county in Ulster could stand aloof from the Home Rule arrangements for a period of three years. To many readers it sounded unconvincing, but 'unimpeachable evidence' generally meant that a Minister had talked, because of personal disagreement with colleagues, in order to make trouble. Whatever the truth of it, the Prime Minister, Asquith, actually voiced this proposal during the debate in the House of Commons on the Bill's second reading. The three-year period given previous publicity, however, was suggested by Asquith as six. Sir Edward Carson, by now the hero of Ulster, described it as a six-year stay of execution in which no loyal Unionist could be interested, and strode from the House amid a mighty roar of Opposition cheers. The Government, however, were sure of their narrow majority, with the support of the Irish members. Redmond, the Irish Parliamentary leader, was keeping the Liberal Government in office and for that he had to be given the Home Rule Bill. They were stirring days.

'The Marvells are going to Ireland at a tricky time,' people said. 'They'll start married life in the middle of a political crisis! Still, they'll probably concentrate on hunting! And on each other, of course. Alan's not in the least politically minded, he's a soldier through and through.'

Francis thought that Veronica, if as passionate an Irish nationalist as Drew's patronizing chuckle and Cosmo's muttered confidences had suggested, was unlikely to be entranced by the Home Rule Bill, whether it passed or fell before the entrenched resistance of Ulster. To the true Republican it was an anaemic measure, distancing Irish administration from London, restoring a Parliament with powers not much greater than those of a county council, and preserving the sacred aura of nationhood to the United Kingdom of Great Britain and Ireland – however much Asquith hoped to persuade the Irish to think they were receiving. Not that any but an extreme minority cared much, it was said, and many Irishmen were highly dubious, whatever public attitude they struck. To the Protestants it was a simple matter of 'Home Rule means Rome Rule'. The North was staunchly Protestant and few doubted that if forced to a change of constitution that alarmed them to the core, Ulstermen would fight. And, in the view of a considerable number of people both in Britain and Ireland, Ulstermen would be right.

20th March was a Friday and Francis had accepted Helena Marvell's invitation to spend 'an entirely quiet weekend' at Bargate. John was to be there. Veronica, he knew, would not. Helena, Francis was sure, would be handling that situation with sympathetic delicacy for John's feelings – for the fact that her younger son had been, and probably would for some time continue to be, madly in love with his brother's future wife. The less he saw the lady until the wound healed a little the better it would be for all, but his mother was a sensible woman and would be unobtrusive in her tact, Francis knew; nor would she be insensitive about pushing fresh feminine faces at John to 'get him over it'. The need would come for that, but not yet. John was damaged, his cousin knew. Outwardly he was his usual amusing, courteous self, but he needed time.

Francis was, therefore, mildly surprised – particularly since Helena had referred to 'an entirely quiet weekend' – when she greeted him with the information that two girls were also staying, and that it was proposed to go to a local point-to-point on the following afternoon.

'I must go,' said Helena, who had hunted regularly in her day but had now given it up. 'I forgot all about it, but I must go. And really it would be too dull for you young men to have nothing but an old creature like me with you.'

Francis doubted whether John would welcome this news, but it was Helena's house and Helena's son. 'People I know?' he asked.

He was delighted to hear that the girls were Hilda Paterson and Angela Forrest. These two tended to be asked to occasions together, to be inseparable. It could be tiresome, but Francis liked Hilda. If Angela had to have female company, it might as well be she.

'They're great friends and live near each other as you know. They weren't doing anything much this weekend. I mentioned that you and John would be here,' said Helena in non-committal tones. The girls were being collected by the Bargate chauffeur. John was driving down in time for dinner.

They gathered in the panelled inner hall at Bargate, used as often as not in preference to the drawing room when the family were on their own or the gathering informal. Francis felt his heart bound agreeably when he saw Angela Forrest again. He had hoped that circumstances would be quick to produce another meeting after the hunt ball which had been dominated by Cosmo's peculiar revelations, but Angela was seldom if ever taken to London and a tentative suggestion that her mother might invite him to stay had born disappointingly little fruit. She was a brown-haired, brown-eyed girl with a small, tip-tilted nose and a very wide smile; and when she smiled her eyes narrowed automatically in what most men found a delightful way. Furthermore, Francis found she smiled a great deal when he was talking to her, which he did as often as possible. Angela seemed a girl – he thought, ruefully, that there weren't many – who was prepared to recognize quiet, sardonic Francis Carr as not necessarily the inferior of the handsome, vigorous Marvells. Hilda Paterson was, as ever, gentle, charming and strikingly different from Cosmo. He asked her how her brother was.

'Which brother?' He discovered she had two. Stephen, still a schoolboy, was described as precocious – 'Mad about politics'. Of course, she knew he meant Cosmo. She was collecting herself, considering how to answer.

'He's abroad, somewhere.'

'Just – "somewhere"?'

'It sounds absurd but we really don't know. He said last Monday – "I must be off, I've got to catch a boat." We asked "boat to where?" and he looked mysterious and said – "I won't be quite sure till I'm aboard." Crazy! We're used to it now. He always writes and explains he's reached somewhere or other. It's affectation! He enjoys mystery.'

'I think he's fascinating,' said Angela. Francis smiled agreement, irritated by the obviousness of this opinion. Cosmo might have fascination for some women, but he was, Francis said to himself sourly, a posturing, theatrical figure, a self-appointed buccaneer who enjoyed intrigue for its own sake, a creature lacking self-discipline or seriousness, in the ultimate an absurd man.

'Absolutely fascinating!' It was Angela, with unbecoming warmth. Francis said nothing and at that moment John came into the inner hall, having just arrived, while simultaneously Froome, the Marvell butler, marched in through the other door bearing a telegram on a silver salver. He approached Helena with a stern expression. Froome liked tragedy and a telegram bore with it a chance of such.

'The boy has just brought this, madam.'

'Thank you, Froome.' Helena waved to John, who went over to kiss her before going round greeting the others, an eye on his mother sitting by the fire, the buff envelope on her lap, the message held between her fingers and causing her to frown.

'Not bad news, I hope, Mother?'

Helena's face was composed but puzzled.

'I don't really know. It's most odd. Here.' She held the telegram out to John, saying, 'There's nothing secret that I can see. Read it to Francis. It's from Alan.'

It was a long telegram. John evidently decided, despite his mother's words, that it was unsuitable for a public reading, perhaps inappropriate to be shared with girls unconnected with the family. He said – 'Have a look, Francis,' and gave it to him. The telegram read –

> 'All officers have been asked if willing to go north where trouble over Home Rule Bill expected from Ulster. Officers living in Ulster exempted. Rest have to choose. If decide not to go will be dismissed from Service. Together with almost all others here have decided not to go. Hope I'm right.
>
> Alan.'

Helena said to the girls, 'Alan has wired that all the officers have been asked whether they're ready to march north in Ireland, to coerce Ulster over Home Rule. If they won't they'll be expelled from the Army.' She said it very flatly. Francis read the telegram again.

'Cousin Helena, I see Alan doesn't actually say what they'd be going north to do. He doesn't say "coerce Ulster" – of course that's what the politicians and the newspapers are saying, but Alan just says "trouble over Home Rule expected".'

'Doesn't it come to the same thing?'

'Not necessarily. I mean, if the Government anticipate some sort of riots or attacks on Government property, they'd be bound to take precautions, I imagine.'

'Why should there be riots? There can be only one reason. He mentions that trouble is expected. Doesn't that mean that the Government expect the Ulstermen to protest and want to move the Army north to shoot them if they do?'

'I doubt that, Mother,' said John. 'There's a difference between protesting and rioting.'

'Not in Ireland, my dear boy. I know it well.'

Francis had been thinking about the telegram. He said, 'There

126

must be things we don't know, that perhaps Alan couldn't say. I can't believe he, or his brother officers, would refuse to do their duty if there were civil disorder threatening, simply because they disagreed with Government policy.'

'But from the telegram nobody is refusing to do anything,' said John. 'He says they've been asked if they're willing. He says, "Rest have to choose." They've been given an option.'

'Not much of an option, if one choice leads to dismissal from the Army,' said Helena, her cheeks rather pink, her voice a little louder. She had been digesting the telegram's contents and her temper was rising. She went on: 'Dismissal from the Army! I don't believe an officer can be dismissed, just like that, unless he's committed a crime! Even then, he'd have to be court-martialled, surely?' She was a soldier's daughter. All this was unthinkable to her, and they could understand it.

John said, frowning, 'I agree, Mother. I don't know anything about military law, but I don't understand what grounds there could be for dismissal. Not if they've been given a choice, as the telegram says.'

'Given a choice, indeed,' said Helena, with inconsistency but not entirely without sense, 'Given a choice! What a way to treat the Army! It wasn't given a choice when I was young! What's to become of the country if the Army can pick and choose what duty to perform?'

'But Mother, your heart's with the Ulstermen. You've often said it would be wrong for the Government to try to bully them into Home Rule against their will.'

'I *do* say that! But I still think it's absolutely wrong to give people choices. And then to threaten to disgrace them when they *do* choose.'

'Dismiss, Mother. Not disgrace.'

'And is not dismissal from the Army,' said Helena, 'disgrace? It would once have been considered so, I can tell you!' Her blood was up, and she said again – '"Choose" indeed! Dismissal! I don't believe the King will allow it.'

'Do you suppose we should send a telegram back, Mother? He doesn't ask anything –'

'Of course we must. Alan says, "Hope I'm right." He needs the support of his family. Of course we must send a wire.'

Nobody was entirely sure what should go in it, and there was a silence. Helena's mind had seized another point, and she said, 'I wonder if he's also sent a telegram to Veronica.'

John said, 'I expect so. I wonder what we should put in a wire to Alan.'

The two girls had been quiet throughout this, embarrassed by their accidental presence at a delicate family discussion. Hilda Paterson now spoke, very directly, addressing her remark to John. What she said was simple but it lifted the tension. Francis wondered how much she knew of Cosmo's dealings with Ulster; wondered, indeed, what exactly these now were. Hilda said, 'I expect Alan just needs to be told that his family are completely behind him, whatever he decides. Only he can make the decision. Nobody in this room can know what he knows. It's for him to choose and you to support without question.'

It was unusual for a young, unmarried girl to address her elders, let alone somebody like Helena Marvell, with such unequivocal authority, but Hilda's words were so honest, so plain, yet spoken with such absence of priggishness or impertinence that all felt relieved. She was, they thought, perfectly right. Nobody could advise or criticize Alan in the peculiar situation in which he and others had apparently been placed by the authorities. All that could be done was to send love and trust.

'Bravo, Hilda,' said Helena, who was fond of her. 'Quite right.' She started to write some words on a pad.

Next day the newspapers were full of the story – there were a number of sensational versions of it. To people of simple loyalty like the Marvells it was acutely distressing. On the one hand Helena, a staunch Conservative, thought the Government totally mistaken over the Home Rule Bill. Her sympathies lay with Carson and his Ulstermen, and the idea of using the Army to 'coerce' (nobody used this word with very clear ideas of what it could entail) the Unionists, shocked her profoundly. On the other hand, the idea of asking officers whether they would be prepared to obey unpalatable orders shocked her stern sense of propriety even more. Finally, she was outraged at what sounded like a threat to dismiss people for following a conscientious choice (however misguided) they had been permitted to make.

'The whole thing is a terrible muddle, a terrible, terrible muddle,' she said several times at the breakfast table. She returned to another point. 'I wonder what Veronica thinks of it. I suppose Alan has sent her a wire as well. If he's about to be dismissed from the Army his fiancée had better be warned!' She tried to smile at the absurdity of the idea, but she was deeply hurt.

John was frowning into his paper. Francis said, 'Cousin Helena, would you like me to telephone Veronica? See if she's heard from Alan?'

'It would be very kind, Francis,' said Helena, 'I know she's got a telephone.' It was not an instrument she herself liked using. 'Get Froome to show you where it is,' she said, 'it's outside the pantry.'

Froome was doing something at the sideboard and led Francis from the room with a resigned expression on his face.

'There are numbers listed in this notebook, sir,' said the butler. 'You will find Mrs Gaisford's. The person on the exchange is a silly creature, more often than not, and there's one that acts deaf as well.'

'Thank you, Froome. I'll do my best.'

After a mild struggle and amid a good deal of crackling, Francis heard Veronica's voice, and asked her whether she'd had a wire from Alan.

'We had one here at Bargate yesterday evening. Cousin Helena wondered whether you'd heard anything.'

'I've had two telegrams.' Veronica sounded excited yet collected, as if mistress of an anxious situation she nevertheless enjoyed.

'Two?'

'Two. Yesterday afternoon Alan wired me that they'd actually been given a choice as to whether or not they were prepared to march against Ulster if it rebelled over Home Rule.'

'Did he say that? "March against", and "rebelled"?'

'No, he put "go north", but it's obvious what he meant. And it's also obvious that the reason they'd get such an order would be rebellion by the Ulster Volunteers.'

'Perhaps. But perhaps they'd be sent just as a precaution – against any sort of trouble, any sort of excesses by the wild men, something the police might feel unable to cope with unsupported.'

'Francis, in that case who would object? Why feel it necessary to offer some sort of choice?'

'I agree. Muddle and misunderstanding perhaps. Did Alan say what he proposed to do?'

'The telegram said almost all the others had said they wouldn't go. Alan was deciding the same.'

'You say he sent two telegrams?'

'I sent one back in reply to the first. I sent a long wire. I said something like – "Impossible believe as many as you say refusing to do their duty. Implore you think carefully before courting dismissal for political gesture not your business."'

'And he's responded to that with a second telegram?'

'It arrived this morning. I'll read it out to you.'

Alan had wired – 'No question of refusing. Received no orders. Simply given freedom to take no part and at same moment told penalty of exercising freedom dismissal. Most feel as I do that sort of bullying intolerable. You say impossible believe as many as I say. You know of –' Here he gave four names, all well known to Veronica – 'All on same side as me.' Two of the names were of Colonels, as well as Alan's General.

Veronica said, 'He wired those names to prove to me it's not just the feeling of nonentities.'

'Anything else?'

Veronica was silent, and Francis thought she might have hung up. He said again, 'Are you there, Veronica? Is there anything else?'

'Yes, I'm here. No more from Alan, no. I'm afraid it's a bad look-out for Ireland. There's bound to be some sort of civil war. They – the Irish people – can hardly respect a Government which is incapable of commanding the loyalty of its own army! They'll have to take the law into their own hands. Why should everything be dictated by the Ulster Volunteers?'

'I don't expect Alan sees it like that.'

'Oh, Alan must of course do what he thinks right,' said Veronica in a different voice. 'Naturally one can't expect anybody to do something completely alone, to strike a pose. Naturally not. And Alan knows and cares nothing about Ireland. Why should he?'

'Will you send him another wire?'

'There's nothing to say. Nothing at all. We're in rather a mess, aren't we?' She sounded perfectly cheerful about it as she said goodbye.

At the point-to-point in the afternoon, people talked of nothing but Ireland and the extraordinary questions which the morning's papers had raised about the reliability of the Army.

In the following days, back in the office, chattering in corridors and clubs, Francis was able to piece together what had happened, or was believed to have happened. Things were said to have moved very fast over the weekend. It sounded to Francis and most people he talked to as if, from any conceivable point of view, the Government had muddled things and Helena's waspish comments, although admittedly coming from one hostile to Asquith's administration, were not very wide of the mark. Seely, the War Minister, resigned. He and Winston Churchill, a close political ally, were particularly unpopular with all those who felt the Army had been treated in a confused and improper way. The King was said to be particularly enraged and to have first learned of these sensitive matters from the morning papers.

Francis next saw John Marvell when the dust had settled. They had learned by that Monday evening that there were to be no dismissals of officers, no 'march to the north', no need for the collective insubordination which had apparently threatened that weekend!

John thought and said that the Government had been feeble. 'They had every right to reinforce Ulster if they expected any sort of trouble, from any quarter. I don't believe Alan, or anybody like him, would have disobeyed orders. Of course not. But they were given a choice – and told if they made a decision the Government didn't want, they'd be sacked. That's bullying. And futile bullying, too, because once somebody stood up to the Government they retreated. Abjectly.'

After confronting Ministers, General Gough, who had taken a leading part in the business, extracted and took back to Ireland a signed memorandum that the Government had no intention of enforcing Home Rule on Ulster. John reckoned that the Government, by mismanagement and disregard for men's decent feelings, had retreated to an unreasonably weak position in consequence. He sighed, 'Alan doesn't care two hoots about Irish politics. But you can't bully or threaten him.'

General Gough had returned to Ireland as something of a hero. The names of those who had taken the same line were well known, as were those, less popular, who had reacted differently. The Press only actually named Gough – he had received an uproarious public welcome, to his embarrassment, and the newspapers were full of it. The attitudes of others were matters of conjecture although there were plenty of rumours about how individuals had behaved. Abroad, the incidents of that weekend were followed with interest by those who relished the embarrassments of England.

A friend in the office showed Francis a report in the *Berliner Tageblatt*. Describing what he called 'Disaffection calling into grave question the reliability of the English Army,' the author expanded on 'General Gough's refusal of duty at the bidding of conscience.' 'Nor was the General alone,' the article ran. 'He was supported by the great mass of his own officers, including a number of senior rank.' The same four names that Alan had used to convince Veronica of majority feeling, were then given. It was not important, and the *Berliner Tageblatt* was unlikely to be widely read in London. It was an unctuous article and Francis found that it angered him.

*

Francis did not attend Alan's wedding. He had no great desire to do so but it was a family occasion and he would have felt an obligation to be there had it not been for a severe attack, that summer, of the congenital asthma from which he had always suffered on and off, which his time in Berlin seemed to have worsened, and his return to London to have cured.

Veronica was a widow so it was not a 'smart' wedding with the usual trappings of a white-dressed bride, but the family turned out in force and a large party was held afterwards. They were married in London and went to Biarritz for three weeks immediately afterwards. John was his brother's best man. Francis felt for him.

In July, John telephoned one evening.

'Alan and Veronica will be back from France next week. Francis, are you fully recovered?'

'Almost.'

'Sorry you couldn't be at the wedding. They both said how sad they were.'

'I was sad, too,' Francis said untruthfully. 'I suppose they're going straight over to Dublin?'

'No, Alan's going ahead and she's staying in England for a few weeks. There are a lot of things to fix, apparently. The house he'd arranged to take fell through, rotten luck. Just before the wedding, the owner died and the executors don't want to let! He thinks he's found another, but it may take a little time.'

'Until then, will Veronica be at Bargate?'

'Yes. I expect so. I'm sure my mother would like to see you. In fact, I think she's going to ask you down.'

A letter of invitation from Helena arrived the next morning, asking Francis to come to Bargate at the beginning of August.

'I suppose the people in your office will be given the day off for the so-called Bank Holiday on 3rd August, so do come down on the Friday, dear Francis, and stay at least until Tuesday, 4th.'

With some unease he wrote a line of acceptance. As he walked to the office, the *Daily Mail* bill board at the corner of the street bore the words –

Serbia had, it was widely believed, condoned the murder of the Austrian Archduke Franz-Ferdinand and his wife at Sarajevo on 28th June, although the newspapers reported that no direct implication of the Serbian Government had been established. Many of the *Daily Mail*'s readers were hazy as to the exact whereabouts of Serbia, which was, by and large, regarded as one of several unpredictable Balkan nations, given to murder, revolution and general trouble-making. No doubt the Austrians would find this murder the last straw and would deal with the Serbs! When Francis arrived at the office, however, the mood was grim. A particular friend worked in the section concerned and they lunched together.

'The Austrian ultimatum's incredible, Francis! No country could accept it and call itself independent! They demand, for instance, the right to order Serbian officials, within Serbia, to be dismissed!'

'When was it delivered?'

'Yesterday. And Belgrade has got to answer by tomorrow.'

'Tomorrow' was Tuesday, 28th July, and on that day, although Serbia had accepted all but the two most offensive of the ultimatum's demands, Austria-Hungary declared war. It was obvious that war had been prepared from the very evening of the murder, that Vienna had determined to take extreme revenge on intolerable outrage. 'What will Russia do?' people were saying to each other, 'The Russians can't accept this! They can't accept the Austrians bullying their way into the Balkans like this, can they? The Serbs are Russia's protégés. The French have told the Russians they'll back them up.'

'We're trying to get some sort of conference called. Mediation.'

Great excitement was in the air that week in London – and, as the newspapers reported, in Paris, Berlin and St Petersburg as well. Francis went down to Bargate by train. John had arrived earlier and met him at the station.

'What's going to happen, Francis? We hope you're going to tell us.'

Francis, now a fully fledged member of the Foreign Office –

indeed, of the Diplomatic Service, albeit temporarily at 'home duty' – was regarded by the family as their domestic oracle on international affairs. Francis, naturally, did not find this role disagreeable. He said sagely, 'There's no secret about one thing. The Russians have ordered general mobilization.'

'What's that mean?'

'It means that their whole army will mobilize. Not only opposite Austria, but opposite Germany as well. It will be in tomorrow's papers.'

'What about Germany?'

In the Foreign Office, they had received different impressions from Germany hourly, as German policy appeared to tack with the conflicting moods, ambitions and fears of an uneasy Government and a volatile Emperor. At one time the Germans had seemed to be joining Britain in urging restraint on Vienna, and the Kaiser had also made a personal approach to his cousin, the Tsar, pleading against actions which would lead to war. On the other hand, it was known that Berlin had, at an early stage, pledged absolute support to Austria-Hungary. It didn't seem, thought Francis, that anybody was fully in control of policy or events. Not anywhere, perhaps.

They drove through the quiet Sussex lanes towards Bargate.

'What about Germany?' John said again. Francis knew enough of the background to be sure of one thing.

'John, if Russia mobilizes her entire army, Germany has to mobilize. Otherwise the door's wide open. And if Germany mobilizes, France must mobilize. For the same reason.'

He did not know, but the weekend news made clear, that the preliminary orders for German mobilization had been issued the previous day. Thereafter there was likely to be a race to get in the first blow.

'What will we do, Francis?' asked Helena Marvell, who was sitting in the inner hall when they arrived, Veronica beside her. Veronica smiled a welcome, looking as enchanting as ever in a pale-blue and white summer frock, a rather watchful expression in her eyes. She said, 'Dear Francis!' and held his hand a fraction longer than customary.

'It will depend on Germany, I think. The Germans have asked the French if they'll keep out of a German-Russian war.'

'And will they?'

'Difficult. They've got a treaty with Russia. And I'm not sure the Germans want them to keep out. They've demanded some pretty undignified sort of assurances of neutrality from France, it seems. The French won't tolerate that.'

'They certainly won't, if I know them,' said Helena emphatically. She disliked the French, but felt little warmth towards any foreigner.

Veronica smiled and said, 'I expect there are plenty of Frenchmen longing for their revenge. For 1870.'

'Very probably.'

'Well,' said Helena again, 'what will *we* do?'

John was polite and distant with Veronica. Nobody would have guessed that he had been wracked with desire for this woman, had loved her, thought he had won her because for a little he had enjoyed her body. Francis thought it likely John still loved her and was suffering. He knew that he wanted to avoid the subject – wanted this very much. He wanted no confidences from John. He couldn't, he decided, help. At times he thought John gave some indications of being on the way to recovery. He was even heard talking on the telephone to Hilda Paterson about some social arrangement. A nice girl, thought Francis, at least old John seems to be over the suicidal stage. But there was still pain there, he was certain of that.

After breakfast on Sunday, Veronica said, 'Church at eleven, I suppose?'

Francis was alone with her.

'Church at eleven.'

'I want to look at my mother-in-law's herbaceous border. She's brilliant with it. Coming?'

'Indeed.'

Helena and John were together in the sitting room, talking like people who sensed time was already limited. The European situation had dominated the previous night's dinner, with Helena holding staunchly to two somewhat opposed propositions – that on no account should British blood be shed to save a pack of quarrelsome Frenchmen from their comeuppance, and that the Royal Navy should now take the chance to teach those arrogant, square-headed Germans a lesson and blow their presumptuous fleet out of the water once and for all. Veronica and Francis went out through french windows. It was a hot, beautiful morning. They walked slowly.

'I was sorry you couldn't come to our wedding, Francis. You sent us a lovely present.'

'I hope you'll be happy, Veronica.'

She said very softly – 'I hope I will. But I somehow doubt it.'

'Veronica –'

'I know I shouldn't say this. You're the only person to whom I could – you are so understanding. A woman is never expected to tell the truth in these things. You said you hoped I'd be happy. I do doubt it.'

Francis had no intention of asking why. All sorts of obvious and intimate speculations came to mind, but had to remain shadowy, unspoken. He found that his feelings for Veronica were, as they always had been, equivocal but that distrust now predominated. Unwisely, as it happened, she said, 'Well, a wife must be loyal, Francis, isn't that it?'

Something snapped inside Francis's head. He listened to what followed as if to a third person, not the quiet, courteous, re-strained Francis Carr. When he looked back on the scene after-wards, he had some difficulty in justifying it. 'It was a time to be straight with her,' he argued to himself. But he knew, with less pride, that a good deal of frustrated desire as well as righteous indignation had built up force inside him and that he derived a certain relish from lashing this girl with his tongue if nothing else. And he knew, too, that Veronica was entirely aware of his state of mind, contemptuously aware.

Francis stood very still, tried to fix her eyes with his and started talking, softly and not allowing interruption although at one moment Veronica drew in her breath sharply as if to exclaim. But she said nothing.

Francis talked for about four minutes.

'Veronica, a wife must indeed be loyal. I can imagine you are going to find that very testing, perhaps rather difficult. And the difficulty is likely to increase.'

He had decided that Cosmo's interpretation of Veronica might well be accurate, that Drew's partial disclosures, his own sight of her with Brendthase, all confirmed the same impression. It was, he thought, good enough to go on. Good enough to try on her, flail her with, watch her damned, lovely, hypocritical face. But he found that, as he talked on, saying unforgivable things in a low, unemphatic voice, he could not, in fact, watch her face. He, not she, avoided the other's eye. She only spoke once, when he – somewhat gratuitously he thought afterwards with regret: she had, after all, herself confided the matter in him – spoke about her unfaithfulness.

'You, now my cousin's wife, used to be the mistress of Dominic Drew. Simultaneously, you were my cousin John's mistress. You changed horses remarkably quickly.'

Surprisingly, and very quietly, Veronica said, 'Yes, I did.'

At the end he said, 'That's all I wanted to say, Veronica.'

There was no sign, but she did not retreat. Francis felt a frightful need to get some reaction. He said, 'And, of course, you may be watched. If you are stupid you can expect no help, no sympathy. I shall be wretched for my family but that will be that. My voice will be added to – to those condemning you. And I hope some of what I've said is mistaken.'

Still no word, and he said, feebly, 'I have thought it best to tell you all this.'

Helena Marvell emerged through the french windows. Seeing the pair of them, she called, 'There you are!' and began to descend the steps to the border and lawn.

Veronica said quietly, 'You have got things entirely wrong, Francis.'

'I think not.' He knew that she was an enemy now. 'I think not.' But he felt sick. Furthermore he felt a great deal of doubt.

He had voiced unpardonable accusations – was it not largely guesswork and gossip? He almost wanted to say, 'Of course I may be wholly wrong', idiotic as it would have sounded. Still, he said to himself, I won't talk about this to others, I won't blacken her name without proof. I don't regret telling her my suspicions. But already he did.

'A new Francis!' Her voice shook a little, and there was some scorn in it. 'You're almost alive, for the first time! Thinking preposterous things, but not quite so impartial and – and neuter – as usual.' She meant to hurt and had a sound instinct as to how she could. He didn't answer.

'Perhaps it would be best not to see much of you from now on, Francis.'

He shrugged his shoulders and moved towards the house. Helena, puffing slightly, had descended the steps.

'Cousin Helena, may I use your telephone?'

'Of course, my dear boy.'

A few minutes later he told them that a prearranged call to the Resident Clerk at the Foreign Office had confirmed that he should catch a train back to London as soon as possible. There was one at midday.

'I'm afraid I must miss church and catch it.'

The Resident Clerk had, in fact, remarked that he didn't suppose there was anything useful Francis could do until at least Monday afternoon. His immediate superior was not expected back until then.

'I'm coming up anyway,' Francis had said.

'Conscientious fellow!' said the Resident Clerk. 'You may not have heard yesterday evening's news. Germany has declared war on Russia.'

'I'll run you to the station,' John said. They drove from Bargate, talking little. There was no particular reason for his return, but he knew that he was best away. The events of these days – and perhaps they would be months, even years – looked likely to overshadow Veronica, Alan, John, Francis, Dominic Drew and their interweaving relationships. Yet Francis felt that Veronica was likely to emerge like Aphrodite from the waves of war, from the storm of the world, to bring her own particular turmoil here and there.

When Francis got to the office that Monday morning, faces were part exultant, part anxious, dependent on the character of the individual. In spite of what Helena Marvell described as the 'so-called Bank Holiday', most of the staff had been warned to be at their desks on Monday and a good many had been active all Sunday as well. The crowds were thronging Whitehall, scenting crisis, avid for drama, and Francis had found it difficult to reach the Foreign Office entrance. Once inside, officials were clustered at every open office door, talking excitedly.

'German demand to Belgium yesterday, Sunday! Unopposed passage of troops! Demand refused!'

'So the decision to invade France has been taken!'

'And Belgium, that's what it comes to. Unless the Germans back down we're bound to be in. Belgian neutrality's guaranteed. And the Germans won't back down. Everything we've ever learned about French and German war plans indicates that the machine's rolling. Nobody can stop it. PM agreed mobilization yesterday evening. Foreign Secretary's speaking in the House later today. Germany can't back down. We're in!'

'In'. That meant that all those smiling hospitable faces in Berlin, as well as the less agreeable ones, belonged now to enemies. 'In' meant that the painstaking efforts to establish understandings, reconcile interests, promote concord were now so many wasted hours. 'Othello's occupation's gone,' thought Francis. But it wasn't Othello's occupation that had gone, it was Francis Carr's.

'Yes,' Francis said, 'I suppose so. Germany can't back down. We're in.'

Part II

JOHN

CHAPTER VIII

People everywhere looked back afterwards at the Great War with such distaste, amid so many private tragedies as well as national lamentations, that they preferred to forget the enormous thrill of its beginning. John Marvell was, he always supposed, a particularly unmilitary man. He had managed to get a commission in the Yeomanry because, Alan had written in a letter, 'One must have something to do if war comes. You'd be miserable sitting in London, publishing,' and John knew he was right. He had a number of friends in the Yeomanry and the rudimentary instruction (his commission was only granted in 1913) was an occasion for merriment, horseplay which John never found congenial, and a certain amount of riding. But he intensely disliked the idea of war. He was thoughtful, even though a young man, and worried by what, even then, he suspected war might ultimately bring to Europe; and it gave him no subsequent pleasure to recall this or to reflect that he was right.

John's comrades, better men than he, as he told himself – were confident that war – and war always meant war with Germany – would be quickly won. Germany was known to have a huge and magnificent army.

'But the French are stronger. They've got these incredible fortresses as well. And the Fleet will be decisive.'

Sea power had frustrated the march of Napoleon's Grand Army in the end, and sea power would do the same for the ambitions of the Kaiser. And when the war ultimately came, the worries of most of John's brother officers centred not on the possibilities of defeat, which were never contemplated, but on the likelihood that their regiment would not be declared fit for service until it was all over. Meanwhile the first wartime ceremony was a parade at which all were invited to attest that they were prepared to serve abroad. The Yeomanry had been enlisted and the commissions granted for home service only, and to extend the engagement required assent. Every man gave it.

Yet, in spite of earlier reservations, John found that in the event he was as enthralled and inspired by the hour as any. He was one of those for whom nothing in life afterwards compared to that August in 1914. His anxiety about the outcome melted, to return later but not yet. All over Britain – and, of course, in every other combatant country on both sides – there was a sense of liberation, unity and purpose, embittering though the recollection might become. Men were freed from the pettinesses of life, they were brothers in arms, joined in one immense and selfless undertaking. The nobility of the *Entente* cause was preached to willing ears by every politician and from every pulpit. The infamy of the Germans (for some reason the Austrians, who, arguably, had started the whole business, were treated to less hatred) was described from the first day as without parallel in history or among nations. As the great German advance swung through Belgium, the stories of atrocities, of bayoneted babies, raped and mutilated women, sacked villages and defiled memorials, fed the general execration. Love of country, hatred of her enemies, fear for loved ones and a sense of invincible righteousness – it was a strong emotional mix. A few, and John was one of them, tried to keep a little balance, a shred of scepticism. It wasn't easy. The enthusiasm and the note of hysteria affected folk of all ages.

Once John found himself going to London in a crowded train where two elderly and not too sober fellow travellers in identical blue blazers and straw boaters told him, loudly, that after victory the entire German race should be sterilized.

'Rather a tall order, wouldn't that be?'

'Sterilize 'em,' said one, with immense assurance. 'Get rid of the problem in a generation. I hope you agree?'

'I certainly don't.'

'Oh,' said the other, rather disagreeably, 'you'd be too kind, your sort. You don't know 'em.'

'Do you know them?'

'Certainly I do,' said the first straw boater with dignity, 'I did a bit of business in Hamburg in the eighties.'

'And you found its inhabitants all vile?'

'No, they weren't a bad lot,' said the straw boater, with massive disregard for consistency of argument. Soon afterwards he went to sleep.

But it was not only the coming of war, the extraordinary and all-pervasive sense of patriotic uplift which made August, 1914, memorable to John Marvell, the most memorable month of his life so far. Somewhat to his shame, private concerns over-shadowed even the exaltation of the hour. For in August came the extraordinary discovery that his heart was beginning to heal from the knife wound it had recently suffered.

Before and after his brother's wedding, John lived in a hell of his own contriving. The sensible part of his mind told him that Veronica had chosen well, and that it was all for the best. Alan was heir to their home, Bargate. He was acknowledged by all to be an outstandingly gifted, attractive person, a figure of some glamour, Captain in a cavalry regiment, on the Staff in Ireland. John, by contrast, was comparatively badly off, starting to make his way as a publisher, always somewhat overshadowed by his brother. Although a strong, quiet man with an agreeable wit and much charm, inside himself – and to a degree which would have surprised the many who admired him – John had a certain unsureness. He was more introspective than ever showed, and part of him had always held a firm if unreasoned conviction that his brother was a better man. It was obvious that Alan had fallen head over heels in love with Veronica and that she had been carried away by his adoration and by the force of his personality. How not? And Alan was a 'good match'. So again, how not?

But John, with another part of his mind, thought there was every reason how not. For Veronica, he believed he knew, did not weigh such matters in the scales of society, count her feelings purely according to the measurements of materialism. Veronica fitted not at all the picture of a woman marrying to be comfortable, established, well placed in life. Veronica was an original, John said to himself angrily, a free spirit, a woman who scorned the conventions if they ran counter to the impulses of her heart. And this part of John's mind told him that Veronica was suffering from delusion, that she had truly loved him, John; that when she had lain in his arms, whispered there was not, there could never be, anybody like him, yesterday, today or tomorrow – that she had meant it, that it was unchanging truth, that she was deceiving herself and Alan by supposing that she was not, at heart, his. In those days before Alan's wedding, John would rush to answer the telephone in his rooms in London, seizing the earpiece from its hook, pressing his mouth against the mouthpiece which would get clammy from his breath, desperately hoping.

One day, he used to suppose, he would hear Veronica's voice – 'John! We'd better meet! It's all been a ghastly mistake! I've been a fool – but I've seen it in time, thank God! Help me, darling – and forgive me. Do you still feel as you did? I've no right to expect it –'

He constructed dialogue for her, for them both. It would be difficult, of course, with Alan, with his mother, with the mockery of the world. Nothing of that would matter a damn. He had a permanent, small pain in the stomach. The telephone call never came.

John got through the wedding rather well by concentrating on practical details and taking on from his brother so much of the bridegroom's side of the business that Alan said again and again, 'You're being wonderful, old chap!'

The Marvells were not a demonstrative family and John had never had praise of that sort from his elder. He tried to look at Veronica as a new person, a sister-in-law, somebody of whom he'd dreamed but was in reality now meeting afresh. He kissed her on the cheek.

'Best of luck! Make Alan get on to me if there's anything I can do here!' After the honeymoon the couple were going to Ireland.

At last it was all over and Veronica was gone. John told himself that he was a self-pitying, fragile fool. Plenty of men loved and lost, and he'd lost to an excellent winner. Unfortunately, Veronica's face came to him when he closed his eyes, in dreams, when walking the streets of London, came to him more not less insistently as those days of summer passed. John did not snatch at the telephone now when it rang, but he could hear Veronica's voice every hour, and could not break himself of the appalling, self-flagellating indulgence of composing sentences for that voice to say – sentences, invariably, of that love peppered with laughter, that romantic sensuality that was Veronica. Sometimes he tried to exorcize her not by 'thinking of other things' – that was beyond him as a rule – but by considering her personality, her appearance, her attitudes, objectively, critically, as if he had been given the task of describing her in exact detail to another. It didn't particularly help, but it was different; and there was, on the whole, nobody he could talk to about Veronica. His mother knew a little of what he'd felt, but John would have found it impossible to confide in her a continuing passion for his brother's wife. Of friends and family, there was only Francis Carr who knew how John and Veronica had been. Francis, John thought, was not a person who encouraged the outpourings of the heart – and John was, anyway, not one to pour out his feelings. Francis had been helpful, certainly – but to recollect that chapter reminded John too painfully of how his hopes had bounded at that time, of how Veronica, warm, naked, giggling in bed beside him that night at Faberdown, had seemed to be his for ever. And there had been other nights.

So John could not talk aloud about Veronica. He told himself that she had, sweetly, deceived both herself and him, that she could not possibly have been the right partner for one so modest and so ordinary. 'Veronica,' he said to himself, 'is a remarkable woman, and I am a most unremarkable man.' All the time he could see her, see her in every detail of physical appearance – her grey eyes, fair hair, her perfect height, reaching his nose when standing, her superb figure, her long, long legs, and skin as smooth as silk, as fragrant as rose petals. A banal image, he thought, but she does bring flowers to the mind, flowers after early summer rain. And, oh! The stimulus, the sheer fun of being with her! The anger, sometimes, the bitterness of thinking of her in another's arms! It choked him.

These physical images, maddening though they were, were still inadequate, thought John, to bring back her spirit and her poetry. For that it was necessary to hear her voice – and he would then immediately hear that voice, hear it all the time. He could hear her expressing her views with enthusiasm, with an aptitude for quotation (she had an excellent memory), sometimes with a mimicry which had enchanted him from the first day he met her. And as he tried to drive his mind away from her during those sultry July days, he could not only hear her murmuring words of love, exquisitely familiar, but could hear her speaking out boldly, inspired by her convictions, on the dangers of the hour. John knew that Veronica was passionate and brave, by nature an idealist, a lover of causes. As the events of that July took on their own threatening momentum, he could imagine Veronica's reactions –

'We'll never be bullied, will we! Nor allow bullies to win, whatever the odds!'

He was sure she was being fiery in her indignation when what Chesterton later called 'the vast empire of blood and iron' erupted into Belgium 'from the darkness of the northern forests'. Veronica, unlike John, had been to Germany and spoke of it with a certain affection, but he could guess where she must stand at this hour.

Then there was her love of Ireland – and her sense of the poetry of Ireland. Veronica loved quoting, quoting passages from Synge's plays, illustrating but never labouring a point, arguing about Ireland, passion always coloured by vivid language and never going far without a burst of laughter.

'"Isn't laughing a nice thing the time a woman's young,"' she quoted. But her feelings ran deep. They had never quarrelled about Ireland, partly because John had a certain sympathy with what she felt, but more because he knew very little about it. Now she was living there, as the wife of a cavalry captain of the British Army, and now he had lost her. Lost this superb woman, this combination of eager, poetic temperament, exquisite body and

148

generous heart. Life, he sadly recognized, had ended. He was twenty-four. And then everything changed.

John had known Hilda Paterson for some time. He thought her a decorative girl, always quick with a remark of such common sense that it struck people like lightning, so that everybody felt that it was what he or she had always thought, that it was obvious, that it made matters clear – but only Hilda had said it. Apart from her prettiness and her good sense, Hilda, John became increasingly aware, had a rare quality of serenity.

Although obsessed at the time in a very different direction, he found the scene at Bargate in March, 1914, often returned to his mind, when they had that odd business of Alan's involvement at the Curragh. It must have been embarrassing for her, John thought, a stranger caught up in such a family matter. But what sense she had talked, with that directness! She compelled us all, he said to himself, when the recollection, irrelevantly, sometimes came to him; she compelled us all. Without her intervention we'd have probably made some blundering attempt to advise Alan – blundering, because inevitably based on too little knowledge. Yes, Hilda said the right thing, he thought; she is an excellent girl. She said the right thing, and we obeyed. And she's only twenty, too. I hope she gets a husband good enough for her.

John saw Hilda once or twice during that summer of 1914: Hilda, brown-haired, brown-eyed, serious, with a rather quizzical expression, and a smile of great charm and gentleness when it came. He found it extraordinarily peaceful to be with her. He liked talking to her, amused, a little sardonic, about her elder brother, that wild man. She adored Cosmo. She felt protective towards him – a strange, *farouche* creature, impossible to protect. He was all that she decidedly was not – an adventurer, immoderate, unpredictable. John could hardly believe they shared the same parents. Equally different from both was a younger schoolboy brother, Stephen; an eager, intelligent, cocksure boy who made them laugh, but for whom Hilda, John thought, felt little compared with her devotion to Cosmo.

Then, one day in that extraordinary July of 1914, John found himself with Hilda, said to himself, as so often, 'I hope she gets a husband good enough for her' – and suddenly found that he hoped nothing of the kind. He found that the idea of a husband for Hilda, good enough or not, was intensely disagreeable. After that, and through that never-to-be-forgotten weekend when the world learned of Russian and German mobilization, John discovered that he was thinking a great deal about international tensions and the imminence of European war, but that he was also thinking, and thinking even more, about Hilda. He still failed to understand exactly why. Understanding came later that month.

John had never realized that Hilda was beautiful before, and he always recognized afterwards the moment when that realization dawned. He had a weekend at home in the middle of August, and Helena asked some people to stay 'and amuse John'. Hilda was one of them. John was training with the Yeomanry, mobilized now for three weeks and in camp not far from Bargate, learning the business of soldiering at which they had agreeably played for a year or so. Cosmo, Hilda's beloved brother, held a commission in their local regiment (astonishingly, it turned out that he had been granted a regular commission two years earlier and after nine months' service had resigned it, to the fury of all concerned). Now he was, of all extraordinary places, somewhere in Persia and Hilda thought he'd received orders to report to some Headquarters or other in India.

They were all sitting in the panelled inner hall at Bargate late one Saturday afternoon, talking, laughing, discussing the war news such as it was, excited, exchanging information about which of their friends was doing what, young men in uniform, girls in summer dresses. Hilda turned from talking to someone else and her eyes met and held those of John. He knew then that she was beautiful. He knew too that he loved her, loved her in a very special way, not before experienced: a certain, peaceful way. And almost at once the pain of Veronica receded. Weeks of mounted exercises, musketry, lectures on administration of men and horses in the field – all these had failed to exorcize Veronica. John had gone on thinking of her living in Ireland (Alan was already in France) and it nagged at him. Now suddenly, at Bargate, he saw

150

Hilda as if he had alw...
which had always been ...
could think of Veronica ...
body, hear her voice, with ...
torment. The catch phrase 'o...
ite. He knew, with utter certai...
something more profound than ...
realize, without regret, that it wou...
longing for Veronica, but it was dee...
ever. Furthermore, John knew, in on...
look they exchanged very seriously tha...
that Hilda felt the same.

That evening Helena said something about Alan, lightly. Suddenly she got up and left the room. It was clear that the picture of her beloved elder son 'somewhere in France' had hit her so hard that she couldn't control herself. It was untypical, it was oddly embarrassing in so strong and conventional an Englishwoman. John was sitting next to Hilda on a sofa, looking at a magazine, chatting, other young people in other parts of the room, detached, unobtrusive. Hilda turned, looked at John, and said, 'Poor you!'

'What do you mean?'

'You know what I mean perfectly well.'

And in that instant John knew, as clearly as if she had enumerated each point carefully and aloud, that Hilda was completely aware of a number of things. That John loved his brother; that John had desired Veronica with the utmost passion; that John's mother, dutiful and dissembling, would always prefer her elder son to him, and that he knew it. All this was utterly certain, conveyed by Hilda's brief, almost gruff words. And there was a final point, equally certainly conveyed. 'I love you,' she had meant, 'I love you, I understand you, I know your heart and it contains mine. And always will.'

In the second week in September Alan's letters began to arrive. John was in England and likely to remain there, training, for

151

y all did, uneasy to be comfortable
in the thick of it from the beginning.
John now found that on snatched weekends,
he could, with luck, persuade Hilda to meet him.
ort notice, I know but . . .'
e would laugh and say – 'Might be managed!'

John's regiment were still not far from both his and Hilda's homes. He had an unreliable car – and life was being incredibly and exquisitely transformed. National anxiety was being accompanied by private happiness of the most delightful kind.

'My mother's going to ask you to Bargate. You can come, can't you?'

'Can't think why not!'

And the weeks of military exercise and endeavour were star-studded with days or evenings of pure enchantment.

Alan's letters were shared between mother and younger son more often than not. By mid-September they knew that the long and disturbing retreat which had marked the opening phase of the war in the west was over. Instead, the papers were full of a great victory, of the defeat of the Germans on the Marne, of a mighty surge forward of the French and British armies to the Aisne; and then – as people in England, eagerly moving pins upon the maps which all possessed, waited for news of what might well be the *coup de grace* – of a great movement through Flanders, encircling the German right wing, racing forward, it was supposed, somewhere between Ypres and the sea.

Alan wrote cheerful, consolatory letters to Helena. He wrote two long letters to John at that time, and evidently reckoned that his brother's standing as a military man, however amateur, entitled him to rather more technical descriptions of what had been going on. In these two letters Alan allowed his imperturbable front to be broken a little, to be creased with a certain amount of indignant emotion – perhaps, John thought, rather more than was strictly proper. Alan clearly felt that such would worry Helena, and had a poor, masculine regard for her discretion. John kept his letters and often re-read them.

Alan was outspoken in his pride for what had been achieved

when British regiments had been enabled to stand and fight.

'Our fellows' shooting has been really wonderful. Time and again we've held attacks by huge numbers of Boches with our rifle fire alone. And, thank God, the cavalry have got the same, excellent, rifle as the infantry – unlike the French or, for that matter the Boche. *And* we've taught men to use it properly. As for our Gunners – they're splendid, but they've got very few shells, so they're rationed all the time. And, of course, our Horse Artillery guns aren't really what one wants out here. They've not got the range.'

The light Horse Artillery thirteen-pounder gun and lighter, faster troop horse were not designed for set-piece battles against or in support of entrenched troops. The Horse Artillery were intended to support the cavalry in mobile operations and to move at cavalry speed. Even John and what he called his fellow-amateurs in the Yeomanry understood that: the Yeomanry were organized into brigades of 'second-line cavalry' and naturally took a particular interest in the experiences of the cavalry brigades and divisions in France. In the north, in Flanders, they learned that the British cavalry divisions were grouped together in a cavalry corps, and the more romantic among them thought of Marlborough handling a mighty array of massed cavalry on the nearby field of Ramillies. Alan wrote about the British Command with considerable lack of enthusiasm.

'We've suffered from some very poor administration – no forethought, no really methodical approach. I've certainly had the impression of a High Command that often didn't know what it was trying to do from one day to the next. And there were too many excitable heads under those red hats at the top! We all pray D.H. will take over as soon as possible. He's got a cool brain and a will of iron, as well as being a professional to his fingertips.'

John was unsurprised at this indiscreet reference to Sir Douglas Haig, now Commander of the First Army, who became Commander-in-Chief of the British Expeditionary Force in place of Sir John French a year later. He knew that Alan greatly admired him. There were a good many adverse rumours in

England about the capacity and temperament of French. Small fry like John were in no position to hold a view, but it appeared from his letters that Alan certainly did. There were grumbles about such matters as the absence of maps (hardly, John supposed, the Commander-in-Chief's fault) and criticisms of the British military system. Alan wrote –

'A lot of our wretched infantry were marched off their feet during the last week of August – and we'd had to embody so many reservists, of course, whose feet were inevitably soft. You may think I've no right to talk, comfortably in the saddle, but we all, Staff and all, walked whenever we didn't have to mount to do a job. A good many horses are in terrible shape and one has to do all one can to spare them. Still,'

He finished his first letter:

'The Boches are in just as bad case! The prisoners we took on the Marne were completely whacked. Fine-looking fellows, but whacked! Men and horses all reckoned they couldn't go another yard! We really had to prod them to move at all. So I dare say both sides will sink to the ground with exhaustion soon, and sit and look at each other until somebody has a fresh idea.'

This letter, John could tell, was written by a very tired brother indeed. He told much that was interesting, some things that were amusing. He described the absolute dependence on aircraft now for information about the enemy 'and about our own troops as often as not!' He told a funny story about the spy mania which infects a retreating army –

'This poor old French *curé wasn't* shot as an Uhlan in disguise but it was a close thing! There had to be an apology at the highest level!'

In his next letter, which gave news of his doings during the advance to the Aisne and the move to the left wing, to the Flanders front, Alan dwelt less on exhaustion, less on confusion

154

at the top (perhaps, John thought, everybody was learning) but more – and for the first time – on casualties.

'We hung on,' he wrote, 'at Messines, we hung on at Ypres. They poured men at us and the shelling was terrific, but we hung on. There was no breakthrough. It was rather sickening that what we all thought was going to be a mighty advance by us round their flank, turned into a desperate show to stop them getting round *ours*! But we hung on, and I think for a while they've had enough. The prisoners were low quality, compared to those we took in August,'

(His letter was written just before Christmas)

'and we know that they really scraped the barrel in Germany to raise new divisions for Flanders. But my God! we've lost a lot. The infantry have lost most, of course, but our regiments have caught it badly too, particularly at the end of October. And as you know, we've got no b . . . y shovels on our establishment, the cavalry are not presumed to need to dig! You've seen the casualty lists of course.'

John had. There were plenty of acquaintances, although since John hadn't many intimates in the Regular Army he had suffered fewer personal losses than the later years were to bring. But he knew these men by name, knew them as friends or comrades of Alan's. He saw the total casualty lists and by now knew enough of military business to realize what a terrible proportion they were of the whole. Nobody fully comprehended at the time what was truly said later, that the old Regular British Army died at First Ypres, as the battles described in Alan's second letter came to be known. John felt a poor creature to be safe in England.

One thing stood out clearly from this second letter.

'We hung on . . . they poured men at us . . . our regiments have caught it badly too.'

Alan was writing of manned trenches, of the wisdom of having armed the British cavalrymen with a good rifle, of beating off massed attacks with well-directed and well-disciplined fire. He was writing of cavalrymen sitting not in the saddle but in exposed and muddy holes in the ground, 'with no bloody shovels on our establishment.' As, in John's Yeomanry mess, they interminably swopped stories from friends and relatives in Flanders, they reflected that this didn't so far sound like a cavalryman's war.

Then, on 30th January, Helena telephoned, voice held very steady, very controlled. Veronica had sent her a wire having herself received the telegram. Alan had been wounded. It sounded, said Helena, as if he had been hit in the shoulder. 'But he's quite all right. Veronica said the telegram was clear there's no question of danger. And,' she said, 'he's being sent to a hospital here in England. Sent home. Veronica is coming over on tomorrow's boat. Darling Alan will, she thinks, for some reason, be in London. When she knows for certain, Veronica can make a plan.'

John was himself in Essex at the time. The first phase of training was over and the regiment had moved.

'I'll keep you informed, darling,' his mother said. 'But he's safe. For the time being. And he's coming home.'

John knew that she had always found Alan a more satisfying son than himself. He never felt inclined to blame her but suffered a stab of resentment that in this telephone conversation she made no reference to his own affairs. They were less dramatic, but they mattered to him.

'Mother, you got my letter?'

'What? It's a bad line.'

'My letter. You got it? With my news?'

Three days earlier, John had written to his mother that Hilda Paterson had accepted him and that they wanted to marry as soon as possible. Wanted to marry before the war claimed John too.

He had to shout his enquiry a third time. Then his mother said, 'Yes, of course, my dear. Of course I got it. I'm writing to you. This business of Alan drove things from my mind –'

'Naturally, Mother. I just wanted to be sure the Post Office hadn't lost it.'

'No, no, it arrived yesterday. In fact, I think it was the day before yesterday. Very exciting, John. She's such a charming girl.'

'Yes.'

'I know Alan will approve.'

'I'm sure he will.'

They said goodbye and John went to his bedroom, to sit at a bare table in the requisitioned billet and write to Hilda. When that satisfying task was over, he reflected that he ought to write a line to Veronica about Alan. He wasn't sure where to send it, however, and the letter never got written.

It was early March, 1915, before John saw Alan. Alan had been in hospital in Hertfordshire, and after that at an officers' convalescent home on the south coast for a fortnight. Now he was at Bargate at the beginning of at least two weeks' sick leave, and John had two clear days. He and Hilda had been very busy during February, and their wedding was now arranged for the first week in April. The brothers greeted each other without reservations. The air was clear again.

'I'm fit. I'm going back on 21st March.' Alan spoke in a matter-of-fact way. He was, however, irritable, and very evidently in a nervy state which he was determined to conceal, failing utterly with those who knew and loved him. He read the war news carefully in the daily papers, allowing himself, now and then, a sardonic comment. There was a headline: 'French advance in Champagne. Germans driven from key positions.' Alan grunted and said quietly, 'And I wonder what that's cost them!'

John heard later – much later – that the answer was 50,000 men. More immediate to British concerns – and actually taking place while they were together those days at Bargate – was the British attack at Neuve Chapelle. Again the papers were exuberant. John had soon learned the sense of saying that truth is the first casualty of war, although he supposed it inevitable.

'Complete surprise achieved in attack by the First Army,' they read. 'Many German positions captured. Prisoners streaming in.'

This was later found to be true as far as it went, but Alan's comment on it was trenchant and perceptive.

'It reads as if we've captured their first positions, their front line. That's not enough – one can generally do that. Have we got the guns and the shells to enable us to keep it up, when we widen and deepen the attack? That's what's going to count. Without that one's simply buying a few thousand yards of muddy trench line with the lives of many, many soldiers.'

And although the news was shrouded in the obscure language of official bulletin, it indeed became clear that Neuve Chapelle was an initial tactical success, and absolutely indecisive beyond that. Sir Douglas Haig, however, was commanding the First Army which conducted the attack, and in him Alan's faith was undimmed.

'At least D.H. will have organized it properly,' he said. 'At least the thing will have been decently prepared.' Alan showed little inclination to talk about his own experiences, although he was keen to learn how the Yeomanry were getting on.

'They're pretty fed up with still kicking their heels in England.'

'Their time will come,' said Alan grimly, 'I wouldn't chafe too much if I were you.'

'It sounds as if we're more likely to be used as infantry than anything else – people are pretty reluctant to face that, in spite of all we hear from the front.'

'Teach them to shoot,' said Alan. 'Teach them to dig if anybody gives you shovels, and buy some if they don't. Teach them to pile up breastworks with anything they've got, including their hands. If they go to the Salient – Ypres – they'll find soon enough that the water table makes nonsense of digging more than a few feet. And those few feet are sheer mud.'

'I think our chaps would simply be relieved to find digging impossible. They're fearfully idle about it. Dodge it whenever they can.'

'Then their life expectancy will be short,' said Alan flatly.

'Anyway, you probably won't come to the Salient. I'd pray not to if I were you.'

He looked at the fire. They were sitting in the inner hall at Bargate, where plentiful wood enabled their mother to keep the fire in until spring came.

'Sorry I can't be here for your wedding.'

'We've tried to bring it forward, you know that. For various reasons it's been impossible. It will feel all wrong not having you as best man.'

'You've got Francis, I gather.' Francis Carr, a chronic asthmatic, was doing something mysterious in Whitehall.

'Yes, Francis will cope well, I'm sure. As a matter of fact, I think he's fairly broody himself.'

Veronica had visited Alan in hospital immediately he reached it, and was now back in Ireland in the house they'd taken the previous year. It made, said Alan, as good a base for her as any.

'I'm going over there on Tuesday's boat. Needed a day or two down here first.'

'She's well, I hope.'

'Pretty well. She's happier in Ireland than she would be in England, I fancy. She might get over to your wedding, old boy. I'll tell her to try.'

'That would be splendid.' But truth to tell, John did not want Veronica at his wedding. He loved Hilda, but Veronica's presence would be, he thought, still disturbing. And he suspected Hilda might, without a word spoken, think so too. Something told him that Veronica could too easily have a part to play still, in all their lives. Banished from the mind and the eye for a little she might be, but she existed, she was Veronica, and it would take more than the gale of the war to drive her beyond the horizon for ever; and she was, after all, thought John uneasily, their sister-in-law.

In the event, Alan sailed directly from Ireland to France, and Veronica sent a charming letter regretting she couldn't manage to get over for the wedding, which took place in Sussex. Hilda and John spent a week of honeymoon in Cornwall, where the weather was disappointing but everything else was very, very good. Hilda was due to return to her own home thereafter, and

159

John to rejoin his regiment in Essex. They spent one night at Bargate before parting. It was 29th April. They found Helena in a ferment of anger, anger disguising renewed fear, every hour of every day, for Alan.

'They're fiends,' she kept saying, 'fiends. Only they could do a thing like this.' 'This' was the German use of gas for the first time in their attack north of Ypres. Even the bland language of the headlines could not disguise that something not unlike a disaster had occurred. Much was made of the horror of the weapon, of German 'frightfulness' as everybody called it. There was, however, little about 'German attacks repelled at all points' and 'ground re-taken by counter-attack' which normally accompanied references to a German push. Reading between the lines, as Alan had helped John to do, he thought it sounded as if the British Army had taken a bad knock at Ypres. It was understandable that his mother fretted even more than usual and showed it. She was a brave but highly strung woman. John tried to look for a bright spot in the news.

'Well, it looks as if our landing in the Dardanelles has gone well!' This had occurred the previous week. A new front, far from home, against the Turks, an enemy few could feel was as directly menacing as Germany.

'The Dardanelles!' said Helena impatiently. 'Gallipoli! Don't tell me that's going to beat the Germans! Gallipoli indeed!'

She said goodbye to Hilda with a convincing show of affection. John looked at his home, a long, relishing look. In war, every pleasure should be taken as if for the last time.

CHAPTER IX

It was John's second bathe. They took it in turns and tried to get every man without exception to the beach at some time. The sand was silver-white, and provided there was no wind the beaches were all delight: unless, that is, enemy long-range howitzers decided to spend ammunition on what military men called 'harassment' – the lobbing over of shells to cause annoyance, kill or wound a few soldiers, a few horses, a few mules. The beaches were inevitably crowded, but all the men could do was to carry on whatever the hazards – swim, move supplies, hump ammunition from lighter to mule pack, care for the horses which mounted officers had, in many cases, had to leave near the beach (the regiment's horses, mercifully, had been left in Egypt except for the chargers of the Battalion Staff and Squadron Commanders, and they had no use for them while in the trenches); hope there would be no harassment. There were a mass of tents on the edge of the beach, where scrubby ground sloped up to cliff-face. Men felt almost safe when on the beach, and carried on with the business of life, until, suddenly, that particular afternoon, death paid them a visit. 'Them' was the regiment. The family.

The shell was, from the Turkish point of view, outrageously lucky. John heard it coming, as one always did – the sound like steam escaping from a valve on an engine at Victoria Station, then the whistle rising to a scream – and then, CRACK. Ears bursting, water everywhere, sand and dust masking the sun, sand in throat and nostril, flying debris, shouts, confusion. Then insistent, frightful screams, human this time. John had been standing in the water up to his waist, the heavenly moment of

161

the bathe almost over, the need imminent to dry, dress, assemble the reluctant soldiery, get the non-commissioned officers to harry joyful, naked men and turn them into sweaty, becapped, booted, putteed troopers. He had floated in an ecstasy of fly-free coolness for one last minute, had raised his head to see the dark outline, to the west, of the island of Samothrace. A barge, empty now of ammunition, was close inshore about a hundred yards away, waiting to return seaward for another load. Few of the men could swim and a number, laughing, ragging, were clinging to struts on the barge, moving adventurously out of their depth in the buoyant water, sensing that their closeness to the barge was probably forbidden, acting like schoolchildren who will break ranks from a disciplined crocodile to climb a railing 'because it's there' – and because disobedience is inherently enjoyable. Sergeants were as little likely to be able to swim as any of them. They clung to the barge, wallowing, ducking each other, spluttering and howling with laughter, flesh cool and clean, the stinking life of the trenches a mile or two inland temporarily forgotten. Then came the shell.

John was unhurt. It took him several seconds to realize it had actually hit the barge itself. A shell hitting the sand – which most of those landing on the beach, of course, did – was innocuous unless one was remarkably near. A shell striking water was a shell wasted. This one, by the sheerest fluke, thought John with a miserable and useless curse, hit that barge. Most of the human limbs which then began to spin gracefully through the air, some landing on water, some on beach, had been smashed and detached by bits of the barge itself as it disintegrated beneath that frightful explosion. John moved as fast as he could to the shore. As he splashed inland, shaking, numbed, a naked human leg, severed at the thigh, floated near him, blood stretching on the water behind it like a delicate, pink cobweb. He could see stretcher parties already running towards the water's edge, and Red Cross armbands on uniform jackets. The wounded were reasonably near first aid, for a dressing station was established below the cliff not a quarter of a mile from where they had been bathing and there looked to be no shortage of willing hands to help them.

Sergeant Bryce at least was unhurt. One of John's squadron and the senior NCO with the beach party, stark naked, he was already gathering the men together to call the roll, a roll he knew by heart without need to dress or consult his book. They were all from John's regiment that afternoon, except two Service Corps men who had been attached to the swimming party and were unhurt. The group was twenty-seven strong. Four had been hurt, one (as it later turned out) very seriously; a wound which led to evacuation and permanent disability. Five men were dead, their pale, severed limbs, their torn flesh, carried here and there by the Aegean waters, their carcass remnants shifted on to stretchers, covered by blankets, destined to join many others on that distant shore.

They had landed early in August, 1915, and been committed almost immediately to the first battle any had experienced. It was a curious, confused business. They marched inland for what seemed an extraordinarily short distance before entering, in single file, a long, sloping trench. The trenches in the Dardanelles had been extended by both sides as stalemate developed. The initial improvised fire trenches and holes had been urgently deepened, connected, made continuous, then strengthened, revetted, crowned by sandbags, pockmarked with dugouts burrowed into the face nearest to the enemy, topped by improvised roofing. So it was in France, and so it was on the Gallipoli peninsula. By the time they arrived, trench systems were complex and elaborate, resembling the maze at some Tudor palace where high yew hedges destroy the sense of direction. Their trenches and the enemy's were seldom more than three hundred yards apart and often much less. And the British trenches were very near the sea. British, French, Australians, New Zealanders had clawed a toehold on the Gallipoli peninsula. To remain there was a hard business. To enlarge the lodgement was harder still.

They moved into that long communication trench leading towards the front, and thereafter each man saw little but the back of the man in front and the shape of sandbags etched along the parapets on each side. It was an hour before dawn – one of those wonderful dawns of the eastern Aegean. Light would soon touch the high points on the peninsula, then rise above them and illumine Lemnos, Imbros, Samothrace – islands of extraordinary beauty not belying for an instant their names. Officers were of a generation into whom the classics had been instilled from childhood. Reluctant or enchanted, depending on temperament, they had grown up on the legends of these places. The Hellespont was before them. Troy lay behind the enemy's left shoulder. Homer marched with them. The Colonel had decreed that there would be a fine, after the first day, levied on any officer referring, even in a murmur, to the wine-dark sea.

They could see none of this as they plodded up the communication trench. From aboard ship the land had looked steep, scrubby, crossgrained, buff-coloured, streaked by dark runners of bush and outcrops of rock, shining when the sun caught some unusually smooth surface and brought from it a luminous orange colour. Here and there was the yellow of gorse. They had gazed and gazed at the shore in those hours of waiting – dry, hot, nervous. Every pair of binoculars had scanned the peninsula for landmarks familiar from the newspapers as well as from the sketchy information passed to them aboard. They could see activity on the beaches. Now and then a puff of dust implied a bursting shell. It looked desultory, unalarming. Of the Turks there was no sign. Then they clambered down into the small craft which took them to the shore. Soon thereafter they were on the march.

John had explained all he knew of the forthcoming action to his troop.

'We'll form up in trenches held by another brigade. They're going to thin out, make room for us at the last minute. There will be one of the heaviest supporting fire programmes Gallipoli's yet seen, including naval gunfire. We go over the top while the barrage is at its height.'

He told them that the first objective, the Turkish front line, would be 350 yards away. When they had covered about 250 of

164

them (it was calculated) the artillery would lift on to the Turkish second line.

'We'll have under a hundred yards to rush them – probably less. They ought to be pretty stunned by our bombardment. We've got to finish them off and occupy their trench. Almost immediately D and C Squadrons will follow up and repeat the process on the Turks' next line.'

The men looked enthusiastic: they had waited a long time for this. The particularly nervous ones concealed it well. They had trained, marched, ridden, skirmished over English countryside, shot on the rifle ranges for many months while friends and brothers fought and died in Flanders. Now it was their turn. Sergeant Janson, John's Troop Sergeant, was a coalmerchant's driver in civilian life – a senior driver responsible for several pairs of horses, a fine, conscientious man, strong and humorous. He said to the troop –

'Sooner you turn Johnny Turk out of his trenches, sooner you'll get home. Someone's got to show these regulars how to fight and it had better be the Yeomanry.'

The first landings of this curious, half-hearted expedition had been in April, at the tip of the peninsula, where an all-regular British Force, combined with the French, Australians and New Zealanders, seemed to have made little headway. Sergeant Janson smiled broadly at the troop. There were still plenty of voices at home to say that the Territorials and Yeomanry could never match the Regular Army for quality and discipline. The Yeomen knew different, of course. They were, they reckoned, the pick of the nation; men who had given their time, often brought their own horses, sweated their guts in time of peace. So they told themselves as they laboured endlessly up that communication trench. It was extraordinarily quiet.

Suddenly, very shortly before they reached their destination and certainly before the barrage opened, a wholly unexpected thing happened. Within a few feet of John's head a sandbag burst, burst like a bomb, its gritty entrails flying round them like bullets. Nobody was hurt. Sergeant Janson was immediately behind John. In outward appearance a slow, deliberate man, a

165

stolid man of peace, his perceptions at such moments were those of the born soldier, the natural man of war he could so easily have been.

'Turk machine gun, sir!'

It was true. Slower witted than his own Sergeant, John now remembered that a high-pitched rat-a-tat had accompanied the sound and sight of the bursting sandbag. Machine-gun fire had turned the rotten sacking into a miniature bomb. It seemed a minor hazard and inwardly he felt a fool for having been surprised.

'We're nearly there, I think, Sergeant Janson.'

They spoke in whispers. It was a quiet night, with only a few sporadic shells, an occasional, apparently aimless, burst of rifle fire. John glanced at his watch. Miraculously, they had taken less time than provided for by orders, for at that moment a muttered word came back from the leading files –

'Squadron halted. Juniper trench.'

That meant they were to wait there until the ordained minute after the opening barrage. The barrage was to last for forty-five minutes and at a given moment they would file forward, line the front-line trench, wait a further five or six minutes for zero hour. Then – up and over!

The guns opened exactly on the minute. There was already a pale light in the east. Soon, if they were above ground instead of bunched in this funnel of a trench, John knew they would see the never-failing loveliness of Imbros and the other islands – Imbros the best, he thought, and dawn the best moment. The Colonel, he who had levied fines for mention of Homer's 'wine-dark sea', had watched it, with the rest of them, three mornings before. The Adjutant boldly tried a joke on him.

'I think you'll have to add 'rosy-fingered dawn' to your list of fineable phrases, Colonel!'

The Colonel smiled his curious, crooked-mouth smile. A bad fall in the hunting field years before had smashed bones in the lower part of his face and given him a distorted jaw and slightly impeded speech, much imitated. They loved and respected him despite it.

166

'I'll think about it.' He said 'fink' instead of 'think'.

The Colonel was an experienced land agent in civil life. The Adjutant was one of the largest landowners in the county. They had their own sort of discipline, their own special set of relationships in the Yeomanry. Military correctness wasn't affected by a man's private circumstances, but these were in the background, subtly pervasive because known by all. They were, John reflected without disquiet, a snobbish lot – mirroring the England of the day, where differences of degree were cheerfully taken for granted, at least in the country districts from which ninety per cent of all ranks in the Yeomanry came. They were a family, for all that, they knew the same places. 'Home' meant the same to all of them, 'England' evoked a similar landscape. And military discipline, hierarchic though it was, had been cohesive rather than divisive. They knew each other very well, would shortly know each other better. But no man, in that testing ground of the front line, was going to be respected because of his private position, only for how he behaved under fire.

John looked at his watch and wondered whether it was fast. Surely –

At that moment the barrage opened.

It was an awe-inspiring sound and sight. For that action they knew they were getting the support of their own artillery batteries, with gun positions near the beaches, and of the trench mortars of the battalion holding the front line. They were also being supported by the guns of the Fleet – those mighty guns they had looked at with trust and respect as they had sailed through the great assembly of warships lying among the islands off the Dardanelles. Now they heard a deep, distant roar; and soon they heard the rushing sound of the naval shells overhead, a sound like a large number of trains emerging from parallel tunnels, almost immediately followed by the ear-splitting crash of detonation about three hundred yards from where the regiment stood huddled before the dawn. They could see nothing but the brilliant light produced by the explosions, so that the northern and eastern sky – they were due to attack in a north-eastern direction – was suddenly illumined as if the sun, already climbing hesitantly in the pale east, had burst through the clouds in some awful, unnatural noon.

'Christ!' John heard Sergeant Janson mutter. The barrage was due so to pulverize the Turkish trenches that nothing would be left for them to deal with, and they could, in those minutes, well believe it. The Colonel had prevailed on two slightly wounded officers, aboard a hospital ship and awaiting evacuation to Egypt, to visit them while confined aboard, to talk about the fighting, visiting squadron by squadron between decks. Each had talked well in his own way – one, little more than a boy, had a great gift for description and had surprised the stolid Yeomen by painting, with what seemed to some absurdly lyrical words, the landscape of those far-off April days when the Allied expedition had launched its first assault.

'There were wild flowers everywhere then – poppies, cornflowers, anchusa. You've missed that, I'm afraid. You'll find it all dried up, scrub, rock, dust. Nothing to look at now. And the digging's hell.'

But he'd talked in cool, sensible terms about the enemy.

'The Turk's a terrific man in defence. They go on till you've killed them. Fatalistic. Not so good at attacking – seem to give up pretty easily, especially under fire.'

It was measured, judicious stuff, and although everybody likes talking as an old soldier to novices, there was, thought John, absolutely no bombast or conceit in it. He had a word with the lad afterwards. The wounded officer looked about eighteen but John knew he was talking to a wiser man.

'You must be looking forward to Egypt.'

'Not a bit. I'm furious. I was happy here.'

He meant it, there was no doubt of it.

His companion, a Captain Mackenzie, had lost three fingers of one hand. A sterner, more methodical sort of man, he gave them a great deal of detail.

'Turkish snipers are excellent. They wear specially camouflaged uniforms and they're very quick. One limb above the parapet for one second and you've lost it. And if it's your head, your family's lost you.'

The soldiers laughed uneasily. He talked well, however, and he prepared them for many things.

'You'll be thirsty all the time. Water discipline's the most important of all disciplines.'

When he talked to the men about it, frowning and serious, they nodded their heads wisely. They had, as yet, experienced nothing. Ship's officers were sitting under an awning that evening, sipping whisky and soda. Soon some of the Yeomanry officers would join them.

'Every gallon of water,' said Mackenzie, 'has to be brought into this part of the peninsula by ship. There are clean wells in some places. Your sector isn't one of them.'

The men instinctively moistened their lips. He talked about Turkish tactics, Turkish guns.

'Their shrapnel fire hit us hard in the early days. It's no trouble when you're entrenched, of course, but it's very effective when you aren't.'

The British bombardment now, however, was due to silence the Turkish guns, and spotter balloons were meant to have pin-pointed them over the preceding few days.

'I reckon there's two minutes to go, sir,' muttered Sergeant Janson. There seemed to be a ripple of movement in the files ahead. Soon they were stumbling into the forward trench, passing silent men of other regiments, single or huddled in ones and twos by the firesteps at regular intervals. They could make out the short ladders for climbing out of their own trench, placed, as arranged, at regular points. They were to go over on the whistle blast. The barrage was due to intensify about now but John could detect no particular difference in that deafening roar beyond the parapet. It was now light enough to see men's shapes clearly. Eight minutes had been allocated for this final forming-up movement from the communication trench. Their Squadron Commander had grumbled.

'It's not enough! In the dark! There are five hundred men to file forward. It'll take much longer.'

He had queried it with the Colonel, who had listened patiently, quietly, unresentful of a subordinate's representation.

'No, Jack. Eight minutes will do us, the Brigade Commander's perfectly right. I want the files to have to step out briskly and to have as little time as possible in the forward trench.'

The Colonel was justified. The last files of each squadron had reached their positions with more than a minute in hand before the dreaded whistle. And the Colonel's view was wise: the shorter that interval, the better.

When the whistles sounded, up and down the regiment's line there was at first the extraordinary relief of finding they could shout, talk at the top of the voice, move freely, uncramped, uncrowded. Up the ladder!

'Up and over, Four Troop! Forward by the left, now!'

John shouted for his own support, not because the men needed orders: they had been told clearly what to do. It was good to find oneself out of the trench, alive, able to command one's limbs without too disabling a fit of shaming funk, the troop lined up and moving uncertainly forward. The ground was uneven and John at once realized that men – and probably himself among them – could fall from a stumble as easily as from the enemy's fire. It was no bad thing, he thought, that the walking was difficult. A man having to look where to put his feet has an object on which to concentrate. One feature, however, was surprising. The dawn showed the skyline perfectly clearly, and about three hundred yards their side of the skyline were, they knew, the Turkish trenches – packed, it was hoped, with dead or terrified Turks, victims of the bombardment, ready for burial or capture. But immediately in front – between them and their objective and only about one hundred yards from the starting point – a considerable fire was burning. They were advancing towards it. Soon they felt its heat.

'It's the gorse, the shelling's fired the gorse, Sergeant Janson!'

As far as John could see, he would have to divide the troop to get round it. The fire's extent appeared to be running away from them rather than laterally. It would, therefore, temporarily separate one part of the troop from the other by a gap of what, as they marched nearer to it, looked to be at least twenty paces. John shouted to Sergeant Janson.

'Take the left dozen men left of the fire, I'll take the rest to the right of it. Take dressing again when we're clear of it the far side.'

'Right, sir!' They were the right-hand troop of the squadron. To his right, John could see the outline of the left-hand files of the next squadron. He felt extraordinarily confident and happy.

'This way!'

The men were carrying their rifles at the 'high port', bayonets fixed, rifles carried across the body, muzzle high. When they cleared the fire there should be, John reckoned, about 150 yards to go. It was important to recover order, to form a good line for those 150 yards. The Turkish trenches must be assaulted by an unbroken line of Yeomen, rifles levelled, bayonets glinting in the dawn light; not by dribs and drabs of isolated men.

'This way!' Suddenly John felt alone with his little party as they strode forward, stepping out round the blazing gorse to recover distance lost in this involuntary manoeuvre. He could now see nothing of the squadron to his right, where the ground dropped sharply and unexpectedly. The burning gorse was extremely hot, the noise of the fire alive with crackle and roar.

John realized that this was the only sound now disturbing that morning. The British guns had stopped.

That meant they were – they should be – nearer the Turkish trenches than he had supposed. In fact, they should be formed up for the final assault! And John's little command was split up by, of all things, some blazing gorse bushes! The fire extended deeper towards the Turkish trenches – or where he supposed the Turkish trenches were – than he had first imagined. A good twenty-five yards wide, it effectively split the troop in two.

John was by no means sure that it had not, at the same time, confused the line of advance. His sense of direction was normally excellent, his feeling for country and whereabouts proverbial in the squadron. But this was a strange place and he was not sure. There were a dozen men with him.

'This way! Get a move on!'

Stumbling and cursing they followed him, moving round the fire. Was he, he wondered with a stab of unease, by now right

171

out in front of the regiment? Or moving at right angles to them? The skyline, monotonous, unbroken by distinctive features, was unhelpful.

'This way!'

At that moment, their ears were deafened by a series of sharp cracks, cracks not unlike enormous fireworks. Simultaneously, the man nearest to John screamed, and John felt rather than saw him drop to his knees, steel helmet falling forward off his head, rifle clattering from his hands, one arm thrown across his face. His screams were dreadful.

It was a slow, decent trooper called Abbott, a farm labourer by profession, a devoted family man, one of the most reliable of the troop, trusted by his mates, trusted instinctively by horses, trusted by Sergeant Janson, trusted by John. The next man to John dropped on one knee.

'Abb!' It was Meredith, a particular friend of Abbott. They had ridden next to each other, marched in the same file, occupied neighbouring bed spaces in troop billets in England, neighbouring bunks on board.

'Abb!'

'GET UP, MEREDITH, AND GET INTO LINE!' All this took seconds only. There was nothing to be done about Abbott. This was Turkish shrapnel. Enough Turkish guns had certainly survived the bombardment to bring down a curtain of defensive fire on the assaulting troops. To John's immeasurable relief, he saw figures the far side of the burning gorse, whose extremity they seemed to have reached. There was a shout.

'Mr Marvell!'

'Yes! Get dressed by the left, quick. Sergeant Janson there?'

'Sergeant Janson's hit, sir. Corporal O'Grady here.'

'Line up, Corporal O'Grady! Quick now! Anyone else?'

'I think so, sir. I think we've lost Hacking and Simkin. And three more, maybe four –'

Corporal O'Grady was a curiosity. He had been accepted as a Yeoman after they mobilized. They had found themselves two men short and by some trick of persuasion and falsehood O'Grady had insinuated himself into the ranks. He had claimed – rightly – expert knowledge of horses. Indeed, O'Grady was brilliant with horses, and this innate gift as well as his humour soon made him acceptable. As to military skill, none of them knew much in August, 1914, and O'Grady learned quicker than most. He had soon been promoted.

O'Grady, of course, claimed a Sussex mother, scenting that they were close-knit in all ranks, tribal. John didn't believe a word of it. O'Grady was from Limerick – indeed had only been in England, they gathered, since May. One evening, John had found himself alone with O'Grady beneath the Aegean stars, trudging through the darkness of the angled trench from one sentry to another. It was a quiet night. Talk had turned to Ireland and John had mentioned that his brother had been at the Curragh on the outbreak of war. O'Grady said, with conversational insincerity, that it was a fine place.

'I was an Irish Volunteer, meself.'

At first John was uncertain of his meaning.

'You mean the nationalist body?'

'Yes, sir. The Volunteers. There was nearly two hundred thousand of us. Fine boys, mostly.'

'And what do they think of all this, do you suppose?'

'Ah well, sir, most of them's in the British Army now. Joined up in August 'fourteen, you see. There's some as didn't, I believe. But many were on the Reserve, you see, sir.'

'The British Army Reserve?'

'Of course, sir.'

Alan had told John of the Irish Volunteers. To the Army in Ireland, of course, they were potential rebels. O'Grady clearly felt no anomalies in his position. Sometimes John heard him humming what he suspected were rebel Irish ballads, but O'Grady justified his rank every minute of the day. He was a born soldier. He, quite clearly, enjoyed the possibilities of killing and being killed, risks and chances which sharpened life for him. He seemed less troubled than most of the troop by the sordid discomforts of trench life. John was extraordinarily glad to see him now.

'By the left, the lot of you,' Corporal O'Grady yelled. Then they heard shouts from further to the left.

'Forward now! Forward! At the double!' Something like a cheer here and there. The rat-a-tat of Turkish machine guns, menacing but as yet unworrying compared to the shrapnel fire, simply and irrationally because making less noise. John felt completely isolated, revolver in hand, unaware how many of his troop were with him, unable to do anything to mend that or any other situation. In that condition – and he never remembered afterwards how he got there – he found himself jumping into what appeared to be a nine or ten-foot-deep hole, and knew that he had wrenched his ankle badly from the force of the fall, although he landed on a yielding surface rather than rock or board. The ankle felt numbed rather than painful as John realized that, possibly alone, he was occupying a Turkish trench, and was standing on the grey-coated body of a Turkish soldier whose head, smashed and severed by a British shell, was lying four feet away. It was the first dead man John had ever seen.

That had been their introduction to the Gallipoli peninsula. The High Command had decided that fresh troops, straight from shipboard, would perform with more zeal in this attack than jaded veterans. They took the Turkish first line, but the attempt to pass other troops through them and take the next line and the next in broad daylight was a horrible failure. They settled down to defend. They learned the routine of trench life, of which the first and by no means least onerous part was to put the captured Turkish trenches into a defensible state – and to clean them up.

John had lost six men, including Sergeant Janson, that morning. Two survived, evacuated to Egypt. Four, and both Janson and Abbott were of their number, died within minutes of the shrapnel finding them.

Everybody had been warned that the worst thing in the trenches would be thirst. In fact, they had a good system of water supply and water discipline. The Yeomen were sensible and – unexpectedly – they were doused within a week of their first battle by two of the most savage thunderstorms John ever remembered. These brought their own special discomfort but men collected water amidst much laughter. There was a curiously great amount of laughter at that time. They felt immensely close to each other. They looked back at the experience with something like nostalgia. Nobody wanted to be elsewhere.

The worst thing was the smell. Two days after they had won their objective the Turks counter-attacked. They shelled the regiment heavily and John lost two more men wounded in his troop, but the Turks were stopped without much difficulty when they came over and two machine guns knocked down very large numbers. No Turk got within fifty yards of John's trench. Then the Turks lay under the sun, dead or dying, and the smell was horrible, drifting over the British trenches like poison gas. And, associated in every man's mind in later days with that ghastly smell, was the dysentery which quite soon began to attack.

Flies were everywhere. When, on that first morning, John had been up and down the line of his troop, talking to men half-exultant, half-nervous, some already wondering aloud when the next meal would be forthcoming, he found himself passing the spot where he'd first dropped into the trench from the Turkish parapet. His ankle wrench was hurting a good deal. The Turkish soldier on whom he'd landed was still there. So was the Turk's head. Two troopers were looking at him and it without particular interest: there were a good many Turkish dead in the trench. The Turkish wounded, like the British, were being laboriously shifted towards the rear, and communication trenches were being pushed forward to make safe a way of evacuation and supply.

Corporal O'Grady was now John's right-hand man, his executant, his support. O'Grady said, 'Better shift him. And it!' he added, nodding at the head.

'Where to, Corporal?' asked Trooper Fane respectfully. His manner was always nicely preserved just the near side of impertinence.

'Over the parapet, that's where they're all going for now!'

There was no immediate alternative. As the men, without visible reluctance, humped those pathetic, grey-clad heaps up and over, a cloud of flies rose and swarmed lazily around them. And flies, fattened on the blood and flesh of English and Turkish soldiers alike, infested the trenches and descended upon food, bodies, eyelids and everything the soldiers did, wore or exposed. Flies, for John, were the Dardanelles.

When John came back from the beach that afternoon, the afternoon when the Turkish howitzer struck them in their hour of happiness, the regiment had been ashore for four weeks. John reported what had happened. Their casualties, as a regiment, had not been heavy after the first battle – and not particularly heavy in that, by the standards of those days. They had beaten off Turkish attacks without much trouble. They had got the trenches in decent order and suffered little from the enemy's periodic bombardment. It was a cruel blow to lose men on the beach, of all places. John's Squadron Commander looked grim. A tough, resilient man, who farmed on the Downs in civil life, he cared passionately for every man of his command. John felt responsible, but his superior was too just to hint at such a thing. Instead he said –

'What a beastly thing for you, John. Unexpected. Not like during a scrap.'

'No.'

'Two letters for you.'

There was also a copy of the *Peninsula Press*, the news-sheet produced by Headquarters which told them a bit about what was going on in the rest of the war. John glanced at the headlines. Their own little taste of battle had given him cynical insights into the realities behind the bulletins, and the news of 'Gains consolidated at Loos' meant to him (accurately, as was later clear) that on the Western front the French and British attacks had achieved precisely nothing at considerable cost. John opened his letters.

One was from Hilda. She wrote every day and sometimes a packet of several letters arrived together. Then John would open them, arrange them carefully in chronological order, and put them aside until he could enjoy them without interruption. Hilda wrote of Bargate, evoked for him the smell of logfires, the creak of panelling, the blessed sound, even, of rain – not the vicious torrents sometimes suffered in the Dardanelles but soft, English rain. With Hilda's letters he could escape from the trenches, the heat, even the flies, and breathe English air.

He could even – almost – in those moments escape the smells. They all got used to them: one gets, thought John, used to anything. But the mixture of putrescent bodies lying beyond the parapet and chloride of lime made a powerful mix beneath the midday sun. Heat, smell, flies feasting on rot and filth, food which no dietician would have recommended, appallingly little water – that these conditions led to widespread dysentery was to be expected. So far, miraculously, John's stomach had been better than most, but the squadron had suffered heavily. Their Major called it 'squatters' fever' and was inclined at first to laugh it off with a touch of scorn, something a man could get over like an attack of indigestion. One evening the Medical Officer came to their squadron sector of the line and spoke in a low voice to the Squadron Commander. He passed John when he left, on his way to Regimental Headquarters.

'All well, Doctor?'

'Poor old Corporal Vestey's died in hospital.'

Vestey had had dysentery.

With a huge effort of will, John put Hilda's letter in his pocket. It was, he noted with relish, a long one. It would help restore him after the events of the afternoon, the slaughter on the beach, but he needed to recover a little first, or the medicine, insufficiently powerful, would be diluted in its effect. There would be time in an hour. He would first get some routine business done, some trench inspection, the completion of a tedious 'return' they had all been troubled with recently. Before this, he opened the second letter. It was from Veronica.

Veronica wrote from Ireland – as far as John could see with no particular motive except to cheer him up. In this she succeeded. It was Veronica's first letter since she – or, for that matter, since he – married, and he was a little disturbed to find that her handwriting, distinctive and slightly childish, was still able to make his heart miss a beat. It was a light, easy, affectionate letter.

'Alan was here on leave last month. They've been having a frustrating time.' (Whether 'they' were Alan's regiment, cavalry brigade or whatever, was unclear. Probably the lot.) 'We talked of you often. Dear John, look after yourself.'

But there was an intriguing postscript.

> 'A Colonel Withers, here, is rather a dear. He knows Francis Carr – in fact, I think he has something to do with him nowadays, when he visits London, but as I don't know what Francis does these days and I have NO idea what anybody in the Army does, let alone Colonel Withers, that's not very informative. Anyway, Colonel Withers dined with us when Alan was on leave, and when he left said to me, "It looks as if we may get your brother-in-law here." I expect you know all about that, and that I shouldn't.'

John certainly didn't know all about that. Nor, astonishingly, had he anything but resentment for the idea that he might, ever, leave the regiment. In war, that close-knit, suffering body of men had become home in a way that no bricks and mortar, no tranquil scene however familiar and beloved, could ever provide. John wondered what on earth Veronica meant. If Alan knew some plan for his future, why hadn't he written? And if the thing were talked about, it must have come to Hilda's ears. Why, in that case, hadn't she mentioned it? Or had she? Now he turned over the pages of her own letter. He would read it at leisure but first see if there was a bombshell in it. There was none.

It was on the next day that John was told to report to the Colonel. He wondered, with a sinking in the stomach not attributable to dysentery, whether he'd been somehow remiss in his conduct of the fatal bathing party. The Colonel was no martinet, but he minded so deeply about the life of every Yeoman that the slightest dereliction of duty by an officer which could be alleged as having led to a man suffering unnecessarily put him into a paroxysm of rage.

On this occasion, however, he said, 'Sorry about that beastly business yesterday, John.'

'It was rotten luck, sir. Too damned clever a shell. Chance in a thousand.'

'I rode round there this morning. Peaceful a scene as you could want.'

The chargers of field officers were kept in horselines near the beaches. Veterinary services were excellent, but it was hard keeping animals fit, and horses were needed all the time for supply, as well as for gun teams and for any movement or liaison beyond easy walking distance.

'Well, there it is,' said the Colonel, 'rub of the green.' A keen golfer, he used the incongruous metaphor on every such occasion, deceiving none about how deeply he felt.

'Quite, sir.'

'I've had a message about you. A number of Territorial and Militia officers are to be attached to the Staff at home for a bit. Seems all the posts at home are filled with old fogies. They want some younger men, not necessarily regulars. Want fellows who've seen a bit of fighting. New blood.'

John said nothing. The Colonel was looking at a piece of paper, holding it at arm's length as if it smelt particularly foul. He had an enormous moustache, which vibrated when he talked. He had long sight, but avoided, when he could, donning his spectacles.

'Says here they want several officers from each active command who've had not less than three years in the Army, including peacetime; and not less than a month at the front. Your name's down here. Picked out of a hat by GHQ.'

'May I speak, sir?'

'In a minute. I've wired back that you can't be spared. I wanted you to know that, before you start telling me what you want or don't want. Can't be spared. Experienced Troop Commander. Know the men. Know your job. We're short-handed. If anything happened to your Squadron Commander – well, there it is. Can't be spared. Sorry. Give anything to be out of this bloody place myself, but just at present we've got to stick it out.'

'May I speak, sir?'

'Go ahead.'

'I've no wish to go home. Thank you very much for responding as you did.'

'Didn't do it to oblige you,' said the Colonel gruffly. 'You're needed.'

'Anyway, thank you, sir. And thank you for needing me.' The Colonel nodded dismissively, with a bit of his twisted smile. John saluted, but before he could turn about, the other said –

'May be overruled, you know.'

John looked at him steadily.

'I hope not, sir. I would formally apply not to be posted.

'Fat lot of good that would do if the powers that be overrule *me*! There's a war on. Got to do what we're told.'

'Sir!' John said, and this time the Colonel did not detain him as he marched from the dugout. It was possible that Lieutenant Marvell of the Yeomanry might have been selected 'for some attachment to a home command', although it seemed to John entirely inappropriate. It was surely, however, altogether fanciful that so tiny a cog as Marvell in the huge machine of the Army of 1915 should have been selected by the authorities at *home* – and, if Veronica's report had any substance, selected by name for a particular post – before (it appeared) the wheel of GHQ Dardanelles had turned to throw his name upon the board.

When John re-read Hilda's letter (he always read them every day until the arrival of the sequel) he found himself very naturally divided. With part of himself he longed to leave that wretched place, where the campaign, embarked upon with a sense of high adventure, was now as static, as tormenting and seemingly as endless as in France itself. He longed to be clean, if only for a little, of the filth and the flies and the corpses. He longed for clean sheets, cool water to drink, fresh English air. He longed to see English colours, subtle tints, to leave those hard, scorched contours, those blinding contrasts of light and shade, beautiful but by now too vivid, too uncompromising. He longed, above

180

all, for his wife. John told himself regularly that he was no hero, certainly no soldier by choice or instinct.

He longed for love, peace and home. And he acknowledged to himself that he longed, too, to be free for a while of the fear which accompanied every minute, acclimatized to it though all became: the fear of Turkish shrapnel, the Turkish sniper's bullet. Fear of death, fear of mutilation, fear of pain.

Fear, above all, of hearing, with mock enthusiasm, plans for their next attack.

But these longings pulled against a more potent certainty. John's place, he knew, was there, on the Gallipoli peninsula. It was only there that he could feel inwardly happy, as things were. It was only there, perversely, that he could be at peace. Not one of them wished to be elsewhere. He stuffed Hilda's letter into the pocket of his tunic – a large pocket in the rough, cloth soldier's coat all officers had quickly adopted to avoid the unnecessary attentions of Turkish marksmen. He felt sad but content.

That night, darkness came suddenly, as always; no gentle English twilight soothed the Dardanelles. One minute the line of the parapet was harsh and bright. Moments later, so it seemed, it was a black silhouette against the stage-set sky.

But that night not only darkness came. A Turkish bombing party had crawled to within fifteen yards of the British trench line. Ten minutes before midnight they all suddenly heard a flurry of shouts, explosions, rifle shots from the sentries on the firesteps. A brilliant light diffused the trench for several seconds. Then another explosion and another. Whistles blew to stand the squadron to.

'Mr Marvell-l-l!'

John remembered afterwards that call, turning into a scream. It was his junior Troop Corporal, O'Grady's colleague, a man called Harrison, whose courage and determination were beyond praise but who suffered from the disadvantage of having little sympathy for his fellow men and none at all for horses. A square peg in the Yeomanry, he was particularly unpopular with the troop. John knew his innate worth, tried to help him, ostentatiously supported him. Harrison was utterly reliable. John was sure Harrison did not in the least like him, as officer or man, but Harrison had true gold in him. In that split second when Harrison's cry turned into a screech, John knew they'd lost a good man.

There was then a sense of the end of the world having arrived as John's brain seemed to explode inside his head. He could see nothing and his body seemed to be spinning, weightlessly, suffering periodic bangs and knocks which he could barely feel. All later recollection of those seconds was blurred. Even the frightful, jolting stretcher journey back faded from the memory. His next clear picture was of water lapping against a porthole as the hospital ship steamed towards Alexandria. The Colonel had needed him and had certainly been let down.

CHAPTER X

'Has anybody told you,' said Colonel Withers, 'that we had arranged your posting to this Headquarters before you were hit? That we asked for an officer called Marvell in one piece, and you turn up with several bones missing? It's most peculiar. Most irregular.'

John had been working for Colonel Withers for ten days. Withers was now standing in John's own office, into which he strode, as he often did, like a man who found it tedious to be more than a few minutes together in one place and needed perpetual changes of scene. John's office – a dignified term for a small, cell-like cubicle, with a six-foot army table, one wooden chair, two trays and a map of Ireland on the wall – was next to the Colonel's, so the latter often crashed into it, waving John back to his chair as he leapt to his feet at this entry, Withers always wearing a look of half-puzzled, half-amused dissatisfaction. He was one of those to whom differences of age or military rank appeared to make little difference if he liked a man; and he seemed, John thought with gratitude, to like him. Conversely, Withers' readiness to make dislike very clear was not in the least inhibited by subordinate military status. Colonel Withers was no respecter of persons. He was an agreeable, sardonic man.

Withers' regular service had ended in voluntary retirement shortly after the South African war. Called from the Reserve, he had been condemned, as he expressed it with what all knew was sincerity, to a chair in Army Headquarters, Ireland. Nevertheless, he seemed to have a finger in every pie cooking in that place. Between retirement and recall he had written two books on Irish history in the time of Strongbow and the Norman invasion. Perhaps this had led to his appearance in Dublin. An

Englishman, he was fascinated by the country. Now he seemed simply to require a chat.

'I met your brother for the first time,' said Colonel Withers, 'on his last leave. And your charming sister-in-law.'

John had been released from hospital at the beginning of February, 1916, after majory surgery in Egypt, a slow journey home and further knife work in England at Christmastime. The Turkish bomb which had exploded in the Yeomanry trench had smashed a good deal of bone in his left thigh and at first the medical men expected he would be compelled, like many others, to leave at least one limb in the Aegean. A skilful doctor aboard ship disagreed. He thought that if John could get to Alexandria they might save the leg and send him, fairly well repaired, to England.

This happened, but on the journey home from Egypt it became clear that more remained to be done. There was a good deal of Turkish grenade inside John, and the patching up of his shattered limb had missed one bit, which gave a disproportionately large amount of trouble. So, once again, a chloroform mask was pushed over his face and he woke up wondering whether or not he still had his left leg. He had. The surgeon had done particularly well, and, although condemned to limp thereafter, what he called his undistinguished wound did not seriously inconvenience him. John exercised his leg as much as he could, as soon as he could. It was a hard February but he decided to start to ride as early as possible. 'Perhaps,' he said to himself without much conviction, 'hunt a bit from Bargate before the season ends.' For John had been given sick leave, and told that it would probably be at least six weeks before a Board could pass him fit for service. He spent the entire time at home, with his mother and Hilda. Six weeks, in time of war, was an eternity.

John knew he would be frustrated by the end of it, however tranquil and joyful a time it was. The sense that all worthwhile men were facing danger when he was cosseted and safe could nag viciously when every newspaper carried a casualty list. But at first, grateful to escape from hospital, reasonably whole although feeble, he was utterly happy, with a sharpness of joy which no previous years of his life had produced. He felt he was consuming a small, rationed helping of bliss and that he should do so as lingeringly as possible. Conscience was a little eased, too, by the news that had come through while he lay in hospital recovering from the latest operation in January. The British and their Allies had evacuated their forces from the Dardanelles. John's regiment had moved to Egypt. Other news drifted through. Before evacuation, their Colonel, he of the heavy moustache, twisted smile and kind heart, had succumbed to enteric fever. He had died aboard ship.

Then, in March, John had been summoned to the War Office and told he was, when fit, to be attached to Army Headquarters Staff in Ireland.

'If I'm boarded as fit, sir, and I'm sure I will be, I hope I may be allowed to return at once to my regiment.'

He was told there was, as yet, no question of it. First, the medical authorities had made clear that for at least six months his 'medical category' would restrict his employment to some sedentary task. Second, because he had, by curious coincidence, already been marked for temporary attachment to a home command. John thought of their beloved old Colonel's 'Can't spare you.' He would treasure that. At least there'd been no move to send him home as an inadequate civilian masquerading as an officer. He knew, on the contrary, that men trusted him, believed in him as one who knew his own mind, talked straight and spoke fair. The Colonel had indicated he'd be needed to lead the squadron 'if anything happened' to his Squadron Commander. Instead it had happened to John. Now it looked as if this assignment to Ireland – so mysteriously mooted before – could be accepted for a while with something like an easy conscience.

He was, as expected, passed 'fit for home duties' at a Medical Board in the last week in March, and never hated leaving Hilda more – there was, for various good reasons, no question of her leaving England just yet. He would be alone in Ireland.

'Alan's next leave's likely to be in July, I gather,' Helena said. 'You'll see him, I suppose. And you'll see Veronica soon, if they give you any free time. I've no idea what people do in Ireland in wartime. I imagine the hunting's very cut back.'

She had been affectionate, grateful for her son's survival more or less intact, had made him immensely comfortable. He was relieved how well she and Hilda were getting on. But her heart was with Alan in France.

John reported to Colonel Withers in Dublin on 3rd April, 1916, a Monday. Ten days later he received the letter for which he longed, and was reading it that day at his desk when Colonel Withers unexpectedly walked in.

'Yes. Met your charming – indeed your enchanting – sister-in-law. Told her I was glad to hear they might send me another Marvell. Truth to tell I'd heard something about you from Francis Carr in London. You know him.'

'He's a cousin, sir.'

'Of course. Carr was over here, too, the other day. Not for the first time. Nice chap, sensitive chap. Carr seemed to think your face might fit. Move to bring some chaps back from the trenches, pass on experience on the training side primarily. Fresh blood. I dropped a word.'

'And I, sir, didn't want to leave my regiment. The Colonel told me my name was down for posting home. I was upset. The Colonel promised he'd oppose it.'

'Idiot boy! One doesn't get "upset" in the Army. One goes where one's told. "Upset"! You sound like a governess who's been treated beneath her station! Anyway, here you are.'

'I was hit, sir.'

'So you told me. And it's properly slowed you up, too! Anyway, get on with reading your letter in King George's time!' He stumped off in good humour, enjoying nagging, pretending to bully a junior, imitating a bluff, hearty conventionality which was entirely unlike his real nature, a nature John was beginning to understand. Colonel Withers was an extremely perceptive, quick-witted and unusual man. John returned to Hilda's letter and read it avidly. He would, God willing, be a father some time shortly before Christmas.

Whatever Colonel Withers' formal description, his own principal duties were concerned with Intelligence, and Intelligence of a particular and specialized kind. John had a small role to play in this. The ostensible reason for bringing back officers with front-line experience (and heaven knew, thought John, that his was limited) was connected with training, with infusions into the home commands of some tactical realism. 'Fresh blood', Colonel Withers had called it. There was, in fact, nothing of this in John's duties in Ireland, duties on behalf of Colonel Withers, almost entirely connected with Intelligence. And John soon discovered that the Intelligence which concerned their branch was only marginally about the Germans. It was principally about the Irish.

The reasons for this were simple, although in the patriotic atmosphere of wartime they were not easily acknowledged. The moves towards Home Rule for Ireland which had dominated British domestic politics in the decade before 1914 had been put in cold storage for the duration of the war. The Irish Nationalist Party at Westminster had declared unequivocal support for King and Country. Irishmen, born fighters, volunteered in huge numbers for the Army. But to those whose dreams were exclusively fixed on Ireland, free, independent, a nation once again, the war with Germany was either an irrelevance or an opportunity. The British authorities were well aware of this. Ireland lay at England's back door and no chances could be taken. It was undesirable that too much military Intelligence effort should openly be devoted to the internal enemy, but it had to be so; and a number of skilful and experienced officers such as Withers – especially Withers – were there to see to it.

John had absolutely no Staff training of any kind and knew remarkably little about the Army. He was, however, quick-witted, articulate and eager to learn. He now was, in effect, what the ordinary world would have described as a private secretary or personal assistant. Withers had persuaded the authorities that he needed such. What he really required, John soon decided, was a fag, a letter-opener, an arranger; but, also, a confidant, a young friend. Withers was lonely: he needed to think aloud, and he needed, often, ears to hear and voices to help him do so. John thus, very soon, came to know more of his Colonel's business than any formal ascription of responsibilities could possibly have justified.

187

Furthermore he knew that Withers respected him as a fighting man, a soldier who had faced the enemy. Despite his affectation of treating John like a delinquent schoolboy, Withers, John realized, was secretly grateful to have with him someone who had walked with death and knew what that meant. Once, in very early days, Withers said – 'They'd never do that!', and John said quietly, 'I think they would.' 'They' were the Irish rebels, if they existed and if they ever came to the surface.

Withers had said, 'And what in hell do you know about it?' But his eyes were serious. John had replied, 'I've seen two Irish regiments in action. I've seen men behave exactly like you speculated and dismissed. It might be mad to you, sir – or me. But not necessarily to them.' And Withers had grunted. They had been closer thereafter.

John did not know whether he was useful, but he was, very soon, enormously interested. He felt instant attraction towards this strange, sad, beautiful country with its maddening combination of humour with cruelty, exquisite and natural good manners with infuriating self-pity. He had seen enough of Irish soldiers to love the best in them and profoundly distrust the worst. He worked on Withers' files and correspondence with growing fascination.

This process had, however, not been long underway when Withers summoned him a few days after he had received Hilda's blessed letter. John opened most messages and letters for Withers but certain particular documents, especially marked, could be opened and seen by none but the Colonel himself.

'Close the door.'

Withers was looking at a piece of buff paper with an air of something not unlike excitement. Most unusually.

'Ship's on the way.'

'Ship, sir?'

'Ship. German ship. Not the first, but a big one.'

John had read enough background to understand. An arms shipment! An arms shipment for those elements, if they existed, of the Irish Volunteers who might actually contemplate armed rebellion. John tried to remember statistics from the relevant summary he'd read on joining the Withers office.

'I suppose they'd take some time to issue them, even if they got them, sir?'

'You don't suppose they *will* get them, do you? Don't be an ass. Navy's shadowing.'

'I only meant that they'd be unlikely to have arranged anything in the immediate future. A rebellion, I mean. If they were taking the timing from this shipment.'

Colonel Withers, as often, gave the impression of not listening to what John said. It was one of those occasions when he needed a sounding board rather than thinking or scribbling alone. He started speaking in soft, disjointed sentences.

'Quite a few arms here already, of course. Enough for a futile effort, suicide, raise the flag. Not enough for serious business. Their problem's always been distribution. We've interrupted arms on the move. So all they've got are a number of widely separated nests for creating trouble.'

He paused. John had found it was necessary to interject, however feebly, in order to help him along.

'And they've got enough people, have they, sir, to use those arms and create that trouble?'

'Enough to use what they've got. Enough to use this shipment – biggish ship – if they can distribute. Distribution's their problem.'

John thought of Corporal O'Grady.

'We think, don't we, sir, that a good many of the old Irish Volunteers are now serving in the Army? In France and so forth.' The Irish Volunteers, a legitimate body although pledged to fight for Irish independence, were not generally quoted as wild men. They balanced the armed Ulstermen of the north; but they were not all committed to violence, murder, revolution, although some in their ranks most certainly were. Recruiting for the Army had been a major issue, of course, with the Republicans angrily denouncing it.

'About ninety-five per cent! Splendid fellows, of course. Record of the Irish battalions in this war, like the last. Splendid. You've mentioned them yourself, seen them in action. Probably

189

serving alongside old Ulster Volunteers from 'fourteen, too! Also splendid fellows.' He sighed, and said, 'That's Ireland!' not without a certain wry enjoyment. They sometimes, at points like this in conversation, shared a Withers dissertation on Irish history, the eighteenth-century troubles, the United Irishmen, the Union. John had the feeling that on this day time did not permit.

'That's Ireland. And ninety-five per cent leaves five per cent. Right?'

'Right, sir.' Indeed, 1,200 Irish Volunteers, with their arms, had marched openly through Dublin six months earlier and again in March.

'That's nine thousand men, you know. Not impossible to arm nine thousand men. Nuisance. But I doubt if more than a fraction of that nine thousand would burn their boats when the time came. A few desperate fellows, maybe. Of course, the Brotherhood have penetrated the Volunteers pretty extensively.'

'Brotherhood' were the Irish Republican Brotherhood, extremists pledged to separatism and known to have resolved, since the beginning of the war against Germany, on armed rebellion while Britain was engaged elsewhere in major war.

John said, 'Well, if they don't get this consignment, sir, what, if anything, will set them off? Won't they just go on waiting, and talking – and singing?'

Rebellion and invasion had been the British preoccupation in Ireland since the start of the war, but even after a few weeks John felt scepticism, although the reports he had read were firm that a rising would happen if certain conditions were right.

'Got something there. Maybe. Anyway, they're not going to get this lot.'

But Withers sighed again and John knew that something was making him uneasy. Though he talked aloud in his junior's presence (rather than to him), Withers knew a lot others didn't. He often, at this time, had long sessions with various senior members of the Royal Irish Constabulary, sessions whose appointments John made. He had direct access to General Friend, the Army Commander. He saw the Chief Secretary himself on occasion. The official 'Military Intelligence Officer' at Dublin Castle, attached to the Civil Government, kept Withers well informed – and learned a good deal in his turn. John never knew whether to withdraw from Withers' presence because obviously without useful purpose, or whether to wait for dismissal. On this occasion, the Colonel was silent a particularly long time and John stood in front of him, wondering.

'Is there anything you want me to do, sir?'

Withers looked at him, the distant look.

'One can just about run this country, so long as one's prepared to pay for one's information. And look after one's friends.'

'I suppose so, sir.'

'Might want you over Easter.'

'Of course, sir.' John lived in the officers' mess, which housed unmarried members of the Army Staff. It was wartime, and 'weekends' were, of course, working days if duty required. But it often did not require and usually Sunday, when church had been attended, was a man's own. On this particular Sunday John had arranged to go by train to visit Veronica. She lived some distance from Dublin and they had talked on the telephone – easy, happy, friendly conversation.

'Dear John,' she had said, 'Alan will be *so* thrilled you're here. I can't get into Dublin for some weeks, could you catch a train out here and I'll collect you in the pony cart from the station? It's only two miles. Come for the day.'

'On a Sunday, would that do?'

'It would do well. There's one Sunday morning train.' She told him the time. John was planning to invest in a motor car but had not yet done so. They had arranged that he would spend Easter Day at Alan and Veronica's home, Ballinslaggart. Early service in the garrison church would be followed by breakfast and a short, leisurely train journey.

Veronica said, 'We'll have a ride in the afternoon, Easter Sunday or not! Is your leg all right for that?'

'Perfectly all right.'

'I've checked there's a train on Easter Sunday. See you then, dearest John.'

Now John said to Colonel Withers, 'I was planning to spend Sunday away from Dublin, sir, if that's all right.'

'Expect so. If I want you, I'll tell you.' That was dismissal.

The next day was Good Friday and was being treated as an ordinary working day, with time off to go to church for those whose consciences so dictated. One of these, as it happened, was Colonel Withers who had told John that 'a few visits' and church would occupy his morning. He appeared after lunch and, as often, came apparently without purpose into John's room. There was a glint in his eye.

'Casement's been caught!'

Sir Roger Casement, distinguished British Civil Servant turned agitator for the cause of Irish nationalism, had been in Germany attempting to raise an Irish brigade among British prisoners of war. The British authorities were well informed on his doings, since he had also been active among anti-British elements in New York before travelling in a neutral ship and reaching Berlin. He was also likely, John supposed, to have been behind the arms shipment to which Withers had referred the previous day. Now Casement had been landed on the Irish coast from a U-boat and been almost immediately arrested. John, too, had heard the news.

'Yes, sir. And the ship's been scuttled in Cobh harbour. It looks as if anything brewing's been stopped, doesn't it? Nipped in the bud?'

'You think in clichés, young man!' Withers was shifting his shoulders restlessly inside his loose-fitting service jacket with its red collar patches. 'Clichés! Why was Casement coming here now?'

'Well, I suppose the arms –'

'What the hell good was he going to do, distributing arms? Local matter. Military Council matter.' The 'Military Council' of the Irish Republican Brotherhood, shadowed by the police at every turn (or so it was supposed), was the directing executive for all subversive activities.

Withers said again, 'Why was Casement coming here? Why now? Must have had a reason. Clever man. Plenty for him to get up to in Germany.'

'Liaison, sir? Planning?'

Withers looked at John without expression. He muttered, 'Well, I'll tell you who isn't here, wherever Casement is. Chief Secretary's not here. C-in-C isn't here. England, both of them.'

John saw Withers at early service on that Sunday. After they had taken Communion among a large congregation of military men and their womenfolk, he left the church near the back of the crowd to find the Colonel awaiting him.

'Look here, come into the office after breakfast. Sorry. Difficult time. Like you in Dublin.'

John was bitterly disappointed. He realized, a little uneasily, how much he'd looked forward to seeing Veronica. But when he reached the mess for breakfast and to telephone, the Mess Sergeant approached him.

'Telegram, sir.'

It was from Veronica. It must, he supposed, have been handed in to the post office the evening before.

'Terribly sorry,' it read, 'small domestic crisis. Easter no good.'

John recognized without pride that he was sorry it was Veronica who had postponed their meeting. It was as if he were again living in those appalling days of 1913, when every hour of every day he seemed to be waiting, disappointed, for her pleasure. There was no need for such a sensation now. Veronica was a sister-in-law, a dear friend, one with whom he'd once shared a secret love, long past. Nevertheless, he disliked the sense of *déjà vu*. Those had been bad times.

'Thank you, Sergeant Smethurst. I'll be in for lunch today.'

In the office Withers said, 'Paying a few visits,' and left. Surprisingly, and unusually for those days, he was wearing plain clothes. He had been in uniform at church. There were a number of reports for John to digest and put in order for him. Withers, John thought with some gratification, was almost beginning to trust his ability to express in clear English the sometimes rather confused raw material which reached the office. The door of John's small cell was, however, thrown open once again at mid-morning. The Colonel's visits had not taken long, he thought rather irritably. Long Withers ruminations aloud undoubtedly took a lot of time. John stood up, composing his face into a blend of the respectful and the long-suffering. But it was not Withers. For a second or two John failed to recognize the slight figure in Captain's uniform who stood in front of him with a wide grin.

'Nice to be in the heart of the family again!'

It was Cosmo Paterson.

Cosmo had so far had what was called a 'good war'. John had, of course, followed his activities of which Hilda, who adored him as ever, had been as fully appraised as anybody, which was not much. He had reported for duty in India, as an officer (with a full nine months' commissioned service behind him, some years before), and instead of being immediately dispatched to England to join a battalion of his regiment, destined as it would have been for France, he had been attached to the Headquarters of some Indian Army formation, based upon his extraordinary, albeit superficial linguistic ability. Cosmo could learn a language as quickly as most people can learn a tune. His method in such things was to decide that he wanted to go somewhere (in wartime this implied wishing to be attached to some specific part of the Army) and then to suggest, with sorrow, that the Staff or troops would fare better if some of them could speak the language of the country. 'Nobody does,' he would be told.

'Well, of course I speak it a bit, as you probably know –'

'*You* speak it, Paterson?' And a little later, no doubt – 'Hang on, Paterson. The Colonel wants to see you.'

And then the indispensable Lieutenant Paterson would find himself with some improbable assignment that he thought would interest him. He would no doubt, that same evening, get busy with dictionary and locally recruited teacher. This had led him to Mesopotamia, where a small British Indian force had advanced from the Persian Gulf in the first months, in order to cover the oilfields. This was Turkish imperial territory and a nasty little campaign had ensued in the valleys of Tigris and Euphrates. Now, after earlier successes, the British were bottled up at Kut al Amara. The newspapers had recently sounded a sombre note.

John had remarked that things sounded pretty beastly at Kut: worse than Gallipoli in fact. The garrison was isolated from the outside world by the Turkish army and it was not entirely easy for an amateur to understand why it had been allowed to place itself in that position. John looked at Cosmo.

'Why aren't you in Kut?'

'I was told to try and get out with some messages. Then I was told not to go back. I was put on a ship and sent home. Told to go to the War Office. Seen some enormously important people. You couldn't believe the circles you've married into, John.'

'But Cosmo, why on earth hasn't Hilda told me? I had a letter from her three days ago.'

'I've not seen her. I only got home on Tuesday. War Box Wednesday. Some rather unrepeatable experiences in London on Thursday, preparatory to spending Easter at long last with my family, getting in touch with my little sister at Bargate, all that. Friday morning, summoned to War Box again. Go to Dublin. Sniffed round yesterday. Now got to see your Colonel Withers. He is yours, I gather?'

'But why, Cosmo? What on earth's so special about either Dublin or you that has led the authorities to bring you together with such urgency? And you must be due for some leave after Kut, for God's sake!'

'Hard to say,' said Cosmo, wearing his wide-eyed, giving-nothing-away, innocent smile John remembered so well. Then he recalled, of course, the days when Cosmo had been alleged to be involved with gun-running to Ulster Volunteers, and kept some curious Irish company. He might, John supposed with some amusement, know a certain amount which somebody in London, with unusual imagination, had thought should be put to use by Withers, by Army headquarters, Ireland. But not, as far as John could see, with the sort of urgency that kept a man from visiting his family after months besieged in Kut al Amara.

'Hard to say. Don't expect I'll be here long. Seem to think I might help Withers.'

'Well, it's good to see you, and congratulations on being a Captain! Wonderful to see you!' John longed to confide in Cosmo, tell him in an offhand way, secretly, privately, proudly that he was going to be an uncle before 1916 was out. He said, 'Cosmo, you're staying in the mess?'

But Cosmo was booked into an hotel and they were discussing that, and where they should dine together, when they heard the heavy footfalls of Colonel Withers.

'Here's my Colonel. Don't go.'

Withers stumped in, wearing his baggy tweed suit and one of the faraway looks that so often presaged time-consuming ruminations. He looked at Cosmo without particular interest. Cosmo saluted.

'Captain Paterson. I was ordered by Colonel Jaques in London to report to you, sir. I believe he sent a wire.'

Withers looked at him without expression, merely observing, 'He did.' To John he said, 'Lord Lieutenant's taking an interest. Wants police to arrest all and sundry. Police opposed. I think they're right.'

'Why does Lord Wimborne –?'

'Trouble coming. Wants to pre-empt. Everything pretty tense. Police want to see who makes a move, comes out into the open. Get rabbits bolting out of the burrows.'

Cosmo, who clearly regarded himself without embarrassment as included in this conversation, and equally clearly followed it without difficulty, said, 'I suppose there are enough guns to deal with the rabbits, Colonel? And I suppose the rabbits aren't the man-eating kind?'

Withers might have ignored or snubbed this gratuitous intervention from a youthful stranger. He did neither. He considered.

'Not enough guns. Rabbits – well, capable of damage, not lethal. Point is whether and when rabbits will actually bolt. May lie doggo still. Hard to say. High-ups seem in no doubt it's coming. Personally, I think –'

He grunted, left the office, turning in the door to say – 'Paterson, come into my office.'

John took up his pen.

*

John agreed to lunch with Cosmo in his hotel in the centre of Dublin on Easter Monday. Surprisingly, Withers had claimed Cosmo for dinner on Easter Day and – rather as an afterthought, John reckoned – had invited him as well. He had had little conversation there with Cosmo and he greatly looked forward to lunch.

'Come early,' Cosmo had said, 'I'd like to lunch at twelve-thirty if you don't mind. I've got a lot of calls to pay on Monday afternoon. Some of them rather odd ones.' He was in his preferred, mystifying mood. There was affectation in it, but reality too. The spurious and the genuinely wild and exotic mixed confusingly in Cosmo. 'Come at midday,' he said, 'and we'll drink some good sherry. The food in that pub of mine's pretty impressive, I may say. We'll get a decent lunch.'

And at midday, John pushed through the swing doors of the hotel. Dublin was rather empty that Monday and the hotel wasn't busy. Where possible, people had left town for the Easter holiday. A friend with a motor car had given John a lift into the centre of the city – the graceful, beautiful city whose dignity and rhythm gave him pleasure on every occasion. How splendidly the eighteenth-century English and the Ascendancy Irish had combined for a little – combined at a certain level only perhaps, and for a sadly short while! Cosmo was occupying a huge leather armchair and installed John in its neighbour. As he had indicated, the sherry was excellent.

'Well, John, you got here.'

'Why shouldn't I get here?'

'Dublin's on the boil.'

John realized Cosmo knew as much as and probably more than he did himself. He said, 'Casement's arrested. The thing will probably fizzle out, if it was ever seriously intended.'

'My friends think not,' said Cosmo.

John found it irritating that he, who by now was beginning to think of himself as an executive part of the Intelligence machine, had to listen to Cosmo discussing his private sources with such lordly authority. He sipped his sherry and said, 'And your friends are knowledgeable are they, Cosmo?'

'Used to be. They reckon boats have been burned. Tragedy's in the air. Blood sacrifice. That sort of thing.'

It was nonsense to John, but he realized that Withers, too, was profoundly troubled and when they had parted the previous evening the Colonel had not given the impression of a man who thought all had blown over. It was only later – much later – that John realized Withers had been aware of intercepted signals between Berlin and the German Embassy in Washington, signals which showed the Germans anticipating important events in Ireland. Nevertheless, Withers, although John did not know it, was sceptical about whether German expectations, however confidently expressed, would be turned into reality by Irish action. Berlin might propose, but Irishmen disposed.

Cosmo looked at his sherry with satisfaction. Then he peered at his watch.

'We'll lunch at half past twelve. Feel like another glass of sherry?'

John had decided he wanted to change the subject from non-existent Irish revolution. Cosmo was the nearest, for a day, he could get to Hilda. He wanted to talk about her. He wanted to tell his brother-in-law that she was expecting a baby. He wanted to recapture something of love and family and peace, even of Bargate, through being with Cosmo. If he blotted out his uniform with his mind's eye, he could treat Cosmo as the embodiment of all that was normal and tranquil and decent. John knew Cosmo wanted to talk about Ireland: they could return to that. He needed Cosmo for something different, for a little. He looked at the neighbouring chair, trying to see something of Hilda in her brother. It was not impossible. Cosmo had turned and was gesturing to a waiter. He'd decided they could do with more sherry and it made the break John needed in the conversation.

'Two more glasses of sherry, please,' Cosmo called.

At that moment the swing doors moved with particular violence. The large hotel lounge in which they were sitting was itself a hall opening on to the street. A man in a brown civilian suit, a man of about thirty whom John had never seen before, came through the doors with an air of urgency. He wore a soft hat and did not remove it. He seemed out of breath and after one quick look round the room marched up to Cosmo.

Cosmo said, 'Hello, Swanson.' He said it without surprise.

'Captain Paterson, would you please come with me. The Castle's been attacked.'

Swanson ignored John, who jumped up.

'Attacked?'

Swanson nodded impatiently.

'They've shot the sentry. The policeman on the gate. And there's some sort of proclamation been made a few minutes ago from the post office. Captain Paterson – please –'

About a thousand Irish Volunteers had dug trenches and formed something of a ring round Dublin that Monday morning. It is a big city and a thousand were not many. Their positions were inevitably isolated from each other. At first, on Monday, they had the streets of Dublin pretty well to themselves. There was something unreal about it, people told each other afterwards, people who'd no idea anything was in the wind. They gazed, open-mouthed, at the attempts to block streets, the sudden threats of armed men to shoot anybody who refused to co-operate, the brutal murder of a lorry driver who failed to bring his lorry and help form a barricade. The stunned silences, the rumours, the low key of the whole thing were astonishing. It was unreal! What were these people trying to do? There were few British troops actually in Dublin that Monday.

But battalions were soon brought in from outside. Withers used John as a general dogsbody; although not a member of the Army Operational Staff, he soon put himself in the thick of it. Although Intelligence had been insistent that 'something was about to break', there had been scares before, and Withers had been reluctant to believe that, when it came to it, the Republican Brotherhood (identified not only as the moving spirits in the rising but probably the only participants) would really seize weapons and take to the streets. But they did. 'All is changed,' Yeats wrote afterwards, in a poem of memorable grief; and all

199

was changed, never to be the same, after that Easter Monday morning when Patrick Pearse declared an Irish Republic from the post office. The unthinkable had been not only thought but expressed in action, however futile. The power of Government had been challenged by knots of men in miscellaneous green uniforms or none, carrying many different sorts of rifles and revolvers in their hands, and, it seemed, extraordinarily ready – even anxious – to die.

John saw little of the streets of Dublin. There was much to do helping out in a rough-and-ready operations centre established by Army Headquarters to manage the movement of reinforcements towards the centre of the city, to keep record of incidents and to plot the course of the counter-insurrection. By that Tuesday evening the large street map he had on the wall showed the rebels to be cut off from each other in a number of areas, each the object of assault by British troops. The British method was to bring up a field gun and pound the buildings which the rebels – there were various organizations concerned but they were generally called Sinn Fein, or 'The Shinners' – had roughly fortified. After a while, fire, destruction, casualties and shortage of food, of water and of ammunition, generally brought them out to surrender. But there were plenty of attempts to storm the Sinn Fein centres, too, and a tally was kept of British casualties. By the end of the week nearly seventy men had been killed, several of them officers John knew, and the final casualty list was a great deal higher. It wasn't Gallipoli, but it was devilish and the mood at Army Headquarters (originally disbelieving, even mocking) became hard and angry. These rebels, these assassins, were British subjects, men whose relations were dying for King and Country in France. They had turned on their own kind and cause – or so it seemed.

Sinn Fein had not been content to seize buildings, proclaim their Republic and defy the authorities to oust them. They had taken the offensive. One British battalion, moving in column towards the city from the docks, was ambushed on the line of march with fearful loss. Everywhere snipers in civilian clothes were rumoured. There were stories – some substantiated later, some not – of the waylaying and murder of individuals whose duty or leisure had placed them at risk, isolated victims. All this made people grim and savage. John reflected that one saving grace was that, except in Dublin, not much was happening. It didn't seem that risings throughout Ireland (predicted by Intelligence) would come off. And after Monday afternoon, the authorities were at a high state of alert everywhere.

Cosmo turned up again on Thursday. Withers had given him exactly the sort of job he liked – a roving commission to make contact with his 'old friends' (most of them, John guessed, men who'd once penetrated the Irish Republican Brotherhood on behalf of the Ulster Volunteers – a dangerous game). Cosmo's friends, he gave John to understand with huge enjoyment, while 'loyal' in the sense of wanting to betray Sinn Fein where it could safely be done, nevertheless were greatly relishing the initial discomfiture of the British Government. Like Cosmo himself, no doubt, they found irresistible the sight of authority embarrassed. Cosmo said that the fires which had lit the Dublin sky since Monday evening had done a lot of damage.

'The fire brigade couldn't get at them because of the rifle fire. A lot of Dublin's destroyed – you ought to see it, John! Quite a sight!'

'I can't. I've been on this damned telephone or at this desk ever since I got back here from the lunch we didn't have on Monday.'

John had worked with quiet efficiency. He knew, and knew that Withers recognized, that a man with combat experience – albeit untrained in this sort of Staff work – had a strength, a sure touch in dealing with situations where men were shooting and being killed, a confidence purely technical training was unlikely to produce. John was effective, and although he found the situation detestable, his own competence satisfied him deeply.

'I've hardly had me own boots off,' said Cosmo. His astonishing facility for languages led him, invariably, to mimic or echo the speech of those among whom he found himself and now, as English as John was, he was assuming (not without passable success) something of a Dublin accent.

201

John looked at the map on the wall. 'Do your friends, as you call them, think the Shinners will hold out much longer?'

'Not them! The thing's over. And it never had a chance – obviously.'

'Then, why –?'

'Blood sacrifice,' said Cosmo, using the phrase John had heard him utter before. 'The cause needs blood. That sort of thing.'

John felt anger and distaste. Cosmo marked the frown and said – 'They've got most of the people against them, for sure. When taken through the streets, after surrender, our chaps had their work cut out to stop the crowd pulling them limb from limb!'

'I know. I was glad to hear it. I'm sure the ordinary decent, patriotic Irishman is as horrified by the whole thing as you and I are.'

'Well,' said Cosmo, 'he may be. But they're a rum lot, John. I got to know them pretty well in the old 'thirteen and 'fourteen days. North, south or in the middle, they're a rum lot.'

Rum lot or not, the rising was over by the end of that week. On Saturday the self-styled 'Army Command' of Sinn Fein surrendered unconditionally. By then, the British garrison had a new General, instructed, as they all understood, to make sure that the embers of rebellion were firmly extinguished, and that such a thing must never, in any circumstances, happen again. Withers, at this time, was more than ever prone to long, rambling dissertations on Irish history interspersed with sharp, crackling comments on Government policy in general and his own immediate superiors in particular.

'Whatever we told them, they told us Sinn Fein was an "insignificant minority". Well, who was right?'

'Do you think now we should have done as the Lord Lieutenant wanted, sir? Taken a lot of them in on the Saturday?'

Withers grunted. He felt sore about this. At the time he had opposed such a move as likely to exacerbate matters. It had been agreed to make no move until the Easter holiday was over.

'In spite of all I know and have read of Ireland,' he said slowly and without his usual irony or affectation of ridiculing John's ignorance, 'In spite of every bloody conclusion I've drawn about this bloody country, I never, God help me, never right up to the moment it happened thought they'd be such bloody fools.'

Relief and a sort of gaiety set in at the end of the week. Cosmo and John agreed another luncheon date, and over good food took to pieces again the course of those extraordinary days. John said that Withers had felt something was bound to happen when he heard Casement had been caught. Casement's appearance must have been a signal – although Withers had disbelieved in a full-scale armed rebellion.

'I think not,' said Cosmo. 'On the point about Casement, I think not. I gather we now reckon he knew little about it. Wanted to stop it, in fact.'

'Really? But he'll hang, won't he?'

'Oh, he'll hang,' said Cosmo easily. 'You can't have a fellow – British Knight, old boy! – roaming prisoner-of-war camps in Germany to persuade our people to join the Germans! No, even we couldn't have that, could we? And I don't think people are in a very forgiving mood. One can hardly blame them,' Cosmo added, 'People are running for cover here, of course, but the fellows who organized this week's little effort at treason, and those who've given them comfort – at German behest, in the middle of a war – aren't likely to get away with their lives, I imagine.'

In Dublin the first executions took place the following Wednesday. Everybody in Army Headquarters knew they were happening, and everybody thought it both just and inevitable. That evening John was handed a telegram.

'Coming to Dublin Claremont Hotel for a few nights on Thursday. Plumbing gone wrong at Ballinslaggart. Need a few days' relief. Make contact at Claremont. Much love Veronica.'

CHAPTER XI

'The name's Seamus Burke,' said Colonel Withers. 'That right?'

'That's right, Colonel,' said Cosmo. 'He was seen, covered with blood, in Merrion Row on the Tuesday. Tuesday last week. And there's been not a sign or whisper of him or his body.'

'Why do we think he's alive?'

'He'd have had a hero's treatment if dead, Colonel. By now.'

For the mood in Dublin had changed. The original stunned repugnance at the act of rebellion and the violence which had accompanied it had been followed by a sort of silent melancholy, as if ordinary folk were saying to each other – 'These were remarkable men, after all!' There were misgivings about the executions. Reason maintained that the State could demand nothing less than their lives from armed rebels, paid and inspired by the German enemy, in the middle of a bitter and costly war in which British (and, of course, Irish) soldiers were dying daily. But reason had no firm roots nor regular nourishment in the soil and climate of Ireland. Myth was being born. There was, as so often, a relish for tragedy in the air. Even at the time, the British in Ireland could feel – while simultaneously thinking it unjust – that the bullet-riddled bodies of the Brotherhood men, swiftly condemned by court martial to die with defiant cries of Ireland on their lips, were winning the last battle. Even Cosmo, quick and cynical, sighed a little.

'Pity we didn't shoot more of them in the actual fighting!'

'Connolly was killed, anyway.'

'Wrong.'

James Connolly, leader of a separate, extremist organization, the 'Citizens' Army', had been shot in the leg. Early reports of

204

his death in the fighting had been overtaken by news that he was disabled but would certainly recover and be fit to stand trial. In fact, Connolly, strapped to a chair, was shot by a firing squad a week after this conversation.

'Wrong. Connolly will be tried like the others. And there's a lot of blood on his hands.'

It was Thursday, early in May, and it was astonishing to them that the rebellion had only broken out ten days before. Cosmo had already been ordered to report to the War Office in London for a fresh assignment. He had been indefatigable in the information he had sniffed out, from heaven knew what sources, about the whereabouts of prominent members of Sinn Fein. Withers regarded him as fascinating, and although Cosmo formally reported to another branch of the Staff, he had established an easy liaison with Withers, and thus with John. Anyway, Cosmo preferred gossip to formal reportage. It was his way of communicating.

'Yes,' Cosmo said, 'my boys reckon Seamus Burke's lying up somewhere, Colonel. He was hit hard by all accounts. But not a sign of him yet. A hard man, Colonel.'

'He's probably left Dublin, somehow.'

'Maybe,' said Cosmo. Roads had been blocked and watched since the earliest days, in so far as the stretched resources of the British Army and the Royal Irish Constabulary permitted.

John had heard a good many similar exchanges. A name, apparently familiar to Cosmo from his earlier days, a name by then notified widely to the military authorities, would be described as 'seen during the fighting', 'recognized near The Green but not subsequently surrendered'. Privately, John thought it remarkable that any such was ever found. The ways across Ireland for a man on foot were infinite in number, and there were many houses where he might lie for a little, although the slums and suburbs of Dublin itself were methodically combed as the weeks went by. John was feeling a certain sense of anticlimax. The whole ridiculous business had both disturbed and justified their lives for a few days, but what now? The news from France was once again dominating conversation. Most of the fighting in that spring of 1916 was in the French sector, it seemed, where there was remorseless pressure on the great ring of fortresses at Verdun. But everybody said a major British offensive couldn't be long delayed.

Meanwhile, office hours at Army Headquarters had reverted to something like normal. Engagements could be made with tolerable certainty of keep them. John's own engagement that Thursday evening was to dine with Veronica. He wished his heart did not jump so disturbingly at the prospect. He loved his wife. He was anxious, proud and happy that she was pregnant with his child. But his pulse beat with unbecoming rapidity as he walked, that evening, to see his sister-in-law at the Claremont Hotel. A taxi had taken him into the centre of Dublin. 'Come early,' Veronica had said on the telephone. But John wanted a little fresh air and a few minutes' preparation before going through the swing doors of the Claremont. He was unsure how it would go.

Veronica was nowhere to be seen when John first looked round the entrance lounge of the hotel. He was about to approach the reception desk but first looked at his watch: he was still embarrassingly early, in spite of her bidding. To discipline himself a little, to test his own strength in what he recognized was an absurd way, he sat down at a desk, wrote some overdue note on hotel writing paper, cheap, wartime stuff, and put the note in an envelope. Before he had sealed or addressed it a voice he would never forget spoke close to his left shoulder.

'John! Oh, John!'

Veronica had an excited air about her. John had seen her only a few times since her wedding, and there was still that curious sense of not knowing how to behave which can beset two people who have been lovers, who have been (in John's case, certainly) passionately in love and then meet in a new, 'correct' relationship. She was his brother's wife. John was, like Veronica, married and 'different'. He supposed they would have to come to terms afresh, thoughts and certainly words about their own shared past set firmly aside, taboo. He imagined that she, too, would feel a certain embarrassment. Any word or glance of recollected love would be a gross betrayal – of his brother, of his wife. She was bound to feel the same, he thought, and they would find some sort of quiet plateau on which to meet, acknowledging that neither must ever approach the cliff-edge of memory that would border that plateau. When John turned at her voice, he was at first almost unsure it was her. Not because Veronica had changed – indeed he was soon acknowledging to himself with regret that she was lovelier than ever – but because the picture he had had of her had become distorted by time, absence, the love of another, and a determination to believe that he had absurdly overrated Veronica's desirability.

In this last, John was wrong. As he looked at her he recognized that he had not at all overrated Veronica's desirability: he found he almost needed to look away. More than that, there came back to him with appalling clarity the extraordinary concentration he had always felt in her, so that a magnetic force seemed to be projected from her and to hold him to her. It took three minutes to establish the lines of force that ran between John and Veronica, not more. And those lines of force were quickened rather than impeded by her bright, rather feverish air. She kissed him gently on the cheek. Her first words, however, were unexpected and by no means agreeable.

'Guess who I've just seen, my darling John?'

'Well, Veronica!' He smiled at her, rather uneasily. 'How are you? And who've you just seen?'

'Printer! News takes him to places. It's brought him to Dublin!'

'Drew!' John frowned. It was the last thing he expected. Not only was Drew an odious creature but he had, at one time, made Veronica's life intolerable. Furthermore, the mention of him immediately transported them from the equable present – two happily married people connected by family links, the past gently buried – to that turbulent time when Drew had tried to blackmail her and John had done his best to save her. To the time when Francis Carr had sympathized and helped, and when Alan had swept her from John's arms and away, while Drew had melted like snow in spring, to be a menace no more. John still disliked the sound of his name. He said –

'Well, I hope I don't meet him! Let's talk of pleasanter things. What news of Alan?'

'Anyway, I've made it up with Printer. He's not too bad, really. And it was all a long time ago, wasn't it? Dearest John! You look awfully thin. The Dardanelles must have been ghastly.'

'What news of Alan?'

'He seems all right. He was on leave at Christmas.'

'I know. I just missed him. Mother said he'll get a decent stretch of leave in July. True?'

'Maybe. These things seem subject to change in wartime, have you noticed?' They laughed. She took his hand and looked into his eyes.

'And, as I said, you're awfully thin. You've changed – you were always determined, now you look, well, stern! Lines! Responsibility! Experience! Oh, John, I can read it all there! Are you really fit?'

'Pretty well. I've another Board – Medical Board – soon. I think I'll probably be kept here a few more months.'

'And then?'

John shrugged. He didn't want to discuss his private, reluctantly formed determination with Veronica. He intended to ask for transfer from his beloved Yeomanry. They were now in Egypt and showed signs of staying there for ever. John had decided that if he was to respect himself he should serve in France. Like his brother.

'One goes where one's sent,' he lied. He returned to the subject of Alan. 'Alan seems to be doing awfully well.' Alan's career on the Staff in France was, indeed, highly creditable. Any soldier of distinction who happened to meet John (an infrequent occurrence) tended to say, 'Alan Marvell's brother, are you?' Alan was now a Lieutenant-Colonel. Alan was known. He always had been. Veronica nodded, her eyes abstracted. They took their places in the dining room where John was unable to prevent himself from quickly scanning the room for signs of the detestable Drew. The coast seemed clear. They talked easily of many things. John found he wasn't very hungry.

'I've got a positive suite here! I had to get out of Ballinslaggart.

No drains! I suddenly felt I'd give myself some comfort for a day or two. The Irish aren't great plumbers.'

'You indicated as much in your telegram.'

'Things are meant to be right by the week's end. I don't believe a word of it, but I'll have to go back.'

'You said something on the telephone about a groom, too.'

'I've sacked him. A Dubliner, not a local man. Filthy brute, never sober. I could stand that, but lately he's been so lazy you'd not believe. If I wasn't there the horses would starve, or worse. I've given Thomas Feely his marching orders.'

'Is a groom essential?'

'Certainly he is. I drive everywhere, and I've got a nice little horse I hunted this season, and Alan, at Christmas –' she checked herself, as she generally seemed to, John observed, choking the conversation when Alan entered it. It didn't sound to John as if Thomas Feely had been very fully employed but Veronica explained that he 'did the heavy' about the place.

'There's nobody else. I must have a man, of sorts. There's a decent brother of the farmer next door, a sort of half-wit who's always been at home, good for very little, poor devil. He's going to come in every day until I'm suited. I've told Feely to clear out. He'll not come back.'

'Did he do anything particularly awful?'

'Accumulation of things,' she said, rather vaguely, 'and drunker than ever on Tuesday. Now, John, I want to hear about you. I suppose you've been particularly busy. We'll have coffee in my sitting room upstairs and you can tell me about Dublin at Easter. God, I wish I'd been here!'

This startled John a little.

'Why would you have liked that, Veronica? It was noisy, violent, muddled and pretty bloody.'

'It was also thrilling, memorable and heroic. Or don't you agree?'

'If you're talking of Sinn Fein, I certainly don't agree! It was a dirty attempt to do the Germans' work for them. And a lot of people have died.'

'Well,' said Veronica, 'people do die in any heroic attempt.'

She'd used the word again. This was nonsense, John thought, looking at her with an attempt at that sternness she had said she found in him. It was also beyond the acceptable limits of dissent which Veronica always explored, on any subject. England was at war.

'A heroic attempt,' said Veronica again, slightly louder, 'and they'll not be forgotten, you can be sure of that. Now we'll have coffee.' She walked rapidly from the dining room towards the lift, and every man's head turned as she passed.

'Veronica, I don't think you – I think you should be careful about talking of the rebels as heroes, things like that. People could misunderstand.'

'No misunderstanding. It's what I think. Why disguise it?' She was wearing a dark-green dress and John was very aware of the smoothness of her arms and shoulders. He decided to leave soon after his cup of coffee. It was, he thought fleetingly, perhaps lucky that he had promised to return to barracks by eleven to relieve another on night duty, and could not stay at the Claremont long. But he felt it important to dent the surface of her scornful, imprudent rebelliousness.

'You ask, "why disguise it?" The answer is because these people – Sinn Fein and the rest – have been taking Germany's side in a war, and people who express sympathy or admiration for them will, very understandably, be thought of as friendly to the enemy. The name for that is treason.'

He expected Veronica to make a scornful response but she said nothing and he thought he could score another effective point.

'After all, there's Alan to think of, too, and your position. If you were just – just one of these asinine Irish lady-romantics, playing at revolution – it would be different. But you're the wife of a British officer –' It was impossible not to make it sound pompous, as was clear from her angry retort. John recognized he had not improved his case.

'So the wife of a "British officer"' – she mimicked his tone, unkindly and with, for the first time he had ever found such a thing in Veronica, a trace of vulgarity – 'can't be an "Irish lady-romantic"'? It compounds the sin, does it? And if the lady is, nevertheless, Irish – and romantic – and historically minded – and patriotic –'

'Veronica, darling Veronica, one can be all these things without backing the rebels!'

'Yes. One can. But suppose conscience comes in? And courage? And shame at keeping silent when others cry out their faith aloud and die?'

They glared at each other. John felt, in spite of himself and his sense of the realities, curiously moved. He knew she was sincere. He recognized, with shock, that this was what really mattered to Veronica, that he was with – that he once had loved, possessed – one of those rare creatures who can give themselves to a cause with little thought of self or of the world. Her ideas were far from John's. She was not only, it appeared, ex-mistress and sister-in-law but also enemy.

John heard himself saying, fatuously, '"A nation once again".' The nationalist song, sung with pathos or defiance or both, not infrequently mixed with drink, said the British, chuckling and mimicking. Veronica stood very still, eyes very wide open. She spoke low.

'Why is that amusing?'

'It isn't. But –'

'Why do the English find funny the love of other people for their country? Why do they look down from their great height on the emotions of other people, the self-sacrifice of other people, the heroism of other people? Why are their faces contorted into one huge, corporate sneer? Why?'

'Veronica –'

'I will tell you why. It is because, first, they utterly lack imagination. To understand the point of view of a stranger, let alone the obsessions of a stranger – Irish, French, German, it doesn't matter – is beyond them. They can only look at others from outside as if observing the behaviour of animals. To make the leap of the mind that could let them see, feel, with other eyes, other senses, is impossible for them. They are too blinkered. And too lazy.'

John said sternly, 'You're being unfair. And you know it.'

'Do I? Then I'll go on being unfair and tell you the second reason for the English sneer, beside lack of imagination. It is because you've lost all sense of history. You can't understand people to whom the past is a reality – not a legend or a pretty story or even just a vivid grievance but a reality. The English –'

'Veronica, you are largely English. And the English have more sense of history, of tradition, than pretty well every other European nation.'

'No,' said Veronica, still very low, very intense, 'they haven't. They like the trappings. They enjoy the sentimental side, however much they mock it in others. But they have no real sense of the past. They have largely lost their feeling of being rooted in their own land. They have driven most of the people into horrible great cities, deprived them of their history and then wonder that they're sullen. They –'

'Darling Veronica,' said John. 'These same unimaginative, stupid, unhistorical English joined up in their millions when the war began and an awful lot of them have died for what they certainly think they love as their country. Why do you give them so bad a name?'

He spoke gently. It was not the moment to say again that she was speaking of part of her own family, and of her husband and his brother.

Veronica's voice was more even now.

'They will have a bad name here for a long, long time. Perhaps for ever.'

'There will be Home Rule, one day, my dear. These things will be settled, time will pass, tempers will cool, grievances be forgotten. Most of Dublin, after all, resents these Sinn Feiners, realizes that we've all got to find a way to live together. And fight together – there's a big war on. And we are, after all, a United Kingdom, however it's to be governed.'

'A United Kingdom!' said Veronica. 'Unity is a matter of feeling, not of laws made in assemblies or lines drawn by cool-headed men on maps! It's a matter of feeling. And we don't feel like you!'

John sighed, and she added –

'Anyway, who wants Home Rule as a present from England, a sweet to a child if it promises to be good and obey Nanny's rules? Independence, nationhood – it's only valuable if you fight for it. Only an Englishman would need a woman to teach him that!'

She was breathing fast and her lovely breasts, half-revealed by the cut of the green dress, heaved with a rhythm he could not fail to find familiar. He said, 'Veronica, I do understand. Your way's not my way, but I do understand. But oh, my dear, I do implore you –'

Suddenly he found she was crying and that his arms were round her. She whispered, 'Oh, John, I'm so unhappy.'

'Because of all this?'

'Not entirely. This is terrible and wonderful. Different. No, it's just that I've made a mess of things. I –'

John found that his hand was stroking her neck and shoulder. It brought back a great deal.

'You see, I was a fool, a wicked fool to marry Alan.'

John was stunned. He was devoted to his brother. Neither Veronica nor he moved and his hand continued to stroke her. He tried very hard to think of his beloved wife, Hilda. Then he tried very hard not to.

'I threw you over, darling John, changed brothers at five minutes' notice! How could you ever speak to me after that? You were so sweet and honourable and forgiving about it. "May the best man win" and all that – I almost wanted you to seek me out, fly at me, beat me!'

'We'd best not talk about it. It's in the past. It may have been best for both of us. It was – yes – it was a bit quick!'

He tried to put a touch of a smile into his voice, which shook.

'I'll never love him, never. I realize it's wicked to say this, to feel it –'

'I'm terribly sorry.' She put her palm against his cheek.

'He's so – so aggressive. We're further apart every time he

213

comes on leave.' Then she whispered – 'I can't bear the fact he's not his brother!'

'Darling Veronica! War is – well, perhaps rather hardening, you know.'

'Has it hardened you? I don't think so. You're quieter, darling, you laugh less. Perhaps that will always be so now. You're less – less young. But not hard, I think. Strong but not hard. It's different.'

John smelt the familiar scent of her skin, like none other.

'You were always gentle when it mattered, John. Strong but with the knowledge of when and how to be gentle. Born in you. Instinctive. I'm sure,' he felt her smiling, voice trembling slightly, 'I'm sure horses know it. And women know it. It's in your hands. It's in your heart.'

John tried, his voice unsteady too, to lighten the air.

'Alan's a better horseman than me, Veronica! Much!'

'That perhaps,' she said. 'That perhaps.'

With as great an effort as any John had made in life to that point, he moved his left hand so that he could look at his wrist-watch.

'Veronica, dearest, the war can't be very good for marriages. You and Alan have had hardly any proper married life.'

'Enough. More than enough.'

'No, I doubt it. He's a wonderful chap – and you're a wonderful woman. Oh, Veronica –'

Suddenly she was in his arms again, and she was whispering – 'Do you have to go?'

'Yes, I must.' Then he murmured in her ear, 'I'll visit you at Ballinslaggart soon.' John found he was kissing and nibbling her ear.

'I'm here till Saturday morning. Will – will you call again? Darling brother-in-law?'

John heard himself saying, 'If you are in the hotel tomorrow at about five, I have to be in Dublin. You might give me – give me a cup of tea! I can't dine again tomorrow. I – I have to go somewhere else.'

It was true. He had been invited to sup with a colleague and his wife, who had rented a house near Headquarters. Would it be possible to apologize, cancel?

She said, 'Yes, I might. Five o'clock! A cup of tea!'

'Thank you for dinner. And Veronica – my dear, do be discreet.'

'I hear you, John, I hear you. Until tomorrow. We'll have tea up here. Or something. You know your way now.' Before he went she whispered – 'Has Francis talked about me?'

'Francis Carr? I've not seen him for ages.'

'He was over here not long ago. He once said a lot of preposterous things to me, accusing things. I wondered –'

John's mind went back to the days when Francis had known of Veronica's relation with Drew and himself. Unreasonably he resented Francis's knowledge, linked no doubt to these accusations Veronica mentioned by some obscure cord. He shook his head, kissed her again, and said goodbye.

John got out of the taxi at the barrack gate of Army Headquarters some time later, still in a daze. There was something of a mist in the early evening air and he could not make out much of the figure that moved unsteadily towards him, a figure that had been waiting in the shadows not far from the sentry box. The sentry, motionless, was within call. John undid the flap of his revolver holster. Officers' weapons were always loaded when out of barracks at that time. A strong reek of liquor hit him; the wheezing, whispering voice was slurred and unfamiliar.

'Would it be Captain Paterson?'

Cosmo and John were not particularly alike. It was a curious coincidence, thought John, but Cosmo had some curious friends. He said, 'No. Do you want to say something to Captain Paterson?'

'It would needs be the Captain himself.'

'I'm afraid that's not possible. He's away until tomorrow evening. Perhaps you can come back.' John spoke curtly.

The figure shook its head vehemently. 'Aren't I taking risks coming the once. Do you know him?'

'Certainly.'

The figure eyed him. The voice was barely audible. 'The name's

215

Tom Feely. Billy Devlin told me the Captain would reward me if I passed a word. As a duty, like.'

Tom Feely. Billy Devlin. A Cosmo-type intrigue. The name Tom Feely was familiar but there must be many such. He eyed Feely and spoke softly.

'Well, if you pass the word to me I'll tell him, and I expect he'll reward you if it's worth it! And if he can find you! Otherwise, as I said, come back tomorrow.'

But although the man was drunk and uncertain, John could see he felt he had been brave to come even the once to the gate of Army Headquarters, and if he was, indeed, an informer of any consequence it was an idiotic thing to do.

The man muttered, 'Billy said it was important, that I should come straight away and the Captain would see I was done right by.'

John sighed to himself. Cosmo was on one of his mysterious tours and was due back, he had said, late the following evening. When in Dublin he was now living in the officers' mess, as was John. John said abruptly, 'Can you write?'

'I can that.'

'Will you write a short message for Captain Paterson? If you will, I'll see he gets it and I'll give you a sovereign.' John pulled out a small notepad he always carried in his pocket and pushed it towards the man, with a pencil. They were standing by the barrack wall, and a broad ledge two feet from the ground gave John's disreputable-seeming companion a writing desk. It was light enough to write by the lamp at the gate. John hoped he was truthful in boasting he was literate, as he fingered the pencil hesitantly.

John took a gold sovereign from his pocket and said, 'A short message, mind.' What a fool, he reflected, Cosmo would think him.

'There's nobody else will know of this, sor, nor see the writing, like?'

'Nobody. I promise you to give it to Captain Paterson personally, and that it will be as safe and secret as if you'd spoken the word to him yourself.'

216

There was no reason for the man to show trust and John cared little whether he did or not, but he preferred to lose a pound than to forfeit a trick Cosmo might have taken. Feely finished his writing. He had found it laborious work, and folded the paper carefully. Then, suddenly, he was clearly anxious to complete the transaction and get away.

'That's it, sor. Did you say a sovereign?'

'I did. And I hope it's worth it.'

They exchanged piece of paper for coin, and when John looked up after pocketing the note, Feely was coughing nervously into his cupped hands. John walked into barracks past the curious eyes of the sentry and then paused by the lamp which illuminated the gate. I'd better have a look, he reflected. His blood was still running fast from the peculiar impact Veronica, her views, her disclosures and the proximity of her body had had on him; still running fast, too, at the thought that he would see her again the next afternoon. He opened and read the folded scrap of paper. Feely's hand was large and childlike –

John was aware that he did not always think as quickly as he should, or act at speed. He was firm and methodical. On that occasion, he moved fast. He was out through the barrack gate like a nervous cat, the sentry puzzled and immobile. John could see a shape moving away down the road and called, 'Feely!'

The shape turned, hesitant. John walked rapidly towards it. In his tunic pocket he had found the note he had been writing to pass time at the Claremont before Veronica found him, that unimportant note in an unmarked and unsealed envelope.

'Feely, perhaps you'd best put your message in an envelope and seal it yourself. That way, there's no chance of other eyes seeing it by accident. Put it in this envelope and write "Captain Paterson" on the outside.'

John shoved the pencil at him again, together with his folded piece of paper and the envelope.

'Come over and rest it here, on the wall.'

John watched him as the thick fingers put note into envelope. Feely looked up, uncertain –

'Captain –?'

'Paterson. P-A . . .' John spelt it for him.

'And you'll give it to him personally, sor?'

'I'll get it to him personally and nobody else shall see it. I promise.'

John slipped the envelope into his pocket. When he looked up, Feely had vanished.

At a few minutes before five o'clock on the next afternoon, John again pushed through the swing doors of the Claremont Hotel. Before leaving barracks he had put Thomas Feely's note in an outer envelope, and round it wrapped a brief message to Cosmo –

> 'The enclosed was given to me by an odd customer who waylaid me returning here last night. He assured me it was worthy of reward and that you would think so. I told him I'd get it into your hands, and I gave him a quid. I suppose you'll tell me I'm half-witted and will refuse reimbursement!

> J.M.

> P.S. Our friend was NOT staying at the Claremont! I had a scrap of paper and an hotel envelope which I gave him to use!'

John was intercepted by the hall porter.

'Will you be after calling on Mrs Marvell, sir?'

'I will. I know where her sitting room is. I'm expected.'

'Indeed you are, sir, and tea ordered.' The man had a particularly cheerful face as he led John towards the lift and, after pressing the call bell, turned with the confidential urgency of the born raconteur. Veronica had said that his name was O'Brien.

'That's a very wonderful lady, sir!'

'She is my sister-in-law,' said John, a little stiffly.

'Is that so, sir? A wonderful lady. Once she came here to stay a couple of nights, and I was not meself at all. Our little Patrick, five years old, had scalded himself near to death. Doctor Magrath

218

had come and put the dressings on, and the little fella – he's the only one, you see, sir –'

John smiled at the lift boy and showed some impatience towards O'Brien, who said something curt to the youngster and resumed his tale.

'Our only one and Mrs O'Brien takes on if there's anything wrong. This time she took on so you'd hear it half across Ireland. She up and told me I mustn't come in to work. I mustn't leave her with a dying child. I was a monster. I said, "Mary, I'm not a monster and Pat's not dying and I'm due at the hotel at three –" I was due to come on after luncheon, you see, sir, and do the duty till midnight –'

'Ah.'

'"And Mary," I said, "if I don't do this job to satisfaction there's plenty would like it, and where would you and Pat be then?" But she went on like a banshee. And Mrs Marvell, sir –'

O'Brien paused. He had the compulsive talker's technique of never breathing at a full stop, never giving an opening to interruption.

'Do you know what Mrs Marvell did? She said, "O'Brien, you look worried. What's the trouble?" And I told her. And she said – "Poor Mrs O'Brien. Children's pain hurts one in a very special way. Where do you live?" she said. And I told her –'

He fixed John with a magnetic eye.

'And when I went back home at midnight I found Mrs O'Brien quiet, and the boy sleeping, and the wife said that's a nice lady, is Mrs Marvell, she was round here in a cab, she said, "Mrs O'Brien I know your husband," she said. "And I'm sorry about Patrick," she said, "and when he's better I thought he might enjoy these –" And she'd a box of bricks with her, the best money could buy, coloured building bricks they were, young Pat had never had such things. And Mrs O'Brien told me the lady had stayed an hour in our place, it's a small cupboard of a place, sir, but decent, and she stayed there with the wife, talking and newsing. And she made her laugh, Mrs O'Brien said, till the tears ran down her cheeks. So that's Mrs Marvell for you, sir, and she'd not known me well. I'd carried her bags now and then

219

– she used the hotel quite often. The boy will take you up, sir.'

John tapped lightly on the door of Veronica's sitting room. She opened it, turned and went over to the window, leaving him to follow and close the door behind him. He moved up close behind her and she leant back, her body against his. She said, very softly –

'I'm going home this evening, now. There's a train at seven o'clock and I'll have something to eat when I'm back. The farmer's brother, the half-wit I spoke of, will bring the trap to the station. You can't dine here, you said so. I've no more use for Dublin.'

John sighed and she turned and put her hands on his shoulders.

'So perhaps, John, we'd better – have tea? I won't have to leave the hotel until half past six or thereabouts.' Her eyes were smiling. Very gently, he took her hands from his shoulders, stepped back and looked at her as steadily as he could. He had been thinking hard throughout the last few hours, thinking and calculating what he should say. And what he should not say. It had not been at all easy.

'Veronica, there are one or two words I must say to you. I don't want you to respond. I just need to tell you one or two things.'

She started to speak, a look of surprise on her face, but he shook his head violently.

'No, Veronica, darling, please listen to me. You see, I can't stay long.

'Everbody knows we're having – the Army and the police are having – to search everywhere, every possible hiding place, every suspect house, for a number of wanted men. People who got away, people who were active in the rebellion, who were seen in Dublin last week. When they're found they'll be tried and some of them will be shot. You know that.'

Veronica said nothing, and he added, very quietly, 'And people who help them, hide them, will, of course, be accessories after the fact to their crime. Treason. And will, I presume, suffer the same penalty.'

'Of course, we all know this,' said Veronica, with a show of impatience. 'These sweeps and searches, everybody knows of them. Not round us, of course – there's hardly a house that's not leased to somebody at the Curragh, hardly a cottage that's not in military hands or in hard, loyalist hands. But of course these searches are going on in other parts. What are you trying to tell me?'

He murmured, so that she could just hear him, as he judged.

'A good many people know the names of the most wanted men, of course. Names like Seamus Burke, for instance.'

Her eyes were on his. Very serious.

'Every possible house will be searched, Veronica. Very, very soon.'

There was absolute silence between them. After a little, he said, 'I think I'd better be going. And you'll want to be packing, to get to that train. Maybe there's even an earlier one.'

Still she said nothing.

'So I'd best do without – tea.'

Veronica came swiftly to him, put her arms around him and whispered, 'Yes, go now.'

'I'll go. And God be with you.'

'Thank you, John. Thank you, my dearest. I'll write, perhaps.'

'Perhaps. In a little while.'

'Yes. In a little while. But perhaps not.' She kissed him on the lips.

When John got into the lift, another figure was also occupying it. The lift boy made way for him. The light was not good, but as the boy started to wind down towards the ground floor a voice said, 'Good heavens! John Marvell!'

'Hello, Drew.'

'And what are you doing on the second floor of the Claremont Hotel? Do our gallant staff spend their afternoons in hotel bedrooms? If so, no wonder they got a little caught out over Easter!'

John looked away, smiled, shook his head, made no reply. As they reached the ground floor and the lift boy opened the creaking grille gate, John said in as friendly a tone as he could manage, 'And what brings you to Dublin?'

'Dear boy, it's where interest focuses for a week or so. And the Prime Minister himself coming, they say! Stories abound.'

'I'm sure you'll tell them well.'

'As usual, dear boy,' said Drew, in a detested voice John remembered vividly, 'I burrow around. I burrow around.'

In the office on the following morning, John heard a hum of conversation from Withers' room next door, and thought he could make out Cosmo's voice. He had not seen his brother-in-law the previous evening: he had gone to bed early, and at ten o'clock Cosmo had not yet returned. When John had been at his desk about half an hour, Cosmo's head came round the door.

''Morning. Would you come in to the Colonel a minute, John?'

John went with him to the office where Withers, as usual, was patrolling the floor restlessly. He was holding a bit of paper in his hand. John thought and expected that it was Thomas Feely's note. He saluted, and Withers grunted and suddenly waved the piece of paper at him.

'Seen this?'

John peered at it. It was without its envelope.

'I think so, sir. It looks like a message a rather drunken Irishman wrote down for Captain Paterson on Thursday night. I said I'd get it to him. I gave him a sovereign. I knew Paterson had some – odd contacts. I thought this might be one.'

'You gave the man a scrap of paper to write on.'

'I did, sir. I also had an envelope in my pocket and gave him that. He was so anxious that Captain Paterson should have this, personally, that I thought he'd be happier if he could see it into an envelope and seal it himself. Childish, I suppose, but he was a pretty primitive character.'

'But could write.'

'Yes, sir. He could write.'

'And spell, for instance, Paterson's name correctly.'

'I helped him with that.'

'You helped him with that,' said Withers, nodding. John was

222

unsure of the Colonel's mind from his tone. He said again, 'You helped him with his spelling. And did you read his message?'

So far John had spoken the exact truth. Now he lied. He was expecting this, but had thought it would first come from Cosmo. There are times, John knew – perhaps very few – when lies have to be told. Such occasions often arise from any intolerable division of loyalty.

'There are a good many things about me,' Veronica had once said, 'you don't know.'

'No, sir.'

'You don't know what Feely's information was?'

'No, sir. He was very firm that it should only be given to Captain Paterson. He said something like "Billy Devlin told him Captain Paterson would give him money."'

Withers now gave John the scrap of paper.

'Read it.'

John took a moment, hoping he was not over-acting. Then he read aloud: 'Seamus Burke is being hidden at Ballinslaggart House, near the Curragh.'

They were both watching him. He said, with, he hoped, a steady voice, steady but unbelieving, 'That is my brother's house, Colonel!'

'I know that, idiot boy,' said Withers. John felt comforted by the familiar abuse, never serious.

'I know that,' Withers said, 'I've dined there. Well – what do you make of it?'

John pretended to reflect.

'I believe I have a clue, sir. I've seen my sister-in-law, whom you know, recently. In fact, I'd had dinner with her at the Claremont before returning to Headquarters that night. She's been spending a night or two in Dublin – domestic problems. She mentioned to me she'd just sacked a groom. I'm positive – I didn't pay much attention, but I'm positive – the name was Thomas Feely. A drunk. Unless it's an extraordinary coincidence, this sounds like the same fellow – I'd forgotten the name until now. This note is probably an attempt to incriminate Veronica – my sister-in-law. To get his own back.'

'Do you think he'd dream up such a thing, imagine we'd ever believe it about the wife of a British Colonel?'

'Unless it were true, that is,' Cosmo said softly.

John was ready for that one, too.

'May I speak frankly, sir? And confidentially?'

'Please do.'

'You know my brother's wife, sir. You know she's a very charming woman, of complete integrity if I may say so. But she's impulsive – and a bit of a romantic. I think she's probably often set out to shock the – the more conventional sort of officers' wives or others, anybody in fact, by expressing pretty outrageous opinions. Political opinions, I mean.'

'Nationalist opinions, you mean,' said Withers. His voice was not unfriendly.

'I expect so, sir. And I dare say this was quite widely known. If Feely had a grudge he might well reckon it would be credible to put it round she'd harboured a well-known Shinner. If her house, unlike other officers' houses, was searched, the mud would stick, and it would obviously upset her.'

They were still both looking at him carefully, silently. After what seemed to John an age, Withers said, 'I expect you're right. But – I don't like saying this to your brother's brother, but I've got to – Ballinslaggart's being searched.'

'This morning,' said Cosmo agreeably. 'I spoke to the police at midnight when I got back. They'd nobody to put on to it until this morning.'

'Beastly for your sister-in-law,' said Withers. 'I'm sure the police will be tactful, but it's bound to be a shock. Will you be seeing her again, soon?'

'No, sir. I don't think so.'

That afternoon Cosmo took John's arm as he was walking down a passage in the officers' mess, about to climb the stairs to his bleak, cramped, comfortless bedroom, one which he was nevertheless ashamed to occupy when he thought of better men in dugouts in France.

'Ballinslaggart's clean! Clean as a whistle!'

John nodded his head. His heart was beating in a way which

he reckoned must almost be audible. He said nonchalantly – 'Of course.'

'As you say, of course. Of course, old boy. Of course, of course, of course!'

CHAPTER XII

John never went to Ballinslaggart. At the end of May, 1916, he had a letter from his mother, expressing pleasure that Veronica had asked to come to Bargate for a few weeks – weeks which would cover Alan's next leave, still hoped for in late June or early July.

'They've had no sort of life together, poor things,' Helena wrote, reflecting words of John's to Veronica, 'Like all of you, of course, darling. But somehow I feel Veronica is so unanchored.' She meant, of course, that unlike Hilda, Veronica wasn't pregnant. But she meant a good deal more.

Then, at the end of June, John heard that Alan had not, after all, come home and that Veronica had taken a small flat in London. Alan's leave was deferred and it was soon clear from the newspapers why. Alan was now a Lieutenant-Colonel on the Staff in Fourth Army of the British Expeditionary Force. On 1st July the divisions of Fourth Army climbed from their trenches in the early morning and walked slowly towards the enemy over the gentle, rolling country north of a certain right-angled bend in the River Somme. Twenty thousand of them had fallen by nightfall. Soon everyone became familiar with new names from the Press reports – Pozières, Thiepval, Delville Wood, the Schwaben Redoubt. At the end of July, Withers summoned John rather formally, unlike his usual habit of breaking into John's own room and striding up and down. A piece of paper lay on the Colonel's blotter and he was sitting at his desk.

'What's this mean?'

John looked as blank and enquiring as he could and Withers waved the paper at him irritably.

'This application of yours. What the hell do you think you're playing at? You've never discussed this with me, your superior. Now you have the cheek to slap down in front of me an application to transfer to the infantry. Why?'

John had done his homework.

'Sir, a number of officers from other Arms, including Yeomanry, are being accepted for transfer for the duration of the war to infantry regiments. I have applied to transfer to our county regiment. I mean my home county.'

'I can read,' said Withers. 'You still haven't told me why?'

John was deliberately obtuse.

'Well, sir, naturally I still have a good many acquaintances in it, and they're mostly local men – particularly in the Territorial and Service battalions – and . . .'

'I don't mean that, you half-wit. Of course you know people in the battalions of your local regiment. I wouldn't be surprised if you haven't been sounding out the Colonel of it and so forth, preparing the ground behind my back –'

This was entirely correct. John remained courteously silent.

'What I mean, as you know perfectly well, is why you want to go to the bloody infantry? Why you want to leave this important job, for which you were requested and where you are just beginning to be something like useful? Why, incidentally, you want to leave your Yeomanry Regiment? They're unlikely to take it as much of a compliment.'

John's regiment, after withdrawal from the Dardanelles, was in Egypt. Little seemed to be happening there.

'May I speak, sir?'

'You'd damned well better speak.'

'I have a Medical Board in September. I'm sure I'll be passed fit. When that happens I want to serve again at the front. That means France. It's infantry that's doing the fighting in France. Even the cavalry, as you know, sir, are often being used as infantry in the line. It seems to me sensible to do the thing properly and transfer. I'm told if it goes through I'll be sent on a course at Aldershot. Then I'd be posted to one of the regiment's battalions in France or Flanders. They've got in all –'

227

'I didn't ask for a lecture on Douglas Haig's order of battle. I asked you *why*! And you've not yet told me. I've not the slightest intention of sending this application higher, I may add.'

'Do you mean, sir,' John said, 'why do I want to serve again at the front?'

Withers was silent and glared at him, and John met his eye and didn't look away. They had always liked each other. John knew perfectly well he would forward the application, and knew he would dislike doing so. John also knew why. The casualty lists were explicit. Cosmo had left two weeks before and was, as usual, doing something indeterminate, temporarily attached to the General Staff in London. John knew he would turn up soon in France – or somewhere else if, improbably, the war took a different turn. Meanwhile, there was nobody in Dublin to tell John he was a fool. And had there been, it would have made not the slightest difference. As Withers looked at this slim, determined young man he knew, without question, how it would be; and he was sad.

John had been careful in letters to Hilda. If the truth, he had certainly not conveyed the whole truth. Their child was due to appear in November.

'My darling, as you know, I've a Medical Board in September, and my leg is so much better I'm bound to be passed fit. I don't want to stay here, in this job and in this Godforsaken country. I don't want to go back to the regiment in Egypt, if I can decently avoid it. It's miles away from you and it's a sideshow. I'm exploring the chances of exchanging regiments, joining the infantry "for the duration", as they say. They need officers pretty badly, and it would mean courses at home and then, I suppose, a battalion somewhere in France – presumably in 1917. Leave at home regularly! I might get command of a company pretty quickly. And I'd never be far from you, my own love –'

Hilda wrote back without equivocation or illusion.

'I think that in Egypt you'd be far from me, but safer and with a better chance of coming back to me in the end. I have to say this, because we both know it's true. I can sense you're unhappy in Ireland. You must do what you feel is right, my darling.'

Withers waved him to beat a retreat from the room.

Exactly a year after this conversation, on 30th July, 1917, John was reminded of it by the arrival of an unexpected letter. It was from Colonel Withers in Dublin, full of exasperated comments on the state of Ireland, the idiocy of Government and the course of the war. Letters home were sieved by a censorship (which officers themselves had to exercise over the letters of their men) but John was never sure whether a reverse process applied, and whether there was any covert scrutiny of those they received. Had the authorities been minded to watch the mail for subversive thoughts being communicated to soldiers, they could have done worse than open any envelope bearing Withers' writing. He was incorrigible – indiscreet. thoroughly disloyal to his superiors, entirely charming, and John chuckled as he read. A sentence at the end, however, aroused mixed feelings.

'I remember that business of allegations that your brother's house was sheltering Sinn Fein. I wonder what he thought of it himself, when his wife told him – I rather thought we'd get an official complaint, and the police were sure of it, but I never heard a word. I've not seen him myself, of course, since they've given up Ballinslaggart, and your sister-in-law hasn't, as far as I know, been in Ireland. I haven't congratulated you, by the way, on your son's arrival.' (Hilda's eldest, Anthony, had been born in November, 1916.)

John, too, had no knowledge of Alan's reaction to the fact that Ballinslaggart had been searched. They had never discussed it at their brief meetings in France. John imagined that Veronica told Alan how Feely had put an evil tale around after his own dismissal, and that everybody had 'been apologetic' but felt they had to make sure no undesirable strangers were lurking unsuspected in the stables, or something of the kind. It wouldn't have been difficult, thought John, although had Alan been less busy he might still have taken it up with a certain amount of indignation. But before coming to France, John had only had one longish talk with Alan at Bargate on an autumn leave of Alan's in 1916, while John was undergoing the indoctrinatory pangs of transfer to the infantry. Alan had seemed very splendid, very authoritative and very knowledgeable. He had asked a little about Gallipoli.

'It was a stupid sideshow. Hopeless planning.'

'Well, Alan, we landed with high hopes, you know.'

'Of course. But it was a miserable business. Typical Churchill folly. The man's a menace.'

Alan had, of course, spent most of his leave in London, in the flat where Veronica was now living. And John, with a little contriving, had not seen Veronica since those Easter days in Dublin. Hilda made small pretence of liking her. She said, 'Veronica's a charmer. And she's got spirit and quality. But I never know what she'll do next. I'm afraid I never feel safe with her.'

'One could say the same of your elder brother, perhaps.' She smiled. Cosmo was now serving, almost prosaically, on the Intelligence Staff of an Army Headquarters in France.

'Perhaps one could. But it's different.'

The principal difference, John thought with affectionate understanding and a good deal of guilt, was Veronica's devastating femininity.

He stuffed Withers' letter into the capacious pocket of his tunic. It was an ordinary soldier's tunic – as at Gallipoli, company officers (and he was now a proud Company Commander), by the sensible order of their Commanding Officer, wore soldiers' uniforms and equipment, and carried rifles. Officers were targets anyway, and the less conspicuous the better. John counted himself lucky to be serving in a battalion which was admirably and humanely organized and commanded. Adaptation to a new part of the Army had not been difficult. John was no professional, had no deep encrustations of habit or prejudice to modify, and anyway had fought on his feet, cavalry Yeoman though he might be called, in his own brief period of battle at Cape Helles. He was happy. He had been with this battalion for three months: months of training, preparation, lecture, ceaseless expositions of forthcoming battle on improvised models in various Flemish village schoolrooms, commandeered like every standing building by troops.

30th July, 1917. And now, in a few hours, they were going to attack: John's first battle with this battalion and the battalion's first appearance in this sector. It would also be its first attack since emerging from the last damp misery of the Somme, in September. John had wondered whether his feelings, fears and reactions would be exactly the same as at Gallipoli, where the aftermath of being wounded had produced in his mind a certain exaggeration of the terrors of war. Two things helped him, and he knew it. First, he had greater responsibilities now. A Company Commander had in his hands the lives of more than a hundred men – indeed, at full strength John's company numbered over 150. The thought that his own performance might save them or destroy them, that his example would affect the conduct of all – these reflections were awe-inspiring, but they were also steadying. They left less room for personal fears to grow. And John knew that he was trusted. Although he had not shared with these men the experience of previous battle (and the majority were new reinforcements, out since Christmas) they had, he knew, summed him up and liked what they found. A modest man, he could not help wondering whether they were right; but he liked their smiles when he spoke to them, their ready response to his talks to the company, their alertness in saluting, their willingness. This was a good company, he thought. And he prayed, in simple, straight-forward terms, to be worthy of it.

The second factor which distracted him from his anxieties was the extraordinary – and, in terms of previous battle experience extraordinarily different – appearance of the landscape. They had, of course, seen a huge number of photographs of the front in general, and the piece of Flanders over which they were to attack in particular. No photographs had fully prepared John for that brown, devastated land.

They had marched through the shattered city of Ypres the previous day, moving up to it from the rest and training area the battalion had occupied in comparatively clean country for the last fortnight. Ypres was little but a pile of rubble. It was near-incredible that this, short years before, had been a thriving, busy market town, a place rich in Flemish history, something of a centre for discerning tourists. Now it was flat, except for the sad skeletons of a few once-soaring buildings, which had managed to preserve an upright wall or two, jaggedly marking the skyline.

Yet Ypres was not a place of the dead, a silent, stricken witness to calamity. On the contrary, the Army had given it an awful simulacrum of life of a new kind. Ypres contained a mass of military traffic. Stuck everywhere on broken walls were signs, many of them with a spick-and-span look which mocked their pathetic supports. Routes, supply dumps, offices in dugouts fashioned snugly from the ruins, were all clearly marked. Signal cable was much in evidence. And in every direction there moved lorries, wagons, columns of horses, guns, ambulances and, un-remitting, the tramp, tramp of marching men. There was music, too, as a battalion's corps of drums or pipe band would strike up at its head. This would go on bravely until a column was clear of the shattered city of Ypres, on the eastern side. On the road to Roulers. Or on the road to Menin. And then there was no music, and columns halted and started filing forward with long intervals between platoons. And nobody sang.

John's company had advanced with a gap equivalent to three minutes' marching time between platoons after emerging from Ypres. He saw then, for the first time, the muddy, shattered landscape which was known throughout the British Army as the Ypres Salient.

It was high summer, but with no green to be seen. No birds sang, no trees stood, no blades of grass pushed through the earth towards the sun. It was a desert – but a filthy, contaminated

232

desert. Everywhere there was mess and destruction. Everywhere there was the debris of an army, broken equipment, splintered wagons, dead horses, shell-cases, paper, and, inevitably, tins, tins, tins. It was a beastly landscape, and, over it, there hung an equally beastly smell. Somehow the frightful nature of the country was a distraction and thus, in a curious way, a help, something at which to wonder, food for the senses offsetting rather than exacerbating fear.

They moved forward in something like silence. They had marched for nine miles to Ypres itself from the west, drums beating, spirits high. Then they had edged forward into this mud-baked scene of desolation, platoon by platoon, moving through their own field artillery gun positions, guns dug into the mud, gunners regarding them indifferently, silently. John had never before seen so many guns. For a while, on their move forward that day, they seemed to have strayed into some sort of forest of artillery. And suddenly part of the forest would erupt into deafening sound.

Then they had passed the gun lines, and John recognized the entrance to the communication trench they had been told to expect. This would slope downwards, a ramp running into a trench, winding forward past a hundred corners towards the front line. He looked upwards as he started into that trench, remembering trenches at Gallipoli. The next time he would look levelly across ground of any kind would be when the whistles blew, John's among them, and the men for whose lives he was responsible would climb up short, wooden ladders and reach the parapet. Then they would all move forward together steadily towards the German trench line, which (he knew from countless presentations and rehearsals) would be 275 yards away.

That had all happened yesterday, and already John felt as if he had been a week in the trenches. They had, he thought, been somewhat lucky. As he entered the communication trench, he had noticed a large number of German observation balloons floating in the evening air high above the enemy lines. Moves forward into the trenches usually took place at night, but so great was the forward press of huge numbers of fresh battalions for the forthcoming offensive that every hour in the twenty-four had to be used. The battalion might have suffered from German shelling while moving in the open, the shelling directed from those balloons. Then, despite the extended order in which they moved, they would have lost some men, and fewer would have climbed those scaling ladders two days later. For tomorrow, at ten minutes to four in the morning of 31st July, they were going to attack as part of the Fifth Army, going to launch one of the greatest onslaughts of the war. But, as it happened, no shells came.

They would start filing into the assault trenches at quarter past midnight. It took – it would take – an age. Meanwhile, the men, except for the few on sentry duty, were kept in the large, evil-smelling dugouts which generations of their predecessors had excavated from the rat-ridden trench walls of the Ypres Salient. John and his officers saw to last-minute preparations, the food, the distribution of the dixies of tea, the cleanliness of weapons. Unbelievably, letters came forward – including John's from Colonel Withers. Commanders encouraged rest, and wondered how to rest themselves. Rest was not helped by their own artillery – ungrateful thought! As they had marched forward, as they had approached and emerged from Ypres, as they sat in the dugouts or went round the trenches, there was a continuous roar of artillery. Field guns fired periodic timed concentrations, largely all were told, at known German forward gun positions and reserve trenches. All the time heavy guns, further away but loud and deeply menacing, kept up a rumble of fire at targets far behind the enemy's trenches, at his dumps and main artillery lines. The Germans, they were told, were short of gun ammunition and their artillery was, anyway, being methodically destroyed. In spite of this a good many German shells fell in every hour. Some of them exploded disagreeably near, although John's company suffered no direct hit on a trench.

'They'll throw what they can at us,' John said to his Company Sergeant-Major, Robson, repeating the official version of fact 'throw what they can but it's not much. Compared to our own stuff.' To applaud his words a brisk and noisy concentration from

234

some of the nearest British gun positions, those through which they'd marched the previous evening, almost snapped his nerve-strings.

'The Jerries are probably saving their shells,' said Company Sergeant-Major Robson, a naturally pessimistic man. 'For tomorrow,' he added unnecessarily. Then he muttered something, saluted and withdrew. John had, for a while, the tiny dugout to himself. And he still had ten hours before the hands of his watch would stand at zero three fifty, 31st July, 1917.

'John!'

John peered towards the dugout entrance. A tall, field-booted figure stood there. At first he thought it was their Commanding Officer: he had been dozing. Then he saw with delighted astonishment that it was a visitor from the higher reaches of the Staff – the one, above all, who was welcome.

'Alan! My God, my dear, dear Alan.'

Alan took his hand, said, 'I've been visiting your brigade, took a bit more time and managed to get here to you. During this last week when you were in decent quarters, believe it or not I couldn't manage it, try as I did.'

John had not seen him for over four months, and laughed from sheer pleasure.

'What news?'

John was getting used to Alan's face again as the seconds passed. There was something amiss. He wasn't laughing when John laughed. He wasn't even smiling. There were one or two ration boxes in the dugout, improvised chairs.

'Do sit down, Alan. I'm afraid I've not much to offer you – I'll get Venner to brew some tea.' Venner was John's soldier-servant, an excellent man, capable of making tea in any conceivable circumstances.

'Thanks – no tea.' Alan remained standing.

John looked at his brother again. No doubt about it, something was wrong. After Alan had first taken his hand, then relinquished it, he hadn't moved. He stood very still in that damp, dark,

235

smelly place and just looked at John. There was a lamp on the table that threw weird, flickering shadows at the roughly revetted walls. John heard himself saying –

'Alan, there's nothing up is there?'

For one terrible moment he thought Alan had come to tell him that something awful had befallen those he loved, now at Bargate. Hilda? Their mother? Darling little Anthony?

Alan stood like a statue. Then he felt in his tunic pocket and pulled out a sheet of paper.

'I've got fifteen minutes here. It will be enough. Read that. It reached me last week.'

'Won't you sit down?'

Alan shook his head. John unfolded the paper.

It was a letter, a typewritten letter. John looked at once for the signature. It was unsigned. Anonymous. A long anonymous letter.

'Dear Colonel Marvell,

I believe you should, as a matter of honesty and decency, be made aware of certain things in the past which have been concealed from you. You have no doubt been informed by your wife and others that at the time of the Republican rising in Dublin last year your house was searched. One of the most wanted members of Sinn Fein, a man called Seamus Burke, had been seen committing crimes in Dublin on Easter Monday, and the police were hunting him. I do not know whether your wife told you that it was Seamus Burke the police were after when they searched Ballinslaggart, or, indeed, what the police told her. Anyway, Burke it was, and, as you know, nothing was found.

What you do not, I suspect, know and what as a respected British officer you ought now to know, is that Burke was, in fact, hidden at your house by your wife when he slipped away from Dublin through the cordon of troops on Easter Thursday. He undoubtedly lay up for some days at Ballinslaggart (he was reported to be wounded) and, also undoubtedly, he left the place before the police visited it. Furthermore, he did so because he was warned. Warned in time to get away.

I say these things are "undoubted", because Burke has now been arrested in Kerry where he has been living in hiding. He was eventually betrayed by a cottager, and has been extensively interrogated. It is possible, however (he has, I am told, been very co-operative), that the more serious charges against him will be dropped. Meanwhile, he has been most explicit about his escape from Dublin. He was hidden by Mrs Marvell, and he was warned to escape by Mrs Marvell.

At this point you are probably exclaiming that the story is nonsense, and wish to discover how I know all this. I am not at liberty to disclose proof; and I think (although this is as yet, I believe, uncertain) that the authorities will be hesitant to proceed against your wife on the very serious charges which could undoubtedly be laid against her. The matter, therefore, is likely to be left dormant, and it is entirely open to you to disbelieve it. Perhaps you are sufficiently skilful to extract the truth from your wife in a form that would set your mind at rest, although I doubt it. Suffice it to say that all this happened, whether you believe it or not. I have excellent sources of information, and I know that what I have written above is true.

Since such incredulity as you may feel is very natural – this, after all, was treasonable conspiracy – I may be able to help you by providing some background of which you are probably also unaware.

Your wife's behaviour has been entirely consistent. Her first husband worked for the Germans (in a small way, and for money). When he cut his throat, your wife, in effect, inherited his mantle. Her sympathies are passionately Irish Nationalist. To give shelter, therefore, to Seamus Burke was in her eyes a natural duty.

There had probably been many others. I doubt if the authorities think they can prove much of this, hence (in addition to ordinary reluctance to have a scandal) the unlikelihood of prosecution, unless they decide to proceed against her on the uncorroborated word of Seamus Burke, whose real use, of course, has been to inform on other and more important rebels. But I assure you that I know enough to be convinced of the truth of what I have written, and I have thought it only right to share the conviction with yourself.

There remains the comparatively small point of how your wife knew (unless, improbably, it were pure coincidence) that Ballinslaggart House was about to be searched. She, as you know, dismissed a groom who had obviously sniffed out the truth, and she may have panicked at her own imprudence and realized the man would get his own back by disclosure, and that Burke must go. I fear, however, that there is a little more to it than that, and that I must, over another matter, cause you additional pain. Again, I have considered carefully whether to do so. But I think you have a right to know. I shall be scrupulous here. Some of what follows is guesswork, unlike what I have written so far.

You probably know that your brother, John Marvell, has for a long time been in love with your wife. Before the war they were, of course, lovers – rather indiscreetly so. At the time of the Easter Rising they met in Dublin. It is probable that they not only met but went to bed together. It is near-certain that John Marvell knew or suspected that your house was about to be searched. And it is, I am afraid, a very fair presumption that he warned your wife – his mistress. Her life, after all, was at risk. I know the authorities did not, in fact, execute any women in the aftermath of Easter 1916, but there was no reason why that should necessarily have been so. I regret that you have, in your immediate family, not one but two malefactors, and I can imagine how painful it must be to you, and can sympathize. But I do not think you should be kept in ignorance for ever.'

It took John several minutes to read this, and during them Alan stood without moving. When John had finished he raised his eyes to Alan's, dimly seen in that fusty, malodorous place. Alan stretched out his hand and flicked the letter away, replacing it in his pocket.

'Well, John. True?'

'Alan, this is a ghastly slander. You can't condemn your wife or anybody else on the strength of an anonymous letter and I'm sure you never would. When did it arrive?'

'Four days ago. True, John?'

'Alan, I'm sure I know who wrote this filth.'

'Interesting. Please answer my question.'

John looked at him.

'What is your question? What parts of this vicious diatribe –'

'Well, let's start at the end, as being the bit that must be within your own knowledge. Did you go to bed with Veronica?'

'In Dublin I had dinner with Veronica, as she has obviously told you, indeed as I told you in a letter some time ago, and when we talked on leave at Bargate. Of course I didn't go to bed with her.' John's voice shook. Alan was looking at him intently.

'Have you ever been to bed with Veronica?'

'Alan – No – I mean –'

'Thanks, John. Naturally I knew you'd been crazy about her, you blurted that out when she and I got engaged. But she told me – and I must say I didn't think – Well, well!'

'Alan, that is in the distant past. Why let it upset you or anything else now?'

'Why, indeed! Something about being jolted by falsehood, I suppose. Something about wondering if there's been only one lie or many.'

'Don't think like that. Don't let yourself think of your wife like that.'

'Another question. Did you warn her that Ballinslaggart was to be searched, was under suspicion?'

'No.'

Alan looked at him and said calmly, 'I don't believe you. On either count.'

'In God's name, why not?'

'Because I know you so well. You're an incurably truthful man. And a rotten liar. You warned her. You'd been lovers, perhaps you were lovers again. You didn't want her shot, you warned her. And you did so because you knew she was a traitor. Or is it traitress? I can't remember.' Neither of them tried to smile.

John said, 'Alan, I swear to you that my relations with Veronica in Dublin were – innocent. And I swear to you that if she sheltered Seamus Burke – or did anything else – she never told me of it. As to that business about inheriting Gaisford's mantle, about working for the Germans earlier – I don't believe it.'

John was sincere. He did not believe it. He would, he thought fiercely, have known. Have guessed. Or would he?

Alan said, 'Hmm! Rather a convincing letter, don't you think?'

'No, it's vile, malicious. And as I told you, I think I know who wrote it. A journalist, a fellow who was once after Veronica and must hate her very much indeed, who wants to hurt her, hurt you and all of us. A fellow called Drew. You know his name from before the war. Don't let him win, Alan. Tear it up.'

'All the same,' said Alan reasonably, 'it would be nice to be sure of the truth, wouldn't it? And I rather think I am. I'm afraid I reckon the substance of this letter is accurate. What I do about it is my own business. As to you – well, if we both survive this war it might be best not to see much of each other, don't you agree? But I wanted to show you the letter. It seemed only fair.'

'I wish to God you hadn't!'

'Yes, well, scenes of violent indignation aren't much in my line, but I think I'll go now. Good luck with your attack tomorrow morning, by the way. A good deal depends on it, as you know.'

His manner made deadly clear that he was expressing conven-

240

tional concern for Fifth Army's operation and in no way for a brother's survival.

John said – 'Alan!' and he knew he had a sob in his voice, but Alan nodded, turned on his heel and was gone. The lamp was burning very low.

It started to rain that night. At ten minutes to four it was raining hard. Men's feet slipped on the rungs of the trench ladders as the whistles blew. John lost seventeen of his men – nothing, he realized later, and others were quick to say, compared to the first day of the Somme. Nothing compared to the later phases of the operation they started that July morning, that which came to be called 'Third Ypres' and reached its beastly climax and conclusion months later with the capture of a spot on the map called Passchendaele. John hated casualties and felt them more and more as the war went on. He hated losing those seventeen men. The opening day of the battle was, nevertheless, accounted a success although the wretched weather soon turned their gains to nothing and their spirits to depression. But of the actions in which John took part, that July morning battle was the one of which he had no subsequent recollection whatsoever. He walked forward, shouting, he afterwards supposed, the usual things, reacting to surprise, danger, opportunity, fear in the usual way. He retained absolutely no remembrance of it. His memory leapt to the middle of the same afternoon when they had not only occupied their objective trench and easily beaten off the first German counter-attack, but had been relieved by one of the follow-up battalions of the brigade and were back in reserve trenches. Their Colonel was walking among the men, cracking a joke here, giving a word of encouragement there, his eyes stern and watchful, his voice quiet and kind. The men thought the world of him. He drew John on one side.

'I want a word with you, John.'

They ducked into one of the dugouts in the reserve trench face and the Colonel said to two subalterns who were in it – 'Just clear out for a minute, will you? I want a word with Captain

241

Marvell.' He said it gently and they moved at once. Tired, inexperienced boys, both had done well, and John took the occasion of his first moment alone with the Colonel to say so.

'I'm glad to hear it. Listen, John, I've bad news for you. I decided not to tell you until the attack was over but I've got to do it now. A shell got your brother after he'd left Battalion Headquarters yesterday evening. Stray shell. He knew nothing. Killed instantly. Heard about it around midnight. No point in telling you then. God knows you had plenty to think about.'

There was a rumble and crash outside. German shelling had got heavier in the last twenty minutes. John looked dumbly at his Commanding Officer and the Colonel held out a flask.

'I'm terribly sorry, John. He was a wonderful fellow, one of the best out here. You don't get many on the Staff with the reputation he had for both efficiency and courage. He was always up, seeing for himself. You know that. I'm terribly, terribly sorry.'

He patted John's shoulder and John said, 'Thank you, sir,' and drank a swig of whisky from the flask.

The Colonel added, 'And thank you for today, John. The company were splendid.'

Then he left the dugout.

CHAPTER XIII

Cosmo said, 'Heard from Hilda lately?'

John nodded. 'Yes, I got a letter yesterday. All well. My mother was knocked over by Alan going, of course.'

'Of course.'

'And although it's nearly eight months ago the wound's as fresh as ever. I can tell that from her letters to me. She's completely unreconciled. Poor mother – Alan was everything to her.'

'I imagine now that you and Hilda will live at Bargate one day, John?'

'Of course. If one can possibly afford such a thing. And if I – well, anyway, I never think about life after the war. One doesn't. One lives from day to day, doesn't one?'

'I think I always do that, war or peace, to tell the truth. Tell Hilda you've seen me, when you write. As a brother, I'm a rotten correspondent.'

He looked with affection at John. 'How enormously older he is,' thought Cosmo. 'Are we all? When the war began he was young – he looked young, laughed young, talked young, walked young. Now he's hard-bitten, grave. At twenty-eight, middle-aged. I suppose the war has done us out of our youth, or greatly foreshortened it. Does he ever really laugh as he did?' Cosmo wondered. 'I've not heard it for a long time. The spring has gone from his stride, too. He's formidable. Stern. Very splendid. But what about the young beau Hilda married only three years ago?'

The front had been pretty static that winter, and Cosmo had found a good many opportunities to visit his brother-in-law. It was comforting, John found, to be able to talk about family, about home, about Hilda, to one who loved her. He looked forward greatly to seeing Cosmo. He had never spoken to him of Alan's final terrible visit. Once Cosmo said, 'I suppose you'd just seen Alan, when . . . he was visiting your brigade, wasn't he?'

'Yes, I saw him for a moment or two.'

Now it was March. March, 1918. John's company had lost a good many men in the final attack put in at Ypres in the autumn. The cruel rain, falling from that first July dawn, had soon turned the Salient, earlier than in most years, into a sickening, squelching inland sea of mud. To leave the duckboards above ground was to find oneself up to the thighs in something the consistency of chocolate mousse, only it didn't smell like chocolate mousse. Men drowned in that mud, though not, John thanked God, any of his. They were never dry. And in the later stages they had to attack – actually move forward towards the enemy – over ground not greatly dissimilar. More often than not these attacks did, however, succeed in reaching at least the first objectives. Day and night shells were poured on to the German positions and behind them. When John's company took prisoners, mostly very young lads by now, they were wide-eyed, shaken, sometimes near-witless from the weight of the British bombardment they had sustained. But they never gave their enemies an easy time, one could never take a chance with them. While there was life in them there tended to be fight also. John's battalion took a large number of prisoners from a Saxon regiment in one of the awful October battles, and he remembered one, an officer, tall and with hair that looked as if it had turned prematurely white. His lined face was that of an old man: his service book showed John that he was thirty. He was erect but manifestly in great pain: one arm was in an improvised sling and there was blood soaking through the inside of his breeches. John walked over to him.

'We'll get you to the dressing station as quick as we can. You'd better sit down.'

'Thank you, Captain. I prefer to stand.'

He spoke in clipped, correct English. John looked again at the book. Major Brendthase. John thought he had heard the name

244

before in some connection. Probably it was not uncommon. The Major stared straight ahead, very pale.

'Well, Major, I expect you're glad to be out of it.'

The prisoner shifted his eyes and glared at John. Wretched, bleeding and captive that he was, he made John feel uncomfortable.

'Sir, I am a German officer!'

John shrugged his shoulders and moved on. What could one do with a man who regarded as an insult the suggestion that he would be relieved to be, for a while, out of the battle, safe from its tribulations? But that was the enemy. To defeat spirits like that was the task. A little later John's Company Sergeant-Major produced a muddied notebook.

'This was on that Jerry officer, sir.'

It was a diary. British officers were forbidden to keep diaries lest they were captured and betrayed information. John supposed the Germans had the same rule. In both armies, no doubt, it was often disregarded. Some men, often the best men, scrupulous and discreet in other things, found their only relief in getting rid of their desperate emotions by writing them down. For no eyes but their own, or so they hoped. John glanced at Major Brendthase's notebook. The man had been commanding a battalion and the Intelligence people at higher Headquarters would probably get something out of this personal record. There should be no delay in passing it back. The Sergeant-Major said, 'Runner going back to Battalion Headquarters with routine messages, sir. Shall I send it with him?'

'Yes,' said John, turning the leaves, 'I'll write a message to go with it.' Then he said, 'Keep him for a few minutes. It may take me a moment or two.' He could understand a little. He began to read, skipping freely but absorbing the general sense of the *Tagebuch* of Major Gerhardt Brendthase. He could not resist it.

'*19th October*

It has been a principle of our General Staff that any officer's promotion on the Staff must be accompanied by a period of proving himself in command of troops in the new rank; but the principle has had to be largely ignored in this war because of the enormous need for trained Staff officers in the expanded army. I had to work hard and make my case with difficulty in order to serve again with troops. I had to intrigue and cajole in order to win a better chance of dying. My application was considered by von Below himself. Anyway, here I am.

Was I mad? I know that the only relief, the only *peace* I could inwardly achieve, was to share to a greater extent the sufferings of these German soldiers in the front line who, as we all knew was imminent, would soon face one of the most terrible experiences of the war, here in Flanders. Yet perhaps I offended against a fundamental human obligation – to survive. It would have been easier to survive had I not taken this step. But I took it, and I am still glad, although the sights and sounds of every day are almost more than a man can endure. For myself I honestly care little. But I am tormented all the time by the sufferings of these decent, innocent Saxon boys who are so patient, so generous to each other, so obedient still; and so afraid.

20th October

Yesterday the English shelled us for four hours very intensively. During that time it was impossible to speak, impossible to hear, impossible to think. There were, at one moment, three shells that fell simultaneously on the battalion's own support trenches, blowing twenty-one men to bits and burying a number of others in mud and debris. In the support trenches, as we moved along them, we were pushing past severed arms, legs, torsos, heads, all covered with both blood and mud. We heard the shrieks of wounded men who had not yet been carried to the medical post, punctuating the occasional gap in the roar of exploding shells, as if a massed orchestra suspended a deafening crescendo for a few seconds and a lone flute, high, touching, was audible. We were unlucky – the men spend most of the time in deep dugouts, well prepared, but a relief was taking place.

The English bombardment, as so often in these last weeks, was followed by one of their attacks. They walk forward very slowly – indeed it would be impossible to do otherwise, to skirmish, double or manoeuvre, since the ground here in front of our positions is a morass of mud and water. The enemy's shells have broken up the landscape on a scale man can never before have dreamed of, it has rained incessantly, and there is, of course, no drainage. So they walk forward slowly and in many cases they reach our trenches and occupy them because nobody on our side is left alive except a few brave individuals who are shot or bayoneted. Then there is fighting in the dugouts and in the trenches themselves as our men emerge from the dugouts and start bombing battles up and down our own lines. No system or order – a confusion of bloody little fights and an atmosphere full of yells and screams, of fury and terror. Then we achieve some sort of stability, men find each other, officers find their commands, it is over for a little, maybe a short distance to the rear, maybe not. But yesterday they did not reach our trenches at all. One minute the uneven, struggling line of Tommies was visible, about two hundred yards away. A moment later one saw nothing – they had disappeared. They had collapsed, dead, wounded, or simply exhausted, in the mud and will have struggled back to their own lines or made new rat-like habitations among the shell holes in front of us. But soon they will come again, shell us to hell again, lurch towards us again, die again, and maybe take a trench here or a trench there.

21st October

We used to counter-attack instantly if we lost a trench.

We have stopped that – and I have had a hand in stopping it. Premature counter-attacks are all right in theory – strike the enemy when he is off balance, relaxing after his success on the objective and so forth – but in practice, here in Flanders, such operations are futile. Any attack, here, must be preceded by a properly organized artillery plan, and that demands system and time. Furthermore, in the immediate aftermath of an English attack, there is such confusion that it is impossible to sort out proper objectives, form up the troops and so forth. There are no features, no landmarks, all is mud, mud, mud. So now we take time and move deliberately. Sometimes we are successful, sometimes not. So that we recover a trench now and then and lose a lot of men doing it; or fail to recover it and lose a lot of men that way too. And, week after week, we are bleeding to death in this hell of Flanders, and still come the English bombardments and the English attacks. And they are in hell too, one imagines.

22nd October

As I see them, the English, walking towards us, or – if they sometimes find a piece of drier ground – making absurd little runs; as I gaze at them through a trench telescope, or suddenly find them all around our men on the rim of the trench, shouting, shrieking, shooting; as I watch them being knocked over by our machine guns, dropping like targets on a range, going down as objects, impersonal – I have sometimes wondered whether, here and there beneath their muddy brown uniforms, there may not be a man I saw, passed in a crowd, even exchanged words with on my visits to England long ago. They were friendly, rather silent people, quite helpful to a stranger I remember. I could never understand them when they talked amongst themselves with their odd slang words, their laughs for no discernible reason. But their eyes, I remember, on trains, or on their omnibuses I took in London, their eyes were patient, long-suffering, not unlike the eyes of my Saxon boys here. Now I knock them over like rabbits, and they blow my lads to pieces, and that has become the only world all of us know. Perhaps one day –'

The last diary entry finished in mid-sentence.

Soon afterwards John's battalion was finally withdrawn from the Ypres Salient and moved to clean rest billets near the old Somme battlefields in Picardy. There they had received reinforcements, repaired their spirits, their clothes and their equipment, rested, drilled, trained and prepared for the spring. But the incident of Brendthase's diary returned to John's mind in a conversation with a newly posted officer, a Captain, posted from another battalion, like John a man of about thirty, whom he had found instantly sympathetic. John told him about the German officer. They had been enjoying a sense of leisure, a long walk in the clean country west of the Somme one January afternoon.

'Extraordinary people, aren't they, the Boches!'

The other laughed. His name was Henry Kinzel, a handsome, friendly man, with an infectious sense of humour. John had been delighted to discover in him a lover of books: Kinzel even had some aspirations towards publishing. They talked of subjects far from war. Kinzel, John gathered, was heir to a substantial family business but his heart was in literature and the arts, already something of a collector.

'Extraordinary people! I suppose I'm one of them!'

'You?'

'Oh, we're German in origin, my family came to England three generations ago. But I suppose I feel a certain itch of resentment when I hear people speak of the Germans as congenitally evil, as condemned through some remarkable inherited defect!' He laughed happily, without bitterness. He said, 'As a matter of fact, my father kept up with our German cousins and was particularly fond of them, though the most loyal Englishman you could imagine. And I know Germany well. We're all bilingual in the family – my father, oddly, thought it right to keep that up. Plenty of Boche in me still, you see! You probably don't know that they've been trying to get me on the Intelligence side, interrogation and so forth, because of it. Damned if I will – I prefer to be with my friends, bloody though it is.'

'What will people feel after all this – this beastly business is over, Henry? Do you think people will ever think straight again? Or have we doomed ourselves and future generations to live with fear and revenge for the rest of time? The rest of the century, anyway?'

Henry Kinzel considered. He looked sad.

'I hate judgements based on the emotions we all find easy to feel in war. It seems to me that to persuade people – perhaps particularly people in great democracies like Britain and America – to fight at all, you just have to tell them the enemy are fiends incarnate. You have to make it a matter of good and evil, black and white. You have to caricature. And they start to believe it. Then they go on believing it, and it isn't true. What began as a, perhaps necessary, propaganda expedient becomes a dangerously untruthful part of people's mental make-up, their prejudices, their perceptions. So the word "German" or "Englishman" starts to convey a fearful distortion, for evermore.'

'I dare say,' said John, 'but what about the Germans? We are told they're being filled up with hate for us by a pretty energetic propaganda machine. Will that hatred last, like ours? Presumably. It's a bleak outlook.'

Henry Kinzel said, 'I suppose the answer to all this lies in what happens after we've won. Because we will win – whatever the turn of events here in the next few months we will, in the end, win. And I think, don't you, that a tremendous responsibility will then lie with the victors.'

'It's going to be hard. People will want vengeance. There've been bad things done and a lot of blood's been shed.'

'Of course. I don't feel optimistic. But I think I know what's right, though I doubt if I'll be in a majority!'

He sighed, and John said impulsively, 'I'm *really* delighted you're with us. Tell me more about your publishing hopes.'

Happily, they talked books, and books again, until the January

250

sun began to sink beneath the frosted horizon of Picardy, delighting in quotation, discovery, enthusiasms joyfully removed from the temporary and sombre realities of the Western front.

After they had walked for an hour, their first of many walks together, Kinzel said, 'We've met before, you know.'

'Really? Not that Aldershot course –'

'No, no. It was in London. Before the war. I was a guest of your firm at a lunch, June, 1913, it was. An extraordinary thing happened – a fellow called Cosmo Paterson pulled a chair away from Dominic Drew, the journalist.'

'Good heavens!' said John. 'Were you there? I'd completely forgotten!'

'You and I didn't talk. Yes, I was there. And I'll tell you a curious thing about that incident I'll always remember –'

'You know Cosmo Paterson is now my brother-in-law? He's out here – Army Headquarters. Intelligence. I see him quite often.'

'I didn't know. Well, after that rather odd business I went up to Drew, to be friendly. I knew him slightly and although I didn't like him I felt sorry for him at that moment. He was rather shaken. You were all talking in groups, slipping away. I just wanted to smile and make him feel the room hadn't turned against him because he'd been on the floor. Odd how civilized adults can revert to the wolfpack – or the child-pack – while still looking impeccably mature.'

'You're right,' said John, impressed.

'Drew looked at me, not really taking in who I was, just needing to speak. He didn't refer to Paterson. Something else obsessed him. He was muttering. He murmured – "She laughed, naturally, but that doesn't matter" – presumably he meant Mrs Gaisford, you remember?'

'Yes, I remember. Since you've started on this, I should tell you that not only is Cosmo Paterson my brother-in-law, but Veronica is my sister-in-law! She married my brother Alan, who –'

'Yes, of course. Oh dear, I have blundered into it, haven't I! I'm so sorry –'

'Tell me what Drew said.'

'He said, "That doesn't matter. But she pitied me, she saw me as an object of compassion. That's the end!" He shook his head, then I felt embarrassed. And of course I didn't know her. I'd no idea what he meant, what was in his mind. I said something banal. Then – and I always remembered this, and wondered whether I'd ever meet you again – he said, to himself really – "John Marvell didn't smile. He was the only one with kindness in his eyes when I got to my feet again." Wasn't that curious? I didn't know you, of course, I'd only just shaken your hand on arriving at that lunch, but I'll always remember the incident, the odd violence of it, and Drew's remark. I hope you don't mind my telling you that. Not that it all matters. Long time ago.'

Kinzel's own eyes were enormously kind. John said, 'No, I don't mind at all. Not at all. I'm very glad you did. Very glad indeed.'

He remembered, with detachment, how he had loathed Drew at that time, resented his attitude toward Veronica, secreted jealousy for him which he didn't dare avow to himself. There had been kindness in his eyes, had there? He felt a curious, disproportionate gratitude. Then he thought of a certain anonymous letter to Alan and made a brief effort to recapture a hatred which came ever less naturally to him, whatever the cause.

'Yes,' said Cosmo, getting up to go, 'tell Hilda you've seen me. And give her my love. I might be over again next week. I've got to go round giving everybody the latest, week by week, day by day, on what the Jerries are brewing up for us.'

'They are, are they? Not just a scare, to keep us on our toes?'

'No, it will be big, no question of it. I wonder whether they, like us, will discover that attacking isn't a very happy occupation in this war! They've not tried, after all, since 'fourteen. Except counter-attacks, local stuff.'

'No. They've not tried.'

They said goodbye.

Hilda's last letter had given the usual tranquil news of Bargate, of Sussex, of Helena, of little Anthony. Her letter transported

John to another world, sometimes remembered with difficulty and never fully recovered during the brief, artificial periods of leave. A world where a different scale of values applied to those which dominated their lives in France.

'Do you remember our meeting at the Winters'?' Hilda had written. 'Mrs Winter died just before Christmas. Your mother says "very young", although she didn't seem like that to us, did she? Formidable but kind! But not very young! I'm sorry. Did you know that her husband is back in the House of Commons? He resigned before the war, said his health wasn't up to it. The war seemed to restore his health, or something, and he came in at a by-election last year! Politicians find it irresistible, don't they! Anyway, poor Mr Winter must be very shattered, she "carried" him a good deal, people always reckoned. I expect it's a good thing he's got Parliament to occupy him. He came here to lunch on Sunday. Your mother's nice to him . . .'

John thought about the Winters. He did indeed remember that weekend at Faberdown, his torment over Veronica, the blackmailing Drew, kind and somewhat ineffectual cousin Francis Carr – Francis who had recently married dear little Angela Forrest, Hilda's friend and companion on that occasion. It seemed a long time ago. But it led his thoughts to Veronica and Alan, and he did not care for that. He wondered – he had often wondered – whether there was anything left of Drew's beastly letter (it could only be his) when the German shell had done its business with Alan. John had seen nothing of Veronica. His letter to her on Alan's death had not been easy to compose. It had received no reply.

Five days later, John saw Cosmo when actually performing. Cosmo was, as he had said, occupied in touring the Army area, acting as a sort of guest speaker about the enemy in the countless presentations held at that time about how to meet the forthcoming German attack. Everybody knew that after the Russian revolution and collapse Germany would launch a major effort in the west. Everybody knew that the Germans were very short of food and much else, and that one more major effort to win the war should be their last. After that, presumably, it would be the Allied turn to attack, once again, as thoughout the previous three years. Meanwhile, in John's battalion, they looked forward with a certain satisfaction to the prospect of the Germans and not themselves walking towards entrenched defenders through a hail of machine-gun bullets, walking over earth heaving from the mass of shells which would devastate no man's land immediately the attacking infantry appeared. They also understood (and Cosmo's description that day confirmed) that there was a good chance that their battalion – their brigade, their division – were in the sector chosen by the enemy to attack. They certainly seemed to have opposite them a particularly large concentration of German troops.

Cosmo spoke well, that day, thought John, who had never before heard him in this capacity, and who, accustomed to the flippant, erratic, unpredictable Cosmo, was surprised at the professional, intelligent presentation his brother-in-law gave. The aerial photographs, enlarged so that all could see them, were impressive. Cosmo pointed out German guns, even tractors for moving ammunition, dumps and so forth. Everybody was quiet and attentive, absorbed by it all, rather solemn.

Company Commanders were dismounted and dressed like their men when in the trenches, but they ranked as mounted officers and John had managed to get a ridable horse, by making particular friends with the divisional veterinary officer. Not only was this welcome exercise – his leg still gave him a good deal of trouble, particularly in the winter, and he had for some time accepted that he would always be lame – but it gave him a certain independence and mobility. On this occasion he had ridden to the village where the presentation was held. Cosmo, too, had ridden over from Divisional Headquarters, where he had spent the previous night. After the performance was over John waited, and managed to detach his brother-in-law from the various exalted figures who were thanking and congratulating him for his efforts.

'Come and ride back with me to the company mess. It's quite near. We'll give you tea.'

He did, and as always it communicated a particular pleasure to John to be with him. It was drizzling, with a light spring rain, but it wasn't cold. 19th March.

'Cosmo, how soon do we really think this is going to start?'

'We picked up some Boche deserters yesterday, who were positive that tomorrow is the great day. I expect they're wrong, but we're taking it seriously. Must be in the next day or two, anyway.'

'We're going up tomorrow. Routine relief. I hope it doesn't catch us in the middle of it!'

'Into the forward zone?'

'Battle zone.'

The British defensive layout was in considerable depth, and included a main battle zone with a number of trench lines, and a forward line of trenches some way in front of that, called the forward zone. John's battalion was due to relieve another in the battle zone on the following day. 20th March.

'Well, good luck,' said Cosmo cheerfully. A little later, after jogging along in a companionable silence, he said, 'By the way, how's your sister-in-law, Alan's widow, Veronica?'

'I don't know. I've not seen her on any recent leave. In fact, I've not seen her since we were all in Ireland.'

'That was an odd time, wasn't it! Ballinslaggart and Seamus Burke and all that. Somebody told me that fellow's been arrested, some time last year. Or did I read it in a newspaper, I wonder?'

'I don't know.'

'It was an odd time. John –'

They rode on for a little. Cosmo said, just audible above the clip-clop of the horses' hooves, 'John, you tipped her off, didn't you?'

'Cosmo –'

'Yes, John, you read that scrap of message, and you guessed it was true and you tipped her off. Don't answer. You were quite right. You couldn't see a woman like that at risk.'

John turned and looked at him as they rode along. He said

quietly, 'You're right, of course. And I knew you guessed, at the time. But Cosmo, I want to say one thing to you. About Veronica.'

'Say on!'

'Francis Carr once told me that you referred to Veronica, to him, as a bad woman.'

'I remember it. I remember the occasion.'

'I want to tell you that you're mistaken, and that everybody who thinks that – and I've no doubt you're not alone – is mistaken. Veronica is a fascinating, attractive woman, she's a romantic, she's unconstrained by convention – all that I agree. But so far from being bad, she's a wonderful woman. She's a truly independent spirit. She does what she believes in. She acts out her convictions. They're not always mine – or haven't been. But she's a human being of rare quality. I don't expect I'll convince you. I don't say it simply because I was in love with her – which you know perfectly well. I say it because we are, we really are, speaking of a glorious person.'

It was a long speech, and in a few minutes their ride would take them to John's company mess: they were already entering the village. The drizzle had stopped.

Cosmo said softly, 'I'm glad you've spoken as you did. And I hope they'll not trouble her because of anything Burke or others may have said.'

'Cosmo, there's more to it than just that Ballinslaggart business. There's something else, a mixture of lie, truth and rumour but I've had to carry it about with me.'

Then John told Cosmo about the anonymous letter. He told him the allegations in that letter about Veronica's connection with the Germans. He told him everything – except what the letter had said about his own sleeping with Veronica in Dublin. That wasn't true and there was no need for his brother-in-law to hear it. The rest John told him. And he told him too, wretchedly, of how Alan and he had parted.

'Cosmo, no other soul knows of this. I expect the letter was destroyed with poor old Alan. But – well, obviously, some of us aren't going to survive this next show. I wanted you to know.

You'll be able – in case of trouble – to, well, orchestrate things so that the least pain is caused.'

Cosmo nodded. He did not appear shocked or surprised. He smiled and said, 'Pity one didn't kill Drew when he was up to his tricks, back in the old days! Perfectly justifiable to get rid of a fellow like that! Save a lot of trouble. Anyway, rely on me if it's ever necessary, dear old boy! Not many people would agree, but you can, believe me, rely on Cosmo!'

'I know I can.' John smiled at him, feeling a great deal of love. 'And Cosmo, I'm glad I told you the real truth about Veronica. You see, people look different, depending on how the mirror is angled. I've shown you, I promise you, that angle of the mirror which reflects the true Veronica.'

'Tell me,' said Cosmo, 'if you don't mind. Did she love your brother?'

John said flatly – 'No. It didn't work. But it wasn't anything to do with me. And I hope he didn't know – or, at least, that he died believing it would all be right between them in the end.'

'Do you think that possible?'

John often asked himself the same question, knowing in his heart that he believed the answer to be 'no' and that it grieved him. They had not found mutual joy, those two – that had seemed certain from Veronica's murmured frankness in Dublin, and John had succeeded in regretting the fact. It had not been easy. Then there was what Alan had died knowing or guessing about Veronica's sympathies in Ireland, her part at Easter, 1916.

Cosmo said, 'Don't answer. Why should you?'

He understands much, John thought gratefully. He is one who doesn't need everything to be spelt out.

Inconsequentially Cosmo said, 'I had a great friend, killed at Loos, who knew the little lady when she was a wild young thing in Ireland and saw her often until her first marriage. He used to hunt in Galway. He said she used to go like the devil himself.'

'I'm sure of it,' said John with feeling and a smile. 'Of that I'm entirely sure.'

'I used to know a cousin of hers once,' Cosmo said softly. 'Patsy. Patsy Dillon. Married that dull fellow Dillon that got himself killed early on, poor chap. She used to go like hell too, did Patsy. Knew her when I was – well, when I was pretty young.'

John nodded, expressionless. Patsy Dillon – a fast lady, slowed down, they said, neither by marriage nor widowhood. And Cosmo. He remembered something now. Hilda's lips had been pursed, loving, sisterly, a little concerned, saying, 'All a long time ago!' Something made him revert to their words of a moment before and he said – 'You probably wonder why Veronica married Alan. Well, she admired everything about him that was tough, and positive, and daring and skilful. She'd got all that herself and I suppose she was always looking for an equal – if possible for a master. Of course she lost her father when she was very young.'

'And so?'

'And so it didn't work,' said John, as before, and this time the conversation was closed.

They had reached their destination, and to John's disappointment Cosmo looked at his watch and said, 'I'm going to ride straight back. I'll have to cut tea.'

'I'm sorry. And thanks for listening.'

'Goodbye, John. Look after yourself.'

'Goodbye, Cosmo. Look after yourself, too.'

There was a thick fog over the whole of the battle zone two mornings later. Contrary to Cosmo's deserters' reports the Germans did not attack on 20th March and the relief by John's battalion took place without incident or disturbance. But that night, at about eleven, every man in John's company heard an increase in enemy artillery fire. Was this – could this be – the threatened offensive? British guns soon replied.

They got their answer in the small hours of the morning. At precisely twenty minutes to five on Thursday, 21st March, John's ears were assaulted by the noise of the most vicious bombardment he had yet heard in the war. He had been sleeping in a dugout and struggled out of it, pulling on equipment and helmet – the whole ground was shaking and trembling as from an earthquake. A man could only make himself heard by shouting.

From the trenches they could see the whole sky lit as if by some immense, simultaneous combustion, a giant striking a match, and a match that continued to burn. Their orders were to keep the men in dugouts until ordered to man the fire trenches. The noise seemed to intensify minute by minute. John had always detested noise, found it one of the most demoralizing aspects of war, and this was worse than he had ever experienced. Ears sang, the mind moved more slowly than it should, nerves tingled. John's Company Sergeant-Major – a new man, Priest by name: Robson had been killed at Ypres – held out a field telephone. It was the Adjutant on the line. His voice said, 'We think this is it!'

John had to shout to hear his own voice. 'I've made the same deduction!'

'The line's cut to Brigade.'

Telephone lines were cut throughout the Army sector. The German concentration of artillery fire had included a special heavy battery programmed to destroy buried telephone cable, and primarily directed, in the first hours, at all British Head-quarters and gun positions. The Adjutant kept them as well informed as he could. Battalion Headquarters survived the first hours unscathed. He rang again at 6 a.m.

'Apparently Brigade Headquarters have had a direct hit.'

It was true. A shell from a German heavy howitzer had done for their Brigade Commander and all but two members of his Staff. Somebody else, John imagined, one of the Battalion Com-manders possibly, would have to leave his battalion and assume some sort of control. It wasn't John's problem.

'Easing up, sir,' called Company Sergeant-Major Priest. 'They may be coming!'

'Keep the men *down*, Sergeant-Major, do you hear? Not a man from the dugouts until I say!'

The lull in the artillery fire lasted about twenty minutes. Survivors were told long afterwards, when the battle was ana-lysed, that the Germans had hoped this would induce British reinforcements to show their heads and make their way forward, from battle zone to forward zone and from reserve zone to battle zone. Then, twenty minutes later, they would be caught in the renewed and even heavier crash, rumble, crash, whistle, screech, crash of shells which now began to fall with even greater fury on the infantry trenches. Mixed into the ear-splitting crack of high explosive they now heard the softer 'phut' of gas shells. The British gas mask was rudimentary and exceptionally uncomfortable, reducing efficiency and endurance; but it seemed to work.

They had never experienced anything like this. John, trying to keep his senses alert, supposed it was what had been inflicted on the Germans before all the great British offensives, but it was medicine they had seldom tasted themselves. It was as if every gun, howitzer and mortar in the German army had been concentrated in one sector of the front and provided with enough ammunition to fire, without respite, for hour after hour. It was one continuous, frightful, deafening curtain of sound, like a thunderclap which, instead of being succeeded by rain and peace, is followed by another and another and another.

For five hours.

At half past nine John looked at his watch and tried to think what was suddenly different. Astonishingly, although the battalion's trenches had been savaged by the bombardment, he had only lost five men: a shell had blown in part of a trench wall and buried them. They had, somehow, dug those men out and passed them, borne by shaken stretcher bearers, down the communication trench towards the rear. John thought it possible that all five would survive although it was clear that one man would never use his legs again. Company Sergeant-Major Priest said, for the third time – but this time with accuracy and an urgent edge to his voice, ''Eased up, sir!'

'Right, Sergeant-Major – Up!'

They moved into the fire trench. It was then they fully appreciated how thick was the fog. There was dust, dirt, debris and smoke everywhere, of course. But now they also realized it was exceptionally foggy.

They could hear absolutely no sound from the forward zone. If the assault was coming in there would be a rattle of machine-gun nd rifle fire from the trenches to their front. There was silence.

'Get 'em up, Sergeant-Major, into the fire trenches, every man!' It might be another feint, a lull before another appalling storm of gun and mortar fire. It might not. The men ran up, still wearing gas masks.

'Masks off!'

'Here we go, sir,' said Priest, suddenly. Simultaneously, John heard a storm of small arms fire from their right front – from a part of the forward zone in front of their right-hand neighbour company – and saw, first doubting, then certain, dark shapes coming towards them out of the fog to the front. Small groups, not extended in lines but moving, ducking, suddenly stopping, then rising to double forward again. Without further exhortation from John or anybody else, the battalion Lewis guns opened up. For a moment nobody was moving in front of them. The fog swirled, thickened, dissolved. John wondered for a second whether he – or the Lewis gunners – had imagined it? He did not think so. He snapped, 'Sergeant-Major, tell Battalion, quick, that the attack's coming in. They seem to be through the forward zone already.'

John noted with part of his mind, unbelievably, that the Sergeant-Major had got through. And, also unbelievably, about five minutes later he heard a grumble of artillery, their own artillery. God knew, thought John, and he John never would, how word got back through the devastated network of army and artillery communications. God knew how any of their guns had survived that terrible, hurricane bombardment. But, however contrived, shells began falling in front of them. British shells.

The men of the company crouched behind the parapet. Nerves were very tense. John walked up the trench.

'Fire at opportunity targets when they come. Rapid fire. They'll come in groups, fire at the same group as your mates on either side of you if you can manage it.' The Lewis guns opened up again. The fog was if anything now thicker and he could see nothing.

He was halfway back along the company front when a very young soldier, a man who had been less than a month with the

261

company, said, very calmly, out of the side of his mouth, 'Here
they come, sir!'

Then he fired, reloaded and fired three times more, all while
John was standing beside him, and then said 'Ah-h,' with a note
of immense satisfaction. He turned his childlike face under its
incongruously tilted steel helmet to smile at his Company Commander.

'God help us all,' John found himself thinking, 'He's happy!'
He peered over the parapet. Again, the Germans seemed to
have dropped. No movement.

'Adjutant, Captain Marvell!'

John reached for the handset. The Adjutant's voice was very
clear and controlled, as if he were dictating a routine message to
some rather slow-witted clerk.

'It sounds as if they're through the forward zone all along the
brigade front. We've got a line though. And to our left they're
into the forward trenches of the battle zone. Are you all right?'

'Perfectly all right.'

'It sounds,' the Adjutant said conversationally, 'as if the battalion may have to go back some time quite soon. To conform.'

Three days later – John discovered only afterwards that it was
Palm Sunday – they were about nine miles west of the position
they had been in when the battle started. They had been extraordinary days, consisting of holding improvised positions, villages, hastily scratched trench lines, ditches; holding them against
line after line of enemy infantry coming forward from the east,
wave succeeding wave. And every morning there was fog and
the fog helped the enemy, helped them horribly. Whenever
John's men weren't in direct contact with the enemy, German
shells seemed to find them – not the prepared concentrations of
the first hours: they realized with sick gratitude that the German
guns were having difficulty in keeping up with the advance – but
scattered shells, a lot of gas among them. Casualties came at all
hours now, a drip rather than a haemorrhage.

By that Sunday, John had no other officers in the company.

He had formed his men into two platoons only, under two excellent Sergeants. Priest was still with him, indefatigable. John himself had not been scratched, but was more tired than he ever remembered. Their battalion had never lost cohesion, as some did. Nor, as he realized afterwards, were they hit as hard as some others; the heaviest and most sustained attacks went in to the north of them, and as often as not they had to go back to conform to others rather than because of enemy pressure. As often as not, too, after giving an enemy attacking wave a stout-hearted volley or two and some magazines from the Lewis guns, the Germans didn't come at them again but pushed somewhere else. They all had to wear gas masks for a great deal of the time, and it added to the fatigue.

Now, on that Sunday morning, they were lining the bank of a canal, and had, for the while, that broad ditch in front of them. Sometimes John could see the question mark in men's eyes – 'Where is this going to end?' That interrogative, speculative look with which every Commander is familiar. 'Do they know what they're doing?' it said, 'Are our lives in good hands?'

John's Commanding Officer walked along the canal line as calmly as if he were sauntering away from the church gate after morning service on that Palm Sunday. An unostentatiously devout man, that is where he would, in different circumstances, undoubtedly have been. He paused by John.

'Do you realize, John, that you and I are the only officers who were in this battalion on 31st July last year, when we attacked at Gheluvelt? That everyone else has changed?'

'I suppose that's right, sir.'

It was a sombre reflection, but the Colonel made of it an easy, relaxing piece of small talk. John wondered how long they would hold the canal line. At the moment all was quiet. It was midday, a warm, lovely day. Men were sleeping where they lay in fire positions, and John encouraged it, merely driving the NCOs to keep sentries posted and alert. Overhead two of their own aeroplanes cruised watching the enemy. John thought that no casual observer would have supposed, at that minute, that they were part of an army which had, according to later reports, largely panicked and run. He thought his Commanding Officer was going to give an estimate of the situation, and of the probability of the Germans assaulting across the canal. Instead the Colonel smiled, very charmingly, and said –

'The worst thing, or one of the worst things in that battle at Gheluvelt, was having to tell you about your brother, about Alan.'

'I'm sure it was, sir. And thank you for the way you did it.'

The Colonel walked on. Next evening they had withdrawn from the canal.

A week later, a week of ceaseless marching, digging, controlled fire at distant lines of Germans, of up, march, march, march, sleep a little, deploy, dig, shoot again, withdraw again – another week of this, another Sunday, Easter Sunday. And the next evening a brief conference at Battalion Headquarters. Although the German advance had pressed them back far and fast there was a certain feeling in the air, perhaps temporary, perhaps illusory, that the enemy were running out of steam. The Colonel however, looked alarmingly anxious. Tired as John himself was he noticed it. The strain was telling. It had been eleven days since the onslaught and they had lived for eleven days in an atmosphere of disintegration. Before they left the conference the Colonel took John's arm.

'John, I've cursed myself for a clumsy fool, reminding you last Sunday of the day I had to tell you about your brother's death. I wish to God I hadn't.'

He paused. He'd not been in the least clumsy. This was preamble. John helped him. Some things were always completely clear, whether words were uttered or not.

'My brother-in-law, sir? Cosmo Paterson?'

'Afraid so. Visiting our neighbours on the railway line yesterday, 31st March, when the Boche started crossing. They knew at Army Headquarters I'd want to tell you myself. Shell. Instant

John nodded, saluted and left the barn which had sheltered their little conference, to return to his company as quickly as possible. There was a lot to do. For the first time in a week it was a beautiful evening. John knew that Hilda would be shattered. Cosmo gone – Cosmo who had cared for nobody, had been ready for anything, contemptuous of rules, of life, of the restraints of conventional proprieties. There'd never be one like him. Cosmo was a man to have at your back if enemies or misfortunes were coming at you from every side. A Boche shell had sent him to his long rest.

John told himself, as he often had since 1914, that he would feel these wounds terribly one day. Just now there wasn't time.

Part III

GERHARDT

CHAPTER XIV

The British had looked after Gerhardt Brendthase well. His wounds were unpleasant but not such as to leave him incapable of work. They required surgery of a kind, and decent care during convalescence. All this he received and was grateful for. One consequence was that, unlike many of his contemporaries, he did not have a long, stultifying period as a fit man in a prisoner-of-war camp. By the time he was fully recovered – or as fully recovered as he would ever be – it was clear that Germany would soon lose the war. He and his fellow captives did not, of course, take for granted the truth of all they read in the English newspapers they were able to obtain, but they knew – or, at least, Gerhardt knew – that after what was obviously the failure of the offensive which began in March, 1918, to achieve decisive results, the German Empire was incapable of another major effort. It took time, of course, to be certain that the March offensive had failed. It was kept going, they could deduce, a long time after its dynamic had expired. But when, in July, 1918, they read of 'Allied offensives'; when they reflected that the United States, as yet unwearied and with huge resources behind her, had entered the conflict and already had an army in France; and when they recalled that the one new circumstance favourable to Germany, the Russian revolution and collapse, had already been fully exploited in this great but indecisive German offensive – when they considered all these things, Gerhardt knew, as anybody with knowledge of domestic circumstances in Germany must conclude, that his country could go on no longer.

The triumphant tone of the British dispatches in August and September, 1918, therefore, saddened but did not surprise Gerhardt. Germany had lost. Germany needed, always, to win a war quickly: that was the eternal teaching of the General Staff. Germany had enemies on all sides, and the coalition of powers that could be raised against the Fatherland would always triumph, in the end, in a long war. For a brief moment this principle seemed as if confounded by the Russian revolution – a revolution at first hesitant, but then (by which time Gerhardt was already a prisoner) taken over by the Bolsheviks, with their determination to make peace with Germany and be free to pursue their bloody programme at home. Gerhardt had no sympathy with what he regarded as their detestable philosophy and barbarous practices, but he welcomed, when he read of it in English newspapers, the Bolsheviks' advent to power. He knew that Lenin would make peace with Germany. The General Staff had always been in touch with him, in Switzerland. Now there might, conceivably, come the moment when Germany could strike a final blow in the west with her full strength and without distraction from the east. It did not work. Germany had already shed too much of her blood. In November, 1918, she bowed to the inevitable.

The prisoners – Gerhardt's camp was in west Yorkshire, with 2,000 German officers behind wire – read the English newspapers with sombre resignation. Two men managed to commit suicide, and several sought Gerhardt's advice very seriously.

'Brendthase, what should a man honourably do? Are they lying, these English newspapers?'

'Of course not. Germany has had to seek an end to hostilities. It has been unavoidable since the summer although it has come more quickly than I expected. As to what to do –'

He shrugged. What was there to do except survive, ponder, hope? It was rumoured that revolution had broken out in parts of Germany. He generally said, quietly, 'Germany does not deserve to lose more of her officers than she has already. There will be a need for us again one day. Somehow, somewhere.'

But it was hard, bitterly hard, to read of British celebrations of the Armistice, to look, disgusted, at photographs of uninhibited carousal, flags waving, crowds cheering their heads off. Germany's ruler, symbols, uniform were now a matter of mockery –

270

exultant mockery – to the British victors. Yes, it was bitterly hard, and November, 1918, was as bad a month as Gerhardt had experienced yet in life, a month in which the agony of defeat outweighed the earlier pain of wounds, even the fear of death. A black, black month. He presumed there would be repatriation after negotiations, but of that as yet there was no word.

In November, too, Gerhardt was subjected to a curious encounter. He was called to a small room in the same hut as the Camp Commandant's own office. The camp consisted of parallel rows of rectangular wooden huts, bitterly cold in winter. In the small room was a table with a grey British army blanket covering it. On either side of the table was a wooden chair. Standing with his back to the window was a tall British officer in uniform. Gerhardt stood to attention and looked at him. The British officer said in excellent German –

'Major Brendthase, my name is Major Kinzel. Please sit down.' He himself took a chair and, after a moment of hesitation, Gerhardt followed suit. What, he wondered, was this? Kinzel. A German name. And an almost flawless German accent.

'Major Brendthase, I have one or two questions I would like to put to you.'

'Major,' said Gerhardt, 'I was interrogated when I was captured. And again on several occasions subsequently. I have given, and can give, no information beyond that required of me by international convention. Of that I am sure you are aware.'

Kinzel said that he of course recognized that, but that his questions were not addressed to military matters. There were certain other areas in which the British authorities hoped for Major Brendthase's co-operation. But before that, Major Kinzel would be interested in Major Brendthase's views on the general situation. The war was over.

Gerhardt said that it appeared so. Kinzel said that it would clearly take a long time to repair the damage done to the fabric of Europe. The majority of the people in the most civilized nations on earth had spent the last four years trying to kill each other. Great emotions had been aroused. Great ferocity had been encouraged. Now all had to be calmed, restored. Gerhardt

271

could not guess where this general discussion was leading, but it did not seem to run counter to the officer's code of conduct which applied in cases of captivity. And, as Kinzel had said, the war was over, Gerhardt thought grimly. Kinzel talked easily, a friendly voice.

'I am interested in your views, Major, because you are known to have travelled quite widely before the war, to have contacts outside Germany, no doubt to have reflected a good deal on the state of Europe.'

'I do not think,' said Gerhardt, 'that my views are of any consequence. I am a soldier, not a politician or a journalist. I dare say the problems will be as great as you say. Statesmen will have to solve them, not soldiers. Statesmen created them.'

Kinzel smiled and said, 'Not all Englishmen would agree with that. In this country it is widely believed that German *Militarismus* had a certain effect on the events which led to the war. I tell you this frankly, not to argue it but to show you the sort of views and, if you like, prejudices it will be necessary to take into account.'

'I dare say, Major Kinzel,' Gerhardt heard himself saying, 'I dare say. And your newspapers are saying, and have been saying ever since I started reading them, that all guilt for the suffering of this war lies with Germany. But I do not think so. And I do not think it wise or right to argue it. Germans will not accept it.'

Kinzel nodded. He had, thought Gerhardt, a sympathetic personality. Perhaps he was, for that reason, a good interrogator. Not that he had yet asked anything of the slightest significance. Gerhardt found himself caring little.

Kinzel said, 'Quite. And it's no good asking the Germans to live with a load of guilt for ever – or even for a short while. Nobody reacts like that. To the vast mass of people in any nation war is a misfortune. It may be that one's own leaders have blundered – if one's side has lost they've certainly blundered! But in no way can people, anywhere, accept it as a matter of personal guilt. And to demand this, as we're doing, is to provoke a reaction. That is what you're saying.'

'That is certainly what I'm saying.'

They talked for a little, amiably despite the bizarre circumstances. It was clear that Kinzel knew Germany well. Gerhardt supposed he came of a German family who had at some time or other settled in this odd country.

'There is bound,' said Kinzel judiciously, 'to be economic disaster throughout central Europe. At first people here will probably shrug their shoulders but that can't go on for long.'

'I presume,' said Gerhardt, for he longed to know, it was crucial for the survival of family and friends, 'I presume the Allied blockade is about to be lifted?'

'Not yet, I think. Not until the Allied peace terms are accepted.'

'Then that will mean further and worse starvation,' said Gerhardt flatly. Everyone knew that. Kinzel looked at his hands. Gerhardt appreciated that a prisoner could not rise and excuse himself, but so far the conversation could not have helped the British authorities, even had he wished to do so. And it had certainly not helped him although he had found himself liking Kinzel. Kinzel now looked up.

'Is the name Marvell familiar to you?'

'*Bitte*?'

Gerhardt thought fast. Certain matters returned to his mind, matters with which he had not been personally concerned but of which he was aware. He looked courteous, interrogative.

'Marvell. There was a British officer called Marvell, killed at Ypres in 'seventeen about the time you were taken prisoner. And his brother, also called Marvell. Captain John Marvell.'

Gerhardt shook his head. Kinzel was staring at him.

'And Colonel Marvell's wife, Mrs Marvell.'

'Major,' said Gerhardt, 'I don't understand what you're talking about, please.'

'I wonder. Major Brendthase, I believe you visited England before the war.'

'I did.'

'And Ireland?'

'No. Not Ireland.'

'You naturally appreciate that the British Government have some important problems in Ireland. During the war the German authorities sought to make those problems much more serious, more embarrassing. I must emphasize,' said Kinzel, gesturing with his right hand as Gerhardt seemed about to interrupt, 'that this was entirely understandable. Our two countries were at war. There has now been an Armistice, an end to hostilities.'

Gerhardt looked at him silent, moving no muscle. Kinzel said very softly, 'But the British Government's problems in Ireland do, of course, continue, as is very generally known and as our newspapers make perfectly clear. My questions, Major, have nothing to do, therefore, with your actions as a soldier. They are concerned with whether you had any contact with – with dissident elements in Ireland before the war, a war which is now over between us. Germany now has no motive in encouraging such dissidence. And every motive, I suggest, in restoring friendship between your country and mine.'

There was complete silence between them. It lasted a minute, during which Henry Kinzel reflected how much he disliked the work he had been briefed to undertake in his last months before demobilization. 'While they're still in the cages,' his superiors had said, 'we really must get anything we can which will fill us in on their previous links with Sinn Fein. We'd be mad to pass up the opportunity. There seem to be one or two names on file who are actually in our hands –'

'And it is in that connection,' said Kinzel at last, 'that I ask you whether the name of Marvell means anything to you.'

'They' had been pretty confident they knew all there was to be known, that it wasn't by now important. But the name of Brendthase had been indexed, and he, Henry Kinzel, had been briefed. He was satisfied that in no way could he be hurting the interests of John Marvell of Bargate, his friend and brother in arms. The file had made that entirely clear. He had seen John Marvell, on leave in London, only a week ago and had felt a certain distaste at his own inner knowledge that he was soon to bandy about the name of this man and members of his family. It had been delightful to see Marvell. Kinzel already recognized how close had been the comradeship of the trenches, how extra-ordinarily, memorably rewarding those snatched moments when a sympathetic personality, another survivor, had for a little while shared thoughts, emotions, memories of better times and even hopes for a peaceful future. Those friendships, often transient, generally terminated by a German shell or bullet before long, had been like no other friendships. Danger and the sense of impermanence had sharpened the affections. Peace, this sudden peace, was natural, blessed and rewarding but it would never include that sort of thing.

Henry Kinzel had only been away from the front for three months but he had greeted John Marvell like a long-lost brother. He had said that he was 'doing an Intelligence job'.

'I hope to get out as soon as they start letting people go. As soon as they're sure it's not going to start up again, I imagine!'

'It won't! But what a mess it all is. Still, I suppose things might be worse.'

'They might indeed. Imagine what it feels like to be a German at the moment!'

'Well,' said John. 'They asked for it. Look at the misery they brought on the world.'

Kinzel had looked judicious, and John remembered a conversation in France, when the other had explained his family's German origins, had talked, even during that time of killing, of the victors' obligation to be generous. He had added, to Kinzel's grateful pleasure, 'No, that was a silly thing to say. Of course it wasn't only they who started it. The causes of the war were more complex than that, although you'd not make many friends by saying so!'

Dear old John Marvell! Kinzel had spent only a short time in John's battalion, and had moved to another on promotion. A wartime soldier, no professional, his intelligence and energy had led him to what people were now calling 'a good war'.

Henry Kinzel brought his mind back to the prison camp and the man sitting the other side of the blanket-covered table. It was just possible, they had said, that Brendthase might be prepared to offer a titbit or two. These trails were old, but in Ireland old trails often survived the generations in a remarkable way. Gerhardt was, however, speaking very quietly.

'Captain Kinzel, I am a prisoner of war.'

'Certainly.'

'You appear to me to be discussing activities linked to espionage and subversion. Your authorities have, naturally, every right to detect such activities and prosecute – if necessary execute – those who carry them out. In peace or war. And whatever the nationality of the perpetrators.'

Kinzel looked at him, straight and frowning.

'They have not, however,' Gerhardt continued, his voice expressionless, 'any right under international law to treat a prisoner of war as a suspect of such activities, a prisoner of war they have not caught in espionage, in subversion, in the encouragement of what you have called dissidence. A prisoner of war captured in battle.'

'I have not suggested to you,' said Kinzel, 'that you are suspected of anything improper or culpable. I have merely asked you questions about events long ago, on the presumption that you might be prepared to help the British authorities, in a way which could not now be in the slightest degree harmful to Germany.' He felt, with irritation, that he was himself on the defensive and was unsure quite how he had got there.

Gerhardt bowed his head and said, 'I am afraid I am completely unable to help you.' He stood up sharply, and a moment later clicked his heels together. Henry Kinzel did not attempt to deny that the interview was at an end.

Gerhardt's captivity – he was not repatriated until the summer of 1919 – at least enabled him to escape the distressing experiences of some of his old comrades in arms when the fighting ceased, as was subsequently related to him. Some found themselves mobbed by revolutionaries, had their epaulettes torn off, were beaten up, lucky to escape with their lives. Some found their own men mutinous – sullen and jeering at best, violent at worst. Gerhardt knew that his own old regiment (with hardly a man in it he knew any more: they had to renew more than half their strength after the fighting on the Yser in the autumn of 'fourteen, and their losses in 'sixteen were appalling) returned in decent order to Saxony, but some of the scenes people told him about, when he ultimately got home, were disgraceful. Berlin, of course, had its own Communist revolution, as did Munich. These were, as he learned, suppressed by the resolution of a few strong-willed men who reacted to the challenge of the hour. But those were frightful days.

Gerhardt returned to find a land and people in the grip of despair. The defeat itself was traumatic. It seemed to render futile all the sacrifices of the previous years – and, heaven knew, he thought, there had been sacrifices indeed, with everybody in wartime Germany hungry and bereft, strikes and labour disturbances, every family mourning a son, a brother, a husband. But as bad as the fact of defeat were the terms which were imposed on Germany, and which seemed to condemn the Fatherland to permanent destitution. Everybody feared that the load of reparations demanded by the victorious powers would be impossible for Germany to bear. The country was shattered by war and could not possible revive – or, indeed, survive – if its entire future was to be mortgaged forever to the Allied debt collectors (a fact that Germans obstinately hoped the Allies would recognize).

As to international standing, it was clear to every German that the victors were determined Germany should be not only savaged to death but should be powerless to defend herself in the process. The armed forces were to be virtually disbanded, their material seized or destroyed, the General Staff abolished. The Germans were to have no modern equipment, no aeroplanes, no mechanized vehicles, no heavy guns, no submarines. The army itself was to be limited to 100,000 men – a derisory figure for a continental nation surrounded by races of unpredictable moods and attitudes towards Germany. Whole tracts of ancient German land, whole territories filled by German folk, were transferred to other nations, to other rule – where, by all accounts, Germans were soon atrociously treated. An intransigently hostile Poland was created on the eastern frontier and given some of Germany. All this Gerhardt learned, and it produced a mood of black pessimism, a universal melancholy it seemed nothing could cure.

Gerhardt found shame, resentment, misery, and shared them all. He also found physical deprivation and a good deal of fear. Nobody knew how the social fabric of Germany – fragile, as in all large industrial nations – could withstand these blows. Confidence, normality – let alone patriotism – seemed to have died for ever at Christmas, 1918. The Kaiser had left, and there was no respected figure to reassure or inspire. The King of Gerhardt's own Saxony had climbed into a motor car and driven off into obscurity. Symbols, as well as wealth and power, were no more.

Gerhardt reported himself, shortly after his return and formal discharge from the army, to General von Seeckt, the Commander and creator of the truncated *Reichswehr*, the forcibly restrained '100,000 *Mann Heer*' which Germany was permitted. He knew von Seeckt well from early days and the General saw him personally. Gerhardt had once been a member of his Staff and wanted to discover whether one like himself, a General Staff officer, having considerable combat experience with troops as well as knowledge of both operational and Intelligence Staff work, might expect again to receive a commission under the new Republic. Von Seeckt shook his head. He had all the men he needed – all the officers he could possibly employ. He was only allowed 4,000.

'*Herr General*, I am prepared to serve in a junior rank.'

'So are most of my officers,' said Seeckt drily, 'and my Sergeants. Everybody is serving in a rank and capacity far below his proper level. It will continue so. There is, however, no place for you, Brendthase. I am sorry.'

Seeckt was a clever, strong, dedicated man, whose beautiful hands and artistic temperament were combined with a will of steel. He was determined that the army should be loyal to the Republic, whatever the Republic's political complexion. Himself a monarchist conservative, he had little time for some of the politicians who drifted in and out of office in Berlin. But he knew that for the army to recover its self-respect and form a nucleus from which revived strength might one day be born, it must preserve its inner cohesion, stand absolutely apart from politics,

278

and place itself unreservedly at the disposal of the State which paid its wages. Not all saw their duty in the same terms in those difficult days and it wasn't long before Seeckt's philosophy of integrity was challenged and disobeyed, particularly in Bavaria. But Gerhardt knew Seeckt's views and reputation and whole-heartedly admired him.

Gerhardt's name was recorded for the army reserve. Military service, it seemed, was to be his life no longer. He knew perfectly well how people had whispered to the General that Brendthase was no longer physically the man he had been, that his injuries would probably have left scars on his mind which could not fail to impair judgement. There is never any shortage of well-wishers, thought Gerhardt, to give a fair wind to rumours of that kind, particularly when there is competition for places, as was certainly the case with the infant *Reichswehr*. He bowed and left. There was nothing to be done. He was an unemployed civilian.

Gerhardt's father had aged a good deal in the war. His mother had died in 'sixteen – suddenly, from an unsuspected heart condition. The elder Brendthase kept up a brave front but he had been lonely and depressed, and, of course, filled with anxiety for Gerhardt's own fate after wounding and capture. He had heard no news of his son for some time.

Herr Brendthase was also much less prosperous than he had been. His South American business, which had once been exten-sive, had suffered considerably from the war. He had always been a dedicated patriot – he had, indeed, gone out of his way in times past to assist the Imperial Government with advice and information, had performed confidential tasks for them when it appeared his duty, even though his personal affairs might suffer therefrom. Gerhardt had, himself, once acted as a sort of un-official agent for the General Staff in several matters where his father's knowledge and contacts had been deemed valuable. This had not been particularly congenial work, and Herr Brendthase certainly got little enough from it, but he was not the man to bother about such things where Germany's interests were concerned. When Gerhardt first sought his father after the inter-view with General von Seeckt, and asked his advice, Herr Brendthase sighed as if this was yet one more burden on an aching back. Gerhardt was a little stung.

'I will look after myself, Father, naturally. I simply wanted your opinion on the best line to pursue.'

'You will find it exceptionally hard. Our economy is shattered. I would normally suggest looking for some sort of position in the commercial world. Naturally, I have – or I had – many colleagues, but –'

'But?'

'But there is no commercial activity. There is no enterprise left, no capital base, no credit –'

Nevertheless, Gerhardt suppressed his pride and Herr Brendthase restrained his pessimism, and soon found his son a 'position' in a small trading company in which he had himself invested fairly heavily before the war. It specialized in business with eastern Europe, and the elder Brendthase thought it possible that, when their convulsions were past, the leaders of the new Russian régime would welcome renewed trade with Germany. Such trade was traditional, a tradition interrupted by war.

'There is chaos there, now,' he said gloomily, 'but someone will have to lend them money, sometime. It may as well come back to us.'

The Germans were in a position, even after the cataclysm of 1918, to sell certain 'services' which an inexperienced and impoverished Russian government might welcome. The company kept Gerhardt alive, and something like a pattern of life began to re-emerge.

One day in the summer of 1921, Gerhardt arrived to have supper with his father to find the old man grey-faced.

'You have heard?'

Gerhardt shook his head. He had been immersed in accounts all day. The Brendthases had no close relative left to lose. The country was crippled. There didn't seem much else that could happen. His father said – 'The reparations!'

'Father, I know about the reparations. We have been living

with them since 'nineteen, since Versailles. Of course they are outrageous but they are not new.'

'The Reparations Committee have finally fixed the sum we have to pay. There is to be no appeal considered.'

'Well?'

'Six thousand, six hundred million marks.'

Gerhardt stared at his father. There had been plenty of rumours, but it was a fantastic sum. Furthermore, it would, without the slightest doubt, be impossible for Germany to pay. It was like demanding hard labour from a corpse.

The following months saw a fearful sequence of events. The German Government, feeble, insecure and deprived by treaty of the means to face the rest of the world, devalued the currency and sought to diminish the impact of imposed and humiliating debt by turning every paper mark into several. The result was horribly predictable. A year later, the German mark which, when Gerhardt first visited England, cost an Englishman two of his shillings to buy, was being traded at 80,000 to the pound sterling. People put up prices, wages and everything else to keep pace. They were only able to pay because the Government printing presses flooded the country with paper money of ever depreciating value. The authorities had turned Germany into a lunatic asylum. Even so, the inmates were unable to pay their foreign creditors who (from their point of view not unreasonably) wanted payment not in a debased currency but in kind.

Gerhardt's father found the whole business incomprehensible. Unable to grasp the bitterness of the feeling against Germany he argued that the world needed a prosperous Germany with which to trade. His son shook his head.

'The French would not agree with you. Britain may like a plump, prosperous Germany. France sees only a military menace from anything that isn't a skeleton or a corpse.' The Germans were desperate: their creditors appeared to them as intransigent, full of hatred and determined on revenge.

Then these same creditors, in the form of the French, quartered their African colonial troops in the Rhineland and occupied the industrial Ruhr. Soon Germany throbbed with fearful stories of

281

the behaviour of these troops and of sexual assaults on German women, unpunished and even (it was said) encouraged by the French authorities. And – less exciting for newspaper headlines but more appalling in the width of its effects – German industry, pillaged by France, increasingly failed to keep turning the already moribund economy of the Republic. Factories went on strike in protest at the French occupation. There were fewer and fewer goods made and marketed, the spiral of inflation rose ever more steeply, and people with savings, people on fixed incomes, people with pensions began to suffer hardships unimagined even in war. The Government's only resource was to authorize the printing of more and more valueless money.

In the middle of this Gerhardt's father died – quite suddenly, like his mother before. Herr Brendthase had seen his country fall from a pinnacle of imperial power to this – humiliation, penury, moral disintegration. Gerhardt found himself glad his father had gone, though he loved him. He could not bear to see the old man's shame. He took stock of his parent's affairs and found that a considerable fortune had all but disappeared. The trading company in which Gerhardt worked had already found it impossible to keep going, after September, 1922. It collapsed under a load of unreal debt – like Germany. Gerhardt needed to do something different in order to live.

A friend said, 'Why not write?'

'Write? Write what?'

'Go into journalism. You were always articulate, you've seen a lot of the world. People are still buying newspapers. Sell your knowledge.'

Gerhardt doubted himself, and jibbed at the idea. Even in such straits he had a stupidly old-fashioned view of newspapers. They were, at that time in Germany, revelling in a certain new-found liberality of mood and were notorious (in some cases) for scurrility and untruth. Gerhardt's friend partly misunderstood his hesitation.

'All right, not here in Berlin. I can see you feel sensitive, and I doubt if they'd have you anyway. Go to Munich.'

'Munich?'

282

'Yes, nobody cares a damn in Munich whether you've been a General Staff officer, commanded a Saxon Guards Regiment, what you've done or who you are. There are some first-class, small-circulation newspapers in Bavaria, keeping their heads above water, family concerns. I'll give you a name –'

Truth to tell, Gerhardt was glad of the challenge of a completely different environment. He knew nothing and nobody in Bavaria.

He decided to change his name to that of his mother's family – Premnitz. Major Brendthase of the King of Saxony's Guards was dead. He would, he thought, see if a new man might be born and survive. He informed *Reichswehr* records of this entirely personal decision. He could barely afford the railway fare, but travelled to Munich with a trunkload of marks and some decent pre-war suits. The inflation, people said, couldn't go on at this rate, something would have to be done, it was unbelievable. But others shook their heads, wretchedly, and said that it would get far, far worse. It was February, 1923. And Gerhardt got his job. He became a newspaper man.

CHAPTER XV

Gerhardt had never before even visited Munich. He enjoyed the easy charm, the broad streets, the trees, the elegant rococo of many of the buildings, the sense of southern warmth mingling with Teutonic order. It was not his Germany but it had appeal, and he soon found it natural to forget the facile contempt with which Germans from north and east had often referred to the Bavarians. He had no intimates. He was, painfully, trying to grow a new identity. He occasionally had brief, courteous exchanges, conversations at arm's length, with colleagues over an evening glass of wine, with companions at the same table in a café. He politely discouraged overtures, still finding something repulsive in the society of creatures so different in sentiment, background and traditions from himself. He also avoided, he was uncertain why, the company of Bavarian ex-officers, men with whom he had shared experiences in a previous existence. He tried very hard to be Gerhardt Premnitz, Saxon stranger, thoughtful newspaper man.

There was, however, no way of avoiding the general sense of chaos. In the office he found that the dignified procedures of salaried employment – the monthly cheque or transfer to a bank account, the avoidance of cash passing from hand to hand, that which differentiated the editorial and regular journalistic staff from the cleaners, the porters, the men who worked the printing presses – these things had, for several months, been necessarily disregarded. Throughout the office all received a pay packet, an envelope containing actual money. It had become not just the demanded but the only practicable method of recompense. This payment with cash or paper heightened the disturbing sense of

284

impermanence which was everywhere in Germany. 'Take me, spend me quickly,' wages seemed to whisper to the recipient, 'I won't buy much tomorrow.' Life went on uneasily, and with every week the unease heightened.

Shortly after Gerhardt had started his new life he was walking home one evening to the lodgings he had taken near Munich's main railway station. It was the spring of 1923, an April evening with a touch of promise in it, the sort of day when it was possible, irrationally, to believe in some future for Germany. Gerhardt was walking by quiet, ill-lit side streets, reflecting with a certain amount of modest pleasure that he was learning his new trade rather fast. Suddenly he was whipped back through the years, and by a reflex action had twisted rapidly into a doorway, his body pressed against a closed street door, protected by two protruding porch walls. Two shots – revolver shots, Gerhardt knew – had cracked the evening air, remarkably close. Next moment a figure, a dark, tall, thin figure, moving carefully, moving like some hungry, cautious wolf, loped past Gerhardt's porch in the opposite direction to that in which Gerhardt had been walking home.

This was not the victim, or the possible victim, of two revolver shots. Gerhardt darted silently and swiftly from the concealing shelter of the porch, caught that dark, tall, thin figure from behind in a cruel grip, arm twisted into small of back, knee applied very painfully. The figure gave a screech.

Gerhardt knew that the revolver was under the left armpit. He doubted whether the nearest policeman was less than half a kilometre away. None of it was his business but he was revolted by lawlessness. If this was a murderer or attempted murderer he'd face a court if Gerhardt could manage it. Using the figure's bent arm, agonizingly, as a lever he twisted him round to look at the face and, at the same time, with a quick movement of his own disengaged hand, dragged the revolver from its hidden holster and sent it skidding along the pavement. The street was still deserted. No alarms, no yells, no response to those shots which had cracked the evening air. Munich in 1923 was like that.

Violence was to be avoided, steps quickly taken in another direction. No shock. No horror. No help.

Gerhardt saw a dark, lean face with a great scar running down the left cheek from eyebrow to corner of mouth, a huge, disfiguring scar. The lights in the street were poor, the face dimly discernible. The face said, 'Brendthase!'

Gerhardt said, 'Krempe!'

Then he slowly stepped back, his grip released.

'Krempe! You've been indulging in target practice!'

'*Fehlschuss*!' said Captain Krempe, his face looking like a snarl, the scar distorting it perhaps permanently. He probably always looks like this, thought Gerhardt, his face was badly burned in '16, I remember well. '*Fehlschuss*!' Krempe muttered, glaring at Gerhardt. 'I missed.'

Gerhardt looked at him levelly.

'What are you up to, Krempe? It's a long time since I saw you! Pozières –'

'Pozières.'

'Who are you shooting now?'

Krempe sighed and glanced at the revolver, lying in the gutter. Gerhardt said, 'Pick it up.'

'Are you going –'

'Pick it up. I trust you not to shoot me, Krempe!'

Krempe gave something like a smile. He stooped painfully to scoop up the revolver. Gerhardt's grip and knee application had been brutal and effective. Krempe stood and looked at his one-time Battalion Commander. Gerhardt's face was grim and Krempe found he was standing erect, his heels unconsciously drawn together. A bizarre scene, Gerhardt thought, standing very still, but Krempe was always all right provided you rode him on a tight rein. A brave man, but a wilful, impulsive man. Now Krempe said, in a soft, sour voice –

'You're not with us, I know that.'

'What do you mean?'

'You know. It's all approved. AK,' he added defiantly.

The *Arbeitskommandos*, known unofficially as the 'Black Reichswehr' had been recruited from the previous 'Free Corps', themselves raised by individual enterprise to resist the Communist uprisings which had swept much of Germany immediately after the war. The Black *Reichswehr*, ostensibly labour units, had been armed and organized, principally in the east, to reinforce the pitifully small army the Allies had permitted Germany. Everyone expected Poland to take advantage of German weakness, and the Black *Reichswehr* were a means of circumventing the Allied Disarmament Commission. Von Seeckt had nodded to them, cautiously. There had been stories, however, of these units punishing any renegades, any who talked of their true purpose, their strength, their aspirations. There had been questions asked in the Reichstag, angry denunciations by some Deputies. There were tales of secret courts and summary executions. The Black *Reichswehr*, Gerhardt reckoned, were one but only one of the dark and violent forces ranging the largely impotent German Republic. He looked at Krempe.

'I thought you fellows were mostly around my old home. Saxony. Keeping an eye on our local situation!' Saxony was a powerbase for the German Communist Party.

'I was – I'm here on duty.'

'You were sent here, Krempe,' Gerhardt said conversationally, gently, 'to kill someone.'

'A traitor! I assure you, Brendthase, I'm not an assassin! It was a just sentence, the swine has betrayed Germany! I –'

'Of course you're not an assassin,' Gerhardt nodded seriously. 'You missed him, Krempe!' He looked at his old subordinate. A good, loyal officer once. No doubt a patriot in his own mind, ready to risk life, liberty, all. A man with a gun.

Krempe said, '*Herr Major –*'

'That's better. Now Krempe, I want one thing from you. You'll leave Munich tonight. You'll report to whoever sent you that you fired and missed. You won't come back. That's all.'

'And you –'

'And I shall say nothing. I've not asked whom you tried to shoot and I don't care. I care – but only a little – about you. You were a good soldier. I don't want to hear of a good soldier dying

287

as a convicted criminal. Or becoming one, for that matter. Now give me your revolver.'

'I –'

'Give me your revolver, Krempe.'

Slowly Krempe did as he was ordered. Gerhardt nodded, slipped it into his pocket. No doubt, he thought, he was as guilty as any – concealing an attempted assassination, shielding a member of an *Arbeitskommando* killer squad because they'd served together. Well, to hell with it. He made a sharp gesture and Krempe moved down the street into the shadows from which he'd come.

The Director of the newspaper company was also Editor-in-Chief. He ran the business, approved editions and made policy. His family had founded and still owned the paper. He was a man of considerable authority, a good employer, firm, fair, autocratic and respected. He called them together – every sub-editor, journalist, secretary and clerk – every one of them apart from the manual workers to whom, of course, it already applied – one Thursday morning in June, 1923.

'Due to the unexpected and unprecedented change in the value of money I have decided I cannot henceforth require that you be paid monthly. Salaries will be paid weekly in future. Starting tomorrow.'

A voice, bolder than most, spoke from the back of the room – 'At what rates, *Herr Direktor*?'

'I have considered that, naturally. There will be an increment, weekly, to take into account the changed value of the Reichsmark.'

'An increment, *Herr Direktor*?' the same voice said. 'Or a multiple?'

There was a nervous titter from several around him. The Director looked stern. His voice, as always, was strong but with a note of justice in it which everybody, including those who disliked him, recognized. He gazed at the back of the room and said, 'It is an honest question and requires an honest answer.

Salaries tomorrow will be fifty per cent higher than hitherto. They will, in fact, have a one point five multiple applied.'

They all moved to leave the room, the younger ones chattering as soon as they got through the door. Plenty of firms – and plenty of newspaper offices – were unable even to attempt to keep salaries abreast of inflation. It depended, of course, on whether the man in the street was prepared to pull out an entire parcel-load of bank notes to pay for his daily paper. If he was – and if his employer could manage to borrow enough from the banks to put those bank notes into his hand – then the printing presses would continue to turn and their salaries and wages would continue, at least for a while, to reflect the ever-rising cost of living. If not, they wouldn't, as the dimmest chargehand perceived.

The Director was invariably correct and courteous where Gerhardt was concerned. Gerhardt knew that his presence as an employee embarrassed his superior, but he did his editorial work quickly and effectively. He could write, he could dissect information, he could compress, he could be clear in print. And he could make others clear – or clearer than their often second-rate minds and abilities would otherwise have managed. Gerhardt, after all, was trained – trained to think and expound with minimum waste of words, fast and in hazardous circumstances. The *Herr Direktor* was employing a man with General Staff training, and knew it. On that Thursday he had spoken Gerhardt's name as they all left the room, digesting the news of salary increases just announced.

'Herr Premnitz! One moment, please. I would be grateful if you would accompany me to my office.'

Gerhardt followed him into a darkly panelled and heavily furnished office. The Director gestured to him to take a chair and proffered a cigar which Gerhardt declined.

'Herr von Premnitz, you are an experienced man, a man of the world.'

The Director had discovered (not from Gerhardt) that his mother's family had been ennobled and was, at least in private, generally punctilious to use the 'von'. He always addressed

Gerhardt in formal, careful, courteous terms, a little stiff. Gerhardt responded in kind.

'Not an experienced newspaper man, *Herr Direktor*. I'm a beginner. You've been very good to me, entrusting me with the editorial responsibilities I hold here. But I'm still learning.'

Gerhardt was largely responsible for a 'features supplement' that appeared weekly, and had little to do with daily news.

'You're learning very fast and I'm delighted. But I'm seriously worried about the future of the paper.'

'Our circulation's gone up every week in the three months I've been here. And throughout last year. I've studied the record with admiration. We're beating our competitors, *Herr Direktor*.'

'It's not that. You know very well what I mean. I'm speaking as a business man. I have just told the staff that their salaries, paid tomorrow, will be multiplied by a factor of one point five.'

'Quite so, *Herr Direktor*.'

'I know nobody in the world of finance, here in Munich, who believes that such a rate of inflationary increase will not continue.'

Gerhardt's own view was similar. He looked at the Director levelly and was glad to see a realist, a man of character. So many people, faced with the apparently inexorable approach of disaster, averted their eyes or started howling. The Director was of the sort who realized that manmade calamities were curable by man, given intelligence and will.

'Have you calculated what that will mean, Herr von Premnitz?'

As it happened, Gerhardt had. He said, without emphasis of any kind, 'Yes, *Herr Direktor*. It means that by the autumn, *one* of today's marks will have turned into approximately one and a half million marks.'

Their weekly salaries even now ran to six or seven figures. Talk of one mark was already totally meaningless.

'Chaos, in fact.'

'I believe so.'

The Director grunted.

'The Government must do *something*. And nobody seems to know what. As you know, this newspaper has always adopted an objective, one might say a central position in political matters –'

'Exactly, *Herr Direktor.*'

'We have firmly denounced extremist opinions and manifestations. The Government needs support, not disturbance, in times like these.'

Gerhardt said nothing. He had never found internal politics agreeable and he had been brought up to regard the manoeuvres of political parties as distasteful and self-seeking. What mattered was the national interest. Its traditional embodiment, the Emperor, had disappeared (having, one was now bound to admit, conducted affairs with an erratic lack of distinction for most of his reign) and the national interest was like a rotting carcass being fought over by stray dogs, each determined to emerge on top. Or so, to Gerhardt, Deputies in the Reichstag often appeared. He realized, thinking objectively, that Germany's problems were fundamentally political and that only through political action would economic disasters be corrected: it was just that he found the subject inherently unattractive. He had done his editorial work in this regard with an impartiality not far removed from contempt.

But as the Director and Gerhardt looked at each other, Gerhardt knew that nobody had the right to stand aside, to shrug his shoulders, to sneer at politics as a dirty game – and then grumble at the outcome. A soldier – and Gerhardt would never cease to think of himself as a soldier – would always find political activity to some extent distasteful, but a soldier was also a German citizen. They had no Emperor. They would have to see to things themselves – or some of them would. It couldn't all be left to Krempe. The Director said –

'Our reportage of political meetings, recently, has been rather superficial. These boys of ours go to a meeting, scribble down what is said and the reactions, make a story of it; but they can't analyse. That is for one of the seniors. Primarily for me.'

Gerhardt said nothing. He thought that as a political analyst, as an editor with political insight, he was useless, or almost useless.

'Premnitz, I try to analyse, to arrange the facts in accordance with some sort of recognizable historical pattern. I was brought

291

up on political theory. I know my German history. But I don't attend political meetings myself. They have become so so . . .'

'Noisy!'

'Noisy. Violent. Irrational. Yet I have a duty to think, to explain – and I have to make the attempt without first-hand knowledge or impression.'

It was true that the Director, although an experienced newspaper man, was by temperament a philosopher rather than an observer, a reporter. Robust and astute, he was, nevertheless, fastidious. Now he said –

'I would be grateful if you would attend one or two of these meetings. It is unlikely to be congenial, but I would like to see through the eyes of a mature man of the world. I would like your impressions.'

'I'm not sure they will be particularly valuable, *Herr Direktor*.'

And so Gerhardt started to go to political meetings. In describing politics in Bavaria as noisy, violent and irrational, the Director was hardly overstating the matter. Bavaria had become the centre for all movements in Germany most opposed to the Republic. The monarchists – the Wittelsbach family had ruled Bavaria for centuries – were strong in Munich, devoted to the Wittelsbach rather than Hohenzollern crown, to an independent kingdom of Bavaria. These people – and a whole assortment of small parties all more or less on the political right – were, therefore, separatists. They disliked Berlin and they wanted not only to bring the new German Republic down, but to see Bavaria arise completely independent from the ruins. When Gerhardt had been working for three weeks in the newspaper office, the head of their sales and distribution office said to him with a smile –

'I imagine you'd be in Saxony, except for the fact the Reds are pretty well running it! You must feel as if you're in a foreign land here.'

'Certainly I'm no Bavarian! But we're all Germans, after all!'

'That won't mean anything much longer,' said the other confidently. 'It's time we went our own way, for good. Got rid of the damned Prussians.'

Gerhardt had frowned but said nothing. He had no sympathy whatsoever with the Bavarian separatists. It seemed to him that Germany must remain an entity, somehow. He had been loyal, once, to the King of Saxony but such small polities were surely an anachronism. Germans had lost almost everything. They should not, Gerhardt reckoned, additionally destroy the last vestiges of the unifying work of Bismarck. Paradoxically, although these parties of the right were loud in their denunciation of Versailles and the outrages of the French, they were, in fact (and Gerhardt had evidence of it in the newspaper office although they were cautious what they printed), secretly encouraged by France. France was not at all averse to the idea of a fragmented German Reich. Increasingly, throughout 1923, political meetings had turned into impassioned pleas for 'Bavarian freedom.' The heir to the Wittelsbach dynasty, Crown Prince Rupprecht, watched the scene with circumspection.

Also thought of as on the political right – although social radicals, and with revolutionary instincts which the conservative separatists regarded with horror – were a number of 'nationalist' parties, rabidly opposed to separatism, but equally determined to bring down the Republic. Of these the best organized, with its own newspaper and a good deal of money, were the National Socialists. They often made common cause with the Bavarian separatists – both detested the status quo and the Reich Government in Berlin. But whereas the monarchists and separatists wanted to divorce themselves from Berlin, the National Socialists wanted to conquer it, to assume the leadership of an undivided Reich. Each of these two wings of what often described itself as the 'Patriotic Front' thought it could use the other and ride towards its objectives with the other's reluctant assistance, to be jettisoned at the appropriate moment. In reality, the aims of the two wings were totally different, although they often came together on specific issues, and on tactics; and their tactics, in general, were to disrupt – to make the Republic unworkable. On the left, the Social Democrats and Communists had been effectively smashed in the aftermath of the Communist revolution of 1919. The survivors kept their heads down and hoped that one day the wind would change and their hour come.

Gerhardt found political meetings a distasteful part of his duties, and until the autumn of 1923 he had only attended four. There was a shrillness, a hysteria on these occasions which he found repugnant. At his very first meeting two young men had shouted interruptions and a number of people around, faces contorted with hatred, had crowded towards them yelling. Gerhardt, who had not even heard the words of the interrupters, had moved swiftly to interpose.

'Please! We are here to listen to the speaker!'

His height, his frown, his authority had cooled them, muttering. It was, he thought with disgust, a dirty business. Reason featured little, emotion – mob emotion – dominated. Gerhardt's dislike of politics did not abate, although he tried to be fair, to say to himself, 'What would you do?' He only attended one National Socialist function – a rather drunken affair, with little coherent speech and a lot of raucous singing. None of the top men were there.

But all the time, in the office, on the streets, the sense of crisis deepened. The feeling ripened everywhere that 'This can't go on.' Gerhardt found the Bavarians as volatile and as disposed to exaggerate as he had always heard, but he shared their prevailing mood, their sense that a climax was inevitably approaching. Everybody said, 'The Republic has failed,' in a tone of either despair or exultation dependent on the speaker's views.

Everywhere there was hunger, acute among the poor, experienced as genteel privation among the professional people, the owners of property, the employed. People said, 'It's crazy!' and shrugged. And more and more they said, 'It's intolerable!'

In September the Bavarian 'Government' – there was a 'Council of Ministers', a sort of local praesidium in Munich – proclaimed a state of emergency, and appointed a rabid separatist and Bavarian nationalist, von Kahr, to be 'State Commissioner'.

Later the same day, Berlin, feeling threatened, declared a state of emergency throughout Germany.

'Herr von Premnitz,' said the Director that day, 'you know General von Lossow?' Von Lossow was the local Military District Commander.

'Only by reputation, *Herr Direktor*.' Lossow was a rabid Bavarian separatist. Gerhardt knew little good of him.

The Director said, 'They're saying Berlin has ordered the suppression of the *Völkischer Beobachter*.' This was the National Socialist newspaper. It had become more and more strident and provocative in recent weeks, pretty well openly advocating rebellion against the Government of the Republic, and saying that soldiers 'loyal to Germany' would not confuse this true loyalty with formal obligations to a discredited régime: all in very violent language. Gerhardt had been increasingly sickened by it.

'They're also saying, Herr von Premnitz, that General von Lossow has refused to act against the *Beobachter*!'

'Typical,' Gerhardt thought.

The Director continued, 'Apparently he is to be replaced by General Kress von Kressenstein.'

A good man, Kress, who had done his damndest to make sense of the Turkish campaign!

Gerhardt said, 'And will the Bavarian authorities accept this replacement happily, *Herr Direktor*?'

The Director smiled wryly.

'I'd like you to make one of your personal appearances at a political meeting this evening.'

Gerhardt knew what he had been leading up to. The National Socialists were meeting in a *Brauhaus* that evening. A good many curious onlookers would be there, and the Press in strength, as well as members of the party in question. Gerhardt bowed his consent. It was to be a big meeting, it had received a lot of publicity and it had been said that all the leaders of the party would attend and that 'history would be made'. Adolf Hitler, the party leader would probably speak.

Although the papers, including his own, were full of Hitler's activities, Gerhardt had never set eyes on this little ex-Corporal from a Bavarian infantry regiment whose photograph was everywhere, who was making speeches that invariably caught headlines and who had, from nothing and without established organization, formed a new party of his own, the National Socialists. Gerhardt's newspaper was prudently caustic about them. They had started in the immediate aftermath of the war as the 'National Socialist German Workers' Party' and from 1920 people had taken to abbreviating '*Nazional Sozialist*' to 'Nazi'. Now, three years later, they were able to hold sizeable rallies anywhere in Germany.

The principal aspect of the 'Nazis' on which Gerhardt's Director tended to fasten was their inconsistency. Their general line was one of fierce, intolerant nationalism – Germany had been betrayed, Germany was being misgoverned by men who did not put Germany first, and so forth – and with this message a good many people felt temperamental sympathy, even if they disliked the brutal, simplistic tone in which the message was conveyed. There was something compelling, too, in the Nazi insistence that culture, genuine feeling, creativity, were indissolubly connected to the land which had nourished the German folk and derived from their feeling for it. It was easy to make fun of such theories, but in a time when love of country was being derided by intellectuals they had, to such as Gerhardt, a certain appeal. But on specific issues – on, as he would put it as a soldier, tactical rather than strategic ground – the Nazis swung from one point of view to another with, it seemed, reckless irresponsibility.

'These people understand nothing, my dear Herr von Premnitz,' the Director often said. 'They've not made up their minds if they're left, right or centre! They think that if you shout loud enough you will solve problems with noise. They have no idea of the delicate mechanism involved in managing a modern state, a modern economy!'

'Is such understanding widespread among the other political parties, *Herr Direktor*!' Gerhardt could not help once interjecting with irony which was, he hoped, courteous. The Director grunted

'German Workers' Party indeed! What's their policy? Everything's the fault of someone else. Find a scapegoat and you've got your answer, and everything will then come right. That i completely false to historical fact. They blame the bankers, the capitalist bosses, the Jews, the other political leaders, the monarchy – everybody and everything, left, right and centre. Find a scapegoat and unify people in the act of crucifying that scapegoat. And from that unity will come strength and health and a solution of problems. It's primitive absurdity, Premnitz. Savagery. They've not a constructive idea between them.'

'Or a man of distinction, *Herr Direktor*?' They had had the same conversation several times.

The Director would sigh. 'One can't say that, unfortunately. Look at Ludendorff, for instance –'

General Ludendorff, styled 'First Quartermaster General' during the war, had effectively been Chief of the General Staff, while Field Marshal von Hindenburg, nominally the Chief of Staff, had been, in practice, Commander-in-Chief. The latter was profoundly respected, despite the 1918 catastrophe. Nobody liked Ludendorff. But he was clever. And he had joined the National Socialists.

'Yes,' the Director said often. 'Look at Ludendorff! Then, of course, this fellow Hitler: a person of no education, background or distinction whatsoever! They can't get far while they're dependent on somebody as second-rate as that. I would only be seriously worried if they recruited more men of real significance and ability.'

On this occasion, before the *Brauhaus* meeting, he said, abruptly, 'Adolf Hitler may speak, they say.'

'If the authorities have challenged them by banning the *Beobachter* I imagine he will be bound to speak, *Herr Direktor*! I presume he will complain about this assault by Government on the freedom of the Press – despite the liberality of modern Germany! A dangerous precedent –'

'They're dangerous times, Premnitz! I can't see Hitler making freedom of the Press an overwhelming point of principle!' The Director snorted and said, 'I'll be interested in our talk tomorrow.' Then he left the room.

*

The beer cellar was enormous. Long tables filled every inch of space, and in the centre of one of the long sides of the rectangular hall was a small stage, made by setting several tables together. It was from this, presumably, that speakers would harangue them. All the tables nearest to this stage were occupied by members of the National Socialist Party – clear both from the fact that they wore an armband with the party emblem (and a good many were in what Gerhardt disdainfully regarded as an absurd sort of uniform, a travesty of military dress) and because they were singing with immense volume songs he recognized as party songs. In fact, some of these were old German refrains, or soldiers' marching songs, with new words adapted to the party's views of its place on the current German scene. Gerhardt found a seat at a remote table with, as far as he could see, onlookers and a few Press men rather than party faithful. He was also pretty sure that he was not among violent opponents of the National Socialists, likely to start a fight. Fights were often a feature of political meetings, and the parties had their own 'stewards' or champions ready to go into action. On that evening the walls of the *Brauhaus* were lined with these stewards, armbands prominent. Gerhardt reckoned they would move on any disturbe of the meeting with energy and, no doubt, with discipline experience. At the moment, however, it was a good-humoured affair. People at the outlying tables round him were joining in the singing (although with, he suspected, rather different words here and there) and there was a lot of excited laughter. This might be a political meeting but it was also, clearly, an evening out. Waitresses in dirndls scurried from table to table, avoiding with indifferent success the bottom pinches which their passag often invited. The band – as far as Gerhardt could see, a professional band, in Bavarian national costume – pounded out the choruses, and smoke filled the air. A half-hour passed, with nois ever increasing, the clank of tankards on tables punctuating song

Then, above the yelling, above the throb of the tubas an bassoons, the singing and laughter, they heard from the street new sound – enormous, insistent. It was a roar of cheering approaching like breakers coming in over surf. A man at Ge ardt's table said, 'Here he comes!' his eyes shining. Then there was shouting inside the *Brauhaus*, the band stopped playing and everybody rose to their feet. The party members near the stage were standing to attention with theatrical punctiliousness. The rest, Gerhardt included, climbed as high as they could in order to see. A lot of people mounted tables and chairs. The leader of the National Socialist Party, Adolf Hitler, had arrived and had taken the stage.

Hitler made a peremptory gesture to the rows of party members at the tables immediately in front of him. All sat down, and the movement was continued until everybody throughout the beer cellar was seated. Without further preliminary, and without any introductory remarks by some other personage, customary at a political meeting, Hitler began to speak.

Gerhardt would always see Adolf Hitler exactly as he was that night. It had been raining, so that a certain steam from raincoats and umbrellas added to the general haze. Hitler wore a grey raincoat, belted and shiny. He also wore a soft felt hat. He removed the latter, but when he first strode on to the stage and looked at his audience he retained his raincoat, glistening with rain. He stood absolutely still for about a half-minute. There was complete silence, a silence which, in succession to the roar of cheering which had accompanied him to the stage, he had instantly commanded by one rapid gesture of his right hand. The atmosphere was tense, the audience rapt and still, hardly breathing. His authority was total. Used as Gerhardt was to the domination, on occasion, of some military assembly by an imperious and commanding personality, he had, he recognized, never before experienced so swift and effective a mastery. Then, without a word, Hitler took off his raincoat and an acolyte jumped forward to take it. The silence was still absolute.

Hitler started talking very quietly. There was no ranting. The issue of the hour was whether Munich should defy Berlin, and if so how the Nazis would or could reconcile the tide of Bavarian separatism with their own strident preachment of the concepts of 'Greater Germany'. But as Gerhardt listened, fascinated despite himself, it was clear that Hitler had no intention of facing,

299

head-on, the question of where the National Socialists stood on 'separatism'. Instead he used the (for him) admirable circum stance that the immediate issue between Munich and Berlin was the dismissal of von Lossow for refusing to close the *Völkische Beobachter*.

'I speak to you,' he said, 'on an evening when a distinguished German General, a man who has devoted his life to the Father land, has been abruptly dismissed from his post by the so-called Government of Germany, sitting in Berlin. Why? Because he refused to suppress the truth. He was ordered to abolish – yes abolish – a patriotic newspaper, to destroy its presses, to arrest its editor,' (all of this was grossly exaggerated, Gerhardt knew) 'to prevent its publication. Why? Because the *Völkischer Beob achter* was telling the truth about Germany.'

Very quietly Hitler said, 'General von Lossow refused to deny the truth. So they removed him. And what is this truth, of which our self-styled masters are so terrified? What are the facts of the German situation, at which every decent Bavarian stands appalled?'

He now sketched for them the outline statistics of the inflation, pausing here and there on a particularly outrageous figure, as if himself incredulous; and at such pauses there was an answering hiss of horror from the audience. Then, as if soliciting their sympathy, almost their pity, he spoke briefly, without morbidity – of what a generation of Germans had suffered, 'with the brave of other nations, let it never be forgotten,' because they, like he, had been betrayed. Those who led the nation – or enough of them – had been influenced by others whose failure of will and whose impure motives had brought disaster to their beloved land.

'To our beloved Bavaria,' he said, nodding, 'and to our beloved Germany.' His voice rose as if perceiving a sudden vision. Then gently but with complete authority checking the bursts of ap plause, he drew another picture before their eyes. He said that recovery was indeed possible; that inflation could, indeed, be mastered, 'given, only, the will to achieve'; that the German working class 'so long the playthings, the tools, the passive sufferers' could be masters in their own land, could move, united,

300

wards a new dawn of employment and prosperity. All this, he
id, *was* possible. A renewed Germany, free, strong, self-
specting and with a decent standard of living for all, *would*
me. But it would only come (and here his voice hardened, and
e rapt looks on the faces of his listeners turned to frowns, as
eads nodded grimly, lips pursed) if Germans themselves re-
lved to change utterly the system under which they now lived.
hey must return to their roots, to the qualities which had once
ised Germany high 'and', he concluded, 'it can and will happen!'
is voice was vibrant now, sharp, immensely loud. '*Das kann
schehen! Das wird geschehen!*'

It was poor, insubstantial stuff if analysed, but Gerhardt con-
ssed freely afterwards that he was powerfully moved. This man
w a vision, and he enabled his hearers to see it too. Gerhardt
uld not say whether the vision was fantasy or ultimately re-
istic, but even he – prepared to be cynical and temperamentally
verse to both politics and demagogy – found himself on his feet
plauding.

Furthermore, Gerhardt retained enough balance to admire
e man's political adroitness. Hitler had given no hostages to
rtune. The Bavarian separatists had nothing in his speech of
hich to complain, nor had those who opposed them. All could
ite in detestation of the Government of the Republic, its
eakness, its lack of spirit, its economic failure. Hitler implied
ther than elaborated the need for that 'national dictatorship'
e had been making speeches about for the last two months.

Several people had left the table at which Gerhardt was sitting,
ying to press nearer the stage in order to see Adolf Hitler
tter. Running through the *Brauhaus* was a remarkable flow
t only of enthusiastic adulation but of a sort of protective
fection. Hitler had placed himself in their hands, solicited their
ust and their hearts. The man had extraordinary, unexpected
arm. Gerhardt had studied and, like most of his acquaintances,
ocked the photographs, the absurd appearance with its single
ack smudge of a moustache, its sombre, brooding eyes, its
gainliness, its lack of distinction. The direct impact was start-
gly different. The cheers were deafening. Newcomers had

slipped into vacant seats and a young man, perhaps twenty or twenty-one years old, was now Gerhardt's neighbour, smiling eagerly and clapping like the rest. He was smartly dressed. Gerhardt thought that if he was not mistaken it was an English suit. The young man was not of an age to have served in the trenches – that marked a man of whatever race, and he was unmarked. He turned to Gerhardt and said in tolerable German –

'I only heard the last five minutes. He's a marvellous speaker, isn't he?'

Gerhardt nodded without expression. He felt a temperamental aversion to discussing what they had just witnessed with a foreigner – an absurd reaction for a newspaper man, he said to himself, reflecting that, anyway, he was rather an absurd newspaper man. He said politely, 'Are you, perhaps, an English visitor?'

'I am indeed. My first visit to Munich.'

'You are interested in politics?'

'Very interested. In fact I hope to write a short piece for an English newspaper – I'm not a journalist, but I'd submit it in the hope of acceptance – about the state of politics here in Bavaria.'

Gerhardt wondered how long a visit the young man was intending to pay. He certainly didn't lack confidence. He was well built, good-looking and had a sort of animal force about him which was both attractive and disturbing. Gerhardt wondered whether this young stranger's impressions might help him distil his own, bring an illuminating crossbeam, so to speak – before composing some sort of report for the *Herr Direktor*. He felt an impulse, too, to practise his English a little. He had been fluent in the days before '14 and there had, of course, been occasions for using the language in prison camp. It would be good to make sure that he was still adept. He did not, however, think it sensible to start this in the *Brauhaus*. The air was full of overcharged and animated colloquial Bavarian, shouted between enthusiasts in the aftermath of Hitler's speech. Hitler himself had left, surrounded by cronies and to a storm of cheers, soon after he finished his harangue. Gerhardt thought it best not to attract attention

302

witching to a foreign tongue. It was unlikely anyone would trouble them, but it was sometimes best to be indistinguishable from one's background.

He said to the stranger in a casual way, 'My name is Premnitz. I work for a newspaper here. Would you like to go somewhere else and have a cup of coffee with me? I'd be interested in what you thought.'

'I'd like that very much,' the young man said promptly, 'Very much indeed, Herr Premnitz. My name's Julius Wrench.'

CHAPTER XVI

Julius Wrench was nearly twenty-two years old and had missed service in the war. Gerhardt had not met an Englishman of his generation before and was instantly struck by how assured he was, how he gave the impression of looking around him eagerly in a world in which most things were good. 'The aura of the victor', Gerhardt thought bitterly, conscious of the self-doubt, the internal divisions, the awareness of imminent chaos, and the introspective scrutiny of German young people (or many of them) at that time. In this, he was generalizing absurdly. Wrench's rather aggressive confidence was an individual rather than a national characteristic, something peculiar to him rather than the consequence of historic circumstances. This became clear as the evening wore on. Wrench wanted to talk – and, Gerhardt acknowledged, to listen – and they spent nearly two hours together.

Wrench had left Cambridge the previous year and wished ultimately to make his way in politics. They began to talk in English, in which Wrench was naïvely surprised to find his companion so fluent.

'You must know England well, Herr Premnitz.'

'Quite well.' Gerhardt wanted to find out this young Englishman's impressions of the Nazis, of German politics, of the inflation, of the future of Europe if Germany were to be permanently a bankrupt invalid. He wanted to know whether a visitor from England – that land of cool heads – thought, as most Germans did, that Bavaria, probably followed by the rest of Germany, was about to burst into a condition of revolution and civil war. Gerhardt did not wish to discuss his own past. He soon found, however, that Wrench was extraordinarily ignorant of European affairs. For one who proclaimed a desire to make a career in politics he seemed to Gerhardt to know virtually nothing. He had found Hitler 'enthralling, but a bit absurd'.

'Absurd?'

'All that stuff about Germans drawing strength from their beloved land, returning to their cultural roots – or did I misunderstand?'

'No, there was a good deal about that.'

'Then he seemed, at another time, to be shouting about doing justice for the working class, telling them they'd been betrayed by their bosses, by capitalists and so forth –'

'Quite right. He did.'

'Well, isn't that a bit absurd? Inconsistent, I mean? The latter point is socialistic stuff, down with the rich, build a new world, all that –'

'It is called the National Socialist German Workers' Party.'

'Yes, but the first part is traditionalist, nationalist, mystical almost –'

'You find the two incompatible?'

'I do rather, yes.'

'In some countries, perhaps. But Hitler and his colleagues presumably think that these two strains – the patriotic and the radical – can and should both be exploited. The mixture might be very effective.'

Wrench shook his head, puzzled.

'I doubt if they could ever mix. Still, this is Germany.'

'As you say. This is Germany. Mr Wrench, the immediate problem is not the Nazis' view of German history, what you have called Herr Hitler's mystical side. The problem is whether or not Bavaria is going to try to secede from the Republic – or overthrow it.'

Julius Wrench nodded.

'Quite an exciting time!'

'An exciting time, yes. But underlying all this foolery –' Gerhardt used the word deliberately. He was somewhat disenchanted with Munich – 'are the economic realities. What do people think of the chances of our Republic, in England? Do they realize we are racing towards complete economic collapse?'

Gerhardt knew England and could see that Wrench was too agreeable to wish to tell the probable truth, which no doubt was that nobody cared a damn. Bloody Huns, Gerhardt thought, as he had often heard shouted between British guards when a prisoner. Bloody Huns, they deserve economic collapse, inflation, starvation, hell, the lot. He knew that at least some sections of British opinion were deeply concerned by the German situation – and all British political parties had denounced France's policy in occupying the Ruhr. But he doubted whether the ordinary Englishman was much moved, or even interested. Julius Wrench made some of those non-committal sounds, those sentences without verb or ending, beloved of the English. And Gerhardt talked with a good deal of warmth about the consequence of the war throughout the continent. He tried to do so without striking any partisan attitudes or sounding disturbingly bitter. Wrench nodded often, said, 'Quite!' at frequent intervals and sipped his coffee. Gerhardt wondered whether he had succeeded in conveying a little of the state of Europe, of an ancient and complex system in ruins. He knew that the victors thought that Germany alone had brought this about, but all, surely, were disagreeably involved with the consequences.

Gerhardt began to rediscover his expertise with the English language. He could even follow most of Wrench's slang, as he began to question him about his own life, of which the young man spoke with great enthusiasm. Despite Wrench's professed interest in politics and his intention to write some impressions about Germany for a newspaper article, he was, Gerhardt perceived, clearly most animated when discussing himself. He had, however, a good deal of charm and Gerhardt did not find this youthful egotism disagreeable: or not for most of the time.

It appeared that Wrench had wished to see something of politics from the inside and that his ambition was, one day, to be adopted as a candidate for Parliament. With this in mind he had, through a friend's influence, got a temporary job as 'secretary' (a more professional term, Gerhardt suspected, than his abilities justified: he was clearly a sort of aide or bag-carrier, an attender to life's more tedious details, little more) to a Member of Parliament. Gerhardt understood that this was an experienced Member, a man of some standing.

'Adrian first won a seat as quite a young man in 'eighty-eight. He's in his sixties.'

'Long, continuous service. He has seen much.'

'Not continuous. He wasn't well at one time, and resigned. Then he came back again, health more or less recovered, during the war. There were a good many by-elections, empty seats, you see –' Wrench looked slightly embarrassed. There was no need. Gerhardt smiled grimly to himself, understanding perfectly. Many of the younger Deputies had no doubt joined the British Army and been killed.

'And what party does your employer represent?'

'Oh, Adrian's a Conservative,' Wrench said rather vaguely. 'You probably know we had a Coalition Government – Liberals and Conservatives – until last year.'

'And you, Mr Wrench, are you a Conservative?'

He shrugged his shoulders and said, 'I think at the moment, yes. I was a Liberal at Cambridge, as it happens, but the Liberal Party is in a good deal of difficulty. I'm not drawn to Labour – that's the Socialists. I think I will, in due course, be offering myself to some constituency in the Conservative interest. If they'll have me!' He laughed. He didn't sound to Gerhardt in much doubt. Nor did he speak as a man of passionate conviction, the other thought.

'You say "in due course". You are young. I imagine that, in England as in most countries, the electors prefer a man of some experience.'

'You'd be surprised how young some of the new Members are, now. But yes, you're right, of course I'm speaking of a few years' time. Anyway, when I finish this German tour with Adrian I'm due to start working in the City. London, that is. It's fixed up. You see I must make some money. It's no good hoping to stand for Parliament unless one's pretty independent, financially.'

'And that will take time.'

'Oh,' Wrench said with undiminished confidence, 'I expect it'll take a bit of time. Meanwhile doing this job for Adrian has introduced me to a large number of people, shown me a bit of politics from a ringside seat. Been quite invaluable. I've had enough of it now, but it's been quite invaluable.' He laughed, rather oddly, and said, 'And immensely enjoyable as well. But I've had enough. Once back from Germany and I take myself off.'

They had switched from coffee to a bottle of wine from the Palatinate and Wrench was drinking fast. They were in a small '*Lokal*' Gerhardt used quite often, by name the *Goldener Hirsch*. Julius Wrench's words were coming more rapidly and his eyes shone. An excellent Rheinpfalz (for which Gerhardt had produced marks to an astronomic total) was having its effect.

'Yes,' Wrench said again, 'once home and I take myself off.'

'You will no doubt keep your political contacts alive through your friendship with –' He had referred to his employer and benefactor, a man allegedly in his sixties, only by the name 'Adrian', presumably a Christian name, thought Gerhardt, used freely between generations in the English manner.

Wrench disregarded the implied question and said, after a short silence, 'You and I are strangers, so it's rather comforting to talk because you know nothing of any of the people concerned. The truth is I'm in something of a difficulty. You know I said I was going to start working in the City?'

'Certainly, to make your fortune.'

'Something like that. Well, the people I'm joining – a very, very interesting finance house I may say, young people, enterprising, understand the sort of new world we're living in – they want to send me to America. To New York. Probably for several years. It's a marvellous chance. If it goes well it might – well, the opportunities might be pretty big.'

'But why does this make a difficulty, Herr Wrench?'

Julius Wrench looked at his companion. He saw a man whose age was hard to guess – forty-five perhaps? A man with thin hair, obviously once fair and now entirely grey, a man with a slightly crooked, sardonic mouth, intelligent eyes, a grave, courteous manner. He sensed that this was a man with whom it would be unwise to take liberties. Nevertheless, he found himself half-resenting the other's formality, the uneasy restraint it produced in himself.

'Look here, do please call me "Julius". I know that's not the German custom but it would make it easier for me. I'm half your age, I feel silly being called "Herr Wrench" by you.'

He was unaware that Gerhardt was certainly not double his age, being thirty-six at that time. Unaware, too, that the German was sensitive about his undoubtedly worn appearance. It didn't matter, thought Gerhardt sourly, but he did not feel inclined to say 'Call me Gerhardt!' as in some absurd novel. If this young fellow thought Gerhardt twice his age he would act accordingly!

'Very well, Julius, why does your imminent departure to New York make a difficulty? You have, no doubt, the good wishes of your friend, your employer, whose name you have not told me –'

'Sorry. Winter. Adrian Winter.'

'You will become rich, independent. You will return triumphant to England, seek election to your Parliament –'

He smiled. 'That's the idea. I say, I insist on buying another bottle of this wine. It's awfully good.'

He had drunk more than half of it and would, Gerhardt judged, do at least as well by the next. Gerhardt bowed his head in assent and flicked his fingers to the waiter.

Julius Wrench said again, 'That's the idea. And of course, as you say, I'll do my best to keep in touch with people here – I mean in England, in London – people on the political scene, while I'm in America. People like hearing what things look like from America.'

'I am sure. And perhaps you, in what you called a "young, enterprising finance house" will be well placed to communicate some useful judgements.'

'I hope so,' Wrench said, obviously pleased with the other's acumen, and certainly unaware of any irony. 'I hope I may get into a position to do people a good turn now and then. Which, as you say,' (Gerhardt had not said) 'may help oneself later. No, I'm not worried about getting out of touch. A few years away will probably be very good for me. And this preliminary time with Adrian – Adrian Winter – has been, as I say, invaluable. He thinks New York is a splendid idea.' He was quiet for a little and the new bottle arrived.

'Yet you speak of difficulty.' He obviously wanted to confide something and Gerhardt was becoming a little bored. The waiter filled their glasses.

'You see, the thing is that she, that Mrs Winter, Adrian's wife, is a very – well, she and I are very fond of each other.'

So it was going to be that sort of confidence! Gerhardt resigned himself and took a surreptitious peep at his watch. 10.30 p.m. He was tired. The *Brauhaus* had been draining of the emotions and Hitler's voice left a man flat and exhausted afterwards.

'Mrs Winter is younger than her husband?'

'Far younger. They married two years ago. She was a young widow – his first wife died during the war. She's half his age.'

All this haphazard mathematics! Gerhardt said carefully, 'Mrs Winter is in her thirties?'

'Exactly! And still very beautiful.'

Why not, indeed? But to Julius, Gerhardt could see, a woman in her thirties was ancient. Soon he would be confiding that Mrs Winter was 'nearly twice his age'!

This was almost correct. Julius said, 'In spite of our difference in age she and I – well, we rather fell for each other. It's been – pretty marvellous. I say, it's extraordinary talking to a complete stranger like this, isn't it? I feel I know you rather well. All this is, of course, highly confidential. Do you mind?'

'Of course not. More wine?'

'Thanks. Well, the fact is I think – by now – I've reached the point where it's frankly rather a good thing I'm going a long, long way away. And I think I'll even leave Munich ahead of them, quite soon. Adrian doesn't need me for the journey home and I've one or two things to attend to for him in London.'

The situation was hardly original. Young Wrench, first excited by and now tired of experienced lady 'in her thirties', seeks to escape. The subject of many a novel. Gerhardt did not wish to sound patronizing, and it was a sad waste to drink the wine too fast. He said, 'Mrs Winter, I suppose, dislikes the idea of your departure.'

'She certainly does!' Julius said, with a good deal of complacency. Gerhardt found himself with a small itch of dislike, just perceptible. The English had a word, 'caddish', for this sort of self-satisfied disclosure by a man. There was no exact German equivalent.

'She certainly does! You see it's a bit one-sided by now.'

Gerhardt could indeed see.

'She's naturally going to miss me.'

Gerhardt said, with a decisiveness which he rather enjoyed, 'You may be sure that Mrs Winter will get over it. Quite soon.'

'You think so? You don't know her.'

'Of course I think so. Believe me, it is a very usual sort of situation. You simply have to go. The sooner the better. A woman of her age – is she fond of her husband, by the way?'

'Oh, yes, he's very good to her, they get on well. But you know, he's –'

'Twice her age.'

'How did you know? Did I say that?'

'Something like it.'

'So I think I've – well, it's been pretty important to her.'

'I expect that the lady will find someone else without too great an interval or difficulty who will also be pretty important to her, as you put it.'

'I very much doubt it,' Julius said with a satisfied sigh, 'very much indeed, I'm afraid. So it's all rather difficult. To tell the truth, I'm meant to be taking her out to supper now. Adrian said – 'Go to this rally or whatever it is, form some impressions, dear boy. I'm going to bed early.' He's not too well, once again. Then he suggested I take his wife out. But it was too late, and anyway I wanted to talk. It's getting a bit oppressive, you know.'

Gerhardt knew perfectly.

'But Adrian almost pushed us together. He's always doing things like that. He's keen she doesn't get bored. He often encourages me to take her out.'

'And doubtless pays on such occasions.'

Julius said firmly, 'He's a very kind man. I'm fond of him.'

Gerhardt thought he had better show some sort of interest in the other's story, if only for good manners' sake. He said, 'Is Mr Winter content with the situation? A '*mari complaisant*' as the French say?'

'Far from it. He knows nothing!'

Gerhardt found this surprising to say the least. For Winter to send his wife out to supper on frequent occasions with a handsome twenty-one-year-old boy, while himself 'twice her age' to use Julius Wrench's overworked phrase, argued a very trusting disposition or a very silly man. Alternatively, of course, Winter knew everything, was philosophic about it, and Wrench was too obtuse to see. Now Julius said, with a good deal of animation –

'He's a jealous sort of man, very possessive. But he trusts me, of course. And she pretends to treat me like a son. But lately I can't help feeling – well, it's another reason why I think it's high time I got away.'

'You would not wish Mr Winter's enmity!'

'Certainly not! Nor to hurt him, either,' he said with a slight change of tone, whether humbug or genuine Gerhardt could not say.

They had – or, to be exact, Julius Wrench had – almost finished the second bottle. To get away from this amorous dilemma, which he found tedious and banal, Gerhardt asked, 'Herr Winter is interested in German politics, I suppose? I imagine the trip was his idea?'

'Yes, that's it. He's on a committee of the House of Commons that sits on the question of war debt.'

'Reparations, in fact.'

'Reparations among other things. Look, you're a journalist. Would you like to meet him? He'd enjoy meeting you, I'm sure of that. He's seen a lot of top people here, officials, bankers and so forth. He said to me – 'I wonder what the ordinary Bavarian thinks?' He's pretty shrewd. The trouble is he doesn't speak German. Your English is perfect. May I telephone you?'

Gerhardt felt he could hardly object, and it was possible – just possible – that he might do some tiny speck of good to his country by talking of its condition to this British Member of Parliament. He thought he had better explain his credentials.

'I should tell you I am not a Bavarian! If Herr Winter wishes to hear Bavarian opinion he should go elsewhere. I am a stranger in Munich. I'm a Saxon.'

'Same thing, more or less.'

'It is not the same thing. Not at all.'

'I'll telephone you,' Julius said enthusiastically, jotting Gerhardt's office number down in his diary, 'tomorrow.'

At that moment the doors of the modest *Lokal* were flung open from outside with a good deal of violence. Gerhardt saw four young men each wearing the armband of the National Socialists enter the place. They were obviously collecting money for party funds. One was carrying a tin into which paper, no doubt bearing million mark hieroglyphs, was being stuffed with ingratiating smiles by people at the first table they accosted. Gerhardt knew that there could be trouble. The young men were slightly drunk and certainly aggressive. When they first encountered a table whose occupants declined to give – even if politely – there would be a row. It was bound to happen – the Nazis, after all, were a minority taste and Gerhardt heard some muttering from the next table. It was unlikely that, in this establishment and in Munich, the fund collectors would find a party of Social Democrats, in which case fists might quickly fly, but soon it was likely someone would simply shake his head, or so Gerhardt anticipated, and say – 'Thank you. No.'

He was wrong. It didn't happen. The quartet went to two, three, four tables. Paper was pushed into their tin. Gerhardt could see the mocking smile of the young man who held it, hear the irony in his *'Vielen Dank'*. 'You know what's good for you,' he seemed to be saying to the donors. 'Safer to give, don't you think?'

Then the four stood at their table. Gerhardt remained seated, looking at his glass.

The tin was thrust forward – a large square tin with the '*Hakenkreuz*' neatly painted thereon.

'*Partei Geldmittel!*'

313

Julius Wrench fumbled in his pocket. Gerhardt held up a hand to him, with authority, and said to the young Nazi, quite pleasantly, 'Thank you. Not this evening.'

There was a silence, and covert observation from the neighbouring tables. The eyes of the other three young men were on the tin-carrier. He was the leader. Now he had been challenged. He looked down with a sneer. Gerhardt was sitting very still.

'You oppose National Socialist ideals?'

Gerhardt said, very quietly, 'I choose when and to whom I give money.'

'And you don't choose us, eh?' the young man shouted, giving a huge shake to the tin. The others echoed him as if in a chorus, and moved, two on either side of the table. Julius Wrench was watching Gerhardt, only Gerhardt.

Very slowly the latter turned his head, looked up, looked the tin-carrier full in the face. Then he spoke, without raising his voice, but spitting out every word with great force and precision. The room was near silent, as people pretended to be absorbed in their own affairs. Quiet though it was, Gerhardt's voice could be heard everywhere.

'I am a German officer, now of the reserve. You dare to come and stand over me and my guest, you filthy young lout? You dare to suggest I must put money into your tin, just because you ask for it? You dare to adopt that tone to an officer? You –'

Gerhardt stood up, very suddenly. He was taller than any of them. They stood absolutely still, gawping. For the first time Gerhardt raised his voice, raised it to maximum volume, at the same time pointing to the door with his hand –

'GET OUT!'

They got out.

A minute after they had left, the proprietor of the establishment, who had been watching the whole affair from well behind the scenes, came forward, bowing. Gerhardt had been to the place a good many times and his name was known.

'Herr von Premnitz, it's a great pleasure – would you and your friend like another bottle of wine? I have something rather special –'

'No,' Gerhardt said. 'Thank you. We are going. We have had enough.'

Two evenings later Gerhardt went to the reception desk at the Park Hotel and asked for Mr Adrian Winter. Julius Wrench had telephoned the newspaper office the morning after their encounter.

'I'm afraid I talked much too much. It must have been very boring.'

'Not at all.'

'I'd no right to impose my personal problem on a stranger. I apologize. To tell the truth I'm not even quite sure how much I did say. We drank an awful lot of that excellent wine, didn't we?'

'Yes, we drank a good deal. Very enjoyable.'

'I can't help feeling I was rather indiscreet.'

Gerhardt said nothing, and the other went on, 'I've spoken to Adrian. He was most interested that I'd met a newspaper man, and at a Nazi rally.'

'I was there, like yourself, from curiosity.'

'Yes, I know. Well, he wondered if you could have dinner at the hotel tomorrow.'

It suited perfectly well and Gerhardt was sure that it was his duty to go. He said, 'Herr Winter is most kind. Please tell him I accept. Will you be present yourself, to introduce us?'

'No, I'll be out that evening. As a matter of fact, I've talked to Adrian and agreed to go back early to London. I'll be leaving after dinner on the evening train, the Paris train.'

After dining with the lovely, possessive Frau Winter, Gerhardt thought. Doing duty of a different kind.

'Just ask for Mr Winter. About eight o'clock, I hope that's all right. He's got a sitting room on the second floor. You'll probably dine up there. Did I tell you he doesn't speak German?'

'You did.'

'But he's a charming man. I'm glad you're going to meet. He's not been feeling too good these last few days, but he's looking

315

forward very much to your dining with him. I'm sure you'll like each other.'

'Of course,' Gerhardt said, feeling a good deal of indifference, 'of course. *Auf Wiedersehen*.'

He told the Director about the *Brauhaus* meeting, and of Adolf Hitler's speech. The Director asked if Gerhardt had been impressed, knowing from his tone that he had. He respected Gerhardt's intelligence, despised the National Socialists, and told himself that a civilized and cultivated man couldn't possibly be taken in by them or by their mountebank leader. Yet Gerhardt sensed he had known it would be so.

'*Herr Direktor*, Herr Hitler has remarkable magnetism. He is a man who draws the affections as well as the attention of an audience. His method is subtle. He has studied the art of an orator, believe me.'

'But the nonsense he talks –'

'Not all nonsense, far from it. Nuggets of gold amongst the sludge. And the whole thing conveyed with immense conviction.'

'You surprise me, Premnitz,' said the Director with some asperity, rather assumed, Gerhardt thought. He had given his superior what he expected. 'You surprise me. The audience I take it, were party members. He was addressing the faithful.'

'Not exclusively. I'm sure a good many people were simply curious, like me. And he was clever – the most extreme monarchists and separatists would have found it difficult to quarrel with what he said. There was, incidentally, a young Englishman at my table. We drank wine together afterwards. He's here *à la suite* of a visiting English Member of Parliament, an influential man it seems. I'm going to dine with the latter tomorrow night. At the Park.'

'Are you indeed? Why Premnitz,' said the *Herr Direktor* with a hint of a smile, 'you're turning into quite a newshound!'

The Park was an old-fashioned hotel, feeling the times hard like all of them. Gerhardt was told that Herr Winter was expecting him, and a pageboy escorted him to a door on the second floor.

Adrian Winter was larger than he expected. Gerhardt had formed a picture of somebody small, ugly and fussy – perhaps

316

unfair knowledge of his cuckolding formed in the mind a caricature. In fact, Winter was large, florid and handsome – a heavy
grey moustache suited his red-faced good looks. Gerhardt
could imagine that he was a popular, jovial member of the
British Parliament, not, perhaps, very interested in power or
particularly clever, but trusted and shrewd in his judgements
of men.

Nevertheless, Gerhardt reminded himself that, if young
Wrench were not a liar, Winter was less than perceptive in the
matter of his own wife. Especially since he had been described
as 'jealous' and 'possessive'. His first words were welcoming and
kind.

'You are giving me great pleasure. Herr Premnitz. I can
imagine how busy you are, as a distinguished newspaper man,
and now I want to learn from you, to pick your brains, and to
give you nothing but a dinner in return.'

Gerhardt smiled and said that he was both undistinguished and
delighted. Winter explained that his wife was sorry not to be with
them.

'My young friend Julius Wrench, whom you met and who
arranged this, is leaving Munich this evening. I suggested my
wife take him out to a good dinner somewhere, I don't know
where, and then put him on the night train to Paris and Calais.
He has been something of a son to both of us.'

'I thought him charming.'

'And efficient. He ought to go a long way. Did he mention
that having finished this sort of a job with me, not a job for a
young man to do long, he is hoping to go to America?'

'He spoke of it. I understand his eyes are on the financial
world.'

'That's right, and if he wants to go into British politics – and
he's seen enough of it in these months with me to decide, heaven
knows – he must have financial independence. That means making money. He's got the chance – he's got brains and energy, and
I've supplied contacts. In fact, we heard yesterday that the
American venture is definite. He's going to spend a month in the
City of London and then off. I'm glad for him, though we'll miss

him.' He sounded to Gerhardt immensely genuine. Even more so when he added –

'My wife will especially miss him. We've no children – and nor has my wife, she was married before, you know – and Julius has been such an amusing, affectionate boy it really *has* been like having a son, as I said! And he's first-class company – and plays a decent hand of bridge, too, which is a favourite game of mine.'

Gerhardt smiled sympathetically and murmured that he, too, was a keen bridge player – not typical for a German of those days: he had learned in prison camp. He inspected Adrian Winter and digested his warm references to Julius Wrench. This could not, he thought, all be humbug. Why expand and emphasize in this (to Gerhardt) rather painful way? Gerhardt was too kindhearted to be amused by such circumstances, and he rather liked Herr Winter.

'Now I want your views, your real views, on what's going to happen here. But first let's have some dinner.'

Dinner, already ordered by Winter, was brought to the private sitting room. It was, for those days in Munich, an extravagant meal. The host complained that he suffered from chronic indigestion and that Gerhardt 'must forgive him if he didn't eat much', but in fact he set to with conspicuous enjoyment. Gerhardt reminded himself of what a pound sterling could buy, as Winter began questioning him closely about the real impact of inflation, the effect on individual businesses, fortunes, salaries. He had talked, he said, to officials and senior people. He wanted to learn the human realities behind the statistics. Gerhardt found him both perceptive and sympathetic.

Once Winter said, agreeably, 'You're a thorough people. Anything you do, or feel, you set about with expertise, with total commitment. You Germans do nothing by halves.'

Gerhardt laughed. 'Mr Winter, that was first said to me by an English friend, in Berlin before the war! I expect it's true.'

'Who was that?'

'He was attached to your Embassy. His name was Francis Carr.'

'Why, I know Francis Carr well,' exclaimed Winter. 'He often stayed at our home in the country when – when my first wife was

318

living. We were fond of him. How interesting that you knew him. My present wife knows him too, of course.'

'I knew him quite well.'

They talked of Carr for a little. The mutual acquaintance helped to get them on equal terms. Gerhardt thought the other could see him, increasingly, not simply as a Hun – a sympathetic, intelligent Hun perhaps – but as somebody who knew people he knew. Almost capable of being 'one of us'. Gerhardt could see all this working behind his host's eyes.

Then Winter started asking about German political parties and their solutions to the crisis. Julius had told him of the meeting at the *Brauhaus*. Winter examined his guest on the state of emergency, the relations between Munich and Berlin, the prospects for the Republic.

'This man, Herr Hitler – to be frank, should one take him seriously as a politician? I'd hardly heard of him until I came to Munich, but he gets a lot of publicity in your papers. He's – I don't wish to sound rude, but he's an odd-looking little fellow, isn't he?' He laughed, deprecatingly. Gerhardt smiled.

'Adolf Hitler will certainly not achieve influence through his personal appearance.'

'Through his ideas, then?'

'Perhaps. Perhaps not at all.'

'Mr Premnitz, I've read several of his speeches now, translated by Julius – Julius is pretty handy at German. Let me ask you something very directly about Herr Hitler. May I?'

'Of course. I am, however, no expert on politics. I had never seen or heard Hitler until the other evening. So, you see, I am here under false pretences. I am not a political man. But please ask what you wish – I have no party affiliations, you could not offend me, Mr Winter.'

'Right. What I want to ask you is – did there strike you, when you listened to him, as something demonic about Hitler? Some of his words – some of his ideas – it's as if some extraordinary spirit possessed him – not like a politician talking at all –'

Gerhardt considered. 'Demonic?'

'Yes – that means haunted, devilish –'

'No, no, I understand the word. I'm simply considering the question. You see, he is a very professional performer, very calculating.

'I could guess that, from what Julius said.'

'So that I don't think any adjective fits him which implies that his actions are in any way involuntary or uncontrolled. He knows what he's doing. He knows what he's saying.'

'Nevertheless – some of his reported words – some, not all –'

'I know what you mean. You are asking is he a prophet or a fiend?'

'That's putting it strongly.'

'Certainly. And perhaps a man can be both. But my answer to you is, I don't know! I've seen him and I don't know. All I know is – and, don't misunderstand me, I am familiar with the sort of remarks of Hitler which have led you to ask the question – all I know is that at the end of his speech in the *Brauhaus* two nights ago I was on my feet cheering, with the rest.'

'You were!' Winter said, nodding thoughtfully. 'You were! And you, a hardened, sceptical newspaper man –'

'Of no great experience.'

'And an officer, an officer with General Staff training!'

Gerhardt had, in the course of the evening with Julius Wrench, inevitably given a brief *curriculum vitae*. The German General Staff had a high international and intellectual reputation, even with their enemies. Perhaps particularly with their enemies.

Winter said – 'The big issue here in Bavaria is whether your conservative monarchists, who want separation, will be able to use the Nazis' popular appeal, or the other way round – am I right?'

'Yes, Mr Winter. Something like that. I think you are well informed.'

They were drinking a red wine from the Main area. Suddenly Winter put his glass down and gazed at his plate with his eyes half-closed. Next moment he clapped his hand to his left breast with a groan. Getting up – Gerhardt thought he was going to fall – he moved to an armchair and collapsed into it, breathing heavily. His eyes were closed. Gerhardt jumped up and ran round the table.

'Herr Winter, Herr Winter! Are you all right?'

Winter had gone very pale, almost grey in the face. He now had both hands to his chest and his expression was contorted with pain. He was very still, his eyes glassy. He muttered, 'My digestion! Oh my God!'

Gerhardt moved to the telephone and ordered the reception desk to inform the manager that Herr Winter was unwell. Three minutes later the manager of the hotel appeared, accompanied by a nurse. She moved straight to Adrian Winter, took in the situation instantly and spoke directly to him. He looked up at her, face still grey and twisted with pain, body very still. He comprehended nothing but took the glass of water in which she had dissolved a tablet.

Gerhardt said softly, 'This is a very important English personality. He speaks no German.'

'He must see a doctor at once.'

The hotel manager started talking nervously and rapidly. The doctor who usually and efficiently dealt with all problems within the hotel had, wholly exceptionally, been summoned to attend an emergency – an accident – in a nearby street. It was an unbelievable misfortune that this had coincided! Another would be summoned at once –

The nurse cut in. She had noticed Gerhardt looked a man of decision, and for the Englishman decisions had to be taken.

'The *Heilige Josef* Clinic is only two hundred metres away. It would be as quick to move him there. I know them well. They are excellent. This man needs attention and care immediately.'

'How would he get there?'

'I will use this telephone,' she said. 'I can have an ambulance here in less than five minutes. It will take longer to get another doctor – at the "Josef" they are excellent but they cannot leave the clinic. It would be best.'

Gerhardt accompanied the ambulance to the clinic, so fortunately near. He explained to everyone he saw that this was a 'visiting dignitary of high international importance' and the usual

321

German respect for rank united with the nurse's efficiency to cut corners, and to get Winter seen by a competent doctor very quickly. Gerhardt left a message at the hotel for Mrs Winter. He considered alerting the police to make an announcement at the main railway station, where she would be seeing off young Wrench, but his recollection of the time of the Paris express led him to suspect she would not be there until after eleven o'clock, and it was still only just before ten. He had no idea where they were dining, and decided to take no further action to discover the wife's whereabouts until Winter's condition was clearer.

He waited in the high, bleak corridor outside the room where the Englishman was being examined. The clinic had originally been a religious house and had the echoing, anonymous quality habitual in such places, something of purgatory about it. After forty-five minutes the doctor emerged.

'Herr Premnitz? Come this way, please.'

He led the way to a sort of cubicle where he told Gerhardt that Winter had had a heart attack.

'There is no reason why he should not recover from it completely. He should have a few days here with complete rest and under proper supervision. He is asleep now and will probably sleep for many hours.'

'His wife does not yet know. Should she visit him here this evening, Doctor?'

'No point whatsoever. He is in no danger, and sleeping as he should. You will see her?'

'Yes. I shall return to the hotel now and explain that there is no cause for alarm.'

Gerhardt telephoned the hotel from the doctor's office. Frau Winter had not yet returned. He told them to cancel the message that he had left and that he would return himself within a few minutes.

Gerhardt found the manager perturbed. He had insisted on coming personally to the telephone. 'Herr von Premnitz, it would have been possible to bring a doctor here, we always ensure –'

'I dare say. In the circumstances, it was best to get him to a

ospital immediately. Everything is perfectly in order and Herr
Winter will be returning to his rooms in a few days.'

Back at the hotel, Gerhardt decided that he had better introduce Mrs Winter to what had happened in stages. She might be
an hysterical sort of woman. She might also be in a neurotic state
already, from another cause, known only to him – the departure
of young Wrench. This mixture of dramatic events might produce
feverish reactions in a highly strung female, if she were one.
Gerhardt wondered whether it would be callous simply to convey
everything by letter and decided that it would. She had better,
however, receive a warning.

He sat at a desk in the Park and wrote a note:

> 'Dear Mrs Winter,
>
> I regret to say that while we were dining together
> your husband had a mild seizure of some kind which has
> necessitated his being taken to hospital. I accompanied
> him. He is perfectly all right, is asleep, and will probably
> be kept there for a few days only, for observation and
> recovery. The doctor there has told me that there is no
> reason whatsoever for you to go to the hospital tonight.
> Should you wish further information at any time you
> should ring –'

He concluded the note:

> 'I wished to give you warning of this. I am waiting in
> your sitting room to give you any further details you
> desire, and to be of any service to you that you require.,
>
> Gerhardt von Premnitz.'

He told the reception clerk to make sure that Frau Winter was
given this and that she read it immediately on her return. It was
now ten minutes past eleven, and, devoutly hoping that she had
seen Wrench off without suicidal Anna Karenina-like aftermath
at the railway station, that she would prove a sensible, decorous
Englishwoman, Gerhardt let himself into the Winter sitting room
on the second floor. He looked at the side table and decided that
he had earned a glass of his host's brandy. He might have a long

323

wait. He thought he would like a little warning – he might well fall asleep in a chair! He rang Reception.

'Herr Premnitz, from Herr Winter's suite. When Frau Winter returns, not only give her the letter as I arranged, but also ring me and inform me here.'

'Jawohl, Herr Premnitz!'

Gerhardt sat in the comfortable chair into which Winter had earlier collapsed and wondered whether the evening had been totally wasted. He feared so. Winter had been sensible and sympathetic and Gerhardt thought that he had made some impression on him, describing the impact of reparations and economic collapse on Germany. He had been talking to one of the victors, to an enemy of yesterday, but, he felt, to an understanding enemy of yesterday. Furthermore, it was clear to Gerhardt that Adrian Winter felt as a citizen of Europe, that he seemed a man who could see beyond national horizons. He was, Gerhardt thought, making a genuine effort to understand the German problem – his visit to Munich itself bore witness to this. German politics surprised and confused him, but they surprised and confused all. The peculiar phenomenon of Adolf Hitler Winter clearly found both compulsive and disturbing – as did many Germans, though most were able to dismiss it with a laugh or sneer. But all this interest which might one day indirectly help, thought Gerhardt, would probably now be overlaid, be obliterated by the heart attack! Winter's energies would now be spent on recovery, not on digestion of political information!

Gerhardt felt sleepy and discouraged.

The telephone rang.

'Herr Premnitz?'

'Yes.'

'Frau Winter has returned to the hotel, has read your note and is already on her way to the suite.'

As Gerhardt put the telephone down, the key of the sitting room door turned and she came in. They stood for a long moment facing each other without a word before Gerhardt's head inclined and his hand went out.

'Why, Mrs Gaisford,' he said, 'It has been a long time.'

CHAPTER XVII

eronica Winter, she of three husbands so far (and, Gerhardt flected, highly unlikely yet to have found her last), was lunching th him at the Park Hotel. He had called, by arrangement, three .ys after Adrian Winter's heart attack, and found the English ember of Parliament back in his suite, not looking too bad :hough a good deal paler in the face. Winter expressed gratitude r what Gerhardt had done, which wasn't, Gerhardt thought, uch.

'They insist I have a nurse here, you know – she's a decent oman, although of course I can't understand a word she says. .e hotel people have been very good. Given her a room next or. I'm under strict discipline, I can tell you!'

Gerhardt smiled. 'I'm glad to hear it, sir.'

'As long as I don't try to go too quickly I'll be perfectly all ;ht. Last thing I want to do is give up the House.'

'The House?'

'Parliament. I resigned once before, you know, when I was ite young. Had a bad time – stomach, all that. Went on some ars. Then they persuaded me to stand again, during the war. .e had to. Duty.'

'And,' Gerhardt thought, 'how you love it!'

'I'll go when I'm no more good to them, of course, but at esent they need men with a bit of experience.'

He was dressed and sitting in the same chair from which he d been carted to hospital. Gerhardt wondered, again, whether ything of their conversation that night had stuck in Winter's nd. He thought he would, despite the other's convalescence, ack the point directly.

'We had a very interesting conversation at dinner that evening, Mr Winter. I must not stay more than a few minutes now, yo' must certainly not let yourself be exhausted by visitors, but I shall remember our talk with gratitude for your interest and you' understanding.'

Winter looked at him, his eyes giving little away. He said, 'D' you want to write it up? Interview with British MP?'

This had occurred to Gerhardt, who thought that a brief articl' recording particularly Winter's shrewd sympathy for the Germa' predicament, could act as a record to which the Englishma' might feel occasionally impelled to be cautiously faithful.

'I would like, sir, to do a short piece – "An English politici' looks at the German question", something like that. Would y' object? I would, naturally, show you a draft, with an Engli' translation.'

Winter nodded, already tired.

'No harm. Might help. I'll give it to my people at home, to' Might be used. I'm known to take a European view –'

Gerhardt got to his feet.

'I should leave you now, sir. Thank you.'

'We plan to return to London next week.'

'I'm sure you'll feel much better by then, Mr Winter.'

Gerhardt was sure of no such thing. Winter looked at hi' without expression. He said softly, 'I hear you've met my wi' before.'

'Yes. I met Mrs Winter long ago, in Berlin.'

'Only in Berlin? She said she'd met you in England.'

'That's true, I'd forgotten. We also met somewhere on a vi' of mine to England. I think it was the summer of nineteen twel' or thirteen. But we first met in Berlin. At my father's house, ' fact.'

'She'd just lost her first husband.'

'So my father informed me, I remember. Very sad.'

'Odd business. Then she married a fellow called Marve' Neighbour of ours in Sussex. Soldier, killed in 'seventeen. Li' so many.'

Winter took the other's hand and held it for a little longer th'

326

handshake, something rather touching. He said – 'You have ach with my wife. Talk about old times. It'll be good for her. e can't sit up here with an old wreck all day.'

'It will give me great pleasure. I will telephone, if I may.'

'She'll be back soon. Shopping. Ring her up here. Fix it .'

'Goodbye, sir. I shall send you the article.'

And next day Gerhardt found Veronica sitting opposite him the Park restaurant. They had said little to each other beyond pressing astonished recognition during that eventful night when inter was taken to hospital. She was still, he thought, a beautiful man. She wore skirts short, in what was becoming the fashion, d her legs and figure were superb. Gerhardt felt no desire for r – that side of life, he accepted grimly, was permanently ashed for him on a certain day in Flanders in autumn 1917. e and he had never been lovers, but he had certainly found r intensely desirable in the old days. He looked at her with preciation still: yes, a beautiful woman. His memory, always curate and retentive, irrelevantly ranged over her confidential from other days. She was eating very little. They had spoken first of her husband's attack, and she talked of him with nuine concern. After a brief exchange they had begun to use t names to each other once again.

Odd, you saving Adrian's life, Gerhardt. You do crop up, n't you! And you've changed your name, like me.'

I did what I could,' Gerhardt said, with a touch of deliberate itality. 'You have already lost two husbands. The experience st have been – harsh.'

You know perfectly well that I didn't feel anything for my first sband. Gaisford was an unsatisfactory creature.'

Gerhardt smiled. 'As you know, we found that so as well. hough I, of course, was a simple young officer with my iment at that time. I was only employed on – shall we say, ernational liaison duties? – rather later.'

Gaisford tried to screw more money out of you and failed. u told me, that time in England. I thought it rather funny. minic Drew put him up to it.'

'I remember.'

'You told me that Gaisford was helpful – and was paid for – by giving your people a whole network of contacts in Sou America. You said that was where a lot of our money came fro You exploited my widow's poverty, you wretch!' She laughe perfectly agreeably, and went on, 'I'd have seen you in h before helping you! But then you found the Irish part of me a we made a deal, didn't we?'

'We did.'

'Then I rather fell for Dominic Drew – "Printer", we cal him – although he was an awful cad.'

'I remember that, too.'

'He tried to put pressure on me, of one sort or another. O or two very decent people were in love with me, believe it not, and Printer's main pressure point would have been to t them that I'd been accustomed to share his bed. We were stu about such things in those days.'

'Some people remain so. It is not an insignificant threat.'

'No. Anyway, it didn't really work. Printer's dead – he v killed in a Zeppelin raid on London. Very late in the war.'

Gerhardt was genuinely surprised. He had never before he of anybody being a casualty from German air raids – they w something of a joke among the front-line soldiers.

Veronica went on – 'But I saw him in the war. He turned in Dublin – in Ireland. You know I was there? Yes, of cou you do.'

'That was always the idea. You were to be a point of cont with those elements in Ireland working against the Bri Government. You were also to act as an agent of influence – speak for our side of the case where it could be done.'

'Ireland was where my heart was, Gerhardt.'

He had no reason to doubt it. Veronica had never appea particularly interested in money. Now she said –

'Yes, I really felt alive at that time. Easter, 1916. It was hopeless, of course. I did what little I could, as I'd promised wasn't much. I helped one man get away. They caught him lat

'Were you suspected?'

'Well, as I told you, Dominic Drew came over there at that [ti]me, sniffing out stories. He guessed a good deal – he knew I [wa]s an Irish patriot. And later he wrote to me, telling me that [I – and the authorities, he said – knew perfectly well what I'd [be]en up to. That was after they'd arrested Burke – the man I [sh]eltered.'

'But you were not arrested or questioned?'

'No. I lived on tenterhooks, I can tell you! I'd left Ireland, was [liv]ing in London. But nobody approached me. I expected it every [tim]e the doorbell rang! I've come to the conclusion Printer was [on]ly guessing – then told me, just to hurt me. He hated me [be]cause I wouldn't sleep with him any more. He was crazy about [me].'

After eating some of her lunch, thoughts away in the past, she [sai]d, 'He – Printer – told me in a letter that my husband, Alan, [wa]s being informed of my past activities. That probably meant [he] himself intended to tell him! It terrified me. It would have [be]en the ultimate sin, in Alan's eyes. Treachery. Betraying the [co]untry. But I think Printer was bluffing there too, because Alan [wo]uld have had it out with me, and I heard nothing. Alan was [kil]led, of course, at about that time. Thank heaven he never [kn]ew – it would have destroyed him.'

'Veronica,' said Gerhardt, 'I must tell you that your name was [pu]t to me, while I was a prisoner of war. They knew there was [a c]onnection with myself. No documents ever passed between [us.] How could they have known the Brendthase name except [fro]m you?'

[V]eronica stared at him. She murmured, 'The person who knew [o]r, anyway, suspected – about me was Francis Carr, whom you [re]member from Berlin days.'

'Your husband mentioned Carr the other evening.'

'Yes, they used to see Francis when he was young – we've no [co]ntact with him now, although I think Adrian runs into him in [Lo]ndon now and then. Francis was jealous – he was keen on me [to]o, you know.'

'I remember that being obvious.'

'He was a cousin of the Marvells, reckoned I was no good, and

329

no good for the family, all that. And he guessed about me. Eve
guessed I was in touch with your people.'

'Dear God!' said Gerhardt, ruffled for the first time. 'How –

'Francis tried to warn me off, just after I married Alan. What
more he knew – or said he knew – that you and your father we
in it.'

Gerhardt was deeply shocked. This had been long, long ag
but the disclosure upset him. These matters had been designe
to be kept secret. Unmasking was failure.

'Veronica, you are saying that Carr knew we, the Brendthase
were involved –?'

'So he said. Guessing, I suppose. Putting two and two togeth
from my visits to Berlin, my first husband's little games
divulged by Drew no doubt, my unhidden Irish sympathies.
was rather sharp of Francis, I must say. I admitted nothing, b
it rattled me.'

'When was this conversation with Carr?'

'Oh, before the war began. Just before.'

Gerhardt looked at her sternly.

'Why did you not report it? It could have been important
dangerous. I ordered you to report –'

Veronica began to laugh. Gerhardt continued, speaking ve
quietly.

'We – or at least our Irish friends – were employing you wh
the British already knew of your activities! And you never warn
us of Carr's suspicions!'

'Dear Gerhardt, I wasn't much good, even to you, was
Disobedient, you see! Undisciplined!'

Gerhardt looked at her carefully.

'If Carr suspected you and linked you with us it explains,
course, why the name Marvell was put to me in the camp. I
if Carr had really known of our – our agreement, you would ha
been more closely watched than I presume you were. If
arrested at once on suspicion.'

'Unlikely, Gerhardt. Anyway, as I said, I'm sure it was gue
work. Francis did come to Dublin now and then and I know
was working, in the war, on confidential stuff in London,

perhaps he opened his mouth about me, but not to the point you've suggested. Perhaps I was suspected – but I acted the tactless, large-mouthed Irish patriot so fully and genuinely that I may have disarmed them. As a matter of fact they could have got me at Easter 'sixteen, when I was hiding a man, as I told you. I was tipped off and got him away. Just. Apart from that I did little, really. A bit of Post Office work, as you directed. Snippets of information.'

'You were "tipped off" – warned, you mean?'

'Yes, warned.'

She did not wish to say, 'Warned, warned just in time, with instinctive goodness, with real love, by the only man who really deserved to be loved in turn.' John's quiet secret of the years was safe with her, whether from Gerhardt or the rest of the world. As safe with her as hers had been with him. She owed that, at least.

Gerhardt sighed. He said, gently,'You loved Marvell?'

'No, I didn't. I was very, very fond of his brother, John, but Alan was a hard man, almost too masculine if you understand me. Clever and successful. But not very lovable. I was rather impressed by his strength and confidence. He was very handsome. And, I have to say it, he was rich. But it was a mistake. Still, I certainly didn't want a break with Alan – I'd made my bed, I was prepared to lie on it, at least for a while. I'd been insecure for long enough. I was appalled at the idea of him – being told things about me.'

'There was the brother –'

'Yes, John was lovable. I never see him now. I think he prefers it that way. No contact. Just as well, probably. Anyway, his wife can't stand me. But I did really love John – I only knew it after I'd married his brother! I know how stupid it sounds.'

'You changed brothers very quickly. We were glad, of course. The cover of being an officer's wife was admirable. Nevertheless –'

'Believe me there were lots of people to say, "Alan took her off his brother very fast," as if I was a parcel, an object! It infuriated me. Whatever I did, and however mistaken and hasty and cruel to John and unfair to Alan – all those things – it was my decision. I made it myself – I always do.'

She looked exactly as he always recalled her.

He reverted to that part of her life with which he was more familiar.

'Veronica, you agreed to help us in Ireland. You have said that you did a little. Even that little was, presumably, enough to hang you if detected. You took risks.'

'Yes. I enjoyed that. I've always loathed safety, playing safe, calculation. I've needed to have my heart engaged. I hate discretion.'

'And your conscience?'

'What's my conscience got to do with you, Gerhardt? You were on the other side.'

'Of course. But I was only sent to talk to you at one time, to act in the uncongenial role of paymaster, because my father's contacts and the services he had performed for Germany in that field made me a suitable choice for such temporary duty. I was sent because it kept that particular matter within the family, so to speak.'

'Well?'

'Well, it was not – or at least it was only for a short while – my profession. I was a soldier. Like your husband. You have said that to him treachery was the ultimate sin. And what about you?'

'Treachery!' Veronica said, her eyes sparkling. 'I detest treachery! But it wasn't treachery. Technically, of course, it was. But in truth, in the heart, it was the reverse. Ireland was my country.'

'You concealed this conflict of loyalties, however. Because it was a clear conflict. Your loyalty was directed to a different cause from that of your husband. And, presumably, of the majority of your friends.'

'Oh,' said Veronica impatiently, 'I never made the slightest pretence about what I felt for Ireland. It's just that nobody – or almost nobody – thought or guessed I'd really do something about it.'

'And help Germany thereby.'

'Yes. And help Germany thereby.'

They smiled at each other, a little cynically. Veronica observed, 'After all, look at all these Czechs and Croats and so forth, who didn't want to be in the Austro-Hungarian Empire –'

'Some of them.'

'It's always some of them. Do people think it was wrong of the British Government to encourage their independence movements, to embarrass Vienna? Of course not – it's all part of a success story, it's called liberation, people boast of it. It's regarded as honourable as can be!'

'I imagine so.'

'So what has Germany to be ashamed of in respect of Ireland? And what have I? People apply a double standard, that's all.'

'Ah well,' Gerhardt said, 'It's just a question, no doubt, of the point at which one is standing and from which one is looking.'

'It's just a question,' said Veronica with force, 'of who wins.'

He looked at her with fondness. She was a self-absorbed woman, self-indulgent in her determination to ride roughshod over conventions, other people, any circumstances which might bring boredom. To Gerhardt none of this was in the least estimable, in human terms. His own standards were closer to those she described in her late husband. This woman, thought Gerhardt, had acted against her own Government in time of war, and the fact that the Germans at the time had thought to profit by it – and used Gerhardt on one occasion as an agent – was beside the moral point. But she was extraordinarily honest. And fearless. God knew, he thought, how she had escaped detection. He didn't suppose her activities had been of much importance, but the Germans could not possibly have selected a more imprudent agent. Her significance, her only significance was as a 'sleeper' in position in Ireland, an agent of influence, conceivably useful in emergency to the Irish Nationalists who had her name, but a little fish, a little, little fish. Such little fishes nevertheless laid their lives on the line. It all seemed a long time ago.

He had, however, been jolted by the statement that Carr had suspected his, Gerhardt's involvement. He said, 'Do you think, Veronica, that anybody knows any of this now? Is your case closed?'

'Oh, I expect one or two people in Ireland remember a thing or two,' she said indifferently, 'and no doubt I'm on some security file or other in London, with a question mark. But Printer's dead, Alan's dead, Adrian knows absolutely nothing, and Ireland's something called a free state now. I've ceased to care. I'd not thought of the matter for years until I saw you.'

She sipped her glass of wine, thoughtfully.

'So they questioned you about me, Gerhardt, did they?'

'They asked if the Marvell name meant anything to me. I said nothing. They had no right. I was a prisoner, taken in battle. The other thing was a separate issue. I was naturally not prepared to answer a word. It was improper.'

Veronica giggled. 'You are a very correct lot, aren't you! Protocol, propriety, whatever the circumstances!'

After a silence and eating a little more, Veronica said, 'Oh dear, Gerhardt, I sometimes wish I'd lived in a quiet time, don't you? A time when people read long books and wrote long letters and had all the hours in the world to examine their own hearts and motives and the truth in them. Time – we never have it! Whenever one starts to think hard about a truth or an emotion there's a bomb or a revolution or a war!'

He shrugged his shoulders and she said, 'Our stories, in our generation, seem composed of scraps of unfinished, unsatisfying, messy drama acted out against a background of noise and violence.'

'Probably. And I see few signs that the noise and the violence will diminish. Not in our time. And anyway, you've made clear that you prefer drama and incident to serenity. Noise and violence – they suit you, Veronica. You were born in the right age.'

She looked at him with a serious expression and said – 'I could always talk to you, Gerhardt. Not just when you gave me money and instructions, or I gave you unimportant, silly little bits of information! I always felt free with you. Not secretive a bit – rather liberated in fact!'

'How complimentary!'

She didn't smile. 'Gerhardt, I'm miserable.'

334

He pretended to misunderstand. 'Mr Winter will, I'm sure, recover quicker than you suppose.'

'I hope so. Listen, Gerhardt, I'm in love.'

He tried to look surprised.

'For the first time in my life. The first time in my life, do you hear? Other men – yes, fun, enjoyable, endearing even, ghastly sometimes, exciting sometimes, but this is different. I'm in love, do you hear?'

Gerhardt went on eating.

'You see, it's Julius.'

'Julius Wrench?'

'Of course. And don't look as if you're going to say – 'He's years younger,' or 'What about your husband's feelings!' or something like that.'

'I was about to say neither. Although either might have been appropriate.'

'I'm tormented with both those things, day and night. I'm fond of Adrian. I don't want to hurt him – especially now, of course. And as for age – well, it's happened before, hasn't it?'

'Certainly. I seem to remember Phaedra and Hippolytus.'

'Don't know about them. Anyway, Julius and I have had something absolutely perfect, age or no age. I just can't bear to lose him, Gerhardt.'

'And have you lost him?'

'He's being sent to America. God knows what he'll feel when he comes back. I've got to decide whether to scrap everything, leave Adrian, go to America too. Follow him.'

'Veronica, that would be unbelievably foolish.'

'How do you know? You know nothing about real love.'

Then, swiftly, impulsively, she said, 'I'm sorry, Gerhardt, I didn't mean that. It was a hateful thing to say.'

He used to be so handsome, she thought, so enthusiastic, romantic even. And now? He might be fifty – and it's as if he's been drained of every drop of blood and feeling.

Gerhardt said, 'What does Julius think?'

'Oh, he tries to dissuade me. He wants to prevent me hurting myself for his sake, all that. But of course he's mad for me to

335

come. It's a ghastly situation. And now Adrian has this heart attack, of all things.'

He looked at her now with genuine pity. Here was a woman who had been blessed by the gods. She was beautiful, brave, had a great heart, moved others by her looks, her charm and her personality. Yet she was a perfect fool. To some. if they knew her story, she would quite simply be a betrayer. Others might see her as an evil enchantress. Others, again, might feel genuine love for her. Gerhardt could only pity her as an unfortunate woman who had made a mess of almost everything, who was now about to discover that a much younger man was bored with her, and had created nothing of permanence to bring emotional comfort to her middle years.

'A perfectly ghastly situation,' Veronica said again, in a low, trembling voice. She lit a cigarette.

At that moment a voice said softly –

'Premnitz!'

Gerhardt looked up to see Christoph Fischer standing by their table. Fischer had an extraordinary voice – caressing and affectionate whether to man or woman, and as enchanting a smile as ever most people saw on a human face. Furthermore, Fischer smiled not for effect but from some sort of inner joy. There was nothing meretricious in his charm.

Christoph Fischer – generally known to his intimates in the southern manner as Kitzi – was as unlike Gerhardt as two people could be, but they had, on meeting in Munich soon after Gerhardt's arrival at the newspaper office, immediately liked each other. They had, despite their differences, certain things in common. Both were strangers to Bavaria – Fischer was a Silesian. Both had served on the Western front – although Fischer had never been a soldier by profession, and had been badly wounded as an officer in a *Landwehr* battalion in Champagne in 1916. Both felt a certain scepticism about the new Germany. In lighter vein, both were keen bridge players and played at the same club.

There resemblance stopped. Kitzi was, by temperament, a poet and by conviction a deeply religious man, almost a mystic. Gerhardt was neither. Cool and sceptical, he was trained to calculate, while Kitzi was impelled by inner fire to a certain emotional excess.

Once he exclaimed, 'You think all the time, Premnitz! You should feel more!'

They were different psychological types, but it was impossible not to yield to Kitzi's attraction. He exaggerated, declaimed, was devoid of prudence. His moral sense, however, was very sharp. His devout faith, which he neither paraded nor disguised, was not in the background of his character. It inspired, directly, all his attitudes.

This included his political attitudes. For another thing divided Kitzi Fischer from Gerhardt. Kitzi was profoundly interested in politics. He judged the parties, the leaders, the programmes according to exacting moral standards, holding up a sort of mirror to them, to their words, their actions. The mirror was uncompromising religious truth, as perceived by Kitzi. Unusually, in the Catholic atmosphere of Munich, he was an Evangelical, but his principles, when they discussed them, seemed universal and most of his cronies were Catholics. Gerhardt had first met him when he submitted an article (he wrote brilliantly, with a musical and inspired command of language) on certain questions the political parties should ask themselves. It was witty, apposite, beautifully composed and most uncomfortable. Gerhardt asked him to come and discuss it – they were a very 'moderate', cautious newspaper. The article's language was like a sword to the reader's heart. The two shook hands and Gerhardt quickly fell under the other's spell.

'Herr Fischer, this is a most interesting article. I believe we should modify certain expressions. Of course the paper encourages independent views, but, as you know, our readers expect from us a certain, may I say "judicious" line –'

The Director had previously observed – 'Fischer! He'll get us all into trouble one day. No sense of the practicalities of life. Take care!'

And on that first occasion Kitzi had smiled sweetly and said, 'Where you find one of my expressions inexact, unjust or untrue, by all means let us discuss and modify it together.'

Very few words of the article were changed. After that they met often, and, through Kitzi, Gerhardt made at least superficial contact with a different world, a more relaxed, artistic and (by his previous standards) sometimes outrageous world. He was never at home in it, but was glad to be aware of it. And, somehow, these people often conveyed, even to Gerhardt, a stranger, something like an affection, a personal warmth, which was lacking in his life. Kitzi could move in any sphere and conquer it. He was a free spirit, barely touched by convention for all his strict upbringing (his father had been a judge) and his military service.

Now Kitzi was standing, resting on his stick, a tall man towering above Veronica and Gerhardt. His wound of '16, which had led to him being invalided out of the army, had left him permanently lame.

'Premnitz! I saw you in the *Brauhaus* the other night! I didn't know you editors reported political meetings! Or have you become one of the disciples?'

'No, just curiosity. Like yourself, I imagine.'

'I've not much curiosity left. I know by now what that lot signify. I had my ears open for another article.'

Gerhardt introduced him to Veronica and he bowed and smiled at her, kissing her hand, entranced and entrancing. He turned again.

'Anyway, Premnitz, I hear you gave some of them their marching orders later in the evening! A friend of mine was in the *Goldener Hirsch*. Most impressed.'

'That was nothing. I don't like sweaty young louts throwing their weight about, that's all.'

'That's all! That's everything, dear Premnitz. And everybody should act on it. But very few do.'

He turned to Veronica and asked her about her husband. He had seen the short news item Gerhardt had released with her approval after Winter's collapse, and Kitzi put two and two together. He was pleased when she replied in easy although imprecise German. Veronica had always spoken some German – she had once told Gerhardt she had a German governess as a child, and she talked ungrammatically but fluently. Although

338

obviously out of practice, she had relished the opportunities provided by this visit to Munich, and she enjoyed trying it on Kitzi. He understood no English and nodded his appreciation of her efforts. She told him that her husband was '*Viel besser*'. Then she changed the subject, still holding Kitzi's eyes. Clearly she had understood some of his and Gerhardt's exchange.

'What did you mean by asking Gerhardt if he has become a disciple?'

'I was referring,' said Kitzi with great precision, 'to the National Socialist German Workers' Party, and to its most articulate spokesman, Herr Adolf Hitler.'

Veronica said, 'Julius – a friend of ours, Herr Fischer, a young Englishman who has been helping my husband – Julius was at the same meeting you've been talking about. My husband asked him to go to see what he thought. The local papers are full of these Nazis, aren't they! Photographs of street marches, demonstrations and so forth. I can't make out exactly what they want. I've stopped once or twice on street corners where one of them has been talking, to listen. But I could never make much sense of it.'

'You were right, Frau Winter, not to make much sense of it. There is not much sense in it.'

'Still, a lot of people seem to be impressed. And it's true, isn't it, that your economy is in a terrible state, with this inflation and so forth –'

'Of course.'

'My husband feels that people are waiting for a strong man, a strong voice, to speak clearly and tell the truth, however hard.'

'Certainly. But they would, I think, prefer that the voice belongs to someone who is not only strong but right.'

'Successful, you mean?' said Veronica. 'Correct in prescribing the right medicine? Able to cure?'

'That, naturally. But I also meant right, *richtig*, just. Morally sound. And of course, we are at present enduring a state of emergency here in Munich, indeed throughout Germany, Frau Winter. We do not know whether the future belongs to those who think our Republic should be saved or to those determined, from one motive or another, to destroy it.'

Gerhardt could see a few heads turn at neighbouring tables, and wished his friend would moderate his voice. He knew what Kitzi thought of the Nazis. Indeed, he was always concerned that sooner or later one of Kitzi's beautiful diatribes would be not only published in full but lead to furious retaliation. The Nazis had a reputation for savaging journalists, physically as well as verbally, who attacked them. Kitzi was talking now with energy, smiling all the time, explaining, with examples, some aspects of the National Socialist Party. Veronica listened, fascinated – more, Gerhardt thought, by Kitzi than by his political exposition, elegant though it was. She understood some if not all of it.

'But what matters, what always matters, is not what these people say is their policy. What matters is who they are, what they truly represent!'

Gerhardt interrupted, speaking quietly. 'Kitzi, you were in the *Brauhaus* the same evening as I. A lot of what Hitler said was sensible and convincing. I applauded it and him. You know very well I'm not a – separatist. Nor is Hitler.'

He and Kitzi both regarded Bavarian separatism as reactionary idiocy.

Kitzi sighed. 'I know. There is the seductive side. But you – we – can only judge by what the whole organism produces. And too much of that is vile. *Darum an ihren Früchten sollt ihr sie erkennen.*'

Gerhardt looked at Veronica. He knew the English Bible. 'By their fruits –'

'Yes, I understand,' she said impatiently. 'But since these people are still in opposition, so to speak, without having had the chance to do anything, without power, isn't it all just talk? Everybody in opposition talks as if the end of the world is coming and they'd like to bring it about themselves! I don't see how the Nazis have yet got any "fruits" to be known by!'

Gerhardt helped a little with the translation of this remark, to make it comprensible to Kitzi. The concept of opposition, in the English sense, was not one Germans naturally understood.

340

Kitzi smiled and said, 'Not just all talk, no. We may well see some fruits, in the sense we've been using the expression, in the next few days, I'm told.'

He rose and kissed her hand again.

'Gute Reise. Und Auf Wiedersehen, lieber Premnitz.'

When he had gone, Veronica said, 'What a charming man.'

'Yes, he is delightful. Very sincere, rather brave.'

'Does it need bravery to say what one thinks?'

'Often, yes. Perhaps soon. Perhaps here.'

'I liked him very much. What did he mean by saying one may see something in the next few days?'

Gerhardt told her that in two days' time there was to be a huge political meeting of the 'Patriotic Associations'. It was generating a great deal of excitement. Veronica nodded with enthusiasm.

'8th November. We'll still be here. I want to watch it.'

'It will be best to stay quietly at the hotel.'

'Gerhardt, I want to attend. I get very little that's stirring, exciting these days. Yes, I know, I'm in love, and I've lost him because I'm middle-aged and he's young and bored with me and he's got a career to make and he'll need a young, ambitious wife one day – No, don't interrupt me, I'm not a fool, I know what I was saying about Julius just now, about him being keen for me to follow him to America and all that. It wasn't true, and you knew it wasn't true. He pretends – most of the time, anyway. He wants to get away! And I – Oh, my God, what I feel! And how I feel! And almost for the first time, or so it seems.'

She was talking very low, looking at the table. Gerhardt wondered whether she was about to weep. He thought not.

She looked up with an attempt at a smile.

'It's rather nice talking to someone whose relationship with one has been as clandestine as yours and mine in the past! Nothing can shock.'

'Veronica, those times are long past. As I've told you, the role of spymaster was not one I enjoyed. Nor was it usual. They employed me as being, in the circumstances, inconspicuous. We had met in Berlin. It wasn't important to them, and neither you nor I were important to them. We are now meeting on a perfectly natural, normal basis. You were once a guest in my father's house.' The past, thought Gerhardt, needs burying. Mine as well as hers.

'Quite so! Don't tell anyone about Julius, will you, Gerhardt?'

'Of course not. And I'm sorry. Really sorry.' It was true. He felt compassion, mixed with a good deal of irritation. He said to himself, She did a little for us once, from whatever motive.

'And, Gerhardt, I want to go to that political meeting, or march or whatever it is. I'm sure you can arrange it.'

Gerhardt told her that he would only consider it if her husband consented, and that in that case, he would see what could discreetly be done – he might manage a Press invitation. The condition of her coming would be that she should do absolutely what he ordered at all times. Later that day, Veronica telephoned the newspaper office to say that Adrian Winter was entirely happy that she should attend if Gerhardt could arrange it. Gerhardt had had no previous intention of being anywhere near the *Bürgerbräukeller*, the scene of the meeting, but knew that unless he did his best to escort Veronica she would go off on her own and probably get into trouble. She was that sort of woman. As for having obtained her husband's consent, he didn't believe a word of it. But in a curious way he found the prospect of an evening with Veronica Winter by no means disagreeable.

Gerhardt was often lonely in Munich. Despite the friendliness he had met, and the agreeable company of such as Kitzi Fischer (but Kitzi was unique), he had nobody with whom he could exchange shared reminiscence of earlier life. He had no old friends around him. It was strange, he thought, but Veronica Winter reminded him of earlier, happier times. She reminded him of their first meeting, at his parents' house: and thus she reminded him of his father. She recalled to him, when lunching, how he had described in romantic terms the great parades in Gerhardt's native Dresden; she had not forgotten his enthusiasm, in those far-off pre-war days, perhaps his innocence. And thus she brought to his own mind those moments of youth, the linden trees, the chestnut trees. Another world. He had put it from him

342

tterly, and much of it had seemed finally drowned in the mud f Ypres and Yser. Now she, Veronica, unconsciously summoned from the past for him, evocative as a song. And he wanted to ear the song again.

CHAPTER XVIII

Gerhardt telephoned the Press Officer of the Bavarian Government. The meeting at the *Bürgerbräukeller* was strictly 'by invitation of the State Commissionary – von Kahr.' There was great excitement in the air as to what would be declaimed at this meeting and there were different rumours every hour. Gerhardt's Director, a bitter opponent of von Kahr albeit himself a conservative, was deeply suspicious. He was interested to hear that Gerhardt proposed to go.

'Not your chosen line normally, Premnitz!'

Gerhardt explained about Veronica, and the Director grunted.

'God knows what sort of impression of Bavarian politics she'll take back to England!'

Gerhardt explained the position to the Press Officer, laying it on thick about Adrian Winter's importance.

'He's genuinely friendly to Germany. He wants to understand our problems. If he can be influenced by what his wife actually sees, it will be more effective than routine Press coverage –'

He knew the official in question pretty well. The man was dubious. 'You want her to have a Press card?'

'It will be the easiest device. She obviously wants to be unobtrusive. Her husband's position – you understand? He must be discreet, and so must she. I'll look after her.'

He won his point. Before ringing off, he said, laughing, making light of it – 'What's going to happen, Scholte?'

Security and discretion were not the hallmarks of the Bavarian Government in those days.

Scholte said – 'What have you heard? Nothing can yet be published!'

'What about *Los von Berlin*?' Gerhardt said lightly. It was the separatists' war cry. 'You know me. It's entirely between us.'

'*Vielleicht! Und mit Rupprecht*,' Scholte said, also lightly. Gerhardt thanked him. Unless he was being deliberately misled they were going to announce not only independence, but a restoration of the monarchy!

Afterwards Gerhardt cursed himself for yielding to Veronica and helping her attend the meeting in the *Bürgerbräukeller*, with all that followed. He tried with no success to find excuses. He told himself that, like many, he could not believe events would turn out as they did. Bavaria was in chaos, but there was a certain operatic atmosphere in the whole affair, a feeling that if matters became too serious the cast would burst into a chorus and the curtain come down for an interval of sanity. That, he said brutally to himself, was misjudgement: when the curtain descended, as it did, there had already been bloody tragedy. He had, he admitted, also secretly wanted to go to the *Bürgerbräukeller* himself, while watching the course of that November week with mounting cynicism. There was no doubt that political drama played by self-important desperadoes made good theatre, and, despite his revulsion, the spectacle had a certain fascination. A 'duty' to escort a distinguished visitor's wife to this historic (and by design, of course, entirely peaceful) meeting was not as uncongenial as it might have been a few weeks earlier. And the visitor's wife was Veronica.

Gerhardt collected Veronica early that November evening. He wanted to arrive in good time and to settle her well in the background. The *Bürgerbräukeller* was in the suburbs of the city, with an atmosphere not in the least resembling the rough, beery places generally used by the National Socialists. It was a fashionable haunt, almost a country club. Hitler had, Gerhardt knew, been invited to this 'meeting'. He had been appointed 'Director' – co-ordinator, in effect – of the *Kampfbund*, the group of self-styled National Patriotic Associations, but Gerhardt didn't know whether he would come. He could recognize none of the better-known National Socialists, as people started to fill the huge hall, chattering excitedly. Nazi armbands, in fact, were conspicuous by their absence. There were a good many of Bavaria's leading citizens, including a number of retired senior officers, wearing full uniform. It was a respectable, even a fashionable meeting. The atmosphere was festive.

Gerhardt watched with interest, guiding Veronica's eyes as well as he could. People were pouring through the doors, waving their invitations. Gerhardt saw members of the Bavarian Council of Ministers being bowed to their places. General von Lossow entered with great pomposity, as one already in control of the armed forces of an independent Bavaria. Gerhardt wondered whether the wheel would turn one day, and von Seeckt have Lossow's head for his insubordination. He also wondered if Crown Prince Rupprecht himself might have been invited. He spoke to a neighbour at their table, a well-known and hard-bitten reporter for a rival paper.

'Rupprecht?'

'Invited – yes. But he's not coming!'

'Sure?'

'Sure. One of his Adjutants is a friend of mine. He'll keep well clear until the cat jumps.'

'Will it jump?'

The other shrugged his shoulders and pointed.

'Look! Friends from everywhere!'

Gerhardt indicated to Veronica several well-known personalities from other parts of Germany. All members of the political Right, they were being welcomed effusively by the Bavarian ministers. There was a hush as the great ones took their seats.

'Who's that standing up now, Gerhardt?'

Veronica talked loudly and in English. There were one or two suspicious looks from nearby and a voice said, 'Sh-sh-'

Gerhardt whispered, 'That's von Kahr! Head of the Bavarian Government. Our host! It's his meeting. Now he'll tell us what it's all about.'

Von Kahr started speaking. He was not an inspiring orator and although everybody had arrived with a high sense of anticipation of an historic occasion, it did not at first appear that the 'State Commissionary' would rise to it. He explained at some length the background to the present 'difficulties' – or the background as interpreted by von Kahr.

'I can't follow all this,' Veronica whispered.

'It doesn't matter. He's not reached the point yet. If there is a point.'

'There'll be a point,' their neighbour muttered, overhearing him. 'He's going to proclaim the Wittelsbachs "by the united will of the people of Bavaria". I'm sure of it – one of his secretaries is a really sweet girl.' He winked.

Von Kahr was, however, losing control of his audience, distinguished though some of them were. Throats were cleared, and the usual November coughs grew louder. The inevitable clanking began to predominate as beer mugs and wineglasses were put down on tables. Von Kahr, most unimpressively, glanced at a piece of paper in his hand.

'Now he'll come to it,' said their well-informed neighbour. '*Gott erhalte unseren König!*' and '*Los von Berlin.*'

'Both? Monarchy and separation simultaneously?'

'Of course.'

Veronica sipped her glass of Mosel. She looked bored and Gerhardt glanced at his watch. It was only eight-thirty – and many, many speeches yet to go, that was certain.

Then von Kahr's voice was suddenly, unexpectedly and alarmingly drowned by the crash of hall doors being thrown open from outside. Next moment he stopped speaking, his mouth wide open, and was standing, silent and aghast, in front of them all.

Through the doors marched a solid phalanx of the *Sturm Abteilungen*, the Nazi SA formed by Hitler two years before. Their boots, marching in time, made the floor quiver. Brownshirted, swastika-armbanded, caps with straps beneath chins, each man carried a revolver or machine pistol. Even Gerhardt, innately contemptuous of these party armies masquerading as soldiers, was forced to concede that they looked formidable. Women started screaming, men shouting, a glass or two were smashed, a table was knocked over. The Nazis reached the platform, while succeeding ranks filed in and round the walls of the *Keller*. Gerhardt took Veronica's arm and held it firmly. He hissed –

'Say nothing. Watch and remember. Keep absolutely still, and with me.'

'My God,' Veronica whispered, against instruct.ons. 'The place has woken up! This is terrific!'

Suddenly a shot rang out.

Gerhardt instinctively pulled Veronica down. Another shot. Then a voice, familiar, dominant. Gradually people straightened.

Hitler was standing on a table. He held a revolver in his hand. It was a different Hitler from the rather appealing figure Gerhardt recalled from an earlier meeting, the figure supplicating support. This was different. This was a creature violent, possessed, an elemental force flowing from him.

There was absolute silence.

Then Hitler barked out two sentences. He yelled that the army and the police had joined the Nazis; that their barracks were occupied. People stared, ignorant not only of what to believe (in fact, Hitler's statement was a lie) but whether or not to regard it as good news.

Gerhardt craned his neck. Hitler seemed to have climbed down from his table. Gerhardt could now see Goering, the ex-Air Force ace who was Hitler's best-known Lieutenant. Goering was shouting in what appeared a rather good-humoured way although it was hard to distinguish his words. The SA stood grimly in the background and stared at them all; and they, the guests at von Kahr's party, stared uneasily back. Hitler had left the hall with von Kahr and von Lossow – nobody had any idea why. People began talking – indeed some began yelling. The atmosphere was feverish and confused. Veronica squeezed Gerhardt's arm.

'I'm enjoying this.'

'Why?'

'Anything can happen. One feels one's in a world that's been turned upside-down. Thrilling. Like Dublin in nineteen sixteen. Just like.'

Her eyes were shining. Gerhardt doubted whether she had the

slightest idea of the issues which might at that moment be being settled, and the fate of Germany with them. His heart was beating over-hard.

Veronica whispered, 'Have they declared for a king, as you thought?'

'Not yet. Nor an independent Bavaria. Last thing the Nazis want. Ah-h-h!'

'What is it, Gerhardt?'

Who is it? was the apposite question. Through the crowd, now parting before them like the Red Sea before Moses, Gerhardt could see Hitler, Kahr, Lossow, returning from some side room towards the rostrum. Their absence had only been for a few minutes. Beside them now was a massive figure, familiar, in evidence for the first time that evening.

Gerhardt mouthed at Veronica – 'Ludendorff!'

It was the first name completely familiar to her, the first name that was a symbol. Ludendorff was square, frowning, his jowls tumbling over his collar, his eyeglass fixed, his demeanour impassive. Gerhardt still found it impossible to look at this man of vanished but terrible power without emotion, even awe. To an Englishwoman, of however ambivalent feelings on the Irish question, the name of the sometime First Quartermaster General practically equated to that of Satan himself! Veronica tiptoed and peered. The name was hissed from table to table.

'Ludendorff!'

Hitler started to speak. The gentleness, the charm, the quest for sympathy from an audience which Gerhardt had discerned on that earlier occasion in the *Brauhaus* were now wholly absent. Hitler shouted his message with enormous ferocity. In Bavaria, 'His Majesty is to be invited immediately to resume his throne.' ('Astonishing!' muttered Gerhardt's reporter friend in the next chair, 'Rupprecht won't accept anything offered by this gang, surely?') 'While in Berlin' – Hitler paused dramatically and then screamed, with mounting emphasis on each sentence –

'There will be for Germany a *new* régime! The torch has been lit in *Bavaria*. Tomorrow it will be carried to Berlin.'

There was a roar from the faithful.

349

'*Nach Berlin!*'

The 'November criminals', Hitler yelled, referring to those who had, willy-nilly, been compelled to agree to the Allied peace terms in November, 1918, would be tried by a tribunal and, if convicted, be immediately executed. That included the present Chancellor, Ebert. He snarled the names, and no person in that huge assembly had the smallest doubt that he meant what he said. Veronica understood enough of that part and turned.

'Bloodthirsty stuff, Gerhardt! Just talk?'

She whispered, but Gerhardt felt eyes upon them and smiled reprovingly, without answering. She gazed at the rostrum where Hitler appeared to have finished speaking. The SA were being marshalled by snapped commands – there were plenty of old non-commissioned officers in their ranks. Gerhardt touched Veronica's hand and nodded towards the rostrum, his eyes narrowed.

'Ludendorff!'

The General was speaking. He was now fifty-eight years of age. Under the Kaiser, and with the tacit blessing of old Hindenburg, this man had been virtually dictator of Germany and Supreme Commander of the army, whatever his title, in the last two years of the war. It had not greatly helped the cause, Gerhardt thought cynically. Now he was, it seemed, giving them all his benediction; and assuring them that these momentous happenings, this 'National Revolution' could, should and must save from anarchy, penury and dishonour both Bavaria and the Reich.

Having escorted an excited Veronica back to the Park Hotel, a journey which took a considerable time through the crowds of cars and people, Gerhardt went to his office. Although not his department he was interested to see how the morning edition was shaping. The paper had been well represented at the *Bürgerbräukeller* and the office was humming with feverish talk. Gerhardt asked if the *Herr Direktor* was personally attending to the issue.

'*Nein.*'

The Director had gone home to bed. He was, they said 'Not very well!' His deputy was in charge, Krettner, a man Gerhardt always suspected of sympathy, if no worse, with the National Socialists. Krettner looked jubilant now. He, himself, had been at the meeting.

'This may be a wonderful night for Germany, Premnitz!' Krettner did not like Gerhardt, who pursed his lips non-committally. The hours would show, he thought. All they had witnessed were two pistol shots, and a cowed von Kahr, who had started the evening supposing that he was about to proclaim Bavarian independence under a restored Wittelsbach monarchy, and had ended by giving his assent to something called a National Revolution. But how would the various authorities in State and Reich behave in the face of this challenge to the Republic? Gerhardt was far from sure that all would lie down without a murmur and agree to give up the instruments of power to Ludendorff and Hitler. In Bavaria, it appeared, von Kahr was to 'exercise authority' in the name of the Crown.

Krettner, although clearly excited, had not altogether lost his ability to sit on the fence. The morning edition was to refer to the 'dramatic occurrences' in the *Bürgerbräukeller,* but purely factually. Gerhardt turned to the editorial comment: there was none! A leading article referred, in the most neutral tones imaginable, to the need for all Germans to 'consult their consciences and, however hard, unite behind those measures which can be demonstrated as truly compatible with national salvation.' It might have meant anything. Krettner saw Gerhardt's raised eyebrows as he leafed though the issue.

'The *Herr Direktor* has instructed me that our tone is to be moderate, judicious, non-committal before – before more is known. I am bound to tell you, Premnitz, that I believe we should be more positive in welcoming the National Revolution. I should like you to remember that.'

'I will,' Gerhardt said pleasantly, 'I will.'

Krettner sniffed. But later that night one of the 'boys' whose business was to patrol the all-night bars and cafés, to listen to

351

every rumour and to bring it for collation to the morning desk, dropped in at Gerhardt's office. He was especially sharp, this one, and Gerhardt had found it useful to cultivate him – the Director thought a good deal of him, although fierce with the youngster's occasional impertinence. Krettner disliked him. He looked about sixteen, was quick-witted and disrespectful.

'Herr Premnitz, the National Revolution is slowing down a bit, it seems!'

'What's happened?'

'Kahr, Lossow etcetera were in immediate touch with Rupprecht after they left the *Bürgerbräukeller*. They all bolted to a barracks, still thinking the SA might decide to hold them. One of the Crown Prince's Adjutants found them there.' Gerhardt wondered whether it was the one known to his neighbour at the meeting. 'Apparently he – Rupprecht – simply told them he was having nothing to do with any movement which included Ludendorff! Told them to do their duty and crush any attempt to challenge the authority of the Republic! Makes Lossow look a perfect idiot, of course. He agreed to pull down the Republic at nine o'clock last night. He was going to march on Berlin, actually be made Reich Minister for War, it seems. Now he's got to order the troops to shoot anybody who *does* want to march on Berlin! Six hours later!' It was four o'clock in the morning. The boy added: 'They'll do as Rupprecht says. Nobody doubts it.'

A busy night indeed!

Gerhardt asked the critical question.

'What about Hitler? What about the Nazis?'

'They don't know which way to go! They're on their own! The talk is that it will all fizzle out by midday tomorrow, today rather.'

'In view of what you say I incline to agree.' Gerhardt felt a huge relief. The boy grinned.

Gerhardt said, 'Von Kahr has now denounced the "National Revolution" he was backing a few hours ago! Rupprecht will have nothing to do with it! Von Lossow, in spite of all his wobbling, is probably going to obey Berlin's orders at last! As you say, the Nazis are on their own. The army and the police are loyal, everybody's agreed on that. Hitler and his gang have made a complete mess of it.'

Gerhardt hoped this summary was right, although he spoke with more assurance than he felt. He ran into Krettner in the corridor a few minutes later, and couldn't resist saying, 'It seems we may have been right to keep our enthusiasm for the National Revolution moderated, don't you think?'

Krettner said nothing and looked at him with dislike.

But it did not fizzle out. The optimists on that score took too little account of Ludendorff. Hitler, they learned afterwards, had panicked, running from one authority to another looking for support, even looking for mercy. His great parade of the National Socialist Party was due the following morning. It was planned to have been joined by troops, police and an enthusiastic population. It was to have marked the 'liberation' of Bavaria, to be followed instantly by a similar movement in Prussia, and a triumphant assumption of the Reich Government in Berlin. Instead, by dawn, Hitler realized this would remain a dream. His men were alone. He decided to cancel the parade, the march. The attempt, he recognized, had failed.

He reckoned without Ludendorff. Ludendorff, empty of faith in most things, believed still in the power of his own name, certain that when they saw that grim figure with its aura of invincible authority, German soldiers would join the march. They would never fire on him or on those he led, and German police would not shoot where German soldiers hesitated. Anyway, the Police Chief of Munich was a Nazi sympathizer. Ludendorff recalled, with stern confidence, Napoleon's march on Paris after landing from Elba, that march of the deposed Emperor alone with a handful of followers, facing the levelled muskets of the former Imperial Regiment sent south by the Bourbons to arrest him.

'Soldiers of the Fifth Regiment, would you shoot your Emperor?' Napoleon had cried, moving towards the cordon of troops, throwing open his coat, showing the orders pinned to it. 'Would you shoot your Emperor?'

They had lowered their muskets, fallen in behind him, cheering wildly, and followed him to Paris. So it would be with Ludendorff. He was sure of it. And when the army joined him, as they would, the road to Berlin would be open. The march must go on! *Nach Berlin!*

Before anybody in Munich, however, was certain what was happening – at about half past nine in the morning – Gerhardt was telephoned by Kitzi Fischer.

'Were you in the *Bürgerbräukeller?* I couldn't get a ticket. None of them like me.'

Gerhardt told him about the evening, and also told him what they thought, from the reports reaching the office, had subsequently transpired. Kitzi's news was much the same. He was, however, positive on one point which was still obscure.

'The Nazis are forming up, you know! They're going to march this morning, come what may.'

'Why are you so sure? Won't they just be sent home? Better luck next time?'

'No, one of them is indiscreet, married a young friend of mine. He's actually rather charming. He tells me things. Believe it or not, they're going to march.'

And Gerhardt could, with reluctance, believe it. Kitzi, charming, high-principled, poetic Kitzi, Kitzi the forthright, the imprudent, was nevertheless an adept at getting people to talk confidentially to him – even people who would be naturally disposed to regard him as an enemy. Gerhardt thought it perfectly possible that this young SA man had, over the last months, found in Kitzi a sympathetic listener, a possible convert, certainly a father confessor in times of uncertainty – if, that is, young SA men ever experienced times of uncertainty. Gerhardt thought with distaste of the unfeeling faces round the walls of the *Bürgerbräukeller*, and of the grinning arrogance of the youths he had kicked out of the *Goldener Hirsch*.

'They're going to march, and march armed, no question about it,' Kitzi said, 'and they're bound to be opposed.'

'I expect our street reporters know by now.'

'Some time around midday, my young friend thinks. I've plained how keen I am to watch the triumph of the National evolution.'

'All Nazis? I mean, only Nazis?'

'Some of the officer cadets from the school as well. Loyalty to e name of Ludendorff! In through the suburbs, across the leonsplatz, I gather. I shall be there. I wouldn't miss it for ything. Do you suppose the *Reichswehr* will fire on them?'

It was a question Gerhardt had often asked himself in the last enty-four hours. He knew that in the previous week a stern ler had gone out from von Seeckt to every command in rmany, reminding subordinates of the inexorable demands of ty. He thought it would probably be obeyed.

He said, 'On whose authority are the troops and police acting? at's what matters. Presumably on the legitimate authority of e Bavarian Government – still part of the Republic, which the *ichswehr* is sworn to serve.'

'Exactly! And Kahr, our revered State Commissionary, don't get, has now denounced the National Revolution! There's no biguity!'

'None!' Gerhardt said. But he was still unsure that German diers would fire on Ludendorff. Nor was he persuaded that he ed the idea.

Kitzi said – 'I've had a telephone call from your charming end, Mrs Winter.'

'You, Kitzi? Why? I took her to the *Bürgerbräukeller*, she obably told you. And escorted her home. I also told her that e should stay with her husband until this business is all over.'

'Yes, she told me she was certain it was not worth asking you take her to watch the demonstration! So she's asked me. She'd ard some gossip in the hotel that it's probably going to happen. onfirmed it.'

'Kitzi, please do not take Veronica Winter to watch this march! ave a certain responsibility. I forbid it.'

Kitzi laughed and said, 'Don't be absurd. Anyway, she's found t where they're starting, and if she doesn't come with me she'll

355

go alone! My dear fellow, unless she's put in somebody's car we'll see her marching between Hitler and Ludendorff in th front rank. Just to be sure of getting a good view.'

It was all too possible.

'Kitzi, where are you going with her?'

'To a friend's flat near the Odeonsplatz. They'll pass that wa I'll look after her. We'll be very discreet. Don't worry.'

Gerhardt asked the name and address of the friend whose fl they proposed to visit. After hesitation Kitzi gave it. Nobo Gerhardt knew.

'Don't worry!'

Indeed, Gerhardt said to himself, frowning, it was absurd worry. They would – if, indeed, this march actually took place see a procession of National Socialists in their brown shirts, oth assorted cranks and desperadoes, a body of foolish boys, all be on exhibitionism and adventure. After the march had pass them, there would be shouting and rumour and that excit mixture of laughter and anger which so marked Munich in tho days. They would probably hear that – 'They've crossed t Odeonsplatz, halted, had a meeting and gone off to start drin ing!' Or (conceivably, but Gerhardt doubted it), 'They've occ pied the Government buildings!' – from which, tired, failed a disenchanted they would withdraw at some later hour. It w already futile, this demonstration, he assured himself. It cou have no sensible objectives. Munich had heard at breakfa time that von Kahr and others had bolted to Regensburg a announced that the Bavarian Government had moved there. V Kahr had had a busy night – at the same time it was said that had ordered the National Socialist Party 'to be dissolved', t from the man who had wept on Hitler's shoulder when th agreed to concert measures in the *Bürgerbräukeller* the eve ing before! Meanwhile Nazis were alleged to have occupi the *Rathaus* and the War Ministry buildings, whatever t meant.

The Director, Gerhardt's superior, was at his desk early a sent for him. Gerhardt had taken two hours sleep.

'Premnitz, these Nazis won't agree to be dissolved, tha

rtain! But what will they gain by marching through the city, hich I'm told they still intend?'

'Presumably, *Herr Direktor*, they hope that the mass of people ill cheer them, in a great popular demonstration! And that the olice and *Reichswehr* will never molest them if Ludendorff arches at their head.'

'Well,' the Director said, as he did rather frequently these ays. 'We shall see.'

Gerhardt told him he proposed to watch the march from a autious distance, if it took place. Half an hour later, with Kitzi's riend's address in his pocket, he drove to a small street near the Odeonsplatz, parked his car and took a brisk walk. Friday, 9th November, a bitterly cold, grey day! There were small knots of people talking to each other and pointing to paragraphs in ewspapers. Gerhardt pulled his hat well down on his head and ug his hands in his pockets. He walked up and down and eriodically looked at his watch. Forty minutes passed.

Then he heard it. Expected but menacing, still far off and rifting on the wind, now clear, now inaudible, he caught the inging. Disciplined singing, like the *Landsers* were trained to do on the march, at the recruit depots. Singing with the periodic pauses which would, when they came nearer, be marked by the disciplined tramp of boots. Gerhardt could hear them coming ong before he could see anything. People started to scurry here and there, some towards the presumed route of the march, attracted by curiosity and excitement; some in the opposite direction, nervous. Several minutes passed. The singing was clearer now. A long, narrow street led towards the Odeonsplatz and it sounded as if they had turned into it. Gerhardt walked fast and reached it. People were shouting and pointing.

'Here they come!'

They were, however, still a long way off. The singing rose and fell with the gusts of a strong November breeze beneath the grey sky. In the far distance he could see people running along the pavements, presumably level with the head of the column. Now and then the wind brought snatches of cheering. The singing seemed to have stopped – the marchers were having a rest.

Gerhardt learned afterwards that the column extended for nearly a kilometre of narrow street. He judged the distance: the head of the march would reach the Odeonsplatz in about seven minutes.

Then he heard shouted words of command from the other direction, and turned his head.

A double file of police, in green uniforms and shakoes had formed up in close order across the Residenzstrasse, barring the way to the Odeonsplatz. They were armed. A police officer stood on their left flank.

'That'll not stop them!' a small man with spectacles and a Homburg hat said scornfully to his companion. 'Anyway, they're coming up the Wein-und-Theatiner Strasse, all of them.'

They were peering down the street in the direction of the *Kampfbund* march. Two convergent streets ran into the Odeonsplatz, with a connecting way between them not far from the Odeonsplatz itself. The marchers seemed to be on the other one, the Wein-und-Theatiner Strasse – and excited voices were shouting that it was blocked by soldiers. By the *Reichswehr*, in force.

'There are three thousand of them,' the Homburg hat man muttered, awestruck. 'Three thousand! They're armed! They're going to take over Military District Headquarters!'

Several heads turned. A man said, 'Three thousand, and Ludendorff at their head! I watched them form up! Came here on my bicycle!'

Now they heard the singing resumed, and it was possible to discern the rhythmic tramp of boots. Four hundred metres, perhaps.

Another word of command brought the police rifles from their shoulders.

The man with the spectacles and Homburg hat murmured something and disappeared into the entrance of an alley, as did several. Gerhardt seemed to be alone. He started to run towards the Wein-und-Theatiner Strasse, the road up which the march was coming.

He had already marked the door of the apartment block where Kitzi's friend was presumably extending hospitality to him and

eronica, and hoped the flat was in an upper storey. He also
oped Kitzi would keep away from the window. His articles were
ten so sarcastic about the Nazis that the party paper, the
ölkischer Beobachter, had christened him 'The Antipatriot
scher', a reference sometimes accompanied by a photograph.
itzi was a well-known figure in Munich's cafés, although he had
ever hitherto been physically molested. But to Gerhardt's great
lief the block in question was on the Residenzstrasse, the
arallel road into the Odeonsplatz, the road with that slender
ordon of green-coated police, the road which the marchers
ould miss. He profoundly hoped that Kitzi had failed to realize
at fact – Veronica would be disappointed, but they'd hear the
in, she'd nearly be a witness.

Suddenly he heard an increase in volume of noise. People
oving, as he was, towards the line of march, started chattering
xcitedly and stopping.

'They've wheeled! They're coming this way!'

It was true. The marchers had seen the blocking line of the
Reichswehr and, instead of pushing straight on to defy their rifles
r receive their homage to Ludendorff, had swung right, down
he connecting road, towards where Gerhardt now was. If they
hen turned left in the Residenzstrasse, towards the Odeonsplatz,
hey'd meet the police cordon. And, at the corner where they
would turn, was the block where Kitzi and Veronica would now,
most unfortunately, have a view of what might be the critical
moment of the whole business. Gerhardt heard the tramp of feet,
he scattered cheers, very clearly now.

On an impulse he darted across the street and went into the
apartment block. He knew that Veronica – and, for that matter,
Kitzi – would be irritated by his interference but he felt a deeper
uneasiness than he could explain. A board showed that Kitzi's
friend lived on the first floor and he ran up the stairs and rang
he bell. To his relief the door was opened by an agreeable-
looking, small, grey-haired woman.

'Excuse me, I am a friend of Herr Fischer. I believe he and
another friend of mine, a lady, are visiting you, and I need to
see them. My name is Premnitz.'

359

'Come in, Herr Premnitz.'

'May I speak to Herr Fischer, please?'

She looked troubled.

'A few seconds ago, they left. Just for a short while they sai You must have almost run into them – into him, anyway. Pleas come in.'

'Left?' Gerhardt said, entering the tiny flat. 'Decided not wait for the demonstration you mean?' He felt short of breat The window of the small living room opened on the street h had left. The singing and the tramp of marching feet were no loud and clear.

'No, the lady, Frau –'

'Frau Winter.'

'Yes, she had a camera, she was determined to get down t the street level to take a snapshot of the – the march as approaches. They feared they might see nothing. They are o the Wein-und-Theatiner Strasse apparently –'

'A snapshot?' Gerhardt yelled and she looked frightened. 'An Fischer let her go?'

'He was in the – the bathroom for a minute. She said, "Te him I want a snap of them, and I must have one of the police it's wonderful." "Wonderful" – that was her word. "I'll com straight back after they've passed," she said. Then he –'

'Yes?'

'He came out – Kitzi – he was furious – he ran down after her –

Gerhardt had not seen them in the street but that was possible Kitzi must have caught her, dragged her into a side alley, some where out of the way. If it was as recent as the woman said would have been clear to both that the march was now headin towards the Residenzstrasse – and, in all probability, towards th police.

'Thank you!' Gerhardt turned to run. There was cheering now punctuating the deafening tramp of boots from the street. Th marchers were singing a soldiers' song –

'Drei tausend Mann –
Zogen ins Manöver –'

360

'Three thousand,' the little man in the Homburg had said, 'with ◼dendorff at their head!'

And within a minute, if they turned left at the corner, their ◼ad would meet that cordon of green-coated police, the levelled ◼les, the shaky authority of the Bavarian State and the German ◼epublic. But as Gerhardt ran towards the doc: of the flat he ◼ard a cry from the little grey lady –

'Herr Premnitz! There they are!'

Gerhardt rushed back to where she was standing at the window, ◼inting. And he saw them. Both of them, widely separated. ◼hey were, sure enough, in the Residenzstrasse, between the ◼artment block and the Odeonsplatz, but by now the march of ◼e *Kampfband* had turned left and was passing them. Veronica ◼ppeared to be flattened against a wall. She was wearing a long ◼ack coat and a small black hat. If she stays like that, Gerhardt ◼ought, she may be all right. I hope she's got the sense to put ◼r camera in her bag. It was possible – he remembered she ◼abitually carried a large handbag. It took him a second or two ◼ see Kitzi. By now there was a press of people on the pavement, ◼arallel to the marchers, people who had joined in as the Nazis ◼rew level, cheering, excited. Kitzi was, obviously, struggling ◼hrough them to reach Veronica. When Gerhardt spotted him he ◼as still only about thirty metres from the door of the apartment ◼lock – as the little grey lady had said, Gerhardt must have ◼lmost bumped into him as he rushed out.

There was considerable hubbub in the street. The leading ranks ◼ad halted. Soon the whole enormous body of men was halted. ◼o singing. Everybody was yelling. Gerhardt pushed his head ◼ut of the window and shouted, 'Kitzi!' at the top of his voice. ◼t was futile – and anyway what did he want to say? The police ◼ordon was about two hundred metres distant, visible to Gerhardt ◼ooking from the window over the marchers' heads.

'Kitzi!'

There was nothing for it but to go down to the street and try ◼o reach Veronica, hoping for the best. Gerhardt had lost sight ◼f her now. The marchers were gossiping with each other, wiping ◼their faces, laughing with onlookers. Then they heard a shot.

Afterwards, Gerhardt learned that the police officer, Freihe
von Godin, had grabbed a rifle and fired it himself. His men we
reluctant – the Ludendorff magic was working.

Then there was a volley.

Gerhardt felt sick at heart, and ran down the stairs. Th
street was chaos, people were screaming, the leading ranks we
turning, gesticulating, yelling. Then the entire column began
move back. As the leading files pressed to get away from th
rifles of the police, panic began to spread. A voice shrieked –

'It's murder. Murder!'

Several brown-shirted marchers ducked into the doorway Ge
hardt had just left, badly shaken.

'Ambulances are needed,' one shouted, trembling, 'they'
cut down hundreds, the filthy murdering brutes!'

It was impossible to make headway against the stream
muddled, frightened humanity suddenly faced with discipline
force, bullets, and the will to fire them. Gerhardt could d
nothing but wait until the flood had passed him, flattened again
the wall. Nobody took the smallest notice of him. After a minut
of this he could see, to his left, the police cordon, still standin
motionless across the street, barring the way to the Odeonsplat
He could make out perhaps twenty bodies lying in the street. H
moved slowly and cautiously towards them, watching the police
After about forty metres, he saw Kitzi; the mob had thinned ou
There was room now for the one-time marchers to run and the
were running.

Kitzi was on the pavement, kneeling down, kneeling beside
still body in a black coat. When Gerhardt reached him and sa
the pool of blood, Kitzi looked up without apparent surprise an
said, 'She saved my life. She's dead, and she saved my life.'

'She saved my life,' said Kitzi an hour afterwards. 'One of thos
brown-shirted thugs recognized me as they were bolting after th
first volley. As you know, when they saw the police mean
business they panicked. Only old Ludendorff, devil that he ma
be, walked forward, daring them to shoot him – walked righ

362

through the police ranks, calm, contemptuous. I wish I'd seen it! I was too far off, but it was a moment of drama, wasn't it! The old devil! Hitler and the others made themselves very scarce, they say!

'Kitzi, Kitzi, tell me exactly what happened to Veronica.' Kitzi was clearly suffering from shock. They were driving towards his apartment having done the sad, necessary things. Soon it would be a duty to go to the Park Hotel.

'I'm telling you. One of the SA recognized n.e. They were bolting, ashamed of themselves. This one yelled, 'Here's the Jew-lover, Fischer!' and came at me. I dodged into a doorway. He was swinging his stick, a heavy wooden truncheon with a thong over his wrist. Strap under his chin. Mad eyes.

'"Jew-lover Fischer!" Two others turned, feeling they might, perhaps, redeem their courage with a little violence. I dodged the next swipe, too, but I saw all three now had their sticks out. All the time the crowd was swirling past. I was completely trapped, of course. Then I heard a cry – "Kitzi!"'

'Next moment, I saw Veronica. She'd managed to reach me, half-carried along by the throng. She screamed – "*Nein! Nein!*" and threw herself between these three louts and me. A stick came down – meant for me, of course – and caught her a terrific blow on the head.

'She fell and must have cracked her skull on the doorstep beside me. Died at once. They saw what they'd done and made off, mingling with their comrades. But I can swear to the first one, I'd recognize him. And it's murder – a criminal assault leading to death, even if not intended as a killing! Murder of a woman, murder of a distinguished foreign observer! We'll make them pay! We'll make the brute pay, and the party suffer! We'll –'

Kitzi, Gerhardt knew instinctively at the time, was quite wrong on 'this point. The 'enquiries' established that Mrs Winter's regrettable death resulted from her having been caught up in the 'disturbance' and suffered an accident thereby. Kitzi, at considerable personal risk, persuaded the police of the identity of a particular SA man who was, he swore, his assailant. The man had an alibi testified to by a dozen of his comrades: he had

363

been in the middle of the column, nowhere near the Odeonsplatz when the whole march turned about, and he could not possibly have been at the place where Veronica fell. The Bavarian State Government acted with the greatest possible courtesy and consideration towards Mr Adrian Winter, assuring him of their profound regret, hinting with delicacy that it was surprising Mrs Winter had decided to witness the 'disturbances' in person. The Embassy in Berlin, having had a full report from the British Consul General in Munich, had been concerned to show that Mrs Winter's death could only be attributed to her own somewhat erratic decision to watch a riot. A stiff conversation with the Reich Ministry of the Interior had drawn conventional expressions of sorrow. The Nazis, in their own publicity, described Veronica's death as a consequence of police violence.

Kitzi reverted to his overmastering thought.

'She saved my life! Why? She could see what was coming at me. She never hesitated. She threw herself between me and the attack. She sacrificed herself, spontaneously, for a stranger, a foreigner, a man she'd met twice. Why?'

Gerhardt said – 'She was a remarkable woman.'

'You had known her a long time, Gerhardt, had you not?'

'Yes, I had known her a long time.'

'She was, obviously, a sort of saint. One who finds it natural, a consummation if you like, to lay down her life for another. I've no idea what sort of life she lived but I would describe her as a saint! And she saved a useless, valueless life, mine. Something impelled her. It was not calculation. It was instinct – an instinct stronger than that of self-preservation. What can we call that instinct but sanctity? Yes, she was a saint if ever I knew one. There was love in her, genuine, spontaneous, selfless love. I thought there was something extraordinary about her from the first minute I met her. Now I know what it was.'

Gerhardt was silent, and, after a little, Kitzi said, his voice raw – 'You don't agree?'

Gerhardt had been remembering Veronica, her twists, her turns, her beauty, her laughter, her perplexities, her enthusiasms, his own ambivalence, his pity.

'Words are difficult,' he said. 'Saint? If you like. I never knew her lack courage, anyway. I don't know the best word to describe her. It depends on what reflection of her one caught, what angles one saw. It depends on the point of view.'

Epilogue

'It's the last day of what we call the Easter recess,' said Adrian Winter. 'The House sits again tomorrow. I've got you a ticket, it will quite amuse you, I think. Bit of a first day of term feeling, you know. Stories from the holidays, that sort of thing.'

The boarding school analogy did not find its mark with Gerhardt von Premnitz. He said, 'You are very kind, sir. And to invite me here to dine, at your club. Too kind.'

Adrian Winter's club in Pall Mall was a large building with dark rooms and a pleasant, panelled card room, seldom more than two tables in use and more generally one or none. On this occasion it was to be one. The dining room, on the other hand, was generally about half full on a weekday evening.

'I wanted to explain a little of what happens tomorrow. You've never been to the House of Commons and you'll get more from the visit if you understand a bit of what's going on, the procedure and so forth.'

'Very, very kind.'

'Also you told me you sometimes like a game of bridge, and I promised you we'd have a rubber if you ever came to London. Didn't I?'

'You did, Mr Winter. I am sorry that –'

But Gerhardt's voice died away. He had been about to say, idiotically, that he regretted nobody had been able to organize a game of bridge for Mr Winter in Munich, but when he thought of the Winters at that time, of the tragedies, the horrors, any suggestion that a quiet game of cards might have passed the time seemed bizarre. Revolting, even. Gerhardt wondered whether Veronica had played bridge. It might have been in her file –

certainly there had been no 'likes to gamble' comment – but he couldn't recall it. Anyway, she might have learned, at any time. From her husband, perhaps. Gerhardt remembered that Winter had spoken of Julius Wrench as a good bridge player. Had they all played together, husband, wife and fancy boy?

Adrian Winter was talking.

'I've got your old acquaintance from Berlin coming, Francis Carr. You said you knew him.'

'I knew him in those days, Mr Winter.' Much, much had happened since then! Berlin, 1912. My God, thought Gerhardt, it was only twelve years ago. Another world.

'Francis belongs to this club,' said Adrian. 'He and I sometimes have a game of bridge together. We're neither of us very expert.' This was unduly modest.

'Nor am I, Mr Winter.'

Gerhardt had learned to play bridge in the prisoner-of-war camp. He played occasionally at the Press Club in Munich. Not often now.

'We'll have a friendly game after dinner. Our fourth is only joining us late, as a matter of fact. He had some sort of appointment down at his home, so he's catching a late train up. He says there's a restaurant car and he'll have something on it. He's got to spend the night in London because he's got a meeting here tomorrow morning.'

Gerhardt asked this fourth person's identity.

'Thought I told you,' said Adrian Winter pleasantly. 'Fellow called John Marvell. Lives in Sussex. Used to be a publisher, still keeps a foot in his old firm. Inherited this place in Sussex from his brother. Brother was Alan Marvell, you see. Killed in, well, late in the war. Alan Marvell used to be married to my wife. To Veronica.' His voice was steady.

'Of course.'

A figure moved towards them across the room.

'Hello, Francis,' said Adrian, getting up rather stiffly. 'You two used to know each other. Marvell's not joining us until after dinner. A glass of sherry? Then we'll go up.'

The men shook hands. Gerhardt said, 'I used to be called

370

Brendthase.' He smiled warmly at Francis Carr. So Carr had guessed he and his father had once 'managed' Veronica! For a little. It was unlikely he would ever trace that guess to its origin, and it was of no consequence now.

'I've never told you, Francis,' said Adrian Winter as he shuffled the cards, 'how splendid von Premnitz, here, was in Munich. I don't want to embarrass him, but he was a wonderful friend – and to total strangers. Of course he'd met – met Veronica before the war, but we were to all intents and purposes strangers.'

Gerhardt had realized during dinner that this evening was the occasion for an unrelenting effort by Winter to come to terms with the past. Winter, so far from avoiding the subject of Munich, the circumstances of his wife's death, all that surrounded Veronica, was, clearly, determined to face all this, to talk about it with a brave show of normality. Gerhardt respected the bravura although he did not entirely understand it. Surely the reticence of grief was still becoming? Veronica had been killed only six months before. But everybody is different, thought Gerhardt, his preference for order and convention a little disturbed. And the English are more different than most.

'Yes, you were a real friend to us, my dear fellow.' Adrian had cut the cards and John Marvell was dealing. When they had all thrown in their hands without calling, Adrian said, 'You two can imagine I was pretty helpless! I'd had this attack – von Premnitz got me into hospital, we were dining together in our hotel – and I was only just up, and making little sense. And then my darling – my darling Vee – was determined to see what this revolution, or coup, whatever it was, in Munich was all about –'

Oh God, can't he stop, poor Adrian, thought Francis Carr. He can't leave it alone. We all know what happened. And Brendthase – why the hell does he call himself von Premnitz now? – Brendthase must find it hellish embarrassing. If he'd been quicker off the mark he might have kept Veronica from getting into trouble, by all accounts. Not that I care a damn whether he's embarrassed or not.

Brendthase! What an extraordinary chain of recollections thought Francis, that name, that face, bring to me. And all or them about Veronica.

He could remember, as if it were yesterday, an evening with Cosmo Paterson, a curious, disturbing talk with the man, walking champagne glasses in hand, talking softly in the great rooms of Anstice Park. 1913. 'Names,' Cosmo had said, 'and one of them's Veronica Gaisford. That's the point.' Francis could remember, could hear in his ears as he now carefully inspected his hand of cards, the gentle, persuasive voice of Cosmo, brave, eccentric, unpredictable little Cosmo, now dead. 'Veronica Gaisford', Cosmo had said, 'that's the point.'

Francis had felt suspended between angry incredulity and a fearful sort of excitement, the sort which accompanies any intrusion of improbable drama, however menacing, into the humdrum tenor of life. Her 'Irish nonsense', Drew had mentioned during that curious luncheon they had had together, all those years ago. Drew was now dead, too. Most people were dead. 'Really, she becomes passionate about it,' he had said. A certain romantic attitude to Irish nationalism was not uncommon among some at that time, heartily disapproved of or mocked by others. But this went beyond legitimate sentiment. Incredulity, but not anger, had diminished as Cosmo had talked on that evening – talked in a Cosmo sort of way –

'They've been doing a good deal of homework, good deal of legwork, too, the Ulster boys. Don't neglect Intelligence in war. Weapons are no good without it. Ever hear of a man, when you were in Berlin, called Brendthase?'

'Yes. A businessman.'

'Quite so. Friend of the late Gaisford. Does a lot for the German Intelligence people on the side it seems.'

This had been entirely consistent with what Francis knew from Drew via Veronica and John Marvell. In the context, of course, of South America. And perhaps Veronica's contact – even if originally a genuinely innocent contact – with Herr Brendthase in Berlin, on what she supposed was legitimate business to do with her husband's estate, had suggested to the Germans that she, too, might have uses? Different uses? How had the Irish dimension occurred to them? To whom had Veronica's passionate Irish feeling been disclosed? It didn't matter. They were no doubt adept at acquiring such information. Everything Cosmo said that evening conformed to a pattern. It had both disturbed and convinced him. He looked across the card table and remembered how Cosmo had continued –

'Brendthase's got a soldier son.'

'I know him.'

'Oh! Anyway, he's used quite a bit, too. Combines it with an ordinary Army career, why not?'

It had all fallen into place. Cosmo had said – 'I reckon Drew may have stumbled on some of this. Has used it to threaten the little lady, keep her docile. That's my theory.'

'I don't think so, as it happens. But whether he has or not, Cosmo, it's important. Alan's going to marry her. You've not said what you – or what you call the Ulster boys – think she's actually done.'

'Very little, I'll be bound. She doesn't know secrets, does she! She's just a nice little lady with a lot of friends. She may hear things, she may one day be useful to spread things. Even do little jobs for them, why not? Point is she's in position.'

'I don't believe Veronica, in spite of everything, would betray –'

'Not necessarily what we're talking about. And we're at peace, old fellow, as you've rightly remarked. Point is she's in position. No criminality. She's a contact, no more, no less.'

'You mentioned money –'

'Quite so. Gaisford had business dealings with Brendthase?'

'So Veronica said. I met him when she was first in Berlin, you see.'

'Dealings which may have made it easy to pass some periodic payments to his widow.' Brendthase, Veronica had said at Faber-down, had been helpful. Brendthase had been kind.

'Still,' Cosmo had said ruminatively, 'I dare say she was given some instructions from time to time. Some idea of what might be expected of her. Expected one day.'

Francis had been silent then, thinking of another evening, in Richmond Park. He pulled his mind back to 1924. They bid, uncertainly, the thoughts of each elsewhere. Francis found himself watching Gerhardt, as Gerhardt concentrated on his cards. And what were they once to each other, those two? thought Francis. He was the contact man, the paymaster, the conveyor of instructions when the Germans ran her for a little, poor Veronica. Much good it did them! But what had Brendthase meant to her, apart from that? Anything?

'Two spades.'

And what about Printer Drew, that nasty bit of work? thought Francis. Killed in an air raid, of all things! He really ought to be here. He'd enjoy the irony, the spectacle. He knew everybody here, except Brendthase. And he'd have quickly assessed what each of us had or hadn't been to Veronica. And he certainly loved her, too. And what a woman she was, thought Francis, and suddenly, blindingly, he saw Veronica as she had first appeared, in an hotel in Berlin, smiling, laying a hand on his arm, concentrating on him. It caught his breath. I've no right even to remember, he thought. One of these men married her, another – perhaps two others, were her lovers. What was I? 'Neuter,' she once called me. And cold.

'Three clubs.'

'Neuter,' Francis remembered. 'Almost alive for the first time!' That's what Veronica had said, that bright, beastly, August morning at Bargate, with war only a few hours away, his own voice, accusatory yet strangely apologetic, saying frightful things to Veronica. He could remember every word of his righteous monologue.

'You see, I know perfectly well that you have been in contact with certain authorities in Germany. You took on the contact role for them your husband played. His area of expertise was South America. Your usefulness – and your motives – were connected with Ireland.

'You are aware that Germany would welcome trouble for Britain in Ireland, and you have given them such information as you ever obtained – probably trifling. You also assured them that ou would act as a go-between, as an influence on opinion where ou found that possible, as a German contact with the Irish Republican movement. One of many, I dare say. But a socially espectable contact, a lady married to a British officer, impeccable.

'You have, in doing this, been inspired by wha' you may think of as love of your homeland, Ireland. That may be the romantic dream of a silly woman, or it may be more reasoning, more calculated. I don't know. I hope the former. Whatever that case, you have, I suspect, been paid for your trouble.

'Your instructions, and perhaps your wages, came from Brendthase; often, I think, through the agency of his son. Whether he, too, was your lover I don't know.'

Veronica had raised her eyebrows and Francis remembered that for one brief, rather awful moment, he had had doubts of whether he was right to condemn this woman in the way he was doing. Then something inside him said, 'Don't weaken!' and surely one couldn't weaken. Not in the circumstances.

'It is extremely probable that we shall, within days, be at war with Germany. The Germans will have every motive to encourage treachery in Ireland. They will need every contact here who can be of assistance, however insignificant. You're very silent, Veronica. I hope you're feeling well.'

She had stood without moving. If he closed his eyes he could see her, in the sunlight. But he couldn't close his eyes. He was playing a hand of bridge. With, among others, Brendthase. Memory of his own accusatory, priggish voice resumed.

'You're married to Alan. I've no idea whether you love him, or pretended you love him, wanted the comfort of sharing his inheritance, or something else. I'd like, however, to spare him and this family pain. I doubt if you have done, at present, any damage to the country. Your trivial act of disloyalty in giving the Germans the names Alan wired to you of officers involved in the Curragh business was unimportant.'

This had been a shot in the dark, but a reasonable guess.

'At least, you probably gave those names, a minor service. There may have been other small things, the passing on of gossip, but on the whole I suspect the Germans have had a poor money's worth from you, Veronica! So far.'

Adrian Winter swept the cards up and began shuffling, distributing kindly smiles all round. He had triumphed in another hand.

Thank God, thought John Marvell, that Adrian can never have heard of any of that Irish business. It would have shattered him. I condoned treason, in time of war, to save a woman and I don't care a damn. Not a damn. He sorted his hand and looked expectantly at his partner, Gerhardt von Premnitz. Interesting that he'd met Veronica in Berlin. That was before John had – come on the scene. He found himself thinking of the lady, very, very reluctantly. She had been – delicious certainly, unpredictable certainly, a woman in a thousand. But God! thought John, pain only beginning now, after nearly seven years, to dim. Oh God! To think of her and Alan! And of Alan and me!

His mind started to go back, he could not stop it, to a filthy dugout in the Ypres Salient, to Alan's face, Alan's voice, confronting the brother he accused as a betrayer.

Within the hour Alan had died, the accusation still lying at his heart. And John had never been able to purge that memory, never confess it to anybody, never talk about it, even to Hilda. Drew, that damned, spiteful creature Drew, had done that. But Veronica had been the occasion of it, that couldn't be denied. Now that picture had to be carried to the grave, the most poignant, in its own way, of all those pictures, some gay, some grievous, some shocking, evoked by the expression 'The Great War'. Anyway, here they were, playing bridge. And his partner had been on the other side. Curiously enough there was something familiar about his face, but John was sure he'd not met him in the old pre-war days. And John had never been to Berlin. He called 'Three no trumps' in a firm voice.

But now, Veronica came to his mind – not simply the associations, the pain, but she herself as he imagined von Premnitz might recall her, before the war, before the horrors, when he, ohn, and Veronica had once dreamed of a future together – for surely, sometimes, she had shared his dreams? He looked at Francis Carr and wondered, as they had wondered at the time, whether it had been old Francis who had gone stumbling along a dark passage at the Winters' house, Faberdown, shuffling along the far side of a bedroom door from the two of them. They had listened, silently chuckling, to slippered and unidentified footsteps recede. In vivid memory he could almost hear his own voice: 'Oh, my darling! Tomorrow night again? Why can't –'

'Sh – sh!'

'You know how much I love you. You know how much I want you to be with me always.'

'Yes, sweetheart. I know. I think you should be going now.'

'Not quite yet, my love. Not quite yet. Veronica, love, can't we meet more often – like this – at your house?'

'Beloved John, there are the maids. It's not easy. Has to be carefully organized. Planned.'

'Then can't you plan it?'

'My – mm. Darling boy, you know how precious you are to me, but you ought to be going.'

'Veronica, you've said you'll marry me, haven't you? I don't want secret visits in spare bedrooms –'

'Don't you?'

'Well, not for ever. I want you beside me, before all the world.'

'I know, darling, I know. And you know my – well, the things that are bothering me –'

'Of course I do. And bless you for agreeing that I talk to Francis.'

'I've asked you to be patient. For a little. And haven't I shown I love you?'

John had sighed at that, but then dropped his mouth again to the delicious recess between her breasts, fearful of seeming ungrateful or importunate. Veronica had stroked his hair and gently caressed his calf with the sole of her foot, saying, 'Well, haven't I?'

'Of course you have, my darling. Of course you have.'

'You must go now, my sweet, my John, and be patient for little.'

'Oh, you are wonderful!' His mouth and hands were bus again. Veronica chuckled.

'Good-night, my darling. No, I mean it, I really do. See yo in the morning – good-night.'

John had smiled down at her as she lay on one side, the bedside candle the only light, flickering on her exquisite body. He had pulled his dressing gown around him.

'I'll go!'

'And John, darling?'

'Yes?'

'You're perfect. Quite perfect.'

Memory, that memory, had ceased to torment long ago. On the whole such recollections were to be treasured as life went on. It had undoubtedly been love, after all.

She did her best for us, thought Gerhardt, that beautiful, unusual woman. She didn't care a rap for us, but she played honestly by us when the Irish business was tried – and what a silly little sideshow it was. She did the few things we asked. It must have been hard for her, with her husband at the front in France. She had to go against her tradition – or one of her traditions. She was obsessed with Ireland, she was a nationalist, a romantic, a revolutionary in her own way. That was stronger than upbringing, stronger than conviction, and stronger than fear.

Yes, stronger than fear, he thought. He dealt the cards. There must have been fear. They might have shot her. We'd have certainly shot her, in their place. But then we'd have caught her, and they didn't. I wonder why not? Helping a rebel to escape, apart from the preliminaries she gave a hand with. They must have been very slow! She told me, in Munich, that she was warned, got the man away. Afterwards perhaps someone covered her tracks for her, just from affection!

He called, 'One spade', and after they had passed and played the hand in silence, he collected the cards and said pleasantly, 'Do you know Ireland, Mr Marvell?'

'I was there – in the Army – during the war, after I was wounded, first time.'

'Ah, you were wounded.' Gerhardt nodded, solicitous.

'In the Dardanelles. Then I did a job on the Staff in Dublin.'

Gerhardt recalled dates and wondered a little. The Dardanelles. 1916. Dublin. He cut the pack to Adrian Winter. 'She's a saint!' Kitzi Fischer had said, his life save ·, perhaps, by Veronica's intervention, her tragic intervention. A saint? No, thought Gerhardt, examining his hand of cards, Not exactly, but brave. And she did her best for us. I will not forget her. And at the end she was wretched with love for a younger man, betraying her husband with a lad who was tired of her! Poor creature, poor beautiful creature! I will not forget her.

I know they think I'm maudlin, pathetic, obsessed, Adrian Winter said to himself. Talking about my wife, refusing to leave it all decently alone, speaking about Munich instead of treating it as a forbidden subject, inviting this nice fellow Premnitz here to meet them. And Veronica was a point of contact between them all so she has to be mentioned. Maudlin, they're thinking, a ghastly, embarrassing evening. They'll say to each other, 'Poor old Adrian, he's an awful mess, he picks at his sores, he can't leave them alone.'

In this he was less than just to John Marvell and Francis Carr, whose own recollections dominated their minds much more than did pity for their host or discomfort at his forced frankness. Adrian bid and made three no trumps, and they changed seats, retaining partners, for another rubber.

But I don't care what they think or what they say, thought Adrian, dealing the first hand. I want to talk about her. I want to hear her name spoken by people who knew her, people who, when they say 'Veronica' can see something of what I see.

He considered his hand and bid, briskly and confidently. He was a better player than the others.

And which of us has the best memories of her? said Adrian to himself, without unease, as he picked up the cards after another successful hand, defensive this time. Which of us is happiest? Premnitz hardly knew her. He remembers a charming young widow in Berlin before the war, and now he's guilt-stricken because he feels responsible for not looking after a charming, middle-aged wife in Munich. Who got – got herself killed. My Veronica. But it wasn't Premnitz's fault. I wanted to make it clear to him I never thought that. I want him to feel I'm a friend, that Veronica introduced us, in a way. Although, of course, young Julius really introduced us. He was obviously upset by her death. In a way.

Bless my heart, Adrian said to himself, She almost went overboard for young Julius, but she didn't and I was sure she wouldn't. I hope my darling didn't die too miserable because of it. I was damnably jealous, but I understood something of life by then! I played that hand well, I think – and she was brave about it. He thought of the letter always carried in his wallet, the letter she had written – why exactly then? – before setting out on that fateful day to watch a National Socialist march from the safety of a flat window near the Munich Odeonsplatz. He had found it between the pages of a book she was reading, in their private sitting room in the hotel. Incurably indiscreet, she had concealed it thus, unfinished, in a place where a suspicious husband would have instantly searched if so minded. Would she have given him the letter, said – 'This is for you, darling. I'm going out for a bit?' It was perfectly possible. Or sent it, during some temporary absence visiting relations in Galway without him, as sometimes happened? Or destroyed it? It didn't matter. He had found it.

He had found it, when, blind with misery, he had gone through her things for the first time in the hotel rooms, gone through them with no thought but to touch things she had touched, unable to take in what they had just told him, what this young German now sitting in his club playing fair bridge had just said. He had found the letter, it had fallen from between the leaves of her book, picked up mechanically. It didn't matter whether or not

380

she had ever meant him to see it. What mattered was its message and that the message had been hers. He touched his inner pocket, felt the shape of his wallet with the hand not holding his cards. Still safe. Still there.

In the letter she had told him frankly about Julius, how she'd fallen for the young fellow, had been foolish, unfaithful, had now got over it – and was being self-indulgent and confessing because she couldn't bear to live a lie where Adrian was concerned. She told him that he, Adrian, had given her a peace she'd always lacked. That she loved him. Adrian had never showed Veronica his suspicions about her and Julius. He had sat with his pain, and with the letter in his hand, in the Munich hotel bedroom and wept, and on the whole they were also tears of gratitude that her heart had led her to tell him the truth in the end. He treasured the letter – it was unfinished and he had no idea whether she would ever have given it to him, it didn't matter – treasured it without reservation. 'I'm prepared to deceive,' she'd written, 'if I have to, in the world of politics, public events, general skulduggery.' Heaven knew what she meant and she'd scratched out a word and substituted 'skulduggery'. But the letter had continued: 'I'm not prepared, any more, to deceive you, my darling, darling Adrian.' That was what mattered, all that mattered. He considered his cards.

And what about Carr? thought Adrian. They were pausing while drinks were ordered and brought. What does Carr see, when he hears her name? He was a cousin of Alan Marvell, of course, and he met her in Berlin and at Faberdown, with us, and I expect he met her pretty often before the war. I think he found her damned attractive, too. I could tell that from his eyes when her name came up. For Adrian was more perceptive than others, who considered his age and health, imagined. Yes, he thought, perhaps he was in love with her himself, once. Poor fellow, he'd never have stood a chance! And I never heard her mention him, as a woman does, usually, if she's ever felt anything for a man. But I expect Carr sees an attractive woman, a charmer, somebody he'd have liked to know better, liked to know more about. I don't recollect them talking much to each other when they were in the same party with us at Faberdown. But then I don't recollect anything as clearly as I did.

Still, he thought with an inward chuckle, My memory for cards remains pretty good!

Triumphantly he took the last trick with a seven of diamonds.

'You thought that was out, didn't you, Marvell'' he said a little primly. Adrian Winter, although club stakes were negligible, played to win. Gerhardt dealt.

John Marvell knew her best of this lot, of course, thought Adrian. He was her brother-in-law. And, come to think of it, he was keen on her before that, had some hopes of marrying her. I remember Mary going on about it. Mary was the first Mrs Winter.

Yes, thought Adrian, he was in love with her. Funny, I'd quite forgotten that, always thought of his brother Alan. I was jealous of Alan. You can be jealous of the dead – very jealous. Anyway, John Marvell's a happily married man now. A well-settled man with a nice wife and a charming place – Bargate's really delightful. So's Carr settled, for that matter. And their knowledge of my darling can never have been anything but superficial – utterly superficial. It's only I, who married her, who had the chance to understand her real quality. But I expect they all felt something, at some time, had a glimpse of what she was really like. I hope so!

No, I don't know about Brendthase, thought Francis, as he inspected his uninspiring collection of cards. He certainly caught fire when he first met her. I remember his eyes sparkling at his father's house, all those years ago. But afterwards – who knows? There's no doubt about me, she fascinated me totally and all my censorious feelings, sincere as they might be, were strongly tinged by jealousy.

And the other two here, John and Adrian Winter, they certainly adored her, Francis reflected, resigned to taking no tricks this time. Poor old John, she nearly broke him. So that's at least three out of four at this table, and maybe all four. Quite a strong bond! And one mustn't forget Alan, who wed her and whom she didn't love, unless I'm mistaken. And crooked old Printer Drew whom perhaps, in a way, she did. Five of us – maybe six!' He sighed, and his partner looked sympathetic. Francis had held bad cards most of the evening.

One mustn't forget Gaisford, too, Francis remembered, following suit with a three of clubs. Poor Gaisford. I expect he loved her, too, in his way. And none of us here is likely to know what his way was.

Adrian considered his cards complacently. He thought – Yes, I'm glad we all at this table knew her, even if only a little!

He smiled at his guests benignly. He could tell from the calling that the hand was his. His cards were strong, the opposition was fragmented. He knew where the only difficulty lay and he could see exactly how to play and win every trick but one. Veronica had taken to bridge like a duck to water. She gambled a bit, but she had luck. She'd have enjoyed this hand.

'Six,' he said. 'A small slam, I think. In hearts. There's no doubt about it.' He continued to smile at them, showing them from his hand, Ace, King, Queen and Knave. 'I've got all the honours, too.'

Brian Callison

'There can be no better adventure writer in the country today.' *Alistair MacLean*

'One of the best writers of modern sea stories.'
Daily Telegraph

A FRENZY OF MERCHANTMEN
A PLAGUE OF SAILORS
TRAPP'S PEACE
THE DAWN ATTACK
THE SEXTANT
A SHIP IS DYING
SPEARFISH
THE AURIGA MADNESS
THE BONE COLLECTORS
A FLOCK OF SHIPS
A WEB OF SALVAGE

FONTANA PAPERBACKS

Hammond Innes

If you are looking for a tough action novel, of man against the elements, breathless but credible, out of the ordinary but authentic, you can't do better than a good Hammond Innes.

'Hammond Innes has a genius for conveying atmosphere.' *Daily Telegraph*

THE BIG FOOTPRINTS
THE BLUE ICE
CAMPBELL'S KINGDOM
LEVKAS MAN
THE LONELY SKIER
THE STRANGE LAND
THE WHITE SOUTH
WRECKERS MUST BREATHE
THE WRECK OF THE MARY DEARE
SOLOMONS SEAL
NORTH STAR
THE LAST VOYAGE
AIR BRIDGE
THE BLACK TIDE
ATTACK ALARM

and many others

FONTANA PAPERBACKS

Fontana Paperbacks: Fiction

Fontana is a leading paperback publisher of both non-fiction, popular and academic, and fiction. Below are some recent fiction titles.

- ☐ THE ROSE STONE Teresa Crane £2.95
- ☐ THE DANCING MEN Duncan Kyle £2.50
- ☐ AN EXCESS OF LOVE Cathy Cash Spellman £3.50
- ☐ THE ANVIL CHORUS Shane Stevens £2.95
- ☐ A SONG TWICE OVER Brenda Jagger £3.50
- ☐ SHELL GAME Douglas Terman £2.95
- ☐ FAMILY TRUTHS Syrell Leahy £2.95
- ☐ ROUGH JUSTICE Jerry Oster £2.50
- ☐ ANOTHER DOOR OPENS Lee Mackenzie £2.25
- ☐ THE MONEY STONES Ian St James £2.95
- ☐ THE BAD AND THE BEAUTIFUL Vera Cowie £2.95
- ☐ RAMAGE'S CHALLENGE Dudley Pope £2.95
- ☐ THE ROAD TO UNDERFALL Mike Jefferies £2.95

You can buy Fontana paperbacks at your local bookshop or newsagent. Or you can order them from Fontana Paperbacks, Cash Sales Department, Box 29, Douglas, Isle of Man. Please send a cheque, postal or money order (not currency) worth the purchase price plus 22p per book for postage (maximum postage required is £3.00 for orders within the UK).

NAME (Block letters) _____

ADDRESS _____

_____

_____

While every effort is made to keep prices low, it is sometimes necessary to increase them at short notice. Fontana Paperbacks reserve the right to show new retail prices on covers which may differ from those previously advertised in the text or elsewhere.